THE CHRONICLES OF URN

KING'S
BRIDE

THE CHRONICLES OF URN

KING'S BRIDE

BECK MICHAELS

PLUMA
PRESS

Trigger Warning: *King's Bride* **contains explicit content, language, graphic violence, parental abuse, and past SA trauma (the act itself is not shown).**

PLUMA PRESS
P.O. Box 341
Camby, IN 46113
Visit Us at PlumaPress.com

Published May 2023

Author: Michaels, Beck

Title: King's Bride / Beck Michaels

Series: The Chronicles of Urn; 1

Genre: NA Dark Fantasy Romance

Identifiers:
ISBN 978-1-956899-11-5 (hardcover) | ISBN 978-1-956899-10-8 (softcover)
ISBN 978-1-956899-09-2 (ebook)

www.BeckMichaels.com

Printed in the United States of America

For all those who believe in the impossible.

GLACIAL OCEAN

UNITED CROWN

XIAN JING DYNASTY

DRAGON LANDS

THE VALE

LEVIATHAN OCEAN

SU
GU

MAG

LUNAR
GUILD

LAND OF URN

ARGYLE

EVERFROST

WASTE
LANDS

HE ELVES

SAXE SEA

MISTY
ISLES

PIRE

EARTH
GUILD

THE EVERFROST

GLACIAL
OCEAN

SKELLING
TRIBE
THE FROST LANDS

HERMON MOUNTAINS

TANNER
CLAN

HARDEN
CLAN

BLACK
WOODS

RULEM
CLAN

TANZANITE
KEEP

MORKHAN
CLAN

SEANA
CLAN

OREM
CLAN

ADHAR
CLAN

ARGOS
CLAN

LAZAR
CLAN

KAZER
CLAN

WILD COURT
THE MOOR LANDS

THE
WASTE
LANDS

SHADOW KEEP

VALE OF THE ELVES

SAXE SEA

MISTY
ISLES

THE SEVEN GATES

Each soul passes through the gates at their beginning and their end.

HEAVEN'S GATE

LIFE'S GATE

SPATIAL GATE

TIME GATE

MORTAL GATE

NETHERWORLD GATE

DEATH'S GATE

Once upon a time, there lived a cruel beast in a castle of ice and roses. His magic coated the land in an endless winter until the day a bride came to burn it all down. This is the grim truth behind their tale, dark as it may be...

1

With life came death, and Sunnëva hunted it now to delay her own. Her boots sank quietly into the deep snow as she moved in on her target, careful not to make a sound. Drawing back her arm, the bow string faintly creaked as she aimed. The crow cawed, and its cry echoed through the sky. It invited paranoia to graze her spine like a whispered breath, but the hollow pit of her stomach won over all reason.

She released her arrow. It landed, hitting the crow. Black feathers and blood splattered bright red in the snow. Sunnëva's breath clouded in the frigid air with a sigh of relief. She quickly ran to snatch up her kill before another creature thought to fight her for it.

Her chapped lips stung as she whispered a quick prayer of thanks to all Seven Gods for granting her this small mercy. She also prayed the King wouldn't notice one of his crows missing. Hundreds of them loitered around his castle. He could spare one to feed her family.

Sunnëva shuddered as the frigid air bit at her numb cheeks. She tugged her cloak tighter around her shoulders. The gray pelt she wore on top hardly kept her warm. Strands of her blonde hair stuck to her frosted lashes as she blinked against the bright sun gleaming over the land beyond the cliffside. Nothing but endless, vile snow in all directions.

Sunnëva hated the sight. Hated that white was all she'd ever known.

Not that the land was ever another color, despite their fairy tales. This part of Urn had always been frozen. So much so that they dubbed it the Everfrost.

Only one person was to blame for it.

In the distance, castle peaks rose above the misty fog. It glinted like a diamond in the sun. How comfortable that tyrant must be in his fortress of ice, living off the wealth he took from the clans while they all simply froze to death or starved because of his cursed magic.

Sunnëva's stomach rumbled, and she sighed. Yanking out the bloodied arrow, she stuffed her kill in a sack. It would barely suffice. Maybe she should have gone fishing instead.

Turning her gaze to the seas in the east, her heart leaped at the sight of ships sailing on the waves. Their gray sails flapped with the white Morkhàn emblem of her clan: a jagged snowflake with twelve points.

They were back.

Sunnëva bolted into the dense forest and hurried home. Leaping over the creek bordering their land, she ran toward the huge Azure Tree outside of her village. It had a white trunk and blue leaves that resembled stars of sapphires. Seeing it always made her smile because it stood out against the landscape, as if in defiance of the perpetual winter.

Passing under its canopy, Sunnëva entered her village.

Few were people out in the cold, but the ones she saw were thin and hungry. Their bleak stares followed the trail of blood leaking from her sack as she hurried past.

"The ships are back," Sunnëva announced. "The clansmen have returned!"

That sparked life into their faces, and their voices rose with excitement as they rushed down the path to the docks to greet their sons and husbands.

"Did you hunt something good today?" an old clansman asked her.

His grandson peeked out from behind him, shivering under his furs.

"A bony bird. Hardly any meat on it," Sunnëva said. At their hopeful expressions, she sighed and handed the old man the sack. "Make it last."

He accepted it with trembling hands and his eyes watered. "Thank you, Sunnëva. We are grateful to you for keeping the clan safe while the Earl was gone—" The old man gasped when he saw what was inside. "Sacred Gods." Insipid fear drained all the color from his face, and he shoved the sack back at her. "I can't take that. You would bring the King's wrath upon my house."

This wasn't the first time Sunnëva had hunted a crow, and no one had come for her yet. "It's not one of his," she lied. "We're too far from the castle."

The old man shook his head. "It's not safe."

No place in the world was safe. The land was a coffin of ice, and they had been buried inside it a long time ago.

Sunnëva frowned. "Is your fear worth starving for?"

"I would rather our souls cross the Seven Gates at peace in our beds than at the end of the King's scythe." He rushed off with his grandson, nearly dragging the poor boy away from her.

She glowered at her reflection in the bloody puddle forming by her feet. The clans believed crows were omens of death, for they were said to caw when a life would end.

It was merely a stupid superstition.

Sunnëva continued toward the longhouse, the Earl's hall. It was a rectangular structure made of dark timber with a high thatched roof. Several runes and the sigil of her clan were engraved on the large, heavy doors. She climbed the steps, and the scent of burning firewood and warmth welcomed her as she entered. Her younger sister was sitting on furs by the large firepit built in the center of the hall, tending to her sewing.

Blonde hair swished around Ansa's soft, pretty face as she looked up. "What did you catch?" she asked eagerly.

"Never mind that," Sunnëva said as she hung the sack on a hook by the door, then propped her bow and quiver against the wall. "They're here."

Ansa's bright smile wavered.

"Come." She sighed. "We should greet Fen at least."

Ansa grabbed her cloak, and they ventured outside, following the last group of villagers on the path to the shorefront. Sunnëva inhaled the brine scent carried by the winds, letting the sounds of lapping waves guide her. A shallow coastline appeared beyond the trees, where their gathered people greeted the clansmen. Their joyous voices almost drowned out the soft weeping of wives and daughters crying over the dead carried off the first ship.

Sunnëva spotted her father and elder brother standing on the dock, overseeing the rest of the fleet coming into the wharf. A majority of the ships had made it back, and they were filled with chests and barrels.

"Father," Sunnëva greeted as she and Ansa approached. They bowed their heads to him as owed to the Earl of the Morkhàn clan. "I am glad you returned home safely, and with plenty of bounty."

Her father was a large man, layered in armor and fur, with a long broadsword on his hip. His blond hair and thick beard looked lighter, tinted gray, his face marked by the seas and battle. His dark blue eyes fell on her like the ocean's cold waves, and he scowled. "You think I would have been gone for the past six months leading clan raids with nothing to show for it?"

At his derisive tone, the little excitement she felt at seeing him after so long settled like heavy rocks in her chest. She shouldn't have hoped for a pleasant greeting.

"More than half the ships carry loot," her elder brother said, crossing his arms. Bjorn looked like a younger version of their father, and he carried himself in the same manner.

Sunnëva glanced past them. "Where is Fenrin? And Rune?"

"I am safe, and no harm has come to me. Thank you, dear sister, for caring."

"If you were harmed, you would not be here now." She stood on her toes, searching among the clansmen as they carried cargo onto the deck.

"I don't see Fen," Ansa said worriedly.

"He's fine," their father groused. "Stupid boy injured himself and won't stop mewling about it." He marched onward with Bjorn, barking at Ansa that he was hungry.

Sunnëva tried not to assume the worst. She stayed put until she spotted a familiar cloaked figure helping her younger brother climb out of the last ship.

"Fen!" she called, rushing toward them. "Thank the Gods you made it."

Fenrin looked tired and pale, but his face lit up at the sight of her. "Of course I did. You worry too much."

His dark blond hair was loosely tied at his nape, tangled in thin braids. Matted strands stuck to his sweaty forehead and temples. He was a lanky boy for his age, and two heads shorter than the one supporting him.

Rune smiled beneath the hood of his long, black cloak. "Were you worried about me, too, Su?" The deep rumble of his voice vibrated through her chest, sinking low past her stomach.

Sunnëva smirked as she admired his sharp jaw, shadowed by his dark stubble and firm mouth. "Not in the slightest."

His amber eyes glinted with amusement. They were flecked with copper, giving them a warm, reddish tint. "You know you missed me."

"I am willing to bet you missed me more." She let her gaze roam appreciatively over his broad frame, adorned with leather greaves, gloves, and boots. He was clad as a warrior.

And she couldn't wait to remove every piece.

His mouth curved as if he could sense her thoughts. The man knew exactly the hold he had over her.

"Rune?" Fenrin sighed as he leaned against him.

"Aye?" Rune replied, not looking away from her.

"I know you haven't seen her in months, but I would rather you not make eyes at my sister while I'm half dead."

Sunnëva laughed at his flush.

"Oh, sorry." Rune adjusted his arm to support Fen's waist and lifted him up, removing the weight off of his foot.

Her laughter died when she noticed the bloodied bandages wrapped around his ankle. "Gods, what happened?" She grabbed Fenrin's other arm and hooked it over her shoulders. They helped him limp across the dock to land.

"The raids in Carthage ended well, but on the way home, Father sent us to raid Orem." Fenrin gave her a grim frown, and she didn't ask why.

Orem was one of the nine clans of the Everfrost, but their allegiance with Morkhàn had long ended.

"Was it a bloody battle?" she asked.

"We caught them unawares, sneaking into their village under the cover of night," Rune said. "Lord Thorstein had disarmed their Earl. It was an easy victory—if not for the wargs."

She halted. "What?"

The image of the bony-faced, wolf-like demons conjured in her mind. Their long fangs could cleave through a body as viciously as any sword.

"One almost took down Bjorn, but I got it," Fenrin said. She raised an eyebrow, and he grinned sheepishly.

"What he meant was that he got in the way," Rune said.

Sunnëva's eyes widened, and she looked down at his leg. "Please don't tell me you were bitten. Warg bites are lethal, Fen!"

He moved back before she could reach for the bandages. "I wasn't bit. Rune killed it. He killed the lot of them, really. I merely cut myself with my sword when I fell."

A relieved breath shot out of her. "I wish the Gods would wipe the Shadow Lord and his demons clean from the earth. Along with the King in his damn castle."

"Aye, that would be a sight," Rune replied evenly.

Sunnëva winced. She glanced at the two axes strapped to his belt, the blades pitch-black. Nightstone. The only ore that eliminated demons. What use was a demon slayer without any demons to slay?

"But it's unusual for them to be this far north," she said. "We are nowhere near the Waste Lands."

She glanced toward the Shadow Lord's territory in the south, but they weren't close enough to catch a glimpse of his black castle, or the poisonous clouds surrounding it. Nothing grew in the Waste Lands. The sky was always dark there. The way demons liked it.

"I also thought it strange," Fenrin said as they continued on. "The demons must be desperate for food to risk coming north."

It was the same reason the clans raided to steal food and wealth from others. To survive. But all it did was end the lives of their youth every year.

Sunnëva frowned at Fenrin's labored breathing. It was too soon to send him off to battle. She was a shield maiden. She should have gone, but their father wouldn't hear it. He said it was time her brother learned what it meant to spill blood.

"How badly are you hurt?" she asked him.

"It's barely a cut."

"I will call on Gyda to tend to it."

Fenrin paled further and shook his head. "Don't bother that old hag. She would probably cast a spell over me rather than heal me."

"Maybe you shouldn't have pestered her with your mischief then, eh?" Sunnëva teased, reminding him of all the tricks he played on her as a child. "And she's a *healer*. Call her a hag again, then Gyda would probably cut off your stones while you're sleeping and use them in her potions."

Fenrin's throat bobbed. "Don't jest about such things. You know I need them."

Rune chuckled and smacked the back of his head. "Do you, now? Grand words for a lad who hasn't bedded a lass yet."

"Why do you think I need them?"

Sunnëva shook her head. Fenrin had returned from his first successful raid. Maidens would flock to him soon enough.

"This is taking too long." Rune hauled Fenrin over his shoulder with graceful ease. "Let's get your weedy arse inside so I can have my filthy ways with your sister."

He gave her a wink and marched ahead. Sunnëva followed behind, laughing as her brother cursed at him. She was looking forward to Rune keeping his word.

2

The longhouse came into view as they walked up the path together. Going in there was the last thing Sunnëva wanted. But she told herself the quicker she did, the sooner she could steal away with Rune. They carried Fenrin inside and laid him on the plank bed lined with furs against the wall. Oil lamps flickered from the posts, casting a soft, warm light. Her father was seated in his imposing chair at the head of the hall, set upon a short dais, as Ansa poured ale into his horn cup.

Rune stood with his arms crossed behind his back and bowed his head. "Earl Thorstein."

Her father grunted, scowling at Fenrin. "Rune, you may as well be my second son. You're more capable than that one. See that the bounty is loaded into the storehouse."

"Aye, sir. Shall I set the King's share aside?"

He spat on the ground. "I'm the one who bled for it, yet the bastard still demands his cut. Set aside forty percent for him, then. Nothing more."

Sunnëva stiffened, sharing a startled look with her sister. Half of the raid's plunder was always owed to the King. Hunting crows was one thing, but withholding gold was a dire offense.

Every territory in the Everfrost paid him fealty, including the wild fae in the Moor Lands. Those who roused his anger would taste his scythe, for he brooked no defiance of any kind. It wasn't merely the army of twenty thousand at his command.

He had strange magic.

The Ice Phoenix, they called him.

The wielder of ice and death.

"Do as I say," her father barked at Rune for hesitating, and he marched out to obey.

Sunnëva picked up the round wooden shields they had dumped on the ground and hung them alongside the tapestries. They were painted gray and white with her clan's colors.

"Father, forgive me, but I must question this," she said.

"It's not your place to question it." He didn't spare her a glance, as if she wasn't worth looking at. He had always made her feel that way.

Worthless.

She glanced down at her scarred hands, knowing she deserved it.

"He has taken enough from me." Her father sneered at the two banners on the wall.

The one colored gray-blue held the sigil of Morkhàn. The other was dark blue with the white sigil of Ice Phoenix: a bird in mid-flight. They were ordered to display it, so they never forget who ruled over them.

Sunnëva shot Bjorn a look from where he sat at their table. He slightly shook his head, warning her to leave it be. But she couldn't, not when it put them at risk.

"We are hungry," Bjorn told her before she could argue. "Bring us food."

"We don't have much, but I caught a bird today, or I can bring some Torrfisk from the larder."

"I don't want dried cod or another damn crow," her father growled. "I want a feast worthy of our return. Butcher one of the boars we brought with us."

Bjorn rose to his feet. "Yes, Father."

"You caught a boar? But we should save it—" Sunnëva cut off at her father's glare. She bowed her head. "The hunts are scarce. There has been no game in these parts for most of the season, and the village ran out of grain last week. We should preserve what food we can and pray it lasts the next two seasons. The lunar eclipse is coming, and we need to be ready."

The King sent measly rations of grain to the clans every quarter, but they were never enough.

Her father's expression hardened. "I earned some damn pork and I will have it. Do not speak against me again."

He never cared about what she did to keep this family alive. Only his own comfort. Sunnëva headed for the door.

"Where are you going?"

She took a deep breath before turning around. "Bjorn can wrestle the boar. I must call on Gyda to tend to Fen."

"He's fine," her father said tightly. "He doesn't need a healer. Useless boy."

Bjorn laughed and jabbed his finger into Fenrin's ribs. "I bet he's playing the sick fool, so he won't have to go on the next raid. Sunnëva swings a sword better than he does. We're better off having her on the next run."

Fenrin rolled over to face the wall. They were always hard on him. He wasn't as big as Bjorn or as fast as Rune, or as ruthless as her father, but that didn't make him useless.

"You leave him be." Sunnëva shoved Bjorn back. "I will go get more firewood to roast the boar."

She rushed outside before her father could command anything else. So much for their return. The village might have been starving, but there had been peace in their absence, however brief it was.

But there was one pleasant thing that came out of it.

11

Rune waited for her behind the longhouse. Sunnëva took his hand, and they ran together into the shadowy woods.

Once they were far enough away, he pinned her to a tree, their mouths colliding. Her pulse thudded with elation at the stroke of his rough hands over her body. She breathed in his familiar smoky scent. He kissed her hungrily as he lifted her, and Sunnëva wrapped her legs around his waist. A low growl rumbled in his throat when she ground against him. His erection was hard and warm against her seam, exactly where she had been craving him all these months.

"You're right," he said against her lips. "I missed you more."

A soft whimper escaped her when his fingers skimmed up her torso and cupped her breast. She was desperate to have him on her skin. They were secluded enough.

She needed him now.

Sunnëva yanked down his hood to remove his cloak and reached for the stays of his pants. The clouds parted and sunlight streamed through the branches, glittering on every frosted leaf.

Rune stiffened under her and broke their kiss. "We should slow down," he said with a chuckle. He moved them under the shade and pulled up his hood. "It's too bright out here. It will be my head if I'm caught with the Earl's daughter."

"No one will see us out here." Sunnëva kissed him again, but he kept it chaste. "You don't want to?"

"Of course, I want to." He set her down, motioning to himself. "Is this not evidence enough?"

She flushed at the impressive bulge in his trousers. "Then what stops you? It's not as if we haven't rolled in the hay already." She traced the ridges of his abdomen underneath his shirt. "If you're worried about my virtue, it's far too late for that."

Sunnëva meant it as a joke, but her tunic had loosened enough that he saw the visible scars between her breasts. They were jagged and puckered against her pale skin. Sighing, Sunnëva nudged him off and adjusted her clothing to hide them.

Rune's gaze stayed on her face as she tied up her laces. He'd been there the night she got the scars, but they had never spoken about it.

He knew not to ask, even when she refused to be naked whenever they slept together.

That night had taken more than her innocence, but she had crawled out of the hole and didn't plan on going back. The past was best left where it belonged.

In the *past*.

"You know that's never bothered me, Su." Rune leaned against the tree, crossing his arms. He frowned at the sunny patches on the ground.

"Then?"

"I shouldn't be using you like this, even though I can't help it." His mouth lifted in a half smile, his eyes falling to her lips.

"Is it really using me if I use you for the same?" Sunnëva walked her fingers up his chest. They were friends who became lovers, stealing away for a moment of release when they could. She didn't expect more than that, even if she wanted more. "Who says you can't have me all to yourself?"

"The Gods and everyone else." There was something in his tone that wasn't his usual jesting.

"What are you saying?"

"I..." Rune cradled her hand in his. Hers was small in comparison, her fingers warmed by his touch. "I want you as my bride."

Air caught in her lungs with an emotion she couldn't explain. Hope or disbelief. "You've never said that before."

Rune sighed. "Because I am bound by certain rules. We come from two worlds, Su. I want you in mine, but I don't belong in yours."

She frowned. "Because my father took you in as a slave?"

Sunnëva still remembered the day she found him half-dead three years ago in the forest from starvation and hypothermia. Rune had been the lone survivor of the Harden clan that had been conquered by Rulem when there used to be ten clans.

He had come a long way since then.

"I have no right to you." Rune brushed his lips up her neck, inhaling her scent. "You're forbidden fruit, sweetling. But that didn't stop me from taking a bite. Several of them." He kissed her deeply, his tongue thrusting into hers in the exact rhythm he liked to take her. Heat pooled between her thighs, and she moaned. He gripped her waist and pulled her tight against him, his mouth curving with a shrewd smile. "If he knew I was touching you like this, he would be furious."

No, he wouldn't.

Rune greatly overestimated how much her father truly cared about her. She doubted it would appall him if he ever caught them one day.

"You know there is no law that says slaves can't bed women, right?" she said.

"Aye, but none of them are fucking the Earl's daughter."

She flushed and shoved him. "And who says I haven't been with others while you were away? I am a woman with needs, you know."

Rune's eyes narrowed. "Go on then, do as you please. I will warn you, Gyda isn't the only one who will geld a man."

He was only half joking. Rune was dangerous, no doubt. It was evident in the way he carried himself and how he fought.

Sunnëva glanced down at the tattoo on the inside of his right wrist, peeking past his sleeve. One end was a spiral that looped up into a circle and crossed into another spiral to level with the first. The mark represented an unspoken history between them better left in the dark, but it bound them together.

There wasn't anyone else she trusted with her body and her heart.

"Yes," she blurted. "I'll marry you."

Rune blinked at her, then coughed a short laugh of surprise. "In all the time we have known each other, you still manage to surprise me."

"You served my father for three years and fought by his side in every raid. You were a demon slayer in your last clan. Prove to him you are worth more than a slave, and he will make you a warrior of ours. Then you can claim me for yourself."

"You want me that badly, eh?"

She curled a lock of his black hair around her fingers. "Only because you're pretty to look at. But are you sure you wouldn't want a younger maiden?"

"Twenty-three is nowhere near old." Rune spoke as if he were an ancient man, but he wasn't much older than her.

But she *was* considered an old maid. The girls in her village were usually married by eighteen. Requests for her hand had stopped coming years ago.

"Do you mean it? You would choose me?" he asked, his face softening.

It was so rare for him to say such things, let alone look at her the way he was now. Like he was earnest and honest and wanted a life with her. Her father and Rune's status were walls preventing that, but damn her for imagining it.

She shrugged shyly. "Maybe ... a part of me was waiting for you to ask."

A smile crossed his face that made her stomach flutter. Rune lifted her chin, slowly kissing along her jaw to her mouth. She ran her fingers through his hair, causing his hood to slide down.

Rune caught her wrist and shook his head. "I better stop now, or I'll take you here."

"I hope you don't think I would stop you."

He grinned. "Wicked woman."

They collected firewood together, then headed to the village once their arms were full. He guided her through the trees, using the shadows for cover in case they crossed paths with anyone else.

"About the bounty..." she murmured under her breath.

"Don't worry." Rune took her firewood and added it to his load. "I set aside some small jewels worth more than all the gold we pilfered." His tone hardened, and his gaze fixed ahead. "The King will get what he is owed."

Sunnëva sighed. "Thank you."

That's why she adored him.

He always did the right thing for their sake, even if it meant defying the Earl. She didn't care if her father approved. Rune was who she chose.

When the village came into sight, he moved a step behind her as appropriate. Unseen and unheard. It irritated her because nothing about him fit the mold of a slave. If luck should have it, he wouldn't be one for long.

"There you are." Bjorn stormed toward them. "What took you so long?"

"It wasn't easy finding dried wood. Help next time if you're to bleat about it." Sunnëva walked past him, but he grabbed her arm.

"Six months on your own sharpened your tongue, hasn't it? Careful, or Father will think you need reminding of your place."

Before she could reply, Rune grabbed Bjorn's face and pinned him against the wall of a pit house. "Pardon me, my Lord. There was a venomous snake by your boots." He smiled, but it was sharp and dark. His large hand constricted, turning Bjorn's skin white under his grip. "Please be mindful of what lurks in your wake. Too many men die young these days."

Bjorn stiffened at the casually delivered threat. His mouth was covered, so he couldn't respond, not that she thought he would.

Rune stepped back. "Would you mind helping me carry the wood your sister graciously gathered? I dropped it."

The firewood was scattered at their feet. He'd moved so fast she missed when he tossed them.

Bjorn scowled indignantly, but the cold look on Rune's face made him crouch down to gather half the wood and rush off. Rune picked up the rest.

"I think you made him soil his trousers," Sunnëva said.

He chuckled. "Then it was worth the whipping I'll likely receive."

Bjorn wouldn't dare.

They entered the longhouse to find it full of villagers in merriment as they gorged on the food brought from the raids. Someone played the lyre, belting a song about the glory of battle and Gods. Her stomach churned when she saw they were roasting *two* boars. She was so angry the smell made her sick.

Damn waste.

Rune left the wood by the firepit and returned to her father at his call. Ansa was in the corner, trying to talk to her twin. Fenrin ignored her, still facing the wall where he lay.

"He won't eat," Ansa said at her approach. She held a wooden bowl of broth made with herbs and pale meat.

"How are you feeling?" Sunnëva touched his forehead, but he nudged her away. That one brief contact of skin startled her. "You're burning, Fen."

"Then why do I feel cold?" He huddled under the furs, shivering. "Please bring me another pelt." He already had three on him, but his lips looked blue, so she did as he asked.

"Have some broth. It will help you feel better," Ansa said.

Fenrin pushed away the spoon she tried to feed him, spilling it. "I'm not hungry," he snapped. "Stop treating me like a child. It's bad enough that Father does it."

Hurt crossed Ansa's face, and she carried the bowl away.

Sunnëva sat beside him. "You know she didn't deserve that."

Fenrin's bloodshot eyes fixed on the ceiling, watching smoke filter out the opening. He exhaled a low, strained breath. It's what he did when he tried not to cry. "Am I really useless?"

"Of course not. You're quick-witted and kind, exactly like Mother." Sunnëva brushed aside one of the braids sticking to his sweaty neck. It was woven with tiny colorful beads and wolf teeth he had gathered on their hunts. "She didn't care for raids, either."

"He hates me because I'm not a skilled fighter. Because I took her from him when she gave birth to me."

"No, my sweet boy." Sunnëva sighed. She had been old enough to see her mother's labor and the way she bled out as well. "That wasn't your fault."

"It is..." Fenrin said faintly as his lashes drifted closed. "Perhaps he will finally give a damn about me when I'm gone. Like Freya."

Sunnëva fought the lump in her throat at the reminder of their lost sister, and she glanced down at the scars on her hands. "Hush, Fen. Rest, and prove him wrong tomorrow."

3

Late into the night, Sunnëva woke to frantic cries. She leaped out of bed, whipping out the bone dagger kept under her pillow. Her heart hammered with the remnants of her nightmare, but no one had come to attack them.

Ansa leaned over Fenrin, shaking his shoulders as she sobbed. "Fen? *Fenrin!*"

Sunnëva stumbled over the blankets and furs as she ran to them. Her brother didn't move. He was deathly pale. She checked his pulse, but it was so faint, she nearly thought him dead.

Sunnëva shook him. "Fen? Wake up, Fen." He was limp and unresponsive. Gasping, she shook him harder. "Fenrin!"

"What's with all the squawking?" Bjorn groaned from the other side of the room, sitting up in his plank bed.

"Have you checked the wound?" Sunnëva asked Ansa.

She shook her head. "He wouldn't let me."

Sunnëva threw off the pelts and yanked down the old, bloodied bandages. She froze. Ansa cried harder. A crescent of teeth had torn into his flesh. The wound was inflamed, puss spilling out of the shredded skin. Purple veins webbed up his leg to his thigh.

Bjorn came up behind them and cursed under his breath.

"He was bitten!" Sunnëva beat her fist against his chest. "How didn't you know he was bitten?"

"I didn't know! I thought a blade had nicked him!"

"Bring Gyda," she told Ansa. Her sister stood wide-eyed, shakily holding the bloodied pelts Sunnëva had torn off of Fen. Ansa was unable to speak or move or do anything but stare at her twin. "Ansa!" Sunnëva screamed. "Get Gyda!"

Her sister dashed out of the longhouse.

Sunnëva took Fenrin's cold hand and prayed to all the Gods, hoping one of them would hear. *Please,* she begged. *Please don't take more from me.*

"We have to cut off his leg," Bjorn said, reaching for his sword. "It's the only way."

"You will not touch him." Sunnëva jumped in his way. "Cut his leg, and you damn him. He'll be cast out of the clan. He won't make it out there as a cripple."

"Fenrin is already damned. Better a cripple than dead." Bjorn shoved her aside, and she fell by the fire pit. He drew out his sword, raising it above Fen's knee.

"No, Bjorn!" she screamed.

Rune appeared, tackling him to the ground. He wrested the sword from his grasp, pinning Bjorn beneath him. His cold eyes were menacing in the low fire, daring her brother to fight him.

Bjorn shrank away.

Her father and Ansa entered the doorway, with Gyda following behind.

The old woman hobbled toward them with her gnarled wooden staff. It jingled with dangling charms of crystals and bones. Her back was hunched over as if she bore the weight of the world.

Gyda's stoic expression didn't change when she came to Fenrin. Only her wrinkly mouth pursed slightly, grunting disapprovingly at the wound. "Warg bite."

Sunnëva pushed off the ground. The old woman was small, barely reaching her waist. "I should have called for you yesterday, Gyda."

"Yes, you should have, foolish girl, but it would have been futile." She lifted Fenrin's tunic, revealing the purple veins traveling up his chest. "The infection is nearly set. When was the boy bitten?"

"Two days passed," Rune answered.

Sunnëva turned to him, confused. Had he known?

"Two days too late, then." Gyda shook her head. "I could have saved him on the first day by removing the leg. Even if I do so now, it won't stop the spread. No human can survive a warg bite after three days." She narrowed her milky eyes at Thorstein with a bravery no one else dared. "You should have seen signs he was failing."

Had he known Fenrin was bit and ignored it because he didn't want a legless son who would indeed be useless? Better to have his son die a hero than to live in disgrace.

"How long?" he asked.

"He will die tomorrow at sunset." Gyda turned away. "I'll make him an elixir to ease his passing."

Sunnëva shook. "That's it?"

"There is no more I can do." The healer hobbled out.

Ansa wept over Fenrin, holding his hand to her cheek. Bjorn rubbed his forehead, at last looking guilty. Her father said nothing. Only scowled beneath the fire's glow.

As simple as that, they all accepted it.

Sunnëva shook her head, her lungs heaving as they compressed in her chest. "No. *No.*"

"That old woman has to know something," Rune said under his breath. "Don't let her leave."

Sunnëva ran out into the brisk night and spotted the healer plodding through the snow. "Gyda! Do not give up on my brother!"

"I can do no more for him."

"You're the greatest healer of the east." Sunnëva cut in front of her and dropped to her knees. "Please. I've already lost my mother and sister. I cannot lose more."

The old woman eyed her grimly in the moonlight, the wind fluttering her shawl and gray hair around her face like smoke. "You will lose him and continue to lose more. That is life."

The words were like blades in her heart, twisting so painfully, her scars burned.

Tears froze on Sunnëva's lashes, and she took the healer's soft, wrinkled hands. "I have seen you heal many on the brink of death. I refuse to believe you don't know how to save Fenrin."

She sighed, her lips pursing. "I did not say I do not know. Only that I cannot. Not with what I have."

"What does that mean? What do you need?"

Gyda shook her head. She tried to walk past her, but Sunnëva clutched her dark dress. By the old woman's grim expression, the answer to saving her brother would be grave, but she didn't care.

"Please, Gyda. I will get it. Whatever it is."

"What Fenrin needs may cost your life, then he dies anyway. Should I save him, he would be cursed all the same. Let him cross the Gates in peace and mourn him in the morning."

Sunnëva drew out her knife, tears streaming down her cheeks. "You will answer me, Healer. Or Fenrin won't be the only one I burn on the pyre."

Gyda chuckled dryly. "Stubborn as you are foolish." She turned away from her blade and continued up the hill. "Very well, then. Come along. You too, lurking shadow."

Rune appeared behind her from the dark cover of the longhouse. He helped Sunnëva stand, and they followed after the healer. The night was quiet, save for the chatter of wildlife and the crunch of their steps in the snow. Stars speckled the sky above the forest behind her small hut made of wood and clay. It was half the size of a pit house.

Opening her door, Gyda parted the thick canvas covering the threshold and nodded for them to enter. The smoky air was ripe with herbs and other raw scents Sunnëva didn't like. They sat by the small fire, and Rune kept close to her, watching the healer warily.

Gyda tossed logs into the blaze and a swirl of embers drifted into the air. A pot boiling with fish bones hung above it on a spit. "To save your brother, you must face death itself. Prepare yourself, for you walk this path to save a life, but it may end another."

"Tell me what you need. Nothing else matters."

"Come tomorrow, you may change your mind, girl."

Sunnëva took a breath to calm her frustration and ignore her dread. She meant what she said. Her brother was more important than what she would inevitably face.

"What I need are the petals of a certain flower that grows in only one place," Gyda said. The wind wailed outside and shook the hut as if to warn her. "Tanzanite Keep."

The King's castle.

A clammy, cold sensation enveloped her in a horrid chill, and Rune cursed. Not only was the castle miles away and guarded by monsters, but to steal from the King himself was certain death.

"Seven Hells," Sunnëva said incredulously. "You need one of his roses? Of all things, why?"

"Because they are no ordinary roses. They are enchanted with the essence of life the King bestowed them with, and thrive in a land of snow. Everlasting. Their magic will revive anything, including your brother. But I warn you, Fenrin will not be the same."

Because the bite would change him, perhaps leaving him without the use of his leg or his mind. Perhaps it would have been kinder to let him die, but Sunnëva kept seeing Freya's face. She had already failed one sibling.

"Sunnëva." Rune took her arm. "You know what it means to steal from him."

"What if I asked him for one?"

His expression hardened. "He would never help you, no matter how much you plead."

"Then I have no choice. It will only be one rose. I will take it before anyone notices." She knew it was rash and hypocritical after chastising her father for stealing, but Sunnëva was beyond rational right now.

Rune shook his head. For once, he looked anxious. "The land around the castle is a frozen boneyard of all who have died there. Gargoyles protect the garden. They would detect you right away and immediately cut you to shreds."

"Only if we enter the gardens at night. They turn to stone in the morning."

"Sunnëva, don't be daft." He moved to stand. "I was wrong to send you here. Let's go."

"Come with me." She grabbed his hand. "You're from the north. You crossed the Everfrost alive. If anyone can get me through, it's you. I can convince my father to form a warrior party. Then we have a chance."

"Tell her this is mad," Rune snarled at Gyda. "You put this in her head, knowing she would never make it out. Tell her *what* he is."

"What does he mean?" Sunnëva frowned at the old woman. "The King is a fae. Is he not?"

That's what everyone assumed due to his eternal life and great power. No one could remember a time without his reign.

"He is not fae. He is worse than that."

A chill prickled Sunnëva's skin, raising the hair on the back of her neck as if phantom claws caressed her.

"What is worse than that?" she faintly asked.

The healer tossed some herbs into the pot and it hissed, releasing steam into the air. "He lived during the time of the Gods when they roamed the mortal world. They eventually left through their Gates, but the Ice Phoenix stayed. He has seen many ages pass and many moons fall while his magic coated the land in frost. For he is as cruel as this endless winter. He's ruled for a millennium, unchecked in his castle of ice, devouring the souls of all those who have challenged him."

Sunnëva's breath clouded in the night air as a tremble sank down her spine. "Are you telling me he is a God?"

The old woman's milky eyes met hers across the fire, catching the spark of embers. "He wields death, girl. What else do you think he is?"

"No."

"But Father—"

"I said *no*, Sunnëva," he repeated through his teeth. His glower was fixed on the decorative tapestry on the wall beside his seat.

It displayed a beautiful green meadow filled with flowers, sunlight, and dreams. The bottom of the tapestry was frayed where it had been ripped off the loom, abruptly cut away like the life of the one who made it.

"If Fenrin dies, that is his fate. I will not risk the lives of my other warriors to get some rose."

Ansa knelt by Fenrin's bed, her red eyes swollen from crying. His complexion looked gray now. The infection slowly stole away his life while they wasted time arguing. Morning had arrived, and they only had until sundown to save her brother. Yet her father refused to help. He liked to defy the King behind his back, but he didn't have the stones to do it to his face.

"Then I will go," Sunnëva said. "As I am the only one man enough to do it."

Her father lunged at her. Sunnëva braced for the blow, but he backhanded Ansa across the face instead. It sent her small body sprawling to the ground.

"Ansa!" Sunnëva shrieked, running to her.

She helped her sister up and inspected her face. An angry red welt marked her cheek. Ansa hardly reacted. She was used to their father's anger. Sunnëva bit her tongue hard enough to make it bleed, so she wouldn't scream. Bjorn looked away from where he stood, waiting by the door. Not once had he ever come to their defense.

"I *forbid* it." Their father's shadow loomed over them, making her chest tighten. She shielded her sister. "You will honor what I say, Sunnëva. Do you understand me? I decide which lives to sacrifice, and another has already claimed yours."

Her eyes widened. "What do you mean?"

He removed his shield from the wall. "We are going on a hunt in the grasslands. You better be here when I return."

He marched out of the longhouse with Bjorn. The clansmen were waiting outside on horseback. So was Rune, his expression grim. He couldn't help her.

At the Earl's command, the ground rumbled as they rode away. Sunnëva stared after his retreating form. Her father would rather embark on a hunt than do everything possible to save his son.

She cupped Ansa's swollen cheek. "I'm sorry."

Ansa winced, blinking away tears. "It's not your doing."

"Yes, it is."

For her every mistake, he hit Ansa. He knew it hurt Sunnëva more to know it was her doing than to bear the beating herself.

"Claimed?" she whispered.

"I heard him speaking with Bjorn during the feast last night," Ansa said. "He plans to marry you to the Chief's son of the Skelling tribe."

Sunnëva balked. "What? He wants to sell me off to those *creatures*?"

"Fae, really. He said it was an alliance."

The Skellings lived in the Frost Lands, past the Hermon Mountains. A land with nothing but ice. And they were enemies of the Ice Phoenix. That must be why her father wanted to align himself with them. What was he planning?

"I don't understand." Sunnëva rubbed her face. "He's never tried to marry me off before. He knows no one would want me, not when I..." She clenched her fists, feeling every scar tighten on her skin. The ugliest one crossed the thumb webbing of her left hand. It continued up her wrist toward her elbow. "I will not be sold off like cattle for his gain. I'm not marrying a Skelling."

"I would..." Ansa whispered. "If it meant I would leave this place ... If it meant I would be *free*, I would marry any monster."

Sunnëva's heart sank, and her throat tightened. Living under their father's control was a prison they couldn't escape from. But marriage wasn't freedom.

"We won't trade one monster for another." Exhaling a heavy breath, Sunnëva went to her brother and touched his forehead. He was so cold. Fen was dying, and they had already given up on him. "This isn't right."

"No, it isn't." Ansa stood beside her. "Which is why we're not allowing it, right?"

Ansa knew her well. She had never been an obedient daughter.

"If I do this, he will punish me by hurting you."

Ansa smiled sadly, and her mouth wobbled. "Then you better come back. Because if you both die, I will jump into the sea."

"Hush." Sunnëva hugged her tightly. "Don't speak that way. I *will* get that rose, and we will leave this place together."

They could do it.

She would take Fen and Ansa to another clan or make their own way somehow. She knew how to survive the land and to hunt. With Rune by their side, they would be strong enough to fight off whatever came after them. They would be free to live how they wished.

It seemed so simple, and yet it sounded like a desperate dream her father would cleave through.

"Here. Gyda made an elixir to slow the infection." Sunnëva handed Ansa a small jar. "It might hold him until dawn."

They squeezed each other's hands. What she was about to do would change their lives. Regardless of what Gyda said, the King couldn't possibly be a God, but his bloody reputation was based on some truth. Today might be the last day she breathed. If so, it didn't matter. She would gladly give up her life if it meant Fenrin lived his.

"Gods be with you." Ansa's blue eyes welled.

Sunnëva hugged her one more time. "Keep him alive for me until I return."

4

Winds raked over the frozen valley with an eerie howl, lashing against Sunnëva. She raced across it on her horse, cloak rippling in her wake. She wore a thick scarf covering the bottom of her face, never looking away from the castle peeking out of the fog.

It was a day's ride away.

She was determined to make it there by half.

The frigid gust beat against her during the long ride. She grew numb, as did the rest of her body, but she didn't slow her pace.

The sun dropped low in the sky when she reached a thick crop of woods. The trees were black and rotten, twisted together by some ill magic. Goosebumps sprouted on her skin in warning. These were the Black Woods. She shouldn't pass through them, but going around would add an extra day to her travel.

She had to go through it to reach the King's castle in time.

Sunnëva urged her horse onward, but as soon as they crossed the tree line, it bucked with a frightened neigh and threw her off. It kicked up snow, galloping away.

"Coward," she grumbled.

Curse her luck. She faced the wretched woods with a deep breath. Distant roars sounded from within. She pulled her sword free, and her hands shook around the hilt. What were the odds of making it out alive? Very slim.

But Sunnëva smirked and banished her fear. She had faced worse odds.

As soon as she crossed the tree line, a clammy sensation crawled over her body. Every instinct told her to turn back, but she kept going. Her light steps were loud in the eerie silence. The dense trees prevented snowfall. Though everything was still covered in frost. Her shallow breaths clouded in the air as she moved steadily, keeping watch over her surroundings.

The further she walked, the darker it became. Fog curled across the ground, obscuring the shadows. She stopped to break a brittle branch off a tree and beat flint and steel together to light a torch. Once the flames burned, she continued. Every distant howl and growl urged her to move faster.

But it was the sense of time passing that worried her the most.

Sunnëva ran quietly and quickly. Chanting a prayer in her mind over and over for protection. But then she halted in the forest, realizing she'd lost her sense of direction. The branches hid the sky, and the shadows stretched in every direction. Panic set in. Her stumbling feet caught on a root and she tripped. The torch clattered across the frozen ground and landed on the edge of a swamp.

The water burbled as something emerged from the surface and slinked forward into the firelight. Sunnëva's veins ran cold. She didn't know what it was. The monster's legs were a tangle of gray spiky tentacles that writhed like worms. They held up a gaunt torso, tentacle arms, and a faceless bald head that split open vertically with sharp teeth. It straightened to its full height, at least nine feet tall.

Sunnëva scrambled backward with a curse. The creature hissed, a long black tongue forking out. She'd faced many beasts, but she drew the line at swamp creatures with teeth for a face. Grabbing her sword, she ran.

Water sloshed as it descended on her. Sunnëva spun around and struck. It dodged, but her sword slashed through one of its tentacles. It screeched furiously and lashed at her with its spiky arm. Sunnëva ducked underneath and drove her sword through its back. The swamp creature snarled, tearing away with her blade still in its body.

That blow should have killed any beast, but this thing was still alive. Either it didn't have a heart or ... it was a demon.

Her entire body trembled, and she backed away slowly. The demon hissed and Sunnëva threw herself out of the way of its next attack, but his tentacle caught her ankle. The momentum slammed her head onto the ground, and the creature dragged her toward the swamp. She whimpered, her vision spinning as she desperately clawed at the frozen earth. It lifted her up in the air and split open its wide, depthless jaws. She screamed.

A black shadow slashed between them.

The creature shrieked and Sunnëva landed on her back, knocking the breath out of her lungs. The hooves of a horse beat on the ground as a cloaked rider in black galloped out of the trees. She immediately recognized him.

Rune dismounted and strode past her toward the demon. The torchlight revealed the hard planes of his face, making his eyes glow like flames. He removed his axes, and the obsidian blades shone in the firelight. The demon keened and recoiled. Even without a face, she could tell it was *afraid*.

It fled for the swamp, but Rune sprinted with frightful speed and leaped in the air. He slashed his axes, cutting clean through the demon's neck. Its head sailed across the forest with a spurt of dark blood. The body burst into black mist and dissolved away, leaving her sword clattering on the ground.

Sunnëva exhaled a shaky breath. "Rune."

He held out a hand and yanked her up to her feet, cupping her head to his chest. "Damn it, Su. I knew you wouldn't obey."

She sagged against him and wrapped her arms around his firm torso. His warmth thawed the cold from her skin, and she stopped shaking. "I had to come. I couldn't simply do nothing."

Rune sighed, looking down at her softly. "I know. And I couldn't let you do it alone."

"My father allowed you to come?"

"I didn't ask for permission. I stole away shortly after we reached the grasslands."

Knowing full well the consequences, he defied orders and came for her, anyway.

Sunnëva hugged him tighter. "Thank you for coming."

"Anything for you, sweetling."

Her heart warmed. He was the only one who cared enough to help her. Sunnëva quickly retrieved her sword and sheathed it. "What was that thing?"

"Bukavac. Swamp demon."

"Why did it run?"

"It recognized the Nightstone." Rune shrugged with a cocky grin. "Or me. I was a renowned demon slayer in my prime."

She quietly snickered. "I highly doubt they know how infamous you are."

"Surely not." He kicked the torch into the swamp and led her to his horse. "Come. We may reach the castle gardens by nightfall. I know the way."

"But we needed the torch. It's too dark to see."

"We'll be fine. Fire will only draw more attention." Rune mounted and helped her climb up onto the saddle to sit behind him. She hugged his large body as he took the reins.

They rode off into a rapid gallop. Sunnëva could hardly see a thing, but Rune must have better vision since he led his horse with confidence through the dense forest.

They eventually left the Black Woods, coming out on a knoll. The ice castle appeared in the distance, glinting orange in the last rays of the sun before it dropped on the horizon. Time was almost up.

"Rune," Sunnëva said worriedly.

He kicked his heels, and they raced down the knoll to cross a large bridge over a river. They galloped under the cover of twilight across the frozen plains. Scattered across the land were white curving spikes jutting out of the ground. Passing through a row of them, she realized they were the ribs of some large beast.

Bones.

Skulls of every creature and human alike grinned at her from the snowy graveyard. She tightened her arms around Rune's waist.

Then the moon began to rise.

It was full and bright, turning the land silvery white. Rune hissed and steered his black steed beneath the veil of the clouds where the light didn't touch.

"We have to keep to the shadows," he called over his shoulder. "If moonlight hits us, we will be spotted. Once we get inside, don't make a sound."

"Understood."

"Take this." He tucked something into her gloved fist pressed against his stomach.

It was a light blue stone, polished into a flat oval, about the size of an egg. Tanzanite. A crystal that could be infused with spells. She had only heard of their existence. It was carved with a marking she recognized.

Raido.

The rune for *journey*.

"It has enough magic to take you anywhere you desire," Rune told her. "It will only work once. When you use it, think of home."

Sunnëva came on this mission with her courage and wits, but had forgotten an escape plan. Not only had Rune saved her life, they would return in time to save Fenrin's.

"If we survive this, I plan to do very filthy things to you," she said.

Rune's quiet laughter vibrated against her chest.

The closer they got to the castle, the clearer the gargoyles on the roof became. Their growls and the leathery flap of their wings echoed in the wind. Crows cawed as they flew around the tower peaks. They finally reached the castle's defensive wall, and Rune brought them to a section hidden by shrubs. He shoved dried vines aside and revealed a broken section in the wall that was large enough to slip inside.

Sunnëva gaped at it. "How—"

Rune pressed a finger to her lips and shook his head, reminding her to keep quiet. He scaled in first, observed their surroundings, then helped her climb through. They linked hands and ducked under the trees as they ran across the courtyard. He brought her to a stone archway leading into the garden, and then she saw them.

Hundreds upon hundreds of enchanted roses filled the bushes, and climbed up the castle walls, glowing vivid blue with the magic they held.

Sunnëva moved forward, but Rune pulled her behind the archway before a gargoyle flew past. It landed on the defensive wall, blocking the way they came. Her heart sank to see there were more of them lurking above the gardens, on the castle peaks. Their yellow eyes reflected in the dark as they surveyed the area. They guarded the gardens as much as the castle.

There was no way they could steal a rose without being spotted.

They were trapped.

One wrong move, and they were dead.

Sunnëva forced herself to take a breath, trying to remain calm enough to think. If she didn't find a way out, this would be another night she failed.

Rune pulled her close and his warm mouth brushed against her ear, whispering faintly. "The King's magic is woven into the castle, the land, and the ice itself. As soon as we pluck a rose, he will sense it." She trembled with dismay. "There is only one way out of this. I will distract the gargoyles and lead them away on a chase to give you a chance."

"What?" Sunnëva stared at him, dread filling her at his words that sounded like goodbye.

"I came, knowing only one of us would make it back." Rune's eyes softened, and he brushed her cheek. "It was always going to be you."

Tears blurred her vision. "No, Rune. I can't leave you."

"Yes, you can. Do what you came to do, Sunnëva. Save your brother. Be quick. Be brave." He kissed her deeply, holding her close. "Once you have the rose, *run*. And don't look back."

She searched for another option, but there wasn't one. They were trapped in the garden.

It wasn't fair that she kept losing people she loved.

Sunnëva removed his leather cuff, tracing her thumb over his strange tattoo. His eyes searched hers in surprise. She memorized his face, black hair, and pretty mouth. "I would have married you," she murmured under her breath.

He caressed her cheek, his thumb grazing her frozen skin one last time. "I will find my way back to you again. I promise."

Then he ran into the garden, shouting a war cry. The gargoyles chased after him. Rune ducked under their claws and let his axe fly. He cut one down as he ran, leading them in the opposite direction of her.

Sunnëva jumped to her feet and snatched the first enchanted rose she saw. The frosted petals crunched in her palm, thorns biting into her skin as she ripped it free.

The gargoyles whipped around and roared.

"Run!" Rune bellowed.

She shoved the flower into her satchel and sprinted for the opening in the defense wall. The sounds of Rune fighting and gargoyles snarling continued behind her. Horns blared through the night, sounding the alarm. Her heart shot to her throat.

She dove through the hole and hit the ground with a grunt. Rolling to her feet, she dashed for the horse and she threw herself onto the saddle. From the castle came a violent screech, and a massive bird of ice spanned the skies, gleaming against the moon.

"Oh, Gods," she gasped.

The Ice Phoenix.

It wasn't only a name. The King was a shapeshifter.

The bird dove for Rune and his scream echoing across the land went silent.

Sunnëva choked back a sob. Kicking her heels, she galloped away, her tears left to freeze on her cheeks. Gargoyles chased after her.

She reached for the Tanzanite crystal in her pocket.

Purple lightning struck the horse, and it crashed, propelling her through the air. She hit the frozen ground hard, and her body rolled across the ice. When she came to a stop, Sunnëva could hardly move. Pain stole the air from her lungs and strength from her limbs. She lay there, gasping for air as she blinked at the moon through her blurry vision. It reminded her of the last time she was left on the ground, waiting for death.

The sound of feathers fluttered through the air, and a shadow of wings passed over her.

She couldn't die yet.

With her last shred of strength, Sunnëva placed the Tanzanite crystal over her heart and murmured the word that would take her home. *"Raido..."*

Black mist flared around her, and the world faded away.

5

The night Sunnëva first met Rune was the same night she lost
Freya. She was shy of eighteen years old, full of pride and wild
ideas. The clans had gathered in Harden before it was
conquered to celebrate a wedding during the lunar eclipse. They
should not have been out there. It was called a blood moon for a
reason, for it was the night demons came out to hunt. But demons
had avoided the north for decades, and the King provided the clans
with salt to ward the villages, so no one was concerned.

The night was bitterly cold, but Sunnëva hardly felt it. She was
happy, drunk, and feeling pretty in her new green dress. She danced
to the beat of the drums and lyre, flirting with various clansmen.
Freya showed her which ones to pick and how to woo them with her
hips.

"That one!" her older sister said, pointing to a young man with
unruly hair and narrow shoulders. "Ask him to dance."

Sunnëva laughed as they spun around in time with the music. The
beads in Freya's braided hair glittered orange in the firelight.

"I will not ask that hopeless boy to dance when he is gawping at you like a love-sick fool," Sunněva retorted. "Give him a smile, and I'd wager he would trip over himself."

With hair like the sun and eyes like the sky, Freya had a face that belonged in songs. The sound of her laughter spoke of warmth and youth, with the beauty of a fabled spring that drew the eye of everyone who desired her.

"Oh?" Freya peered over her shoulder to gift the gawking young man a simpering smile. He dropped his mug of ale, and they fell into fits of laughter. "Oh, dear."

Sunněva's smile turned into a glower when she spotted Luc walking through the crowd toward them. "Gods, here he comes," she said under her breath.

No matter how many times Freya refused his proposal, he continued to insist. It was insufferable.

"Lady Freya of the Morkhàn Clan," Luc greeted with a sweep of his arm as he bowed. He'd worn his fine leathers and armor today, displaying his status and the yellow sigil of a bear that belonged to his clan. Taking her hand, he pressed his presuming mouth onto the back of it. "Indulge me in a dance so I may plead with you once more to join our Houses. You will find no better man than me, son of the Earl and warrior of Orem. You know I have the means to provide for you and keep your bed warm."

Sunněva scoffed, pulling her sister away. "What a *generous* proposal, but Freya has enough warriors and hunters offering to do what I do for her every day. Her betrothed must meet several requirements, and I doubt an untested *warrior* of the Orem Clan could achieve it."

She had no respect for a clansman who posed as a soldier when his armor still shone. He had yet to join the raids.

Luc's mouth pursed as if he'd eaten something sour. "If you weren't a woman, we would cross swords for that insult."

"I don't need stones or a sword to defeat you. A shield would suffice." Sunněva looked around and motioned to a clansman. "Here, let me borrow yours."

She grinned as cackles broke out. No one sang songs about her beauty, but they did about her battles.

"Stop it." Freya moved her back when Luc looked ready to meet that challenge. "Pardon my sister's rudeness, my lord. Pay her no mind."

He frowned. "Then tell me what I may offer to win your heart."

Freya glanced at her, and Sunnëva gave her a look. Best to break his arrogance and wound his pride, so he thought better of insisting again.

Freya tapped her chin as she thought about it and smiled sweetly at him. "Very well. I will marry you," she said aloud. The music halted, and all attention fell on them. Triumph crossed Luc's face. "The day you have the power to melt the snow and make our land green."

Which was the same as saying *never*, because the land was forever frozen.

Their audience hooted with laughter. Luc flushed red. He shoved his way through the crowd and stormed toward the tables where the ten Earls of the clans were gathered.

Sunnëva held her stomach as she laughed and laughed. "That was better than anything I could have said."

Freya flushed. "I think that was too terrible of me. He has gone to Father to complain."

"Or to beg him for a marriage contract," Sunnëva said as she adjusted her sister's kransen circlet, and Freya fixed hers.

They tittered when Luc stood at the end of the line of men waiting to speak to their father. Bjorn stood beside him, his beefy arms crossed, trying to appear important.

"By the end of the night, he will be drowning in petitions for your hand."

"Hopeless souls." Freya pouted with false sadness. "He will ask too much of them and still not give me away."

They headed to the tables to drink more ale.

"Do you really think the land was once unfrozen?" Sunnëva asked.

A dreamy smile crossed her sister's face. "That's what Gyda told me, and I don't think that old crone is a liar. She said in a past age, the land was once filled with meadows of flowers in every color. Can you imagine?"

Sunnëva almost could. But it was difficult to envision green replacing the white. It was merely a fairy tale they told themselves to hold hope.

"It sounds impossible."

"Impossible is a word used by those who don't believe." Freya winked. "And I believe if I dream of it enough, it will one day be."

Sunnëva rolled her eyes and laughed. "Then you can be the dreamer and I the skeptic."

Before she could reply, little Ansa and Fenrin came running and threw their arms around Freya's waist. "Dance with us!" they pleaded.

Freya became their willing prisoner and let them pull her into the fray. A rare smile lit their father's face as he watched her prance around the fire with their twin siblings.

Freya was his pride and joy.

The doted one.

Sunnëva always saw it there in the hard features that only softened for his first daughter. If he was capable of holding any love for his children, it was reserved for her. She never held it against her sister, even if she was born to an Earl who only wanted more sons. So Sunnëva trained as one. Freya could be the lady, and she would be the shield maiden who protected his happiness because at least she could earn his approval of that.

"I found you another prospect," Freya said when she twirled by.

Sunnëva frowned. "I think I am finished with prospects tonight."

It was fun to flirt and dance, but she had no interest in clansmen. They only wanted her to rut or to wed for convenience. If anyone was going to use her, it was herself.

"I think you might change your mind about this one." Freya nodded past her. "He can't keep his eyes off you."

Sunnëva turned and noticed a man sitting alone by a small fire.

He was clad in fine leather armor the color of coal, with a fur pelt on his shoulders. Black paint patterned with white runes completely covered his face, the mark of a northern warrior. His raven black hair was braided around his ears, falling down his sharp jaw. The baldric strapped to his chest displayed the Harden sigil of a black stag. Sunnëva couldn't measure him beneath all that paint, but what caught her attention were his eyes. They were light, their color indistinguishable against the flames.

And they were not on Freya but on *her*.

Sunnëva's heart leaped under the intensity of his stare. It thinned the air. Her veins thrummed in time with the drums as if it called her to him.

"Ask him to dance," her sister said. "Or ask him for a kiss. Whatever you choose, be brave."

Be quick. Be brave.

Freya pushed her forward and Sunnëva's leather slippers slid over the frozen ground. She tripped and fell into the stranger's lap. He caught her by instinct, his cool hand holding up her back, the other resting on her knee.

His large body was thick with muscle, his strength palpable. The stranger didn't push her off or touch her inappropriately, as others would. He regarded her stoically. Even with the layers of paint on his face, she could tell he was attractive by the curve of his jaw, the line of his nose, and the firmness of his brow. She glanced at his soft mouth, wanting to feel them against hers.

"I ... was sent to ask you for a dance or a kiss, stranger," Sunnëva said. "I will only ask once, for I am in my drink and may not be so forward again."

His gaze was still on her when he shoved aside a drunkard who almost stumbled into them. She glimpsed the tattoo on his wrist— two spirals curving into a loop. The hand supporting her back slid up to her neck, and his cold fingertips brushed her skin, shooting currents down her arms.

She shouldn't be sitting on his lap, proposing such a thing. A moment ago, she had no interest in prospects, or perhaps it was because they didn't stir this response. Her heart beat so fast, the stranger had to feel it thundering against her spine.

"Claim of me either as you wish," he said, his voice deep and lush as velvet, so smooth it thrummed through her body like music. "I shall grant it at the lady's choice."

With as little as fifteen words, he enamored her with his gallant response and rich tones.

Sunnëva looked at his mouth again.

She had kissed others before, from boys behind the stables and warriors leaving on raids. Quick, insignificant kisses given to try, for luck, or favor, but this one she would take for herself.

"Then it is you I claim," Sunnëva said. "On this night, and in my dreams thereafter."

He cupped her head, cradling it in his palm. Her lashes drifted closed, and she pressed her mouth to his cold lips.

She expected a chaste kiss, but that wasn't what he gave.

He devoured her mouth. Staking his claim. Owning her in every way he could. No one had ever kissed her like this. Her palms wandered over his chest, feeling the muscle underneath, her body arching toward him. Beneath the musk of male, fur, and leather, the stranger smelled sweet. Like a winter garden from a world she never thought to find.

Then he pulled away, leaving Sunnëva breathless. Her lips followed in a daze as her eyes opened, staring hazily at him. The stranger seemed equally surprised, as though the kiss struck him, too.

She must be drunk because the firelight haloed the atmosphere. The air seemed to pulse with something magical that made her feel like this was indeed a dream.

His nose skated over hers, speaking raspy words against her mouth. "One kiss for you to claim..." He dipped his head forward again, barely licking her top lip, before stealing another kiss. "And the other I give to pay for the price of a dance."

Sunnëva flushed at the flowery petition. Freya was watching them with a huge grin. "Then I'll dance with you, stranger. But first, I must spare a moment with my sister."

Leaping off his lap, she scampered to Freya. They ran off into the woods to relieve their bladders and giggle to themselves as she recounted every detail.

"I think he was fae," Freya said once she finished. "When you kissed, I swear you sparkled."

Sunnëva laughed. "What?"

"It must have been your innocent heart falling instantly in love."

She shoved her playfully and adjusted her dress. "If he kissed you the way he kissed me, you'd fall in love, too."

"Shall I go ask him then?" Freya teased as they headed back.

Sunnëva shoved her again, but their laughter vanished when they were cut off by four Orem clansmen, Luc included. She moved in front of Freya as the men circled them.

"We hear you like to laugh in our faces and think yourself too good for our clan," the largest of them said. "We will show you the only thing you're good for."

Sunnëva's heart raced, her body stiffening. The men leered at them, fouled by their drink or the evil in their souls. Sunnëva told her sister to run to their father, and she launched herself at the man. But without her weapons, they quickly subdued her. Freya was caught before she made it three steps.

"I will enjoy this," Luc said.

His fist smashed into Sunnëva's stomach, wrenching the air out of her. The next blow struck her jaw, and she buckled to the ground.

They dragged them deep into the woods, away from the feast. Ice crunched beneath their stumbling steps and whimpers. The drums and music of the wedding dance faded beneath the wind, as though that was a different world and she had fallen into this one.

Luc and another hauled Freya away. Sunnëva cursed the two that held her down. She bit and scratched, kicked, and fought. But they beat her half to death, and ripped the kransen circlet out of her hair, tearing strands from her scalp. Then they took turns cutting her flesh as their malicious laughter mingled with Freya's cries.

Her sister screamed and screamed somewhere in the trees. Sunnëva stopped fighting them. She called for Freya, begged them and the Gods to spare her. Over and over she pleaded until her sister no longer made a sound.

Tears rolled down her temples. *Her fault. It was her fault...*

Inward she crawled to a place where nothing could reach her.

Sunnëva looked up at the trees, the branches stretching like claws for the red moon. Snow drifted down, landing on her wet lashes as her blood soaked the earth. She couldn't move or hardly breathe. Every beat of her heart slowed. Her life would end here in the frozen dirt to feed the worms.

And she didn't care.

Everything perished in the Everfrost, and hope was always first.

Sunnëva's mind fogged as she let herself wane. But then a distant sound tugged at her consciousness.

Screams.

Guttural cries of terrified men.

Luc's frantic begging rang through the night. They were the pitiful sounds of someone who knew they were going to die. His pleading was abruptly silenced. Something wet and heavy landed near her. Luc's head. One by one, their cries ended. The forest was filled with the wet tearing of flesh and snapping bones.

They must have stepped out of the protective salt circle when the clansmen dragged them here. Something foul had come, and Sunnëva weakly smiled.

She would rather fall prey to a beast than to a man.

May it kill her quickly and eat her whole, so no one found their bodies. It was better if their family believed they had been spirited away.

But that was not her fate.

The beast stalked forward, its steps almost soundless. It was big, too dark to distinguish properly in her fading vision. But as it got closer, the beast disappeared. A hand reached for her, and she glimpsed the spiral tattoo on his wrist.

It was the stranger. Her Rune.

He gently lifted her in his arms and carried her away beneath the snowfall. She closed her eyes as the cold vanished, and so did her pain.

But Sunnëva wished she had never left those woods.

Because when she woke days later, it was to her father's hatred and to the ashes of Freya's remains on the pyre.

6

The world was shaking. Sunnëva's eyes snapped open with a gasp. There was a pressure on her chest that made it difficult to breathe. Her vision cleared, and she saw Ansa and Gyda kneeling beside her, looking at her worriedly.

"Gods, what happened?" she asked, her voice raspy from thirst

"You dropped out of the ceiling," Ansa said, letting go of her shoulders.

Gyda held up two pieces of the broken Tanzanite crystal. "The Gods are on your side, girl. You returned in time. And *alive*."

Everything rushed back, leaving her mind spinning.

Sunnëva lurched up and winced at the ache that shot through her throbbing body. She was in the longhouse. Villagers were crammed inside, gawking at her. She ignored her father's harsh stare from where he sat in his seat, Bjorn at his side. The light of the full moon shone down on her from the window.

Her throat clamped, and her lungs constricted, choking on the sob she held inside. Because of Rune, she made it back again, but he never would.

"Did you get it?" Ansa asked her hopefully.

"Yes." Sunnëva grabbed her pack and opened it for them to see. The single enchanted rose glowed inside, its petals still glimmering with frost. Her people murmured in awe and Ansa gave a cry of relief.

"Come," Gyda ordered.

Sunnëva limped after the old woman. The clansmen stepped aside, revealing Fenrin in his bed. She gasped. All the color had drained out of him. He already looked dead.

"He clings on," Gyda assured her.

Ansa sat and rested his head on her lap. "She's here, Fen. Sunnëva made it."

She had placed a cloth with runes over his wounded leg and wrapped it in dried ragwort flowers said to nullify magic. But they probably couldn't do much against demon venom.

Sunnëva carefully drew out the blossom, and its power hummed in her palm. The rose was pristine, not a wrinkle or blemish in sight. Only a small speckle of her blood stained the petals.

She passed it to the healer. They fell silent as Gyda plucked the petals and tossed them into a clay bowl. A sweet floral scent filled the air as she ground them into a poultice until it produced a radiant blue oil.

"Lift his head, child."

Ansa shifted her knees further under Fenrin's back and supported his head.

Gyda waved Sunnëva forward. "Help him drink. My old hands may drop it."

Sunnëva's hands trembled as she carefully took the bowl. But something made her hesitate. Was this right? Would the consequences be worth it? After everything, it had to be.

Fenrin wouldn't share Freya's fate.

Sunnëva poured the rose oil into her brother's mouth. It turned his lips bright blue, a drop leaking down his chin like blood. Everyone stared down at him, waiting.

But the seconds stretched without change, and her heart quivered. *Please.*

Fenrin let out a horrible scream.

Flaming light blazed from his eyes and gaping mouth. He writhed on his bed as his veins turned black and webbed across his body.

"Fenrin! What's happening to him?" Sunnëva fought to hold her brother down as he convulsed violently, then he dropped onto the plank bed. Still as death. Her shaking hand touched his cold cheek. "Fenrin?"

What had she done? Had she killed him with magic she didn't understand?

Ansa shook his lifeless form, weeping.

"Leave him," Gyda said. Her wrinkled fingers searched for a pulse on his neck, and she nodded. "He is only unconscious."

"What was that?" her father demanded. "What happened?"

"That was forbidden magic, Earl Thorstein," the old woman replied. "Exactly what was needed to counteract his curse."

Sunnëva's shoulders slumped. "What do we do next?"

"We wait to see if he survives, for he is very weak. His life rests in fate's hands now." Then Gyda gathered her belongings and hobbled out.

The villager's voices droned around her in a dull hum, speaking of witchcraft and curses. Most quickly left, wanting no part of it. Once the longhouse was empty, she moved in front of Ansa and faced her father. Sunnëva's chest tightened painfully, bracing.

He hurled a chair, and it crashed into the wall, splintering to pieces. She flinched but refused to cower. She would take the beatings and words that cut like a whip. Her brother's life was worth whatever befell her.

Her father's eyes simmered. "You disobeyed me."

"To save his life," Sunnëva said. Which was what his father should have done, but she kept that to herself.

"No, stupid girl," he said scathingly. "Do you think you can go into the King's castle and pilfer without him knowing? This is not gold hidden from a raid. This is an insult. You have damned us."

Sunnëva twisted her hands together, scratching at her scars. "The King doesn't know it was me. He didn't see me."

Yet, in the back of her mind, she recalled the Ice Phoenix's shadow in her wake.

"Doesn't he? Where is Rune?"

The sound of his name was a punch in her gut. Sunnëva lowered her head, unable to stop the tears welling on her lashes from spilling.

Her father spat out a curse. "My best slayer was wasted on your idiocy. Wearing my colors. My sigil!"

She shook her head. "He wasn't—"

He closed in on her, his next words cleaving through her bones. "You saved *no one*. If Fenrin lives, it's only to die tomorrow. The King will come. He will come for us all."

Sunnëva stood guard by Fenrin's bedside. She constantly checked his pulse, making sure he was breathing. Trepidation hung over her like storm clouds threatening to pour. She kept hearing Rune's screams in the garden and the flutter of wings chasing her. But the King didn't see her face, and she was sure Rune hadn't worn any livery. How would he know?

But Sunnëva secretly packed a bag, anyway. She couldn't risk staying when it put her clan and family at risk. She filled the bag with rations, clothes, and weapons. Then hid it under the steps of the longhouse with her shield and spear. As soon as morning came, she would take Fenrin and Ansa away.

The hours dragged as she watched the sky, wondering if the King would come.

She didn't need to wait long for an answer.

The Ice Phoenix came like a shadow in the night. The neigh of horses and the beat of hooves galloping into the village signaled their arrival. Sunnëva's heart sped wildly and her hands shook. Ansa's wide eyes met hers across the room. How did he get here so fast?

Her father appeared from his room, his expression harsh and accusing. Her stomach sank. He glanced at Bjorn, then went outside, and she followed with her sister.

The King rode into her village on an enchanted crystal horse that glimmered in the moonlight. A steel helmet hid his face, his eyes glowing a vivid blue. Plates of metal layered his body. He was tall, broad-shouldered, and wore a long dark cloak and fur pelt over his shoulders. A group of riders in black followed him, their faces covered by hoods.

They dragged her people from their beds and made them kneel in the snow. The King dismounted, his heavy boots thudding on the frozen ground. His horse dissolved behind him into flurries. Cerulean magic sparked around him as a scythe materialized in his hand. The handle was black and welded with bone, the wickedly long blade the color of midnight. His riders spread out, lighting torches and spearing them into the ground until the entire village was lit.

Sunnëva kept her head low, quivering. She risked peeking at him when he walked past them. All she could see were those icy eyes that glowed like falling stars. They were cold and merciless, leaving her body to freeze.

The King didn't speak to anyone, but they all knew why he came.

One of his riders stepped forward. There was nothing to distinguish him from the others but a silver pin of the phoenix crest on the right side of his chest.

"Earl Thorstein," the rider called to her father in a cool tone. "Your clan has been marked for death. As is the punishment for stealing from his majesty, King Jökull, ruler of the Everfrost."

Ice sank through Sunnëva's body. *No.*

"But the King is merciful," the rider continued. "Return the rose and give up the thief. Then you will be spared."

This was merciful?

Her father looked at her with contempt, because he told her this would happen. The cost of her actions arrived, and she had no choice but to accept it.

Sunnëva shifted forward on her knees and bowed until her forehead touched the snow. "I am the thief, sir..." she said, the words trembling on her lips. "I alone went into the King's garden and stole the rose. But I cannot give it back. I humbly beg your pardon."

The rider crouched in front of her. He took her wrist in his gloved hand and inspected the minor cuts on her palm left behind by the thorns. "Where is it?"

She swallowed, stiffening. "It's gone—"

"It's here." Bjorn came outside carrying Fenrin. He lay him in the snow at their feet. Fen moaned and shuddered from the cold.

"Bjorn," Sunnëva gasped. "What are you doing?"

"What I have to," he murmured.

The rider stood, looking down at her brother.

"A warg bit him," her father said. "She could not accept his death and did something foolish to save a life that should not have been saved."

Silence fell over the King and his men. The rider turned to his master, and there was a long pause between them.

Sunnëva sucked in a breath. "It was the only thing that would heal him," she said desperately. "It wasn't his fault. This was my doing!"

"The rose was not meant for humans to consume," the rider told her, a hint of regret in his tone. "We cannot allow it. His life is forfeit."

"No!" She lurched toward Fenrin.

Her father stepped in the way and grabbed her arm, his hard fingers digging into her numb skin. "Leave him. There is nothing you can do."

"No, please!" Sunnëva cried. Why did she leave Rune to perish if it was all for naught?

Riders grabbed her brother's arms and legs, carrying him off. Fenrin woke and whimpered, calling her name in confusion.

"Fenrin!" Sunnëva shoved off her father and tried to run after him, but Bjorn pinned her down.

They took her brother into the woods, and the King followed. She pleaded for his life, choking on her cries. But it was the same as when Freya died. She could only listen to Fenrin's screams in the forest, powerless to stop it. Wild beast sounds reverberated in the night as they tore him apart. Sunnëva screamed with him, Ansa crying at her side.

Then all fell silent.

Bjorn let go, and Sunnëva sobbed wretchedly in the snow.

You saved no one.

The King came out of the trees, his armor speckled with blood. Her stomach twisted and bile lodged in her throat. He slaughtered her brother like it was nothing. Tore him apart for what?

All for a rose.

He marched away and shifted into an enormous white bird as big as the longhouse. Moonlight glinted over his ice feathers, illuminating the focus of her hatred.

She was tired of those in power taking from her. Tired of losing those she loved. Tired of not being enough to keep them safe. Simply tired of it all.

Sunnëva elbowed Bjorn in the groin and stole his sword. "Curse you," she screamed at the creature's retreating back. *"I curse you!"*

He turned, and she swung the sword with all her might, releasing a primal scream of rage. It whipped through the air, cleaving through the snowfall toward his face. The phoenix tilted his head a mere inch, and the sword zipped past, fluttering his feathers.

Those icy eyes bore into her.

For a brief moment, all was still. The shock of his riders, her family, and her clan smacked into her sharply like the bitter wind. Sunnëva drew out her shield and spear from where she'd hidden them beneath the steps of her home. Both shook in her hands. Attacking the King was a death sentence, but if she was to die tonight, then it would be on her terms.

"Fight me," she said. "If I draw first blood, we will no longer live under your rule. If I lose, my life is yours."

S unnëva didn't give him time to react. All she had to do was hurt him. She would make him bleed, even if it meant dying. She ran at him and lanced the spear. It arced through the air for her target, soaring through the veil of sleet.

The Ice Phoenix let it come.

The spear hit his chest and bounced away. She froze, blinking at him. He was a solid glacier. Her spear couldn't penetrate his frosted feathers. He flapped a wing, and the sheer force of the wind threw her across the clearing. Sunnëva hit the ground with a grunt, and her face smashed against a sharp stone. Blood leaked down her cut cheek, landing bright red in the snow.

He won without trying.

The Ice Phoenix shifted back to his other form, and the King strode forward. She rolled to her feet for her shield, but his riders had their swords at her neck before she could grab another weapon. They parted when the King reached her.

He towered over her, at least seven feet tall, his body large enough to block the gust passing over them. The sharp plates of his armor reflected the flame. She stilled beneath his glowing stare as all else fell quiet. He removed his helmet, revealing the man behind his dire reputation.

Sunnëva didn't know what she expected.

Anything but what she saw.

His long hair, as white as snow, fell past his sharp jaw to his chest. The torches flickered, sending firelight dancing across his features. She took in his gleaming armor, the sharpness of his cheekbones, the rigid planes of his body, and the softness of his mouth. Dark tattoos crawled up his neck, writhing on his skin. His blue eyes glowed ominously in the dark.

Jökull was devastatingly beautiful. Almost too beautiful, like something only found in hallucinations.

And he was frightening.

His cold presence filled the void between them. A knot formed in her chest. It tightened and shifted inside of her as if merely looking at him consumed all the air out of the atmosphere.

She couldn't breathe.

"Well, vicious little thorn," the King said. His voice was a velvety rumble, sending goosebumps down her arms. She flinched when his armored hand took her chin. "What do you plan to do now?"

Sunnëva glanced down at her boot, where she'd hidden her bone knife.

His icy fingers grabbed her throat, and he lifted her a few inches off the ground, the pressure nearly strangling her. She clutched at his arm, her toes struggling to find footing in the snow. His hold was unyielding.

The King lowered his head, his piercing eyes boring into hers. They were splintered with white threads, like cracks in a frozen lake. "I do admire your tenacity," he mused. "But don't make another choice you will regret."

Her heart pounded wildly behind her ribs. By the sharpness of his grip, she knew it wouldn't take much to remove her head. He would snap her neck faster than she could reach for the knife.

God or not, he held her life in his hands.

"You steal from me, then challenge me," the King said in that smooth rumble again. It pricked her flesh, sending shivers down her spine. He released her, and she fell, gasping for air. "You care little for your life."

"Why care when it's no longer mine?" She glared at him, rubbing her neck. "Do what you will with it, then. I don't fear death."

Jökull's dark chuckle fell over her like a blanket of barbs. "At times, death is the kindest gift fate has to offer." His voice sank into her soul, her body trembling with something that wasn't cold. "What is it you cursed me with?"

"My face," she hissed. "May it haunt your every waking hour until you're mad, and it's the last thing you see when you draw your final breath."

He studied her as his riders cackled. Maybe it was a stupid curse, but she wanted him to remember this moment and for her blood to eternally stain his soul.

Her people huddled behind her, terrified. Her father and brother looked grim. Ansa held Gyda's hand, softly weeping.

I'm sorry, Sunnëva mouthed at them. *Take care of her.*

Jökull's scythe materialized in his grip. Sunnëva shifted to her knees and lowered her head, exposing her neck. Shivering, she closed her eyes and withdrew into that dark place, ready for the end.

"By all rights, I can kill your entire clan." The King's proclamation echoed in the silence.

Sunnëva's lashes flew open to find him analyzing her people.

Her breath caught. "You won't touch them! Kill me, and be done with it. That is all you're owed."

His eyes flared brighter. "I decide what is owed, fragile mortal. Not you."

Flurries whirled around him. The wind picked up, and the air turned so bitterly cold it burned against her skin. Her rapid breaths curled around her face with each exhale. Ice cracked over the snow, and her heart raced as the torchlights went out, one by one.

"Please spare them," she said in a panic. "Please!"

"I have never been swayed by begging." He looked down at her coolly. "But your life is now mine. Therefore, that is all I will take."

Sunnëva sagged with relief so heavy she collapsed in the snow.

"Spare her, my King." Her father bowed beside her, shocking Sunnëva. "My foolish daughter is spirited and acted out of desperation. Take her as a bride. She is a worthy prize. Fierce in battle and of noble birth. She would make a fine wife and bond my clan's loyalty to you."

Jökull gazed at her for a long moment, truly considering it.

Disgust roiled through her stomach, and she bared her teeth. "I would rather die."

A gasp went through the crowd.

Her father snatched her arm, his grip bruising. "Your life is no longer yours to decide, stupid girl."

Jökull snarled at him. "Do *not* touch her."

Thorstein jerked back.

The King's frigid gaze fell on Sunnëva again. The wind blew against them, weaving her hair around her face. His gaze flickered on the fresh cut on her cheek, then to the scar on her temple, coursing into her hairline. "What is your name?"

She gritted her teeth when he took her chin again. "Sunnëva."

"Sunnëva..." Jökull repeated, sounding each syllable. "A name that means gift of the sun. It suits you." His mouth twitched, perhaps finding that amusing. He leaned in close, his mouth parting to reveal the tips of his fangs in the moonlight. Whatever he was, it wasn't human. "I will give you a choice, Sunnëva Morkhàn. You either accept my hand in marriage, or you and your people will die tonight. Choose."

She was speechless in the windy silence, as was everyone listening. Her mind spun with his proposal, unable to make sense of it.

Sunnëva struggled to speak, her throat becoming dry. She licked her cracked lips, and he followed the action, watching as her tongue darted out. "Why?"

Surely he must have noticed she wore no kransen, the mark of a maiden. She wasn't from a royal family, nor any beauty to behold. Not a moment ago, she tried to kill him.

Yet he wanted her as a wife?

The King's mouth curled with the barest hint of a sneer. "Perhaps I am taken by your devotion and ferocity."

She didn't believe him, yet he offered no other explanation.

Her people shivered in the cold fearfully as they all waited for her answer. There wasn't really a choice when denying him would end her entire clan.

Maybe luck was on her side after all. What better way of getting close enough to bury her knife in his throat than by getting into his bed?

Sunnëva lowered her head demurely. "I accept."

Satisfaction glinted in his eyes, and Jökull straightened.

"My House is honored, sire," her father said, clearing his throat. "And ... what of the bride price? It is customary to pay the bride's family to secure her hand."

Sunnëva almost laughed at her father's nerve.

"And what is your price, Thorstein?" the King said, shocking her next.

"The land from here to the end of the Hermon River, in addition to ten years of ten percent levy," he replied without hesitation.

"You would sell her for ten years of reduced taxes?"

"I would sell her for ten bags of grain, sire. That is how desperate we are for another day of life."

Jökull chuckled, the low rumble startling Sunnëva. "Humans. So fickle and ignorant to the real value of life." He nodded at her. "And what say you, daughter of the Morkhàn clan? What do you think you're worth?"

"She does not speak for—"

Jökull silenced her father with a look.

He asked her to set a price for herself? She could either risk angering him or her father. She had her pride, but her clan suffered enough. He wanted her for some reason. Then she may as well take more in return.

"Make it fifty years, then. No matter my lifetime," Sunnëva dared to say. "And fifty bags of grain each quarter."

"Done."

He so easily agreed? He didn't even pause to think. Food was more valuable than fortune in the Everfrost. If he was so wealthy, she should have asked for fifty cattle then, or fifty roses, or fifty damn chests of gold.

The King was never generous. Why now? Perhaps to make her come willingly. She should have thought better about her answer.

Jökull canted his head at the look on her face. "What else do you desire?"

She swallowed, considering what she wanted most. "Protection."

"You are the King's bride. No one will ever touch you again," he replied, his voice suddenly deathly quiet. "None other than I."

She ignored the flush creeping up her neck. "Not for me, but for my sister. If I am to leave her, then I want your word that *no one* will put their hands on Ansa ... lest he lose those hands."

As if he knew the reason for her request, the King pointed his scythe at Thorstein's throat. "The Morkhàn clan is now under my protection, as well as my bride's sister. Swear it now."

Thorstein swallowed. "On my vow, no one will touch my daughter."

"If you break it, I will remove more than your hands." Jökull's cool stare fixed on her father until the message became clear, and he marched away. "You have until tomorrow to say your goodbyes. We will wed at sundown."

The air pulsed with magic, then Jökull shifted into the Ice Phoenix and flew away. His riders mounted their crystal horses, and the ground rumbled as they rode off in his wake.

Sunnëva watched his form shrink until he vanished behind the clouds. She did it. She lost her will and brother, but Ansa was safe.

"Well done, daughter." Thorstein snatched her arm, forcing her to look up at him. "You wanted to kill him, well here is your chance. Earn his trust. Learn his secrets and find his weakness. End his reign so the Morkhàn clan can rise. That is how you avenge Fenrin. That is how you atone for Freya. Bring me his heart."

Atone.

The word lit coal in her stomach, searing her from the inside. He left her there with the blood of her siblings on her hands.

Ansa dropped in the snow and hugged her tight. "Why did you do that?" she cried. "Why?"

"Everything dies in the Everfrost..." Sunnëva said as her tears fell.

They eventually stumbled away together to recover Fenrin's body. All that remained was a chewed-up arm, feasted on by the crows in the dawn.

The superstition was true, after all.

Sunnëva built a small pyre in the woods for Fen and on top she lay Rune's cuff. It was all she had of him.

She lit it on fire, and they watched it burn together. *May you cross the Seven Gates in peace. May the Gods receive your souls.*

The Ice Phoenix took lives as he wished, ruling over their bones and spilling blood with none to challenge him. But her defiance grew from the poison of her hatred. She would marry the King, but not because her father ordered her to.

This was for her.

In the silent snowfall, Sunnëva swore to all the Gods she would be the one to end him.

8

Sunnëva had one day to figure out how to kill her husband-to-be. And there was only one person in the village who could help her. But when she came to Gyda's hut, the old healer tsked and shut her door.

"Gyda, please."

"I can't help you anymore," came her raspy reply behind the door. "I warned you, foolish girl."

Sunnëva's eyes burned with unshed tears as she folded over herself, gripping her mourning garments in her fists. All of this was her fault. Yet she still breathed.

"I should have burned on the pyre," she said. "But why? Why does Death pass over me? Why does it take others in my stead?"

Freya.

Rune.

Fenrin. Her clothing was stained with his ashes.

Why were they gone instead of her?

"Because you have been marked, girl." Gyda stepped out, looking at her with pity. "Death claimed you a long time ago."

Sunnëva had felt its touch on the night of the lunar eclipse. That should have been her end, but fate cruelly spared her. She always asked herself for what? They lived in a miserable land shackled by a tyrant king, but maybe now there was a chance to end his curse.

"I tire of seeing my loved ones die," she told her. "I must do this so our people can thrive. So life can change and the Everfrost can be green again. Those are the stories you told us. It's what Freya dreamed of. Help me make it real."

The old healer sighed heavily, and her wrinkles creased, aging her further. "The King is indestructible. *Immortal*. I told you what he is."

Jökull was undoubtedly powerful, but that didn't make him one of the Seven Gods of the Seven Gates.

"He isn't a God. Otherwise, why be among mortals?" Sunnëva said. "Whatever he is, there has to be a way to kill him."

"You come to ask what I cannot give."

"Because you do not know?"

Gyda hobbled past her and sat on a log placed for seating outside of her hut. She looked out at the frozen forest beyond. "I am old. I have learned and discovered many things others should never see. Every creature, spell, and curse has a flaw. That is the natural law of life. The Ice Phoenix must have a weakness, girl. But what it is, not even I know."

She wilted.

The old woman regarded her grimly. "However ... there are those out there with the curse of knowledge. They know dark secrets and futures that have not yet come to pass. The one with the answer to your question would be the Druid. He is *Seidr*. A fae Seer with eyes cursed by the God of Time."

A shiver sank through Sunnëva's already numb body. "Where can I find him?"

"*He* finds *you*." Gyda tapped on the charred stones circling the ashes of her dead campfire. "Go into the woods and build a circle of stones with an offering inside. Food or treasures to tempt his interest. Call on him, and the wind will carry your message. Should he care to answer, that will be up to him." She shook her head. "Take heed of my warning. Sometimes it's best not to know your fate."

Foreboding hovered in the atmosphere like the coming of lightning. Her pulse quickened, but Sunnëva already knew there was no turning back from this path.

"Even if I tell you not to do this, your heart is heavy, and it seeks retribution. Can you let go of your need for revenge?"

She smirked faintly. Perhaps in another lifetime.

Gyda sighed. "Gods be merciful, then."

The married women of the clan gathered in the longhouse to help Sunnëva bathe and cleanse herself for the wedding. After they dressed her in traditional bridal garments, her father came in. He watched stoically from his seat as they braided thin strips of silk cloth into her hair. Ansa placed their mother's ceremonial crown on her head. It was made of woven driftwood and adorned with crystals and charms.

She'd never planned to one day marry. The desire hadn't crossed her mind ... until Rune. He was the one this should have been for.

Ansa held up a round mirror. Sunnëva didn't recognize the woman in the reflection. Her blue irises, threaded with dark gold in the center, were stark against her pallid complexion. Faint bruising flowered around the scab on her cheek. Her blonde hair shone in soft waves around her shoulders, her lips stained red, and her eyes lined with kohl. She looked thin and fragile.

Afraid.

Pretty frills and beads hid the warrior beneath.

Perfect.

The women excused themselves, leaving them alone. The fire crackled in the silence as Sunnëva waited for him to say something fatherly. Of course, he didn't. And she hated herself a bit more for pathetically wishing for some sliver of approval.

"Did you think this day would come?" Sunnëva asked. "That I would wed, let alone wed the King."

"Not for you." Bitterness laced his tone with the barest hint of melancholy underneath. Her chest compressed with another invisible boulder.

They had always been mercilessly honest with each other. So why did she keep hoping he would care for her as a father should? But even as a child, he spared her no kind word or affection. He didn't even cry when their mother died in childbirth.

Only one had reached the pitted shell of his heart.

"Do you wish..." Sunnëva swallowed, daring to ask what had lurked in her mind for the past five years. "Do you wish Freya had survived instead of me?"

His gaze lifted to the tapestry on the wall. The one her sister had loomed with the design of a green field full of flowers and trees. Free of snow. It looked like a land of daydreams. But now Sunnëva realized it was merely an unattainable reality while the one she lived in was a nightmare.

"Every day," her father said.

The sting of tears burned behind her eyes and nose. Not because she wanted him to love her, but because it confirmed he never would.

"You know the purpose of this marriage, Sunnëva." His harsh stare returned to her. "It's not real and not for love. Never forget that. Don't betray me. No amount of protection will prevent Ansa from suffering your failure."

Her lungs tightened with a shallow breath, and she straightened her spine. "Nothing will make me forget."

"Good." He headed for the door.

"Whether I fail or succeed, I hope to cross the Gates with your forgiveness," Sunnëva said, and he paused with his back to her. They both knew it was unlikely she would survive this. "Should you recover my body, burn me under the full moon."

Thorstein glanced at her for the briefest of moments. Whether it was with regret or agreement, it was too fast to know. He stepped out of the longhouse, leaving her to stare into the fire until her wet eyes dried.

Sunnëva braided her hair away from her temples, then painted her face with runes as was custom, but continued to smear paint over her eyelids and drew a line down her lips to her neck.

War paint.

She was going off to battle and wanted everyone to know it.

Sunnëva stood, and her crimson garments flowed like blood around her feet. Despite her white, fur-lined cloak, the cold sank into her bones.

She took the main path to the village square where the ceremony would be held. Her people had put together a wedding fit for royalty, at least within their means. Tables were decorated in colorful cloth, displaying a full feast. That must be all of their winter rations. The Morkhàn banners were up, and the musicians were ready.

Her father stood on the podium in the center. The clan watched in solemn silence as she walked toward him and climbed the steps. Sunnëva was stiff, her limbs frozen as they all waited to witness her union with the beast of the land.

Orange and pink streaks painted the sky when the cloaked rider who had spoken the night before arrived on his crystal horse. The Ice Phoenix broke through the clouds. It let out a screech that pierced the air, its icy feathers catching the fading light. The bird dove in a gust of flurries, and Jökull shifted as he landed.

Her people bowed low, and she lowered her head. His heavy steps vibrated through her feet as he climbed onto the platform. Jökull wore no armor today. He was dressed in a fine black jacket and a gray pelt over his heavy cloak.

Distaste coated her tongue as she peered at him beneath her lashes, taking in his eerie glowing eyes and firm hands tipped in sharp, black talons. How would this day be told in the ages to come? Would it be the fairy tale of an impoverished girl who caught the

King's eye and all her wishes came true? Or would they tell the dark fable of a girl who sank into Death's clutches with her own claws?

The ceremony commenced. Per tradition, Jökull presented her with a sword. Instead of steel, it was made of Nightstone with a pitch-black blade and a polished hilt so fine it had to be pure silver. It was a symbol of his protection.

In turn, Sunnëva gave him Fenrin's sword.

A symbol of her spite.

The King handed it to his rider and drew out a ring. The band was gold, weaving delicately like vines around an iridescent gem as white as fogged ice. "Do you choose to bind yourself to me by accepting this ring?" he asked.

Such a strange way to put it. Not would she be his wife, but would she bind herself? Whatever customs he had, they were all the same. She would become his captive now and did so willingly.

Sunnëva raised her gaze to his, fueling all of her hatred in one single word. "Yes."

Retracting his lethal talons, Jökull took her hand with an unexpected gentleness and slipped the ring onto her finger. It glinted beautifully in the firelight, but it felt like a fetter of snow. They drank from the bridal cup, sealing her doom.

Her father's faraway voice sounded like a distant crash of waves as he chanted the prayer for marriage and handfasted their hands together with a sash of braided cloth. She braced herself for the kiss at the end of their vows, but her father didn't mention it, and the King didn't try.

The rider brought out a scroll with their marriage contract detailing the bride's price of land and the provision her father gained with her purchase. Jökull signed his name at the bottom. Thorstein signed hers, then his as a witness.

And the ceremony was over.

Sunnëva sat at the bridal table with her new husband as her people feasted and drank honeyed mead. Girls pranced around the fire to the music, the drums beating in time with her pounding heart. For the briefest of seconds, she saw Freya dancing among them and heard the echo of her laughter.

I will make the land green again, Sunnëva told her. *I swear it.*

She tracked the last golden rays of sunlight as it vanished across the horizon.

It was time.

Ansa came to the table and curtsied. "Sire, our house is made ready for your stay. May I take my sister to help her dress into her consummation robes?"

Sunnëva lowered her head, attempting to appear timid. It wasn't hard. Heat rushed up her face at the thought of someone touching her who wasn't Rune. She intended to bury her knife in the King's throat before he had that chance.

He took a drink, letting the question ripen in the air. "No need. She is coming with me tonight."

Ansa stiffened, and Sunnëva's heart sank. No, this ruined her plans.

"I trust you have no complaint against this, Earl Thorstein."

Her father, sitting at the table beside them with Bjorn and his war chiefs, lifted his horn of mead. "She is yours now, sire. I care not where you bed her."

Sunnëva ground her teeth at the callous response. She forced herself to place a hand over Jökull's on the table. It was like a block of ice. "My dear husband, forgive me. I do not wish to speak against you, but it's tradition for every maiden." She grimaced through a smile, knowing she had no right to be called that. "Even if we do not ... consummate here, please allow me to dress myself as is proper. If not for my honor, let it be in my late mother's name, as she is not here to see her daughter wed."

Jökull looked down at where she touched him, then up to her face. Her heart raced under his glowing stare. "As you wish."

Her stiff shoulders relaxed in relief.

"But I will no longer indulge your *traditions*." He stood. "I'll wait for you on the rise outside the village. Come shortly. I do not like to be kept waiting."

She bowed her head. "I am grateful for your kindness."

Jökull left the table with his rider, taking the path out of the village.

Sunnëva stood and faced her father. "I leave my clan, but my heart stays. The Gods be with you always."

Bjorn nodded. Her father continued drinking and eating as if she didn't exist at all.

Their goodbyes were already said.

She climbed down the steps to Ansa and hurried into the growing darkness. When they were out of view of the wedding party, they ran to the Azure Tree. Sunnëva pulled out a wrapped bundle from a hollow in the trunk and took out her white robes, along with a pink pearl she stole from her father's storehouse.

Ansa quickly helped her change and folded up her wedding garments. The wind blew against her thin robes, pebbling her skin. They hugged tightly.

"I made you this." Ansa tied something around her wrist. A bracelet braided with golden threads, decorated with beads and wolf teeth.

Sunnëva's vision welled when she realized what it was. Her sister had added a small dial made from the white bark of the Azure Tree, carved with the rune for protection.

"I cut off one of Fenrin's braids last night … in case he…" Ansa's tears spilled, her mouth trembling. She wore one of his braids, too. "You did right by him, Sunnëva. You do right by him now. I am proud to call you sister, and I will pray for your safe return."

The love and sadness on her sister's face both warmed her heart and broke it.

Sunnëva kissed her cheek. "I love you, Ansa. If I don't return, search for me in the brush of the wind and know that it's me. Now go."

Ansa nodded. She walked backward a few steps as they shared one last look, then ran toward the village. Sunnëva wiped away the wetness from her eyes. Her fingers came away smudged black.

She gathered stones into a circle and placed the pearl inside. She stepped back and took a deep breath. "I call upon the Druid," she said

65

into the night. "Come and share with me your knowledge—at whatever price you choose."

It was the most awful thing to offer the fae, but she could think of nothing else that would guarantee his appearance.

Only the rattle of leaves and branches answered. No. He had to come.

"Please." She clenched her shaking fists. "I beg you."

"*Oh.*" Low laughter came deep from within the forest. Goosebumps sprouted across her skin at the sound of his gleeful voice. "I do like begging."

A branch snapped behind her, and she whipped around. She couldn't see anything in the shadows. When she thought his form hid behind a tree in front of her, a rattle of bushes came from her left.

"More so from the desperate who beg so recklessly." His eerie words carried a forewarning.

She scowled. "I am desperate. I want to know—"

"I know what you want," the Druid hissed in her ear.

Sunnëva gasped and spun around.

He moved among the trees, his steps prowling around her. "There is a cost for the answer and a cost for the result. Both you will pay. One to me and the other to your heart. And they will be painful. Do you agree?"

A horrible, clammy sensation climbed up her back. Here was a choice. Two paths into the future, but she had already decided which one to take. Because Sunnëva could still smell Fenrin's ashes and feel Rune's last kiss. She heard Freya's screams and bore her father's hate.

And because all she had was vengeance.

"*Yes.*"

"Splendid."

She glowered at his mocking tone. "What is the payment?"

"The latter is fate's price that you will pay in due time. My price is that which brought you here in the first place."

Sunnëva stiffened. "You want an enchanted rose?"

"Aye, but this one must be given, not stolen."

"How?" she hissed. "The King kills for those roses."

"When your hatred begins to thaw, the rose will fall into your hands."

"Then you play your tricks. That will *never* happen."

The Druid laughed, the sound weaving among the branches. "Never say never."

Fingers brushed against the edge of her hand, and she jumped. A tingling sensation crawled across her palm to her fourth finger. She removed her wedding band and saw a glowing spiral wrap around her finger like a worm or the root of a tree, before settling into a dull brown mark.

"A geas to seal our deal," the Druid said.

Sunnëva replaced the ring, covering his mark perfectly, like he had planned it. "Now give me what I came for." She searched the forest shadows for him, hearing the soft crunch of his steps in the snow as he circled her. "How do I kill the Ice Phoenix?"

"Many have tried and failed to achieve this. His power is beyond your comprehension."

Her stomach pitched with dread. "Are you telling me it's impossible?"

"*Nothing* is impossible."

She took an eager step forward. "Then how?"

"The answer you seek lies where you do not see."

"Speak clearly, or I will pluck out your eyes," Sunnëva snapped, tired of his games. Time was running out, and soon the King would wonder about her delay. "Tell me how to save my world."

The jeering laugh came again, and it made her teeth clench. "Very well, I will give you exactly that. What is not a God but gives life? What bleeds but doesn't die? And is as unpredictable as the rising tide?"

Sunnëva shook her head. "I don't know what that means."

"And you won't know, scheming mortal." Golden eyes surfaced from the dark, glowing unnervingly as they peered at her. "Until the day comes, you'll wish you didn't."

She waited for more, but his dark form retreated into the shadows. "That is not an answer!"

"It is a riddle for you to solve during your stay in the castle of ice. By the time you unravel it, you will have led your husband to his demise."

"Why not simply tell me?"

"This way is much more fun." The Druid's laughter faded away. The wind rushed through the trees, howling like a wicked creature.

The pink pearl was gone.

A terrible shudder crawled down her spine. Sunnëva ran toward the village, cursing her stupidity. She didn't get a clear answer, but he confirmed the King could die. That was all she needed.

She grabbed the edges of her robes and ran down the path to where everyone waited at the base of the hill. The wind whipped around her, pressing the thin fabric against her nakedness and exposing her scarred legs. Her face burned from embarrassment.

Jökull said he would be waiting, but he wasn't there. She rushed up the hill and looked for footsteps, or the hoofprints of his rider's mount. The snow was untouched.

She took too long. Maybe the King was insulted and went to demand an annulment from her father.

A screech called from above.

The Ice Phoenix circled the night sky and dove for them. Her people screamed and scattered in every direction. But it was coming right for her. He cawed again, the sound tearing into her ears. Sunnëva ran and leaped off the hill.

Talons caught her arms mid-air and hauled her off into the sky. The wind stole Sunnëva's scream, shoving it back into her throat.

9

They soared high among the clouds. The howling wind muffled her panicked cries and curses. It thrashed against them so hard Sunnëva was terrified Jökull would drop her. He had her securely trapped in the cage of his black talons, but she screamed anyway. She clung to the leathery part of his legs, crushing the ice-cold feathers in her fingers hard enough to make him screech at her.

The dark ground was too far to see, but the Ice Phoenix seemed to know where he was going. A tall highland came in the distance, with some sort of structure. She squinted at it past the sleet. *What was that?*

The Ice Phoenix flew down to it and dropped her. Sunnëva's shriek cut off when she landed in the plush snow.

She pushed up on her wobbly limbs. The frigid air bit into her skin and it rendered her instantly numb. Past the whip of snow was a towering, stone archway on a set of steps with a hollow center. It had a domed roof with elegantly carved pillars leading down a short passageway. The other end merely opened to the rest of the frozen hill.

The Ice Phoenix landed and shifted. His glowing gaze fixed on the archway ... waiting for something.

Sunnëva frowned. The structure wasn't for shelter and it didn't lead to anything. She didn't understand what it was or why they were there.

"What are you doing?" Sunnëva called. "What is this place?"

The King didn't answer. He gritted his teeth, scowling at the structure. He snarled a demand in a foreign language.

The longer they stood there, the more sensation she lost in her body.

"I can't be here," Sunnëva said tersely. "Are you listening? I will freeze to death!"

That got his attention.

Jökull's gaze shot to her face, then raked down to her exposed cleavage and trembling legs. Frost coated her hair and lashes. She shook violently, her arms wrapped tightly around her torso as her thin white robes flapped in the wind like a veil. What she wore was meant to be removed, not to keep her warm.

Sunnëva moved away before he could grab her. "I need to get out of this wind."

She noticed a shallow cave in the cliffside and ran to it. But the ground vanished when he snatched her into the sky again. Sunnëva screamed curses at the stupid bird, demanding to be put down. He ignored her or didn't hear her past the roaring wind as they flew higher.

The Ice Phoenix let out a loud caw that echoed through the night, and from the darkness appeared the glinting spires of his ice castle. Monstrous creatures moved on the battlements. Some howled and called back, welcoming their master.

He flew to a large open balcony in the highest tower and dropped her again. Sunnëva screamed as she landed on the frozen stone. The Phoenix circled, and another screech ripped through the sky. A warning before he dove straight for her. Sunnëva scrambled to her feet and ran into the dark room. There were no torches inside. Moonlight glinted on the floor-length mirror in the corner, reflecting fractures of light over every frozen surface. The chambers had an elevated ceiling, made to accommodate the gigantic bird coming inside behind her.

Sunnëva backed away, bumping into a round table with chairs, tripping further until she landed on a bed. It was large and lavish, made with dark wood and an elegant canopy that framed it with velvet curtains. The icy black sheets were stiff and cracked under each of her movements.

Everything in the room, from the furniture to the candles, glimmered with frost. It was so cold, her breaths clouded in the air as she clutched her arms to herself.

The phoenix assessed her violent tremors. Talons scraped the floor as it stepped closer, moonlight glinting off his ice feathers.

Sunnëva climbed further onto the bed and pulled the blankets and furs around her. Needles jabbed at her nerves now that she was out of the wind. "You nearly got me killed, vile beast," she hissed at him. "You may be immune to the cold, but humans are not."

He stared at her in silence, tapping his talons contemplatively.

"Why did you take me to that place?"

Jökull shifted and strode to a bureau with a basin without answering. He punched inside, and she flinched at the sharp sound of ice cracking. He splashed water on his face and leaned over it, his hands resting on the edge of the bureau. His broad back was stiff, and she sensed he was angry at the frost forming in the air. His irises glowed in the mirror's reflection.

What was he angry about? It had to do with the arched structure. Something about it warranted nearly freezing to death.

The King raked his fingers through his white hair, and his jaw flexed as he summoned a deep breath and exhaled it slowly. Some of the rigidity left his broad shoulders. He grabbed a bottle of wine from a stand and poured himself a drink. He brought it to his mouth, his head tilting back as his pale throat bobbed with the swallow.

It was odd to see him, to be here, watching the King do such normal things as have a minute of anger, then calm himself with a drink.

Jökull caught her staring at him in the reflection. Blood rushed to her cheeks, and she quickly looked away. Her heart was racing, but this time with nerves. She heard the pouring of more wine and listened to his boots crunch across the ice-covered floor toward the bed.

"Drink. It will help."

Sunnëva glanced at the offered goblet in his pale fingers. Whether he meant it would relax her or bring warmth to her bones, she was too thirsty to care.

She took a swig and let the wine pool on her tongue before swallowing. It sank in her stomach heavily and sent a rush to her head, heating her face. Her limbs painfully tingled as more of her slowly thawed. The feeling reminded her she was still alive. She drank the rest to the dregs.

Jökull's thumb swiped a drop of wine from her lips. The touch startled her, and she hissed at him. He canted his head, watching her again. Calculating the way a predator did before it lunged.

Sunnëva stilled as they stared at each other. Her fingers itched to reach for the hidden knife strapped to the top of her thigh, but she didn't dare while he was so close. His eyes flickered to the hollow of her throat as if he could hear her racing heart.

"You're shivering," he said in a gruff tone. The cold didn't appear to bother him. Of course it didn't.

"That's what happens when you're sitting in a chamber of ice."

She needed to get warm. Once her eyesight adjusted, Sunnëva noticed a shadowed fireplace in the corner. She ran to it, but there was no wood to light a fire inside.

The balcony doors slammed shut, cutting out the harsh breeze. She jumped and spun around.

Jökull removed his thick furred cloak. "Come here, wife."

Oh, Gods. He wanted to bed her now.

She backed away. "I will not—"

He flicked a hand idly, and ice grew under her feet, sliding her across the room to him. Catching her arm, he shoved her onto the bed.

Her heart thrashed wildly against her ribs, and she scrambled back. "If you try—"

Jökull dumped his heavy cloak on her head. "Get warm. Your lips are blue."

Sunnëva stilled, stunned that his intention wasn't to force himself upon her, or that he even cared for her wellbeing.

"Whose fault is that?" She pushed his cloak off and her messy hair fell around her face. But the chilly air prickled her skin, so she grudgingly wrapped the cloak around her shoulders. It smelled like him. Like winter, cedar, and … something floral. The roses from his garden, she realized.

The scent elicited the memory of Rune's last moments.

Sunnëva ground her teeth and focused on what she came to do. Kill this man and flee. But she needed to bring the feeling back to her body first.

"I'm cold," she said evenly. "I need fire."

Jökull's gaze turned sharp as he took in the sight of her. "No, you don't," he said, a hint of disdain in his tone.

He removed his gloves and his boots. The veins on his hands shifted as he removed his clothing, piece by piece. He tossed aside his jacket, then loosened the laces of his long-sleeved tunic, tugging it open. His skin was the color of the bright side of the moon, and black tattoos coursed over his bare chest in strange shapes. From his neck, they snaked like a maze over the rest of him, past the ridges of his abdomen, disappearing beneath his trousers.

"Are you finished gawking?" Jökull asked.

She flushed because she had been gawking. "What do those markings mean?"

"You will find out soon enough." Lying beside her with comfortable ease, he grabbed her wrist in his large grasp and pulled her toward him. Her face landed against the cool, rigid planes of his chest.

Sunnëva squealed in horror. "What are you doing?"

She tried to shove him away, but he held her firm.

"Don't get excited quite yet." Jökull's icy palm pressed against the small of her back.

Her curses halted when her stiff body began to thaw. She couldn't help moaning as she sagged into him. He was extracting the cold from her limbs or matching her temperature to his. Whatever magic this was, it made him feel like a heated rock that had her curling into him.

Was this real? She was cuddling her brother's killer, clinging to him desperately for warmth. It had to be madness.

Still, the tremors wracking through her body made her stay.

Or maybe it was the wine.

"Don't think anything of this," Sunnëva bit out. He grunted when her knee nudged too close to his groin. "This is for survival, nothing more. At least until I can light the hearth."

Jökull's mouth hitched as he studied the cornices on the ceiling. "I see you and I are going to get along well," he said, his voice rumbling in the back of his throat.

He hauled her up, sliding her body across his torso to bring them face to face. Her breath caught. The moon's grace painted his features in strokes of silver and blue.

"There will be no fire in this room, wife." A shrewd smile curved on one end of his lips. "If you're cold, then I will gladly be the one who keeps you warm."

10

Sunnëva decided to wait until the King fell asleep before she killed him. He was too powerful to attack head-on. Better to make her move when he lowered his guard. It might have been unfair, but she didn't survive because she fought honorably. He, least of all, deserved a good death. So she lay perfectly still beside him and waited.

Being in bed with this man didn't feel real. Yet the space that Jökull took up in the room, the power of his energy, was very real. There was something otherworldly about his presence. It made her skin crawl.

His hand rested on her hip with familiarity. She clenched her jaw, counting down the minutes until she drove her knife into his throat. The only thing that kept her still was imagining she was lying beside Rune. It was his breath tickling her scalp, his large warm body she was nestled into. But no matter how much she tried, Jökull's scent overpowered her imagination.

She gnashed her teeth when his finger twitched on her hip. He was still awake. If he expected more out of tonight, she would give it to him soon enough.

Sunnëva let out a sleepy sigh, closing her eyes. *Sleep, sleep, sleep.* Eventually, patience paid off.

It wasn't long before his body slackened. Anticipation thickened as his breathing slowed. His hold on her loosened next. Her heart beat wildly as she waited longer to ensure he was truly asleep. The moonlight tracked across the wall for another hour before she carefully sat up.

The King didn't move. His white lashes cast shadows over his cheeks, his chest rising and falling with even breaths.

Now was her chance. She would never find him so defenseless again.

Sunnëva swept her robes away from her legs and drew out her knife. It was made of demon bone, with black leather woven around the hilt. A gift from Rune on her last birthdate. She ran her finger along the sharp edge. It seemed fitting to kill the man who killed her lover with his blade.

Jökull really must not find her a threat if he could sleep beside her so relaxed. His tunic had fallen over his left shoulder, revealing his tattoos continuing down his arms beneath the fabric.

How many of the rumors were true?

With those pointed ears, he had to be fae. The bastard looked like a fairy prince with the deep voice of a beast.

Maybe she should have brought iron, but the fae weren't immortal. They may have endless lifespans, yet they could still bleed to death.

Even if this failed, she most likely wouldn't live long.

Before she could change her mind, Sunnëva straddled him and brought her weapon to his throat. Jökull woke and regarded her lazily through his white lashes, eyes softly glowing. Not at all concerned by the sharp edge against his pulse. If anything, he looked amused.

"How charming. Is this another tradition of how the women of your clan bed their husbands?" he asked, his voice raspy with sleep. "With a knife to the throat?"

"No," Sunnëva replied through her teeth. "It's how we kill them."

His chuckle vibrated up her thighs from where they were wrapped around his waist, curling through her center. "You will fail with that pathetic knife."

"You haven't seen how well I can use a knife," she hissed. "I'd wager you bleed as any other man."

At his smirk, she bared her teeth and thrust the blade into him, but it didn't pierce his flesh. It was like trying to cut stone. He lifted his hand, and she recoiled when he drew a sharp talon across his throat, slicing himself open. The wound healed in seconds, leaving a small bead of blood to slide down his pale neck and stain the white pillows beneath.

"I am not like any other man."

She stared at him, her grip shaking around the hilt.

The King is indestructible. Immortal.

Jökull's mouth curved in a slight sneer. "If you thought to kill me tonight, I am afraid you will be sorely disappointed. No manmade weapon can harm me."

It took her a moment to speak. "You knew I would try again."

"I would be disappointed if you didn't." He was so at ease with her on top of him, straddling his waist. No, he looked comfortable. *Content.* Her sharp knife was still at his throat, yet it was no more dangerous than a soft feather.

"Are you so immune that this does nothing to you?"

His cold hands glided up her warm thighs, the sharp contrast in temperature making her flinch. "Lower those hips, wife, and you will know exactly what it does to me."

She threw herself off him, scooting to the other end of the bed, pointing the useless weapon at him. "I am not your wife."

Jökull sat up. "We exchanged vows. We are wed. In turn, I spared your clan. Was that not our deal?" Bindings of ice wrapped around her arms and legs. So cold they could have burned her skin if he wanted. They pulled her helplessly onto her knees. The pressure of his power filled the air, and she realized how much he had been containing it.

Her lungs heaved with heavy breaths. His cloak slipped off her shoulders, revealing her rumpled white robes. They splayed open, leaving her cleavage exposed and her stomach bare, revealing all of her scars. He stilled. His frosted blue eyes blazed as they roved over her body. Not with lust, but with a shocking fury.

Because Jökull now realized the bride he bought was tarnished.

Sunnëva covered herself and looked away. "If you expected a pure maiden, then you'll be the one who is sorely disappointed."

His lip curled with disdain. "Of all the things I expected tonight, that fact is not on my list of disappointments."

Sunnëva stared at him for a moment, not sure what he meant.

He looked at her scarred chest again, and his fists tightened on the sheets, shredding them beneath his claws.

"Stop looking at me like that," she snapped. "Do not ask what happened or ask who did this to me. Those responsible are already dead."

Jökull's glowing gaze lifted to hers, seeming to see beyond what she said. He was quiet for a pause, perhaps still waiting for something.

"Do not hope to consummate. You can add no sex to your list of disappointments. If you try to take me by force—"

Jökull cupped the back of her head and hauled her toward him. His talons lightly prodded against her scalp, shooting goosebumps down her arms. "I take *whatever* I want. But I will *never* force you to take me."

An iridescent sheen rippled through the air, and magic prickled against her skin.

"What was that?" Sunnëva whispered.

"That was the promise of a God. Once given, my word cannot be broken."

Whether he was one or not, her body inexplicably settled with relief at knowing he wouldn't hurt her that way.

"I have no need to force you into my bed, vicious thorn. When you're ready, you will beg for it."

She clenched her teeth. "Not *ever*."

Smirking, he let her go. "How do you desire to spend our first night together, dearest?"

"Alone."

"As you wish."

She stilled at his unexpected compliance, and magic rippled around them again.

The bed dipped as Jökull rose to his feet. When he readjusted his tunic, she caught a glimpse of something on the back of his upper right shoulder before it was covered.

"Tonight, you will stay in my chambers." He faced her. "There are three rules you must follow. One: do not wander the halls alone. Two: do not remove your ring. Three: do not leave this castle. Break those rules, and there will be dire consequences. Understand?"

She glared at him.

"Goodnight." Jökull bowed his head with mock gallantry. "My Queen."

The title left her staring after him as he strode out of the room with his tunic unfastened. The heavy doors closed quietly behind him.

Queen?

Sunnëva supposed she was one after marrying a king.

Now what?

Failure roiled in her stomach like spoiled food.

She glanced at the drop of blood on his pillow and shuddered. Either it was his infrangible abilities that unnerved her, or the room's temperature dropped again with him gone. She slung Jökull's thick cloak around her shoulders and folded her knees against her chest to conserve warmth.

Her mind turned over everything he said and the moment of his departure. It couldn't have been a trick of the light. She saw it.

A jagged scar beneath his shoulder blade.

Whatever injured him, the wound hadn't healed seamlessly, like the cut to his throat. That had to mean he wasn't invincible.

Now to find the weapon that made that scar.

Sunnëva repeated the Druid's riddle in her mind for clues, but the cold and exhaustion didn't help her come up with any answers. She sank into a fitful sleep, with Jökull's voice still haunting her thoughts.

No manmade weapon can harm me.

How about a god-made one?

Sunnëva hardly got any sleep. Her mind was too alert. She was startled awake whenever the gargoyles growled outside, or a gust beat against the balcony doors, convincing her some beast had come into the room. But when the wind started to wail, the cries sounded too much like Freya.

She had nightmares of the dark trees, of jeering faces and screams.

But then came that pale hand with a tattoo on his wrist. He picked her up and cradled her close as he carried her away.

Rune? She tried to call out, but her mouth wouldn't work. *Leave me, Rune.*

If he didn't leave her there, his life would end because of her, too. *Don't save me. Let me die. Let me die...*

"We don't ever truly die," he said, his voice no longer the same as it once was. *"We only change worlds. And I need you in this one."*

Sunnëva jolted up in bed with her heart pounding and clammy sweat on her forehead. Dawn's gleam shone against her wet eyes, bathing the King's chambers in golden light. She sighed tiredly and wiped the tears from her cheek.

Sometimes when she dreamed, she forgot why she kept living. She silently thanked Rune for reminding her she wasn't finished yet.

While her breath still clouded, the walls were no longer coated in frost. Jökull's scent was so strong in the room, she rapidly rolled over, expecting to see him in the bed. But it was empty.

He kept his word about leaving her alone last night.

A God's promise.

Sunnëva was beginning to consider it might be true. If so, fate may be on her side. While manmade weapons couldn't harm him, Jökull had made weapons, too. It was said he created the Nightstone ore from the dark itself. And he had a scythe constructed entirely from it.

Could she destroy him with that?

It was a theory worth exploring.

Now that she had some time to rest and think, Sunnëva realized sending him away had been a mistake. She had to learn more about him.

And about this place.

Rolling off the bed, she padded to the balcony. Beyond the frosted doors, the white land spread far and wide. The whole world could be seen from up here. The pewter door knobs were shaped into roses with a ring for the handles. She touched the glass, only for it to hum with a pulse of blue magic. She tried the handles, but it was sealed shut.

He spelled her inside.

Sunnëva tried the chamber doors. The knob was stiff, but after a few tries, it creaked open. *Not locked.* She frowned. *Why lock the balcony but not the door?*

Sunnëva peeked out and found the stone corridor empty. Light streamed in from a window at the end, reflecting off white stones embedded in the bricks. Taking a breath, she dared to wander out. This broke one of Jökull's rules, but she didn't care. The corridor brought her to an open foyer with a rug and seating, brightly lit by sunlight coming through the glass ceiling.

As she went on, Sunnëva found the castle wasn't as dark and eerie as she had expected. It was the windows. They'd been strategically placed in a way to assure natural sunlight filled every corner by reflecting off the white, iridescent gems decorating the walls.

There were hardly any torches needed. Whenever she did pass through a shadowed hallway, the walls had more of those white gems and Tanzanite crystals.

She probably shouldn't wander in a castle full of beasts, but morbid curiosity pushed her onward.

Oddly, there was no one around until she heard the distant hum of voices.

Sunnëva followed the sound to an alcove high in the castle that overlooked what must be the throne room. The walls were covered in frost, displaying a large banner with the King's sigil. The cloaked rider from her wedding stood at the foot of a tall set of frozen stairs. They lead to a dais where Jökull sat on a throne of jagged ice. He reclined against the armrest lazily, his chin resting on his fist.

The gallery circling the walls was full of fae and creatures she couldn't name. They hooted and jeered at the beast in the center of the room. It looked like a monstrous hound with dark fur, sharp claws, and the bare skull of a wolf for a face. *Was that a warg?* It was huge. Nearly twice the size of a normal one. The creature howled, fighting against the chains a group of goblins were using to hold it in place.

What were they doing with a demon?

"Submit," the rider said.

The warg growled, its fur rising on end. It lowered into a crouch, ready to lunge.

"Does it even understand?" Jökull asked.

"Oh yes, it understands clearly, sire." The rider pulled down his hood, revealing a handsome man with short, silvery white hair. He clapped his palms together and spread them apart, forming a glowing purple whip.

The creature snarled savagely. It reared up on two legs and stepped back warily, or perhaps afraid.

Jökull came down the steps. The warg was bigger than him by at least three feet, yet he was completely relaxed, hands in his pockets. "Serve me, and no harm will come to you."

The warg flattened its ears, snapping its teeth.

The King canted his head as he studied it. "This one is already sired."

Was he trying to control the Shadow Lord's demons?

His rider sighed. "If so, you may have to get rid of it. What good is a creature that does not obey?"

"Indeed." Jökull glanced up. Sunnëva ducked down with a quiet curse.

Did he spot her?

The grunts of other beasts loomed down the corridor. She ran to his chambers and tripped over her own feet as she slammed the door shut. At the snicker behind her, Sunnëva whipped around. A fae female sat comfortably on Jökull's bed, as though she had done it many times before.

Like most fae, she was beautiful.

Long hair like black silk spilled down her perfect features. She wore a dark green dress adorned with silver embellishments to resemble a scaled pattern. The high slit on either end left her thighs exposed. Sharp fingernail guards tipped the end of her slender fingers. They were also silver, with delicate chains attached to the bracelets on her wrists. It matched her dangly hairpin adorned with red jewels.

Sunnëva scanned the room to make sure she came to the right place. She had. "Who are you?"

Her plush red lips split in a smirk. "I am Donelle."

"Are you my servant?"

Donelle's smile vanished into an affronted glare. "Do I look like your servant?"

No. Which she had already guessed. No maid dressed half-naked like that. But her presence meant one of two things.

Beneath Jökull's cloak, Sunnëva readied her knife. "Then why are you here?"

Donelle's lip curled at her rumpled appearance. "I wanted to see what the King decided to marry. Clearly, something lacking."

That answered her question.

Sunnëva may not know much about demons or fae, but she knew envy when she saw it. Jökull most likely had a harem of women, and one had come to stake her claim. Not that Sunnëva cared, but she also wasn't going to let someone exert dominance over her.

"You must think yourself something important to enter my husband's chambers uninvited." She crossed her arms. "Get out."

Donelle hissed at the command. "Do not fool yourself. Your union is a farce, and you're not a true queen of this castle. Jökull is only using you. Once he gets whatever he wants, he will cast you aside like all the others."

Sunnëva smiled sharply. "You mean like you?"

Her face twisted in a sneer, and she curled her claws. Sunnëva readied her bone knife, but they were interrupted when a knock came at the door. It opened, and the rider from the throne room walked in.

He was strikingly pretty.

In the sense that he had angular features rather than roughhewn, with smooth pale skin and pale purple eyes the color of a coming twilight. The sunlight danced over his silvery white hair. It was close-shaven on the sides of his head, while a few inches longer on top. He had traded his black cloak for dark purple robes trimmed in white fur. And looked to be perhaps a few years older than her.

He frowned at the scene before him. "You should not be here, Donelle. If I find you in the King's chambers again, I will personally drag you to the dungeons myself."

Donelle scoffed and stormed out of the room.

He turned to Sunnëva and introduced himself with a bow of his head. "Good morrow, my Queen. I am Aero Astron, Chief Advisor of the King. I have come to see how you're faring and if you require anything. Whatever you desire shall be provided."

Chief Advisor?

That was too high of a position to be tasked with asking about her necessities.

"Hello..." Sunnëva replied hesitantly. "Why did he send you?"

Aero paused. "The King thought you might be more at ease with me."

Because he was one of the few who didn't look like a monster.

Sunnëva crossed her arms. "If *His Majesty* cares about my comfort, he can ask me himself. Not through a messenger."

Unfortunately, she needed to be close to Jökull to complete her goal.

"Very well. And meanwhile?"

"A meal would be wonderful," Sunnëva said when her stomach cramped with hunger. She adjusted her rumpled robes. "And clothes."

"Of course."

As if they were waiting, four little gnome women entered behind him. Leathery brown skin stretched over their oval faces with hooked noses. Long ears poked out of their wispy, braided hair. They wore little aprons over their gray frocks. Two carried a large tray of food as big as their three-foot bodies between them. Another pair brought forth a dress in their bony fingers. It flowed like a pool of moonlight, decorated with glittering gems on the bodice.

Not exactly what she had in mind for clothing.

Three of the gnome women curtsied, then promptly left. The youngest one tugged Sunnëva to sit in the chair at the vanity. Her shoulders were stiff, unused to being this close to fae.

She grimaced at her reflection in the mirror. Her blonde hair was a tangled mess, with paint smeared over her face, the runes long blurred. She adjusted the cloak to hide her many old scars. The gnome woman brought over a basin with water and started cleaning her face with a cloth.

"May I inspect your hands?" Aero asked from the door. "You seem to have a bit of frostbite."

Red patches covered her fingers and knuckles. She hadn't noticed them until now.

"I was burned by the cold. Your beast of a king carried me through the snow in nothing but my consummation garments."

Aero had the restraint not to blush, but his mouth did twitch. He came to the table and gently took her hand, inspecting the red rashes. He hovered his palm above hers as it glowed purple, releasing an electrical charge in the air. A soft mist of the same color fell over her skin with soothing warmth, and the red burns slowly vanished as he healed her.

She gawked up at him. "You're a sorcerer."

"Something of the sorts."

Sunnëva looked him over, not sure what she was searching for. No claws or fangs, no pointed ears. What kind of creature was he?

Aero gave her a polite smile. "I am a Lunar mage of the Magos Empire."

Her mouth dropped open with awe. *A mage!* She had heard stories of them but never met one before. Now that she was paying attention, she heard his faint accent that wasn't native to this side of Urn.

Aero finished and released her. Not a mark was left on her skin.

"If I wanted to send a message home?"

"That could be arranged."

At that, Sunnëva was able to take a full breath and some of her tension eased. She supposed Jökull was right about her being more at ease around the mage. "Thank you, Lord Aero."

"I'm at your service, my Queen. If it should please you, Aero will do fine." He bowed his head and took a step toward the door. "I will leave you to prepare."

She frowned. "Prepare for what?"

"The King summons you to be introduced before the court. And he asks that you leave the knife behind."

11

Sunnëva's steps were loud in the vast throne room, heels clacking against the frost, the heavy train of her gown flowing behind her. Her hair was up in an elaborate knot that pulled her tresses from her neck. She wore a white fur pelt on her shoulders, but she was freezing.

Her stomach rolled when she noticed the skeletons dangling from the ceilings with lit candles melting from their ribs and open jaws like chandeliers. Dark blue banners hung from the walls, displaying the white crest of the Ice Phoenix.

Sunlight poured through the windows, making the frosted walls gleam with rainbow refractions. The room was so bright it made her vision water.

Even the throne glittered.

The backrest was jagged and sharp, with peaks of ice that matched Jökull's crown. The King looked rather bored where he lounged in his throne with one leg crossed over the other, but the touch of his gaze tracked her approach. Propped against the armrest was his scythe, the blade as black as ink.

Aero, who had escorted her, bowed when they stopped in the center.

She fixed her dull stare on the tall windows behind the throne. "You called?"

Jökull's heavy gray cloak shifted over his elegant leather jerkin as he leaned forward.

"Sunnëva." The rumble of his voice sounded out her name as if he was savoring each letter. She hated that it immediately drew her eyes to his. "You are expected to bow before your King."

Titters came from the high galleries where creatures lurked. She heard the flutter of their leathery wings and the scrape of their claws as they moved. A griffin perched on a ledge near the domed ceiling with open windows, tail flicking. The castle was full of monsters. The next words out of her mouth would determine whether they would eat her, and she wasn't here to die.

Jökull straightened as she climbed the steps to the dais.

Sunnëva stopped before him, holding his stare. "I will bring you to your knees and make you beg before you ever see the day I bow to you."

A stark silence hovered in the air.

Sunnëva's heart sped under the intensity of his wintery eyes. She flinched at the icy stroke of his black talon slowly trailing down her jaw.

Jökull pulled her close, close enough to feel his perpetual cold prickle her skin. "Delicate mortal. The day I fall to my knees, you will be the only one begging."

Heat rushed into her cheeks.

"Unbeknownst to most of you, I have taken a wife," Jökull said, his voice projecting loudly in the vast room. "I present to you, your Winter Queen. A beauty with a searing tongue, and I come to find, as dangerous as a thorn."

She clenched her teeth as their audience snickered. Was this all to mock her? She was no queen nor a beauty, not when she was as ugly as the rest of them.

Inside and out.

He held her gaze as he continued, "I trust you will show her the courtesy owed to the mate of your King, even if she does not show it to me."

Mate? Sunnëva curled her lip with disgust. She would *never* be anything of his.

The court made a mock show of bowing to her while others hissed and bared their fangs.

"Leave us."

Beasts lumbered away at Jökull's dismissal. Some flew into the air and went out the high windows in the ceiling, others trudged out the large doors leading into the main hall. A few stayed behind to lurk in the alcoves.

"Where is your ring?" Jökull asked, noticing the black ribbon she tied around her ring finger. It completely hid the Druid's geas.

"I removed it," she said stiffly. "The ribbon is a symbol of my time in mourning. Therefore, I am not fit to perform the role of a wife."

In case he assumed she would bed him later.

Jökull's mouth curved with a tight, knowing smile, and his talons tapped on the armrest. "That ring was more than a symbol of our blessed union. The Moonstone is to protect you."

Moonstone...

It must be another magical ore. It matched the gems on the walls.

"I can protect myself," she said, aware of the bone knife still strapped to her thigh.

"Nonetheless. I know the beasts of this castle and how little control they have over their ... inclinations. If you're going to wander, precautions must be made."

She inwardly cursed. So, he *had* spotted her.

Aero climbed up the steps behind her and presented a box inlaid with dark red velvet. Nestled inside was a Nightstone dagger with a blade like liquid night. A Moonstone decorated the beautifully engraved steel pommel.

"You will need this." Jökull took out the dagger and offered it to her.

Sunnëva's pulse leaped with smug satisfaction. How perfect that he should hand her the weapon that would end him. She reached for it, but he held on a second longer.

"Use it wisely."

Oh, she planned to.

As soon as Jökull let go, Sunnëva flipped the dagger expertly and aimed it at his heart. He caught her wrist. His firm grip held her tightly, his strength impossibly strong. She couldn't budge, no matter how much she squirmed. The air chilled with his reserved expression and silence filled the near-empty throne room.

Sunnëva held Jökull's icy stare even as she panicked inside.

"What a treacherous, vicious little creature. For someone in your current quandary, I have to admire your spirit."

Then he drove the blade into him. It hit his chest and shattered into a thousand pieces, falling to his lap like black stardust.

Sunnëva's next breath wedged in her lungs. Nightstone had no effect on him. Was he really so indestructible?

He would probably kill her now. She tried to yank out of his vice grip, but her heels slid against the ice, struggling to stay upright.

"I am not a demon," Jökull rumbled.

Sunnëva glanced at his pointed ears.

"Nor fae. I can lie quite easily, and iron does not burn me." He handed the dagger-less hilt to Aero.

The mage accepted it, placing a gold piece in Jökull's waiting hand in return. "I will have another made, sire."

Jökull played with the coin, and it caught the light as it danced through his clawed fingers. "I will wager more next time I put a weapon in your hands."

It was infuriating the way he ridiculed her. "Maybe I will try poison next."

One way or another, she would destroy that frozen heart in his chest.

"Oh, I do love how murderous you are." Jökull smiled.

There was something dark and feral about it. Goosebumps sprouted down her arms. It was her only warning before he snatched her throat. She pushed against him, but his hold was made of steel. The disparity of strength between them was astronomical, and the first seeds of helplessness planted themselves.

His grip slightly tightened, and her breath cut short. "I wish to be lenient, but you're wearing my *very* little patience, vicious thorn. Try as you might, your efforts to kill me will be futile. All those who have attempted it have not lived to speak of it. Do you truly think it wise to challenge your King?"

"I do not fear you," she hissed.

"Fear?" he growled. "You have no idea what fear is." Jökull's talons grew into razor-sharp blades around her racing pulse. He pulled her closer and his icy lips brushed her ear. "I have witnessed the founding of life, watched worlds form from a star, and seen creations begin from the dawn of time to their conclusion. I am the cold breath on the neck of those on the brink. The wielder of endings and decay. Nothing can take my life, for I am Death itself."

An icy chill sank through her body, the hair on her arms standing on end.

He pulled back slightly to meet her gaze. The whites of his eyes bled to black and his irises glowed pure white. A whimper lodged in her throat. And at that moment, she knew what she'd been told about him was true.

A haunting moan resonated through the throne room. Looking over her shoulder, she gasped to see the faint white outline of a person hovering in the air. It soared right for them.

Sunnëva screamed as it plunged through her. An awful cold shudder shook her entire being. The soul passed through her and went into him. His tattoos pulsed with cerulean light. He let her go at the same time she shoved against him and Sunnëva fell at his feet.

Jökull stood, towering above her. "I wonder how your soul tastes."

Oh gods, he was going to kill her.

"Not yet, wife." His cold hand gently brushed her hair in a way that was almost affectionate. "We both must be patient for that."

Shock rocked through her. Had he read her mind?

Jökull's dark chuckle sent shudders down her spine. His sharp talons teased her cheek. One wrong move and they would split her open.

Sunnëva had always considered herself a fighter. Someone who never backed down from a fight, no matter what she faced. But as she looked at the God of Death, a feral instinct rose inside of her, urging her to flee. This wasn't her, she didn't cower, yet she was frozen in panic. Her heart was racing so fast she was wheezing for air.

"Sire," Aero said warily.

Jökull held her captive with his glowing gaze, his immense power squeezing all the air out of the room. Sweat slicked her forehead. Her heart drummed loudly in her head. A cold, creeping impression crawled over her flesh that she couldn't escape. Every instinct was urging her to *run*. Tears blurred her vision as a growing scream threatened to rip from deep in her throat.

"Jökull," Aero called again with more force. The pressing energy in the room evaporated, and she sucked in a breath.

The creatures that had lingered by to watch snarled, baring their teeth at her as they started to prowl forward.

"They smell your delicious *fear*," Jökull said, watching her with those frightful eyes. "Do not run. If you do, it will trigger their need to hunt. And mine."

Sunnëva bolted.

Her white gown flared around her feet as she fled down the frozen steps from him like an animal running from a predator. Because that's what he was.

Jökull's quiet chuckle floated to her as she dashed down the hallway.

Who was she to kill a God?

Sunnëva had never felt so small and insignificant than in that moment as true fear wrangled her heart. Her panicked breaths filled in the hallway. Idle footsteps echoed behind her, and she drowned in her terror, feeling Death would catch her at any moment.

She tried the windows, but they wouldn't open for her. Her fists pounded against the glass, and it pushed back.

He had spelled the entire castle against her.

She sprinted down another hall with no windows. The light faded the further she ran. The loud thrashing of her heartbeat thudded in her ears. A monstrous roar boomed from the end of the hall. And Sunnëva did something stupid—she looked back.

Her body slammed straight into a wall, and the scab on her cheek tore open.

Sunnëva fell and hit the ground hard. What had halted her escape wasn't a wall, but an enormous ogre. It towered over her, bulky and thick as a tree with claws and sharp teeth.

And it had its sights on her.

Leaping to her feet, she drew out her bone knife. Fighting to survive on the Everfrost taught her to look for weak points first. Its chest was plated with thick scales, the torso melting into its head, which made it difficult to locate the vital parts of its neck.

It lunged at her, and she rolled out from under it to the other side. Without a sword to defend herself, she should've kept running, but it was so large it filled the hallway, cornering her.

Black slashed through the ogre from groin to skull. It slowly split apart, exposing innards and bones. Her stomach heaved as hot blood splashed the icy floor with a hiss. Steam rose where it pooled.

The ogre dropped to her feet.

Footsteps came forward in the dark. It was his glowing white eyes she saw first. Moving with a predator's ease, Jökull came out of the shadows into the light, scythe in hand, red speckled on his cheek.

Sunnëva slipped on the blood as she lurched around. She ran into the open foyer with sunlight streaming in from the glass ceiling. Jökull was in front of her in a blink, stealing the air from her lungs. Sunnëva skidded to a halt before crashing into him. Backing away, she bumped into the iron railing with a high drop down a spiral of stairs.

The scythe dissolved, and Jökull caged her within his arms, his hands clutching the banister so tight the ice coating it cracked. "What did I tell you?" he growled, each biting word laced with wrath. "Do not run from me."

An answer couldn't form past the whimper in her throat. Her wild heart thudded against her ribs with an immobilizing terror brought on by his presence. Sunnëva drowned in her panic, and her chest heaved with gasping breaths as the world closed in on her. She wanted to run, but fear stole her strength. She fell against the banister as her vision skewed. Her lungs crushed under an invisible weight. It felt like she was dying.

"Sunnëva." The anger melted from Jökull's features, and he reached for her.

She flinched away, whimpering. "Please. Please. Please." It was the only frantic word she could say. *Make it stop.*

"Look at me." Jökull's cool hands came around her face.

She trembled violently, gasping for air. She was rooted in place at the touch of his frigid fingers brushing over the bleeding cut on her cheek. A trickle of magic washed over her skin, healing it. He shifted closer as his eyes lowered to her mouth.

His voice murmured in the pocket of space between them. "Don't be afraid, little thorn."

Then he kissed her.

Sunnëva was frozen beneath the softness of his lips, cold to the touch. He drew her closer, his hands sliding down her throat. She lifted the bone dagger to drive it into his back, but he caught her wrist. The energy of his power hummed between them as he kissed her, lulling all the fight out of her body. Jökull seemed to sink into her being, and she let him. He extracted the roots of terror he had planted in her soul one by one. As soon as they were gone, the ice in her veins thawed with shocking heat.

Yet she didn't push him off.

Because something was stirring inside of her, lighting a craving that sank past her stomach. His scent was everywhere. Intoxicating her senses. His touch was maddening. So much she was quivering. Her thighs squeezed. A deep rumble vibrated in Jökull's chest, and he kissed her harder. The bone knife slipped from her fingers, clattering at their feet. He released her wrist, and she tugged at his tunic, searching desperately for his skin. He groaned deeply, like he was stretched between torture and insanity.

No. Sunnëva told herself. *Why...*

She didn't want this.

Yet she found her way under his tunic and dragged her nails across the ridges of his abdomen, perfectly honed. It gratified her when he jolted from her touch and his hips pressed into hers. Jökull's hands roamed over her waist and gripped her harder, pulling her closer. Her arms circled his neck and her mouth parted to meet his tongue.

Why couldn't she stop kissing him? What was this?

His body pressed into hers, stirring feelings she shouldn't have. Not want. It couldn't be *want* when she hated him so much. But there was an irresistible thrum in her body that she couldn't contain. It was need or confusion brought on by the way he continued to caress her. She hadn't been touched like that in a long time.

Her pulse was dancing. It made her feel alive.

She traced the smooth hardness of his skin, tracing the slab of muscle as she explored his broad back. He shuddered, and his fingers threaded through her hair, cupping her head. His other hand went to her breast. The stroke of his thumb sent fiery shocks all over her body, pooling heat low in her stomach. She shouldn't be doing this. Why was she doing this? His mouth traveled over her jaw to her throat, licking her pulse. Sunnëva whimpered and ground against his thigh, needing friction. Needing him.

No, stop!

Jökull jerked back.

Both panted as they stared at each other mutely. His lips were wet and flushed. Beneath his thick white lashes, his pupils had dilated so wide, his irises were nearly black.

He turned and cast out a lance of ice. It swiftly speared a harpy's skull into the wall across the foyer. Dead before she even noticed it was there. Jökull's tattoos flashed bright blue as he reaped the soul.

She stood there stupidly. Still disoriented from the kiss, the carnage, and the ache between her thighs. The distant roars below drew away.

"You kill your own?" Sunnëva asked breathlessly, when she could finally speak.

Jökull blinked, and his eyes returned to their pale blue color. "When it comes between me and something I want, no one is safe."

Her mind finally cleared, and rage reared in her stomach like poison. "How dare you?"

"Better they taste your ire than your fear. Otherwise, I would have to decimate everyone in this castle."

The kiss was to anger her? But he had also been inside of her being. He took her fear … and replaced it with arousal.

"You put me under your spell!" Sunnëva swung at his face.

Jökull caught her fist before the punch landed.

"I know what you are," she hissed. "Out of every vile depravity in the world, you're the worst one!"

His gaze darkened as he chuckled, the sound low and harsh. "There are only beasts in this castle, and I am the cruelest one of them all." He yanked her toward him with a sneer. "But I won't take credit where it isn't due. That, *dearest*, was all you."

The startling reply struck her silent.

Lies.

The only thing she felt for him was unadulterated loathing, so potent it tainted the air between them. As soon as she found out how to get rid of him, the land would be free, and so would she.

Jökull nodded at the look of disgust on her face.

A spiral of blue light appeared next to them. She flinched away, staring as it formed into a glowing, circular gateway that revealed a room. Not his bedchambers, but a different room with a smaller bed.

Jökull hooked his arm around her waist and hauled her off the ground onto his shoulder, carrying her through the magical doorway. Sunnëva kicked and punched his back, cursing him with every foul word she could think of. He planted her in a chair and gripped the armrests as he leaned in close, his nose inches from hers.

"These are your chambers, wife. Whatever you desire will be given to you. But you are *mine*," Jökull said in a rough rumble. Sunnëva dug her nails into her shaking fists, itching to strike him. "Do not run away from me again. If you do, you better run fast. For I will hunt you to the ends of the earth. And you don't want to know what will happen when I catch you."

Then he strode into the spiral of light, and the portal vanished with him.

12

Queen she may be, but only in name.

Sunnëva was his prisoner, that much was clear. The chamber Jökull left her in was perhaps a fourth the size of his, but still lavish. The stone walls weren't coated in ice or any ore. It held a wardrobe, a desk, a small dining table, and a four-poster bed with fine velvet bedding. It was also darker. The only large window faced away from the path of the sun. At least the balcony looked over the castle gardens below.

The door was locked this time. It struck her with a soft charge of magic when she tried to pull on the handle. *Damn beast.*

And she lost her knife.

Sunnëva clenched her fists, glaring up at the molding on the ceiling. She reviled him with the depths of her being. The adrenaline had long gone, leaving her trembling and bewildered. A shudder went through her when she recalled his frightening white eyes. And Jökull had killed his own people. He sliced one completely in half.

When it comes between me and something I want, no one is safe.

What did that mean?

Sunnëva dropped onto the stiff bed with a sigh. At least there were fur pelts and thick blankets. Jökull's scent drifted to her, and she realized they were the same ones from his bed. She rubbed her mouth roughly at the memory of his lips on hers, scowling. A faint throbbing echoed deep in her core. She flushed at how aroused she'd been by his touch, and cursed. Why did she kiss him back?

It was only a reaction to his magic. He put a spell on her. Nothing more.

Guilt stirred inside of her when she thought of Rune. His remains were probably rotting in the garden while she was here kissing the one who slaughtered him.

Sunnëva wiped away her tears before they frosted on her lashes and lay down on the bed.

She wanted to go home.

The sky was painted with gradients of orange and deep purple when a knock came at the door. Sunnëva didn't move from the bed, where she shivered under the mound of blankets.

The door opened, and soft footsteps entered. "My Queen."

She glared at the stoic Chief Advisor. "Don't call me that, Aero. I am *not* his queen."

He bowed his head. "Pardon, Lady Sunnëva. Dinner is served. You're welcome to join the King in the dining hall if..."

She smirked at his perceptible hesitation. "If I don't attempt to skewer him with my fork?"

Aero was quiet, filling the space with awkward silence.

"What did he say? Repeat it as he said it."

He cleared his throat. "The King said 'My wife is formally invited to dinner if she is capable of behaving as a proper lady, and not a ... savage.'" Aero cringed as he recited the last word.

She scoffed. "Well, you tell that beast I would rather starve than eat at his table. He can shove a roasted gargoyle up his—"

The abrupt rumble of her stomach interrupted her rant.

Aero must have been practiced in discretion because he had the gallantry not to laugh, or show he heard it at all. "I would rather you not starve, my lady."

"I refuse to eat as long as I am kept prisoner."

"You are not a—" He cut off at her glare and sighed.

Then she noticed the creature lurking behind him. It was as tall as Aero, with the face of an eagle and the torso of a lion, large gray wings tucked against its body. The griffin she'd seen in the throne room.

"Ah, this is Cael. My dear friend. He is also the castle messenger." Aero entered, and from his pocket came a swirl of gold dust as he presented her with scrolls, quills, and ink. "So you may write your letter."

"Oh." She blinked, surprised he complied with her request. Not that she could write. "Thank you. I ... didn't think he would allow it."

"The King won't refuse you, my lady. You will want for nothing."

Sunnëva crossed her arms, contemplating this odd imprisonment. "And does the King plan on reading my messages?" At Aero's hesitant expression, she glowered. "All except privacy then. What about my bone knife? I want it back."

It appeared with another swirl of magic, and the mage held it out to her.

Frowning, Sunnëva took the offerings and placed them on the table. How far did this leniency go?

"What if I wanted to leave this room? Would he allow that?"

"Your confinement is temporary. Merely for your protection. The occurrence in the castle has riled up the court, and His Majesty wishes to keep you out of harm's way. The scent of blood and fear, especially of humans, can revert some in the castle to their baser instincts."

A crawling sensation shuddered down her spine.

"What did he do to me in the throne room?" she whispered.

The mage hesitated before saying, "Instilling fear is one of the King's abilities. But rooting primal terror ... that only happens when he loses control."

Did that mean Jökull didn't intend to terrify her?

She touched her lips, remembering the way his power seemed to sink inside of her and extract the emotion away.

"Does that happen a lot?"

"Losing control?" His purple eyes flickered to her, an unreadable expression on his face. "I have only seen him do so once before."

She didn't know what to think about that. If he wanted to hurt her, he easily could have.

"Is he really a God?" Sunnëva blurted. She didn't know Aero, but he seemed kind and honest. And she sensed he would answer trustfully.

"Yes, my lady. One of the Seven."

She swallowed. "Are they all here ... in the Mortal Realm?"

The mage was silent a moment before saying softly, "Not all."

A cold sensation washed through her body. She didn't dare ask which ones.

"Well, I will have the kitchen send up a meal later, in case you have changed your mind."

"Wait."

Aero paused.

Why did he agree to marry me? Sunnëva wanted to ask him, but it seemed too personal.

"Can I get you anything else, my lady?"

Twilight had arrived, and with it, the nip on her skin. Sunnëva was going to say she was cold, but she didn't want Jökull to touch her again. No fires were seen around the castle. Probably not permitted due to all the ice, or the King preferred it that way.

"Could you light the candles?"

"Of course." He snapped his fingers. Purple electricity crackled over the candles and flame lit the wicks.

She smiled. "Thank you, Aero."

With a bow of his head, he silently stepped out, leaving her with more questions than answers.

Sunnëva glowered at her dreary chambers and sighed.

Her breath clouded in the frigid air. It was getting colder by the minute. She decided to check the wardrobe and was relieved to find it full. Not only with dresses, but with less formal clothing like trousers, tunics, and cloaks. She quickly changed out of her flimsy gown into a warmer one.

Night had fallen, leaving only the flickering candlelight. She found some old books on the mantle above the hearth and threw those into the fireplace, promptly lighting them on fire. Making herself a bed on the woven rug in front of it, she held her stiff hands over the dancing blaze. She would probably freeze before she got what she came for.

She needed to find out how to kill her husband and escape soon— preferably alive.

He was the *Ice* Phoenix. Maybe fire was his weakness. But could it be that simple?

Rune probably would have found a way to do it already. Her throat tightened, and her heart ached with the loss of him. How she wished to see him again and tell him she was sorry he sacrificed his life for her. And it had all been for nothing. Her brother still died.

"I'll destroy him," Sunnëva said to the stars, hoping Fenrin and Rune could hear. She grabbed a candle. "I swear it."

First, she was going to burn his castle to the ground.

A low chuckle surfaced from the other end of the room. "How does one kill a God?"

Sunnëva leaped up and spun around. But there was no one.

"If you wish to vanquish the God of Death, it will require much more than fire." The voice was distorted and layered like many speaking at once, and it seemed to come from the darkest corners of the chamber.

"Who are you?" She turned in place, searching for him. "How did you get into my room?"

The shadows stretched across the walls and the floors, crawling for her.

"You're asking the wrong questions, Sunnëva."

Goosebumps shot down her arms. It knew her name.

"Yes, I know who you are, and I know what you desire." Something darkened the corner beside her bed and she stiffened, her pulse climbing. Whoever it was, she had a feeling it wasn't human. "I can give it to you."

Her pulse raced. "In exchange for what?"

Because she wasn't stupid. Everyone always wanted something.

"In exchange for you."

She stiffened as the speaker stepped forward into the low candlelight. He had the shape of a tall man. A veil of shadows shrouded his face. Long black hair fell to his shoulders. He was dressed in a fine dark coat that fell past his knees, trimmed in black silk. Wisps of smoke and embers loomed behind him. The back of his knuckles were coated with iridescent ebony scales, sharp talons on each finger.

Her instincts immediately marked him as something dangerous. Behind her back, she gripped her bone knife. "What do you want with me?"

"Your company." He shrugged. "I am lonely in my castle."

Nervous laughter bubbled out of her at the ridiculous answer. She must be hallucinating, or she had gone mad. Nevertheless, this was intriguing.

"Why do you want Jökull dead?"

He deliberated for a pause. "Let's say you aren't the only one with debts to settle."

She played with the knife's hilt, rolling it between her fingers. "Go on."

"The Ice Phoenix rules the Everfrost with none to defy him, save for two. The Lord of the Shadow Keep and…?"

"The Skellings." Her eyes widened. "They have the power to kill him?" At his nod, she asked, "If you know that, why have me do it?"

He looked down at his hand, clicking his talons together. She couldn't see his face, but she sensed he was frowning. "Unfortunately, there are rules I must follow."

"And I am not bound by these rules," she guessed.

"Indeed."

"What is it? This weapon that can kill a God?"

He chuckled and held out a clawed hand to her. "Come with me, and we will discuss it on the way."

Sunnëva stared at his dark form, her body coiled tight with adrenaline. "Would you guarantee my safety?"

"I swear." He placed his hand over his heart. "I mean you no harm. Now or ever."

A sheen of magic swept through the room, and a quiver sank down her spine.

Sunnëva placed the candle on the mantle, weighing this new option. Was she really considering it? She needed help, and here it was. But it all seemed a little too convenient, making her suspicious.

"I have already tried to kill him, only to fail time and again. How do I know this will work?"

"Because someone came very close to succeeding with it before."

She recalled Jökull's scar. Then it was true?

"Everything in the universe has a balance. A *weakness*. Nothing is ever invincible, and the same is true of Gods."

There was an undertone to his words that she immediately caught. *Not all...*

She took a hesitant step toward him, and another until she was in the middle of the room. That was as close as she dared to get. "Who are you?"

Shadows moved around him like living smoke, writhing up the wall behind him. "Dear Sunnëva, you're smarter than that." His voice distorted around her again. "I am eternal darkness."

An awful chill coursed over her shoulders, prickling her flesh.

Sunnëva suspected what he was the moment he came into her room, and it was confirmed when his promise rippled through the air.

He ruled over the Keep in the Waste Lands. A place bathed in darkness and where demons prowled. The people called him the Shadow Lord, but they had been mistaken in the title.

"The God of Shadows," she said faintly.

She came here to vanquish a God, and another was offering his assistance. While a tempting offer, she didn't trust him in the least. Not when he was equally responsible for the fatality of the Everfrost.

Better to stay with the evil she knew.

A thin stream of silvery moonlight trickled in through the window as the moon rose above the thick clouds, making the walls shimmer. Light spilled across the floor toward him, and he took a slight step back.

It occurred to her then why Jökull's castle was covered in ice.

And other things.

"If all Gods have a weakness..." Sunnëva reached into her tunic pocket where she had left her wedding ring. It hummed at her touch, and some inexplicable instinct surfaced. She slipped it on. "Shall I take a guess at yours?"

She stuck her hand into the light. The Moonstone blazed so brightly it bounced off the frosted walls and refracted into his misted face. He snarled at her furiously and elevated himself into the air in a spiral of embers and shadows that whipped through the room. It knocked the candles off the mantle, and they tumbled onto the blankets she had left on the floor, catching them on fire.

The door ripped off the hinges and Jökull burst inside with a furious roar. The Shadow God's power blasted him, and the force threw her backward into the wall.

Then everything went dark.

13

Ringing sharpened in Sunnëva's ears, and she winced. Her eyes were heavy, her mind foggy. The back of her head hurt, but she hadn't been this warm in days. The soft sounds of a crackling fire slowly brought her to consciousness.

Faint voices drifted from nearby.

"How did he know she was here?" Jökull snarled quietly. "It has hardly been a day."

"We have long suspected there were spies in the castle." Aero sighed. "Lady Sunnëva is in danger now that he knows. Perhaps if you told—"

"No."

Sunnëva held still, quieting her breath. *Told her what?*

She peeked through her lashes and found herself in a huge room full of books. Walls of them, at least three levels high. She lay in a large chair with a thick pelt covering her. It carried *his* scent. Jökull's cloak.

They were not in sight, but their voices drifted from where candlelight flickered past a bookshelf.

"As your *advisor*, heed my counsel," Aero said, following a soft *thunk* of a book. "Everything depends on this marriage, sire. You will not succeed if your bride is against you."

What did that mean?

Jökull's sharp exhale floated through the shelves.

"You must try to understand her."

"Demons, I understand. Fae, monsters, and the like. I understand the threads of the universe more than *humans.*" He sighed with audible aversion. "I rue the day Elyōn created them. As if he made them to spite me."

Sunnëva's eyes widened. He spoke of the God of Life.

"Why didn't it work?" Jökull murmured as their steps drifted away.

She only caught snippets of Aero's faint voice. "I couldn't say ... the Gods ... no records, but ... they had in common..."

Jökull's reply was lost beneath the creak of a heavy door opening. She strained to listen, catching only one last line.

"Are you sure she is the one...?"

Sunnëva sat up, waiting for more, but the door closed and they were gone. What did Aero mean by being the one? The one for what? What did she have to do with the Gods?

Whatever he meant, it was the reason why Jökull married her.

And it was somehow connected to the unexpected guest in her room.

Standing, Sunnëva went to huddle by the hearth. The Moonstone ring glinted in the firelight.

Another God was lurking in the Everfrost, and he wanted Jökull dead. She couldn't help but wonder why, even if she wanted the same thing. Her first day here was a failure, but she only needed to bide her time and jump at the slightest show of weakness.

So deep in thought, Sunnëva yelped at the sudden voice behind her.

"You're awake."

She spun around, her hackles rising with the jump of her heart. How did he return without her hearing? Had he come through one of his portals?

"How is your head?"

Sunnëva eyed him warily. "It's fine."

"As I understand it, you have not eaten." Jökull placed a silver platter on the table near the hearth. "I hear you would rather starve, but unfortunately, I need you alive."

She glanced at his offering. A covered plate with a pot of tea, steam spiraling out of the spout. Was this his poor attempt at a truce?

"If I don't?" Sunnëva challenged, almost on impulse now.

His eyes narrowed. "Sit *down*." The rumbling command flipped her stomach. "Unless you prefer, I feed you myself."

That made her obey.

She slowly approached the table, sitting stiffly in the chair furthest from him. Only because it was near the fire. It had nothing to do with the gruff order shocking her pulse. And not related to the way the firelight highlighted the edges of his face. He looked larger without his heavy cloak, a simple tunic clinging to his broad frame.

"It's warm," Jökull finally said, as if he had no other comment.

He paused before taking the chair at the opposite end of the table. It seemed the King wasn't used to serving others, but he was trying to follow Aero's advice.

Very well.

Perhaps she should play along. Attacking him first without knowing all of her options would only get her locked up. Again. She would never find his weakness if she didn't learn more about him first.

But tonight, she received her first clue.

"You must be hungry," he prompted.

"Hunger is common among the clans. It's difficult to find food in winter's misery."

Jökull fell silent at her accusing tone. He looked at the fork and knife set by her plate pointedly. A silent reminder of what he would do if she didn't comply.

Sunnëva uncovered the plate to find meat, bread, and steamed root vegetables her people hadn't been able to farm since last season. Her mouth watered at the delicious aroma, but she hesitated.

"It's not poisoned," Jökull said. "If I wanted you dead, you would be."

And he wouldn't stoop to such trivial methods when he could be much more violent.

"How can I ever show my utmost gratitude?" It came out more sarcastic than Sunnëva intended. She amended it with a false smile.

"Eat. That will be enough."

Her empty stomach won her over. She cut a sliver of meat, and at the first taste, her eyes fell closed, a small moan escaping her. A flush washed through her cheeks at losing her composure.

Jökull's talons scraped the table, his hand curling into a fist. He looked tense, his shoulders rigid.

"I haven't had venison in over a year." Sunnëva licked the juice from her lips, and he followed the drag of her tongue.

His pupils dilated, making his gaze darken beneath his white lashes. He had the same look when he kissed her. *Interesting.*

She hid a smirk and continued eating. At her next bite, she exhaled a quiet, breathy moan.

He growled. "Stop that."

"Stop what?" She looked at him innocently, biting her bottom lip.

The wooden table cracked under the force of Jökull's talons as he glowered at her. He rose from the table and strode to the hearth to toss another log into the fire.

Smiling to herself, Sunnëva finished her food. When she ate the last bite, she sank into her chair with a contented sigh. She couldn't remember the last time she felt this full. But guilt made her stomach churn, knowing her people were starving.

"I noticed you used the books in your room for kindling," Jökull said. "They are meant for reading, not burning."

"What was I to do when you left me there to freeze?" she replied tersely. "I can't read anyway, save for runes. Books aren't exactly valued in the clans."

"Then you will learn," he said, surprising her. "Knowledge is as equally valuable as swinging a sword. And as Queen, education is a rudimentary requirement." Jökull browsed the shelves and pulled out a small leather-bound book, placing it on the table for her. There were strange shapes on it, maybe runes in another language. "We will start with this one."

She frowned. What would she want with a book? And what did he mean by *we*?

He was avoiding the subject that hovered in the air between them. It was about time she got answers.

Sunnëva crossed her arms. "I say we start by discussing what happened tonight."

He returned to his seat. "You have questions."

She decided not to dither. "You're not the only God lurking in our world."

"No."

"He is..."

"The God of Shadows," Jökull confirmed. "And not fond of light, as you saw."

"The ring..." Sunnëva looked down at her hand.

"Its magic will protect you. As long as you wear it, I will know where you are and if you're in danger." His gaze swept to the ring, then to her face. "Keep it with you always."

Jökull had barged into her room seconds after she put the ring on. His expression had been pure rage. He only cared about her safety because he needed her for something.

"When he came, I had the impulse to put the ring in the moonlight. And when I did, light burst out of it as if the moon itself was in my room."

Jökull nodded. "I created that ore to reflect the moonlight."

"*You* created the Moonstone?" she asked.

"I have created many things."

Like this castle. The library walls were coated with more ore beneath the frost, white and a pale blue.

"Tanzstone," Jökull said, following her stare. "Or Tanzanite, as humans call it. Bloodstone is another ore I've made. That one I have come to regret. Among others." He picked at the sleeve of his dark tunic. She heard something in his tone. Regret, but also resignation. "I have yet to create something I deem great."

"And Nightstone? You made it to kill demons."

"All Gods can create in different forms. Sometimes those creations become an infestation that must be quelled."

Sunnëva straightened in her seat. "How do you create things?"

"I weave life from death. People. Animals. Nature. When they are on the brink of dying, I remake them into something new."

The gargoyles screeched outside, and she wondered what they used to be. They were vile things that only came to life at night and turned to stone in the sun when the rest of the world was awake. Perhaps intended to guard the castle against certain unwanted guests.

"What did you do to anger the Shadow God?"

Jökull's mouth curved cynically. "Why do you assume I did something?"

"Well, he wants you dead," she bit back. "Clearly, you did something to him."

"Is that what he told you?"

"It's not difficult to guess." Not when she wanted him dead, too.

"You take an eager interest in him," he said flatly.

She sneered. "Maybe I'm interested in what he has to say."

The firelight danced across the sharp planes of Jökull's features. His eyes were bright as they roved over her face, heightening his otherworldly aura.

He tapped his talons on the table in a pensive rhythm. "And what did my petulant brother have to say?"

She paused in shock at the reveal of their relationship. "That everything in the universe has a weakness. Including Gods."

"And you're determined to find mine. You won't stop trying to kill me—for you despise me."

"*Vehemently*," Sunnëva said. The harsh word left her mouth faster than her better judgment. "I hate you more than you will ever understand. Each day I have to look at you, I curse fate."

Her hatred was never hidden. She wanted him to see it. To feel it. To know if she had the power, she wouldn't hesitate to finish him.

Jökull linked his fingers together and rested his elbows on the table. "Make me understand."

He really couldn't be that stupid. She was forced to marry him under threat to her people. He spilled her family's blood. Rune's blood.

At her silence, he said, "I do not want you as my wife any more than you want me as a husband."

"Then why marry me?"

"I have my reasons."

"Oh yes, of that, I am sure." She glared. "Whatever you want, I will make sure you *never* have it."

He clenched his jaw, and a muscle in his cheek flexed. "Have I not treated you well?"

"By treating me well, you mean taking me from my home and keeping me locked up in a tower in your castle full of monsters that would eat me?"

"You have not exactly made it easy."

"Easy?" Sunnëva repeated, furious. She grabbed the dinner knife and hurled it at him. It flew past his pointed ear and skewered the bookshelf behind his head.

Jökull's eyes flared ice blue.

He shot to his feet and prowled toward her. She scrambled out of the chair but held her ground, her heart beating wildly as he closed the distance between them. Grasping her arm, he swung her around and pinned her against a bookshelf. The force knocked the air out of her. He caged her with his towering body, taking her throat. It was effortless the way he moved her. His strength was inhuman. Her skin tingled as he leaned in close, fury etching every sharp edge of his face.

"Do you realize how much restraint I've shown you?" Jökull asked, his voice deadly soft.

She swallowed, shrinking away from his talons as they extended, lightly pricking her skin. His presence was so cold goosebumps scattered down her arms.

"You call this restraint?" she said through her teeth. "You're quick to temper."

"Temper?" He chuckled quietly, the rough sound sending a rush through her stomach. "If only this were merely *anger*." His head dipped, his nose skating across her cheek to her throat. The sensation of his frosted breath coasting over her chest sent a shiver through her body. He inhaled her scent, and she grimaced at the faint touch of his tongue darting out to taste her racing pulse. "I am maddened by how enticing you are." The vibration of his guttural words sank into her bones. "Every time you attempt to kill me, I am tempted to devour your soul or do other more beastly things that end with you screaming."

Her heart shot into her throat at the dark heat in his voice.

"The worst thing you can do is kill me," she said venomously. "So, if you want to kill me, do it. *Do it!*"

Her dare echoed in the vast library.

"Scornful woman." His white lashes lowered as he leaned in closer. "There are worse things than dying." The fire dimmed at the sudden drop in temperature, and the library darkened. "I could peel the very life from your body and hold it in my claws forever, never letting you know peace."

Ice coated the floor and crawled toward her feet. Sunnëva's heart raced, her shaky breaths clouding in the frigid air. Frost climbed up the shelves behind her, crackling over the books. The sound brought her to that day in the woods when she had been helpless and broken. She closed her eyes, not wanting to give him the satisfaction of her fear.

The ice melted away as quickly as it appeared, and the fire blazed to life.

Jökull's hold slid from her neck, and his thumb lingered at the hollow of her throat, tracing her pulse. "Stop provoking me, little thorn," he murmured. "You seem to always forget who I am."

"That is the one thing I will *never* forget."

Sighing, he tipped her chin. "As hard as it may be to believe, I do want this marriage to work."

The look on his face ... it seemed genuine. Jökull clearly wanted her for something. Whatever it was, it was significant enough to marry her.

Sunnëva scoffed a shocked laugh. "Did you think I would love you like some sweet, innocent maiden from a fairy tale? Well, I am neither and I never will be."

A spasm of pain struck her chest at the truth behind that statement.

Her vision misted and blurred. Jökull blinked, his expression shifting. It infuriated her that she was crying in front of him, yet she couldn't stop.

"I never had much," Sunnëva admitted, her throat constricting. "There wasn't much to have when my people constantly died in the tundra of your making. Every day is a fight for survival, for territory, and for food. We *hate* you because we struggle to survive, for you have built your kingdom on our bones. But I hate you more than all of them for taking the little I had." She inhaled sharply, the pitch of her voice breaking. "Fenrin was a sweet boy. He was *good,* and he would have had something good to offer the world. But ... you tore him apart." The tears rolled down her cheek and dripped to his sleeve, sinking into the fabric. Her mouth trembled with quiet fury. "On his pyre, I swore to him I would take your life, even if it cost my own."

Jökull remained still, his gaze on hers. The library filled with a heavy silence, the only sound coming from the crackling wood in the hearth.

"I had to take him," he finally said.

"Why? Because I stole one of your stupid roses? I only wanted to save him. For once, I needed to save someone. But I..." She wept. "I couldn't."

She couldn't save Freya or Fenrin. If she failed again, she wouldn't save Ansa, either.

Jökull turned away, falling quiet for a moment. "Come with me."

He walked out of the library without looking back.

Sunnëva hesitated, confused. She wiped her face and followed him. Grabbing a torch off the wall, he led her through the dark halls toward a part of the castle she hadn't seen before. They climbed down stone steps with narrow walls and no windows. The air grew colder and rancid.

"Where are we going?" Sunnëva asked warily.

"The dungeons. It's where I keep the beasts that cannot be controlled, or they would be left to devour every last human alive."

She tensed and reached for her knife.

"You won't need that," Jökull said without turning around. "Nothing will harm you."

His cool tone was definitive. But it was *him* she worried about. Since she was also something he couldn't control, did he intend to lock her up as well?

"I don't keep your kind down here, little thorn. If you were wondering."

It unnerved her how he sensed her thoughts so accurately. They reached the bottom of the steps, coming before a heavy door carved with runes and embedded with Tanzanite. A blue sheen of magic hovered on the surface, prickling against her skin.

"Why have you brought me here?" she asked.

"You will see." Jökull knocked three times in a distinct rhythm.

There was a turn of a lock, and the heavy door creaked open. A goblin with scaled green skin appeared inside. He wore armor with the Ice Phoenix crest.

"Sire." He bowed his head as they entered, eyeing her with distrust.

Sunnëva followed Jökull through the dark dungeon. Torches lit the path but didn't reach into the rows of large cells. Creatures howled and snarled from the shadows. In one cage was a spider-like creature, with sharp pincers for arms, and a long neck that curved downwards, as if made too heavy by the three heads it supported. It had no eyes, yet it stared straight at her. Its mouths stretched wide, baring jagged yellow teeth in a feral grin.

She shuddered and stepped closer to Jökull.

He kept them prisoner instead of letting them run rampant? Why? Better yet, why did he care if they hunted her kind?

They reached the last cage, the largest of them all.

Two eyes glowed brightly with flames in the darkness. A deep, rumbling growl reverberated against her. The beast prowled closer, its snarls growing louder. First came a bony snout with sharp, drooling teeth, the inside of its jaws glowing with more flame. Closer it came, revealing a massive hound with dark gray fur and the elongated, exposed skull of a wolf. Its hunched body rose on two legs to its full height, at least ten feet tall. It had thick corded arms ending with clawed hands, and a tail flicked behind it.

It was a monster with the face of a warg and the build of a man. But when it fully stepped into the light, its eyes stopped glowing. They became ocean blue, flecked with golden brown streaks in the center—exactly like hers.

Sunnëva sucked in a gasp and spun to Jökull. His expression confirmed her fear.

"It can't be." She shook her head, air lodging in her throat. "I saw the blood. A hand!"

"He turned in the woods and bit one of my riders. So, I brought him here."

She covered her mouth, drowning in horror and relief. "How?"

"The roses carry my magic, but I have never mixed mine with another God's," Jökull said as they looked up at what Fenrin had become. "A demon infected your bother. That was certain death. Yet you changed his fate with the rose. You created something, Sunnëva."

"Me?"

"Somehow, you gave him life."

Her brother was alive, but she did *that* to him. The creature whined and stuck its bony snout through the bars.

"Oh, Fen." She reached out with a shaky hand.

Jökull took her arm. "Don't get too close."

But she wasn't afraid. She stroked his skull, feeling the thick bristles on his jaw. "I am so sorry."

He keened softly, crying too. He understood. Fenrin was in there.

Sunnëva reached in through the bars and hugged his bulky arm. "I will find a way to fix this. I promise."

14

After sighing for the hundredth time, Sunnëva sat up in bed and frowned at Fenrin. Her brother lay by the fire like a puppy, resting his head on his large paws. She promised to fix him, but she didn't know where to start.

The morning sunlight shone across the crystalline surface of her table, windows, and decorative moldings. Only a few scorched stains marked the mantle and floor by the lit hearth. Now that her bedroom was warm, the surface frost had melted. While she had been in the library, she'd gained an extra window and someone had embedded the walls with decorative plates of Moonstone and Tanzanite.

Rising, Fenrin padded to her, his claws tapping on the floors. He sat beside her on his haunches and made a questioning chuff, no doubt worried by all of her restless sighing.

"By the Gods, you're enormous."

He puffed out his chest proudly.

Sunnëva smiled weakly and petted his furry arm. "Father sent me to assassinate him, Fen. And I had planned to. I was so determined to take his heart because I thought he killed you, but now what do I do?"

He rested his head on her lap, huffing a sigh, too.

She traced the shape of his skull face and scratched behind his furry ears. "Father said if I failed ... he would hurt Ansa."

Fenrin growled.

"And if I told him what happened to you..."

They shared a look. Both knew their father would sooner put him to the sword than allow him to remain this warg mutant.

"I have to find a way to get her away from him." She groaned. "Now I don't know what to do about Jökull. Not that he is innocent. He is responsible for the land's conditions ... and Rune."

Her heart pitched.

She was powerless against him, but he had a weakness. The Skellings, storm birds of the Frost Lands. But in what way? She needed to find out.

Fen straightened, his head turning to the door.

"What is it?"

A soft knock came shortly after, and Aero entered with a weepy young woman at his side. She kept her head lowered, hiding under her wavy, dark hair and clutching one of her arms to herself. She was dressed in the gray robes of a servant. This was the first human Sunnëva had seen in the castle besides herself.

"My Queen, this is your new handmaiden..." Aero trailed off, his eyes widening once he noticed Fenrin in her room.

"Where did she come from?" Sunnëva asked.

Aero composed himself, but he remained by the door, keeping an eye on her brother. "The Rulem clan."

The young woman burst into sobs and covered her face.

"Good Gods, Aero." Sunnëva rushed up and pulled her into her arms. She was a petite thing, hardly reaching her shoulders. "There, it's all right. Don't be afraid."

She glared at the mage. The poor girl was probably terrified of this place.

Aero dipped his head. "It was not my doing. His Majesty thought you may be more comfortable here with human companionship."

"So he simply stole her for my comfort?" she said sarcastically.

Aero frowned. "The King is not a thief, my lady. She was given."

"Of course she was. All he has to do is snap his fingers, and the clans would give him anything out of fear of retribution." Sunnëva wiped the young woman's wet cheeks. "What is your name?"

"Tally, Your Majesty," she said, her bright green eyes shining with tears. She took the ends of her frock and dipped into a clumsy curtsey.

"Call me Sunnëva, please." She patted her arm. "And don't you worry. I will be sure to have you sent back to Rulem this instant."

Tally gasped. "Go back?"

Aero shook his head. "I'm afraid—"

"She's going home." Sunnëva stormed out of her chambers. Fenrin followed on her heels, and Tally scurried back, clutching Aero's sleeve.

"Hold a moment," he said, hurrying after her. "The King is presently engaged."

"I don't care."

"My lady, I must insist—"

"No, this is completely ridiculous, and I will not have it." Sunnëva continued on, but realized she didn't know her way around the castle yet. "Fenrin, can you find that pig-headed block of ice?"

He sniffed the air and prowled ahead. She followed him until they reached a tall set of doors.

Sunnëva slammed them open. "You can't merely steal girls from their homes, Jökull!"

She came to a stop, finding she had entered the dining hall. The table was full of fae and monsters. All conversation halted, every eye falling on her. Jökull was seated at the head of the table, his legs crossed on top.

Aero bowed. Tally immediately dropped, her hands and knees slapping the ground as she prostrated herself on the floor.

"Good morrow, wife," Jökull said, his mouth curving into a tight smile, the edges sharp. "You appear displeased. Pray tell, what is your complaint now?"

Suddenly, with all attention on her, she thought better of disrespecting him before the court.

Sunnëva cleared her throat. "I ... would like to discuss the matter of my handmaiden."

"What is wrong with her?"

"Nothing. Only that she was taken away from her family, and I want her returned," she said, then added, "Please."

After last night, Sunnëva felt a little indebted to him for her brother. She should at least be cordial.

Jökull took a drink. "Your handmaiden was given. Rulem was short on their levies this quarter, and Earl Bram thought she would make up the deficit. Generally, it would not, but I assumed her presence might please you. I see I was wrong." His icy gaze fell on the poor girl. "Human."

"Yes, sire?" she replied in a small, shaky voice.

Sunnëva started to regret coming here. By speaking out, she may have put a target on the girl's back. She moved in front of her protectively. "Her name is Tally."

Jökull arched an eyebrow at her reaction. "*Tally*, it seems we are no longer in need of your services. I will have you returned to Rulem immediately."

"No, please!" She threw herself at Sunnëva's feet, clutching her skirts. "Forgive me, Your Majesty. I will no longer weep. Please, don't send me there. I beg you."

Sunnëva frowned at her in confusion. "You don't wish to go back?"

Tally shook her head wildly.

"She was a slave," Aero whispered. "The spoils of conquest when Rulem defeated the Harden Clan."

Sunnëva's heart sank. Harden had been the tenth clan before it was destroyed. That meant Tally had no home either, and Sunnëva had seen how awful Rulem treated their slaves. Wanting to stay *here*, of all places, proved it.

Jökull had saved the poor woman, and she yelled at him for it.

Sunnëva glanced at him sheepishly, cringing under all their stares. "All right, hush now." She helped Tally stand. "No one will send you there. You can stay."

Hopefully, she hadn't traded her handmaiden's suffering for another.

Tally bowed repeatedly. "Thank you, Your Majesty. Thank you!"

"No need to call me that," she murmured under her breath.

"Join us," Jökull said.

Sunnëva deliberated, but Tally was so thin. The poor thing probably hadn't eaten a proper meal since her clan had fallen. Sunnëva took the chair on the opposite end of the table and motioned for Tally to sit on her left. Her new handmaiden hesitated before stiffly lowering in the chair. Aero took his place on Jökull's right. Fenrin laid down beside Sunnëva, curling his body around her chair protectively. His soft growls rumbled in the room.

"*This* is who you chose to be our Queen?"

Everyone looked at the fae who spoke.

He was a reedy male with pointed ears sticking out of his dark purple hair. "She is a lowborn human without a shred of respect." His red eyes turned to Jökull. "You have received marriage propositions with fine dowries from all corners of the world. You could have chosen any princess from a reputable kingdom to strengthen our army and fortify territory lines. Yet on some whim none of us understand, you chose this impertinent mortal we all have to bow down to?" He sneered at her with disgust, revealing a pair of long fangs. "I would rather chew on her bones."

He was a Nightwalker.

Dark fae that liked to consume blood. But he was out in the daylight. How?

She glanced at the garnet brooch pinned at his neck. The vivid gem reminded her of fresh blood. The other Nightwalkers beside him also wore the same gem as jewelry on their pointed ears or their clawed fingers.

Bloodstone.

"Your entire speech was a slight, Valden," Aero said sharply to the one who spoke.

Jökull flicked his hand, unbothered. "No, please, continue. As an emissary of the Wild Court, you are free to speak."

"I feel the warm blood in her veins." Valden's claws scratched against the table's surface. His focus locked on her like prey. "Let us feast on her flesh and find you a new wife."

The other two male Nightwalkers with him hissed, drool spilling from their fangs as they all looked at her with obvious hunger.

Sunnëva stood and reached for her bone knife. These creatures she was prepared to kill. They were fast, but she could be, too.

Aero got to his feet, a blaze of purple filling his hands. Currents of electricity danced along his arms and flickered around his head. A powerful electrical current charged the air.

Fenrin also stood to his full height, growling at the Nightwalkers. They hissed back. The only one not alarmed was the King.

If Valden hadn't been looking at her, he would have noticed Jökull's smile. An icy smile that made the hair stand on her arms.

"You want to eat her, Valden?" he asked. *"Be my guest."*

Her heart stopped.

That was all it took to snap the tension in the air.

Valden blurred into a burst of speed down the table. Jökull was in front of her faster than she could blink. The sound of their bodies collided like the clash of thunder. Valden was thrown into the wall, and he ruptured into flames. His screams filled the dining room, bouncing off the frosted walls bathed in firelight. Tally's trembling fork rattled against her plate as they watched him burn.

Something dropped from Jökull's hand, and it landed by Sunnëva's plate.

The Bloodstone brooch glinted in the sunlight.

The other Nightwalkers leaped from their seats, and they bared their fangs at him.

Jökull regarded them coolly. "Bow or burn."

They fled for the doors. Glimmering wings of ice unfolded from Jökull's back, and with one flap, he was on them before they ever reached the threshold. He tore off their Bloodstone jewels, and they were consumed in flames.

It was quick.

Nothing left of them but ashes and charred bone.

Jökull's tattoos pulsed blue as he reaped their souls. She stared at him, her heart thrumming wildly with several emotions she couldn't process. Shock, maybe. Because it couldn't be gratitude, and certainly not fascination. It had to be shock by the swift brutality of violence.

"It seems I need to repeat myself. After today, I never will again," the King said to his court, his glowing eyes rising to her. "Touch my wife, I take your life."

Sunnëva held still, her heart doing all sorts of strange beats beneath the coolness of his stare. *Who knew he was a poet?*

Straightening her shoulders, she sat down again and schooled her expression, her mind reeling.

Jökull's footsteps carried in the quiet dining room as he returned to the table. His wings vanished in a dusting of frost, and he sat in his seat. Taking a drink from his goblet, he nodded. "Continue, Garr."

Everyone retook their seats.

"As I was saying," one of the orcs said with a clearing of his throat. Garr was large and bulky, with skin the dull green of a swamp, dark green hair, and pointed ears. His yellow feline eyes glowered at the ashes on the floor. "Fae loyalties are wavering, my King." Large incisors protruded from his bulbous lips as he spoke.

Jökull smirked. "Clearly."

The warriors at his table chuckled. They acted as if murdering members of their court were a daily occurrence. Perhaps it was.

"With them being so close to the Waste Lands, the Shadow God's influence is beginning to spread," Garr said. "It may be something to be wary of."

"Prince Dagden knows what I do to traitors. And soon he will be shortly reminded." Jökull nodded to Aero. "Send word to the Moor

Lands that I need his representatives replaced. Preferably with those who don't attempt to suck my Queen dry."

"Right away, sire." Aero made a note on a small scroll, rolled it up, then tossed it up in a purple mist of magic. Cael swept down from the alcoves to snatch it in his beak and flew out of a window in the glass-domed ceiling.

"There is the Sea Queen to consider," said a dark-skinned male with large horns curling over his head, his voice a deep rumble. He was strapped with fine armor. "She holds no associations with us or anyone. We could propose an alliance."

Aero shook his head. "The sea fae prefer to stay out of any war with land dwellers, Quill. Their Queen has enough uprising beneath the surface."

"What of the Dragon Princess?" Garr asked next, perking Sunnëva's interest.

She'd never seen a dragon, as they lived on the west coast, but she heard they were incredible.

"We are allied with Xián Jīng by trade," the orc continued. "But perhaps she would be willing to part with a hatchling. Having a dragon among our ranks would dampen any uprising."

"The princess considers her dragons family, General," Jökull said. "She would probably have them eat you should you ever have the stones to proposition such a thing to her face."

Garr stiffened in his seat.

Sunnëva secretly smiled. Now that sounded like someone worth meeting.

They rambled on about politics as Jökull lounged at the head of his table with mild interest. The slaying of the Nightwalkers spun in her mind. The way Jökull had moved. He hadn't hesitated for one second. If he had, it would be her remains on the floor.

Her stomach churned as the servants cleaned up the charred bones. She'd lost her appetite. Sunnëva grabbed a whole roasted bird and tossed it to Fenrin, who ate it in one bite.

"They keep trying to push into the south," Garr said. "Kyrr threatens war again if we do not renegotiate territory lines."

"I *don't* negotiate." The sharpness of Jökull's voice drew her attention to the conversation again. The room became frigid, making her breath cloud. "Kyrr has no grounds to be a threat."

At every encounter, Jökull had always been cool and composed. Even when he killed the Nightwalkers or was provoked by her. But he was now visibly angry, his teeth clenching.

It appears the clans weren't the only ones fighting amongst themselves for territory.

Aero set down his goblet. "Perhaps it might be worth considering, sire. The Skellings only wish for—"

Jökull's eyes flared to a menacing ice blue. His gaze cut to the mage, silencing him. "I rule everything from the Hermon Mountains to the shores of the Saxe Sea. This is my land, and I will not give up an inch of it. Not an *inch*, Aero. If either of you bring this up again, I will rip out your tongues by the root."

The dining hall filled with the tension of his anger. Exhaling sharply, he stood, and a portal opened behind him. Beyond it were the gardens, the roses bathed in bright sunlight. "Come along, Fenrin. I will show you the hunting grounds."

Fenrin gave her a soft whine, perhaps worried about leaving her alone with their guests. But if Jökull wasn't concerned, she didn't feel the need to be. Her brother was going to need more than chicken to fill him.

Sunnëva nodded. His paws padded softly in Jökull's wake, and they vanished into the portal.

"You must convince him, Aero," said the orc as the rest of them stood. "The value of peace is higher than pride."

The generals excused themselves, and it surprised her when they slightly bowed their heads to her. Then they promptly left the dining room.

Aero sighed. "Are you all right, my Queen?"

"Yes..." She picked up the brooch, turning it in her fingers. "I see now why you tried to stop me. I should have listened."

"Truthfully, such an occurrence was bound to happen in a castle full of creatures. Some are more compelled by their appetites than their sense. The simple ones can't help themselves. The same cannot be said of Valden." He frowned at the black stain on the floor. "I prefer to keep the castle in order, but in this case, an example needed to be made among the gentry. Meanwhile, please do not wander the castle without me or the King. I have employed knights from far out west. You will have a proper Queen's Guard to protect you. It will take some time for them to travel by ship, but they should arrive within the month."

She would have a Queen's Guard? They must certainly be something if they could be trusted around a human.

Sunnëva was more interested in Jökull's reaction to the Skellings. They were enemies, but there seemed to be history there.

"What is this trouble with the border territory? Sounds like rebellion, yet the generals aren't interested in escalating this further."

Which she found unexpected. The clans knew Jökull as someone who crushed any uprising before it could grow.

Aero pressed on his temples. "They did, in the past. But they are content now, having grown fat and wealthy in their castles. None of them are interested in disrupting that. The last time the King battled with the Skellings, half of his army was decimated."

Her eyes widened. "Are they that formidable?"

"When a flock of them comes together, yes, very." The mage's brows curled together.

"But ... ?"

"It's not a matter of concern, my lady. Kyrr is not a risk anymore."

Well, the God of Shadows thought otherwise. What did he know that they didn't?

"Kyrr is their leader?" she asked.

Aero nodded. "The Tribe Chief, and the sire of the Skelling race."

That meant he was the first.

Sunnëva read the concern on Aero's face. "You wonder why he threatens war if he is not capable of keeping it."

Despite what Jökull said, Kyrr must still be dangerous.

"Sometimes desperation makes us do foolish things."

Sunnëva turned over his answer as she took in his tense expression.

Aero cleared his throat. "Speaking of foolish, I see you have let your brother out of his cage."

"He didn't belong there. Fen is perfectly fine with me. Jökull allowed it." Not that he put up much of a fight when she refused to leave the dungeons without him.

"Until instinct strikes, and he decides to make a meal out of someone. Those jaws could easily snap a body in half."

Tally squeaked, lifting her head.

"Fenrin won't hurt anyone," Sunnëva assured her, glowering at Aero. "He may not look the same on the outside, but he's my brother. I only need to find a way to return him to who he once was."

The mage crossed his arms, his brow pinching thoughtfully again. "I have been working to find out what he is since we brought him here. He is not full warg, made clear by the fact he is not bothered by the sunlight as demons are. I've taken samples, and I am experimenting in my workroom. I don't quite have it yet, but I may be on to something."

Sunnëva jumped up from her seat. "Show me."

15

First mission: Kill the King—was now on temporary post-
ponement due to many factors. Foremost, Jökull hadn't killed
her brother. He was immortal, incredibly lethal ... and he had
saved her life. Sunnëva didn't want to think about any of it yet.
Instead, she gave herself a second mission: Cure Fenrin.

Aero led them up three flights of stairs to a corner tower and
opened the heavy doors to his workroom. Sunnëva and Tally
marveled at his shelves full of glass jars, each filled with shimmering
powders, bubbling liquids, preserved animal parts, and herbs. Some
contents glowed with magic. The end of the room led to an outdoor
garden enclosed entirely in glass. It was full of plants and flowers of
every type, including enchanted roses. Their sweet aroma filled the
space. She was awed by the sight of so much green. It reminded her
of Freya's tapestry.

"I didn't know you were capable of this," Sunnëva said. "Do you
use magic with all of your experiments?"

"Only if necessary. I mostly experiment with the fauna of the
land."

"How did you come by this knowledge?"

"Well, I have not always been the Chief Advisor. Before I came to serve the King, I studied medicine in Magos. That's what he originally hired me to do. I was meant to be the castle's healer, but there wasn't much use for my skills when the courtiers here either heal on their own rather quickly—or die instantly. In time, His Majesty made me Chief Advisor when the position became available. I had no experience with such things, but it works, I suppose."

It's because they were friends, even if neither acknowledged it. Jökull was stubborn, but he valued Aero's advice. She could see why. The mage came off as very reliable and clear-minded.

"You're a mage from the west?" Tally asked in surprise. Catching herself, she bowed her head. "Pardon me."

"It's all right, you may ask," Aero said. "Yes, I am a mage. I was born and raised in Magos until I came here."

"I ... I was told there were three Guilds your people are born into," she said timidly. "Sun, Earth, and Lunar."

He nodded. "That is correct. We draw Essence from our element."

"Essence?" Sunnëva asked.

Aero lifted his palm, and it blazed a brilliant purple. "That is what we call the life-force energy that powers our magic."

Oh, that explained the pull of electricity in the air whenever he used it.

Tally stepped closer, her face lighting up. "May I...?"

Aero nodded. He smiled faintly as she ran her fingers through the glowing mist with wonder.

"That's remarkable," she said. When Tally looked up at him, she flushed and stepped back.

Aero continued to his desk. "It's unfortunate what befell your brother, Lady Sunnëva, but I must admit, I am enjoying this case. It is not often I am able to make use of my original studies on herbology and science."

She went to see what he was tinkering with. He was grinding dried herbs in a white mortar made of marble. Stacks of old books, scrolls, and other trinkets cluttered his desk. On the table beside it were stands of glass orbs boiling with unknown substances over candles. One held a glowing blue liquid, and she leaned in closer to see the enchanted rose petals inside.

"What are you making?"

"I am testing the samples I took from Fenrin by mixing them in a solution with the roses," Aero said. "If they should react negatively, it helps me deduce certain aspects of his physiology. What we want is a positive reaction."

"And that will tell you what, exactly?"

"It will help me determine *what* he is. Normally, such questions are easily answered by the God who sired their creations, but no God made him."

She had.

"But I used the magic of Gods. Is that not the same?" Sunnëva asked.

He shook his head. "It seems as if it would be in theory, but something changed the magic. You must have introduced some other matter to Fenrin at the same time."

She frowned. "All I gave him was the rose."

He sighed. "There has to be something."

"Perhaps because I am human?"

"I have warg samples and human samples, but those are only pieces." He frowned at his work. "The answer is here somehow, but I am not seeing it. How was the rose administered?"

Sunnëva gazed at the bowl of blue petals, recalling what Gyda did that night. "Our Clan Healer ground the petals until it defused the rose oil, and she had me give it to him by mouth."

"Thus, siring him to you." Aero leaned up against the table, his fingers tapping on the edge absentmindedly. "What I don't understand is that he should have turned right away when you gave it to him."

"He didn't."

"Yes, I saw." Aero crossed his arms. "More must have happened that we are not taking into consideration. Other factors could have affected his blood. Did your healer add anything to the rose oil? Perhaps given him something to ease the pain or treat the bite?"

"Oh!" Sunnëva gasped. "She did. She made him an elixir with aconite to slow the poison from reaching his heart."

Aero's eyes widened as he seemed to work through something in his head. "Aconite is a purple bloom. Highly poisonous and a deterrent against wargs." He went to his bookshelf and pulled out a book. "Do you know what it's called in the West?"

"Wolfsbane."

At the soft reply, they turned to Tally. She was studying a jar, holding it up to the light. At their silence, Tally noticed them and turned bright red.

"F-forgive me, milord." Flustered, she rushed to put the jar back, but tripped and went sprawling.

The jar flew out of her hands. It should have shattered on the floor, but with a snap of his fingers, Aero caught it in a mist of Essence. He levitated it onto the shelf.

"I-I am so sorry!" Tally exclaimed. She started to rise on her knees, but when Aero approached her, she cowed and covered her head. He froze, and so did Sunnëva.

It reminded her of Ansa cowering in the longhouse, and her heart sank.

"Tally." Sunnëva went to her.

Her handmaiden looked up at her frightfully, tears on her lashes. "Please forgive me."

The fact that she had recoiled and profusely apologized for such a small mistake made Sunnëva embrace her. "Your slave keeper, he hurt you. Didn't he? Was it the Earl of Rulem?"

Tally lowered her head.

"No one will touch you in this castle." At the dark rumble of Aero's promise, they both looked up to find his eyes glowing purple. "*Ever*, do you understand?"

Maybe it was the threat in his voice, or the menacing static in the air that sent a shiver rolling down Sunnëva's spine. He didn't say it because Tally would be impervious to the monsters wandering the halls, but because Aero decided he would kill anything that made her shrink in such fear again.

Sunnëva had been wrong about the mage.

He wasn't Jökull's Chief Advisor because he was kind. Aero was as dangerous as the King. He was merely more reserved.

Tally's wide green eyes stared up at him, slowly nodding.

Aero held out a hand and helped her to her feet. "As you were saying," he continued casually, the magic fading from his irises.

The action dispelled the crackle of energy from the workroom.

Sunnëva frowned when he didn't help her up, too. The mage was taking the *no touching* rule Jökull placed to heart.

She stood and asked Tally, "How do you know about wolfsbane?"

"I-I was once an apprentice of the Healer in my clan," she said shyly, looking down at her feet. "Before we were conquered, I mean."

"I see." Aero nodded at the jar she almost broke. "Have you deduced the contents of that jar?"

Her handmaiden hesitated. "If I were to guess ... white peony root, milord. For pain and fever." Tally bit her lip as she glanced at the dark glass bottle on the desk, twisting her fingers together. "I noticed the drake oil was left out near sunlight. The oil retains its medicinal properties better when placed in a dark space."

Aero jerked to a stop, completely taken aback. "Right, of course. I normally do, but I was using it last night and forgot to return it." He put the bottle away in a cabinet.

Tally blushed and nodded, hiding under her dark hair.

"Her talents may be wasted as my handmaiden," Sunnëva murmured to him as she approached a barrel containing shimmery black sand. "What is this for?"

"Ah, this is the base form of Nightstone," Aero said. "Demon blood and crushed meteorite."

She took a step back. "*Demon* blood?"

"Yes. It must be gathered during the lunar eclipse to work. Like salt, the dust can be used to make a warding circle, which we call Night Ash. Primarily, we forge it into weapons."

That must be a fascinating process.

Sunnëva was enjoying herself, learning about all of this. They spent the remainder of the day discussing theories about Fenrin's condition.

When evening arrived, they realized they had missed dinner.

"Thank you, Aero," she said. "I didn't know how I was going to help my brother, but you have given me hope."

"Think nothing of it, my Queen. It's my pleasure. I will continue to investigate with the information you have provided."

"Would you mind if I returned to work on this with you?"

Aero's silvery brows quirked. "No, not at all. Should the King approve, of course."

"Approve of what?" Jökull's large form darkened the doorway. He leaned against the frame with his arms crossed. He took in the view of them huddled together at the worktable in the middle of the room. "What are you doing alone at this hour with my wife, Aero?"

The mage replied evenly, without missing a beat. "Purely science, sire. Chaperoned by her handmaiden, as proper."

Tally came around the corner from the glasshouse garden. When she saw the King, she nearly dropped into a bow on the floor again, but Sunnëva caught her arm. "If you keep doing that, His Majesty's royal head will grow bigger."

Jökull's mouth hitched on one end. "It's already big, I can assure you."

Tally's face turned bright red.

"Charming." Sunnëva glowered at him.

"As for my question?"

She almost retorted that he had no say over what she did, but didn't have the energy to argue. "I would like to join Aero in finding an antidote for Fenrin."

Jökull hummed and nodded. "Very well. That could be a good use of your time. Then you may come here in the late afternoon, should Aero be accessible outside of his duties."

The mage tilted his head in acknowledgment and returned to his work.

"Come, I will escort you to your room." Jökull moved into the hallway, and Sunnëva headed for the door.

"Tally," Aero called, not looking up from the thick tome he was reading. "You may return, as well, during your leisure time. To continue your healer apprenticeship, if you wish."

Tally's mouth opened in surprise and happiness lit her face. She bowed deeply. "Thank you, milord."

Sunnëva hid a smile as they trailed after Jökull, noticing a new liveliness in her handmaiden's step.

16

Jökull may not have cared about her evening activities, but he was serious about her education. She was made to sit every day with a stern elf during the mornings in the library to learn history, arithmetic, and government, along with reading and writing.

Boring stuff.

Jökull was present as well, probably to keep an eye on her or to make sure no other came wandering in, lured by the scent of a human. He made himself a spot on the other end of the library at a desk that his advisors filled with endless documents he had to sign or revise. Occasionally, she caught herself studying him instead, perplexed by the sight of a God doing something so *normal,* such as work.

Whenever Aero finished his duties, she eagerly joined the mage with Tally in his workroom to conduct experiments and make notes on their findings.

Jökull helped Fenrin in his own way.

She didn't ask him to, but when he wasn't busy being King, he went off with her brother in the woods past the gardens. *To learn his capabilities,* he said when she asked what they were up to. Her brother seemed more relaxed, and she couldn't help but feel ... grateful.

As the weeks merged into a month, Sunnëva found herself becoming accustomed to the castle, though she was still wary of the creatures wandering the halls.

They hissed at her, their strange eyes glowing with hunger or disapproval. The more temperate ones, like the fae, regarded her with mild indifference. She was curious about them, but very few spoke to her. All gave a wide berth or fled in the opposite direction whenever she walked past with Jökull or Aero. No one else attempted to attack her again.

Life was surprisingly simple here. She was sheltered, fed, and finally warm. But she couldn't fully enjoy such things when others didn't.

Above all, Sunnëva worried.

Her father was waiting for results while he held her sister hostage. She had Aero write a message for her and send it home two days ago with Cael, asking how Ansa was, but the griffin returned with no reply. The silence was deliberate because her father knew how to write. He could have sent a message.

Was her sister all right?

Sunnëva blinked at her reflection in the vanity as Tally brushed her hair. She touched her cheek, noticing her face no longer looked so gaunt. Her dark circles were also disappearing. The nightmares hardly came now. Perhaps because she was too mentally tired after her long days to dream of more torture.

"Shall I pick out a dress for you today, my lady?" Tally asked.

"Ah, no, I will wear the usual."

She was more comfortable in trousers and a leather jerkin under her cloak. It made it easier to run or fight if needed. When she finished dressing, a knock came at the door.

Tally went to answer it, revealing Aero and two armored fae. One was a male with long dark green hair tied back at his nape. The other was a female with the same colored hair falling past her jaw. The phoenix crest marked their black chest plates with swords at their waist.

"My Queen, allow me to introduce you to Ren and Riona Willowglen. Knights of the Summer Court. They are to lead your Queen's Guard."

They bowed to her.

"It is an honor, my lady," Riona said.

Ren smiled at her kindly.

"If you'll excuse me. I will leave you to get acquainted." Aero bowed and continued on.

The knights stepped in and shut the door, taking their posts beside it. Sunnëva couldn't help observing them curiously.

Fae were rarely seen among the clan territories, but the few she had met were either terribly ugly or starkly beautiful. Ren and Riona fell into the latter sort.

They held an allure that drew the eye. With graceful features and lithe forms, they looked too inhumanly perfect. The sunlight shimmered on something past their elbows.

Sunnëva canted her head. "Are those wings?"

"Yes, my lady," Ren said, and they turned around to show her.

Each of them had four translucent wings with patterns of crisscrossing veins, like a dragonfly. Riona's were lustrous purple tipped in sapphire, and Ren's were an iridescent emerald that turned aquamarine in the light.

He glanced over his shoulder, and his moss-colored eyes met hers. "Beautiful, aren't they?"

She smiled at his swaggering grin. "Yes."

Riona nudged him, grousing under her breath. "Don't flirt with the Queen, Ren. That's why we were dispatched from our last post."

He chuckled. "I can't help it when I see a pretty lady."

Already trying to get on her good side.

"Aero mentioned you're from the Summer Court," Sunnëva said. "Where is that exactly?"

"It's located in Arthal, my lady," Ren said.

From her studies, she'd learned Arthal was another country far across the ocean. "So, not part of Prince Dagden's court, then?"

"No, my lady, those are wild fae," Riona answered with a hint of condescension to her tone at the mention of them. "Seelie and Unseelie, who have abandoned their courts in Arthal and gathered together here, calling themselves a *court*." She tsked. "Prince Dagden has no right to such a claim when he is not yet king and is very unlikely to become one. He is the petulant grandson of the Autumn Queen, too far down the line of succession to ever sit on the throne." Catching herself, Riona ducked her head. "Forgive me. I have said too much."

"My sister gets riled up with fae politics," Ren said. "To answer your question, we are pixies. Woodland folk of the Nadair Kingdom, ruled by the Summer Queen."

Sunnëva wondered how many fae queens there were. Perhaps one for every season. "And they sent you here as punishment?"

Her flirty guard grinned slyly.

Riona glared at him. "You are shameless."

"What did you do?" Tally's quiet voice piped up beside her.

"Do you really want to know?" The knight took her handmaiden's hand and brought it to his lips. He gazed into her eyes so deeply, her cheeks turned bright red. "My sweet, there is something about your eyes I find so intriguing I could get lost in them for an eternity."

"That." Riona smacked his head. "He did that! With the Queen, her sons, and her daughters. It caused a riot."

But Sunnëva was staring at Ren's hand. On the back of it was a brown symbol of an oak tree. A geas. It seemed he, too, had struck a bargain with the Druid.

Ren pouted. "I have a lot of love to give."

"Yes, well, thanks to your indiscretions, paramour, we have been shipped off across the world to serve in a foreign court like wet-nosed squires until our Queen has decided to forgive you," Riona snapped. "Which may not be for decades, mind you. Thank the Gods you still have your neck."

Sunnëva watched their interaction with great amusement. She didn't mind a little gossip, and Ren was full of it. "Why were you sent here?" she asked Riona.

"I volunteered." She glared at her brother. "Someone has to watch his back."

"That's why you're my favorite sister." Ren put an arm around her shoulders.

"I am your *only* sister."

"Precisely."

Seeing how close they were made Sunnëva miss Ansa a hundred times more.

"Well, shall we escort you to the dining room for your morning meal, my lady?" Ren asked her.

"Oh, no, I have already eaten."

"She prefers to take her meals in her room," Tally informed them. "It is time for her lessons."

"Ah, wonderful. Shall we go?"

Sunnëva nodded and followed them out into the hall. They passed the foyer down another set of steps. It was the long way to the library, but she liked it because it crossed an open veranda with a view of the land. She paused by the balustrade, looking in the direction of her village. Sunlight glinted over the snow and the trees beyond.

Before she left, Gyda promised to look out for Ansa. She didn't worry about Bjorn. He was an obedient son, eager to please their father. But her sister was left defenseless without her.

Sunnëva reached out, and her palm landed on the invisible wall of Jökull's magic. It pulsed blue at her touch, humming gently against her skin like cool water.

"Are you all right, my lady?" Tally asked.

She considered the question. "Yes. I merely wish to see the ones I left behind."

"You miss home."

"I suppose you could say that. You must also miss your home."

Tally looked out at the woods on the northern horizon. "Every day."

In the far distance toward the south, the outlines of the Zafiro mountains were partially obscured by black storm clouds near the Waste Lands. The castle was supposed to be guarded against the God of Shadows, but she had a feeling she would see him again.

"Pardon, Your Majesty," Ren called.

The title reminded Sunnëva she was Queen now, and her *accommodating* husband said she could have whatever she desired.

She knew what to ask for next.

Sunnëva turned away. "Yes, lead on."

Her steps were hasty, now urged to get to the library and speak with him. But much to her surprising disappointment, Jökull didn't join her that morning. She glowered at his empty desk as her instructor blathered on. The rest of her day endlessly stretched while she waited for him to make an appearance. Of all the times she wanted to see that beast, he chose now to be absent.

The dining room at lunch also lacked his presence. She checked the throne room and even the war room with no success. Sunnëva sighed and hurried to Aero's workroom. Surely, the mage had to know how to find Jökull. But only Cael was there. The griffin handed her a note in his beak, and Sunnëva took it excitedly.

She passed it to Ren to read. "Lord Aero expresses his apologies, my lady, but he will be preoccupied with his duties until late tonight."

Sunnëva groaned.

"It also says here that the King would like you to join him in the courtyard this evening."

17

Sunnëva had run halfway across the castle when she stopped. Ren and Riona skid to a halt behind her. Why was she running so desperately to see him? She didn't want to seem too eager to ask for Jökull's help, in case he decided to hold it over her. Though, if he wanted to force her obedience, he could have done that with Fenrin.

Taking a breath, Sunnëva forced herself to walk at a normal pace. They crossed the throne room as her guards led her through another hall, finally reaching the courtyard. She found Jökull outside, but he wasn't alone.

Donelle stood before him, scantily clad in red silk. She gazed at him with soft doe-eyes, speaking too quietly for Sunnëva to hear. Jökull's attention, however, remained on the forest, despite the beautiful fae stroking his chest with her fingernail guards.

Donelle glanced past Jökull's shoulder and noticed her. She flashed Sunnëva a sharp smile as she bowed. "I will wait for you tonight," she said aloud, then walked away with a sway in her hips toward the castle.

Sunnëva rolled her eyes. Gods spare her.

Ren and Riona took their posts by the courtyard doors as she came to stand by him.

"You called for me, dear husband," she said sweetly in greeting, forcing a smile on her face.

His mouth hitched on one end. "I hope it was not to your inconvenience, wife." Jökull's light tone matched hers, almost teasing. Completely different from his usual growl. "I trust your studies are going well?"

She glowered at the garden dully, scratching at the scar on her elbow. "Splendid."

Jökull didn't physically harm her, but he certainly found an effective way of torturing her. Those hours of lessons were a bore.

"And your handmaiden has finally settled?"

"Yes, she is getting on well. I think your mage has taken it upon himself to make sure none of the other servants torment her. Don't be surprised if he obliterates some of them by the week's end."

A faint smirk rose on Jökull's face. "Aero is one of the kindest men you will ever meet unless you give him a reason not to be."

Was that his way of saying he could also be amiable if she didn't provoke him so much?

His gaze lingered on her, but she didn't look at him. Not yet. She pretended his garden of roses held her attention. A particular tree with a white trunk and blue leaves stood out among all the rest.

Sunnëva faintly smiled. "You have an Azure Tree."

"I do." Jökull crossed his arms behind his back.

"Did you make them, too?"

"They are Elyōn's creations. He seems to have a fondness for trees." Jökull canted his head at it thoughtfully. "These, in particular, appear at random in places of strong magic or intended fate. Azure Trees hold an unpredictable power and not even I know their true intention."

"Hmm." Sunnëva studied it curiously. She didn't know how to bring up the subject of her sister now that she was with him. "And what brings me to join you on this fine evening?"

"I thought you might like to see whether Fenrin was successful. He is out hunting in the Black Woods."

"What?" She balked. "You sent him *there*? It's full of monsters and demons."

"Fenrin is capable of holding up his own. However, the woods are spelled. If they sense he is a danger to the land's balance, he will remain trapped there."

Sunnëva whirled around, her chest heaving with a sharp breath. "You made a decision about my brother without consulting me first?"

Jökull frowned. "You may survive each night with him unscathed, but he is sired to you. Perhaps it is due to your shared blood. I have to test him against nature now. But I believe his chances of leaving the woods are substantial."

"He would never hurt anyone," she said sharply.

"Best not gamble the lives of others if you're wrong."

Sunnëva clenched her fists, trying to keep herself from an outburst. He fully turned to face her and his body towered over hers, blocking most of the wind.

"You carry your heart in those sultry eyes of yours, little thorn," Jökull murmured. "The deepest blue threaded with gold. They burn with anger and hate. Yet they burn brightest when it is with love."

Sunnëva looked away from the intensity of his stare. She could count on one hand how many people she cared about and she would do anything to protect them. "Why let me think you killed him?"

"Would you have believed me if I told you the truth?"

No, not without proof. Which was what he provided.

They both knew she wouldn't trust him otherwise, not that she did now.

"If Fenrin was successful, he should arrive any minute. Your timing is impeccable, as always."

Sunnëva took it as a jab, even if she was summoned. "Forgive me if I *interrupted* something. It seems your mistress is in need of you."

"She's not—" A slow smile tugged at the ends of Jökull's mouth. "Is that jealousy I hear?"

"For *you*? Never."

He chuckled quietly. "Good. There is no need to be jealous of her." His eyes roved over her face, falling to her lips. "There is no one else in the world for me but you."

Whether it was the unexpected low rumble of his words or the way he shifted a step toward her, an electric current sank down into her stomach.

Sunnëva crossed her arms, ignoring the sensation. "Oh please, do go on and tell me more sweet nothings, beast. Then the court might finally be convinced you're madly in love with me."

"I am sure once Valden's ashes coated my floors, they think exactly that."

Sunnëva studied him against the backdrop of snow. The wind fluttered his long black cloak around his tall frame, plated in armor, his ice crown glinting in the light.

She was torn between asking why he killed the Nightwalkers or asking for what she came for. But Fenrin's return interrupted them.

His large, lumbering form came through the trees with something hanging from his jaws. It looked like a stag, but the head was missing. He lay on the ground, tearing it apart with his sharp teeth. Bone crunched as he ate, blood splattering on his bony skull and spilling from his fangs.

"You were successful," Jökull said. "Well done."

"If he had failed, did you expect me to leave him out there?" Sunnëva asked, with a spark of defense rising within her again.

She took a step to approach her brother, but Jökull caught her wrist. "While he does retain human intelligence, he still has wild instincts. Best not to intrude when he is feeding."

Fenrin looked at them with eerie, flaming eyes, then resumed snapping bones in his teeth. Bits of carnage painted the snow red around him. She shuddered, and Jökull pulled her away.

Sunnëva glanced down at where he held her and couldn't help but notice the veins that curved over his knuckles. "Have you found his weakness yet?" she asked because she assumed that was Jökull's true intention.

And because she wasn't ready to return to their previous subject.

"It's only a matter of time. I have, however, come to find he is very durable. Watch." Jökull suddenly grabbed her throat. Fenrin snarled and charged for them. He was *fast*. So fast she blinked, and he was already coming down on them. Jökull conjured his scythe in a flash of ice and struck. The blow tossed him across the courtyard into the trees.

"Fen!" Sunnëva screamed.

She was sure he was dead, but her brother leaped to his feet, and the cut on his chest healed in seconds.

"We have been working on his aggression. Haven't we, Fenrin?" Jökull said, the scythe dissolving away.

Her brother growled mildly and returned to his meal.

"He is very strong. With incredible speed and senses. It's quite interesting."

She scowled. "*Interesting?* You could have killed him!"

"Nightstone has no effect on him. As you saw, he is fine. If one were determined to kill him, they would need to be much faster and get really close."

She didn't imagine many would attempt to approach Fenrin, seeing how terrifying he already was. If she didn't know that was her brother inside, she would probably be frightened of him, too.

"Don't do that again." Sunnëva heaved a breath to release her temper. He went out of his way to help Fenrin, even if she wasn't fond of his methods. "Have you tried Moonstone?"

"I did. Along with iron, salt, and steel. He is neither demon nor fae. I think he is a new species," Jökull said thoughtfully. "Now that we are on the subject, this is why I called you here."

He held out both hands, and a sheathed sword materialized in his palms, along with a new dagger.

Sunnëva's breath caught faintly as she admired the beautiful weapons. The dagger had a pointed pommel adorned with pale blue gems. The sword's hilt design matched her dagger, but it was adorned with small iridescent Moonstones. She drew it out, revealing the

Nightstone blade. No light shone through the pitch-black sword, and she sensed the magic it held.

Others may have valued rare gems, but she fantasized about weapons. Good ore was difficult to find and steel held a high price. Yet, she had never owned something so luxurious as this. It wasn't merely pretty to look at. She could tell from the sharp edge, the blade would cut through any man like a torch through snow.

He was trusting her with another sharp object? Two, in fact.

"Try not to break these, vicious little thorn," Jökull said, a hint of a smile hovering on the edge of his mouth. "If only to save me the trouble of fashioning another."

"I will *try*."

They both knew the blades wouldn't shatter as long as she didn't attempt to use them on him again.

"The hilts are made of iron," he mentioned. "One can never be too careful, especially while residing in this castle."

Because there were all sorts of creatures wandering the halls, and the fae were as dangerous as the rest of them.

"Between your studies and experiments, acquaint yourself with these weapons. I will train you myself."

Sunnëva blinked at the offer. "There's no need. I'm already trained to use a sword. I learned long ago what it means not to know how to defend yourself in this world."

The statement invited a heavy pause.

Jökull glanced at the scar on her brow, then at the visible ones on her hands. "Nonetheless. These blades will be different from what you're used to. Fighting is a skill, especially when adjusting to a new weapon. Let's see if you have any." He stepped back as well, motioning for her to come. A sword of ice appeared in his hand, crackling with blue magic.

He wanted to spar? It had been a while since she had a good sparring match, and he would certainly be a challenge. Good thing she wasn't wearing a dress.

Sunnëva whirled the blade, but it was so light it slipped from her fingers and clattered on the cobblestone. She blushed. "I see what you mean." Her body was used to moving with a heavy sword. "It does not weigh much."

"Nightstone was created to be lighter than steel. You will need to move quickly when battling a demon. I imagine you have not fought many."

"I haven't." Sunnëva flipped up the sword with her boot and caught the hilt.

She had only fought in battles amongst the other clans or raids, but everyone knew how fast and violent demons were.

"I will attempt to teach you how to survive when facing one," Jökull said.

Smirking, Sunnëva fell into formation and they circled each other. "I think you underestimate me."

"Hmm, you're probably right."

Then she launched at him, and their blades clashed.

By the time the sun was low on the horizon, she was drenched in sweat and oddly ... enjoying herself. Once she got a hang of the sword, she adjusted her movements to Jökull's speed. He taught her how demons liked to attack from above and how to evade them. After that, she managed to keep up with him.

He handed her a skin of water to drink. The cool liquid was crisp against her tongue as it slid down her throat.

"You move well," Jökull said. "The sword suits you."

Sunnëva wiped her mouth and sheathed the weapon. She still wasn't sure why he cared enough to give her one. "Thank you ... but..."

"It is a gift."

She hoped he wouldn't say that because she still had to ask him for more.

Sunnëva shifted on her feet. "It's customary when one gives a gift to receive one in return, but I have nothing to give you of equal value."

"Well, if you feel inclined..." Jökull closed the distance between them. He reached for her hair and gently tugged away a single blue bead from one of her braids. The edge of his finger brushed her jaw, eliciting a shock of energy down her neck. "This will do."

She stilled.

What was he doing? Why was he not growling at her? And why was she standing so close to him?

When her mouth opened, she asked him a different question instead. "Why did you protect me against the Nightwalkers when the previous night you were ready to kill me and take my soul?"

"And what a delicious soul it is." Jökull reached for her again, and she flinched. He paused, his expression darkening at her reaction. "I would love nothing more than to consume it whole. But I cannot."

Jökull's cool hand glided down her cheek, and he took her chin, the pad of his finger grazing her lip. "I alone am worthy of being feared, but you need not fear anything from me." Her skin prickled with the ripple of magic in the air at his promise. He invaded her space, forcing her to look up at him. "Nor will I allow harm to befall you. I will rip out the spines of anyone who touches you and display their innards on my walls."

Her breath shuddered at the bloody assurance. A current went through her stomach as she was suddenly aware of how close they were. It made her feel more alive than she had in years. But the only thing she should feel at this moment was revulsion.

"I'm the only one allowed to touch you." The late-afternoon sun gleamed off his thick white lashes, leaving his eyes to flare. His every word was a low growl. "You are mine. Your soul is mine. Your life and every breath you take, every beat of your heart, and the blood flowing through your veins belong to me. And no one touches what is *mine*."

The savage possessiveness behind his statement made Sunnëva's heart lodge in her throat. He didn't mean it like that. He didn't care for her in that way. To him, she was merely property.

She narrowed her eyes and stepped back. "I am not another jewel for your trove."

"No." His mouth curled. "You are far more than that."

He needed her alive for a reason. There were thousands of humans he could have taken, but he married *her*.

Sunnëva questioned the purpose behind their marriage. She knew her reason to marry him, but not his. He said he wanted it to work. Perhaps it was time to find out the answer.

"Why did you choose me, Jökull?" she asked. "Why marry me?"

Jökull fell quiet, observing her past the flurries of snow. He was an immortal being. King above them all. He didn't need to explain himself, and she expected him to say as much, but she saw a decision cross his face.

His lips parted with a soft inhale. "I need you, Sunnëva. I need your help to open my Gate."

18

Windy silence filled the courtyard as they stared at one another. Sunnëva repeated the revelation in her mind, too slow to make sense of it.

"Before the beginning of the age, Elyōn brought the Gods into existence amongst the burning stars," Jökull said, looking up at the sky. "He is our father. Each of us serves a purpose to create worlds and bring balance to the universe. Once this world was created, we came here through our Gates and spent centuries filling it with everything you see. The seasons, the creatures, the sun and moon, the depths of the ocean, and the laws of life and nature. When our work was complete, the Gates pertaining to my brothers opened so they may return to the Heavens, but Elyōn did not open mine."

For the first time since they met, she saw a new expression cross Jökull's face. It was thoughtful. Forlorn.

She recalled the frozen hill they came to on their wedding night and how he had waited for something to happen.

"That structure you took me to..." Sunnëva's eyes widened. "That was your Gate."

Jökull nodded. "Yes, but it remains dormant. Perhaps due to my disobedience for being imprudent and impulsive with my abilities in. my youth. But I was not the only one left behind."

The God of Shadows.

"We didn't know why we had been discarded, and we fought each other for dominion of the world. My brother desired chaos, but as Gods, it is our duty to ensure balance." Jökull turned to face her. "It's taken all my power to keep him in this corner of Urn. Should I lose my hold on him, the land will fall into an age of darkness, fire, and brimstone."

Her breath caught as she pictured it. A world without sunlight. Right now the light shone in the courtyard, gleaming off the ice, so bright it made her vision water. Her breath caught because she finally realized something.

There was a reason demons avoided the North.

Sunnëva covered her mouth. "You turned this land into the Everfrost ... because the ice reflects light..."

The snow—it was a means to protect against the darkness. And he made Nightstone to slay demons. His power was the only thing keeping the Shadow God at bay.

She sat on a stone bench, staring blankly at the white fluff at her feet. The one person she hated the most wasn't the pure evil she thought he was. Otherwise, he wouldn't have cared.

"The perpetual winter you made us suffer..."

His expression became stoic. "It was either death by starvation and cold or being ripped apart by demons. I made the necessary choice. I bear the soul of each one who dies because of it."

It reminded her of the wailing soul diving into him in the throne room. He cursed the land because he had to, and she didn't know how to feel about it.

"And me?" she asked faintly. "What do I have to do with your Gate?"

"I questioned for many years what my brothers had done to have their Gates open until I realized they all had one thing in common. They married humans."

She blinked up at him.

"But not any human. Each of their brides tried to kill them." He smirked. "My father seems to enjoy such jests. He created wild, delicate, impulsive creatures meant to balance us. We would know them by their need to take our immortal lives ... and our craving to take theirs."

Jökull frowned as he studied her. "I have my bride, and yet, my Gate does not open."

"You think the answer lies with me?"

"The other difference between my brothers and I is that their brides came to accept them once they found their balance with each other. Out of impatience, I forced you to take my hand."

"You threatened me," she clarified.

"I didn't threaten you." His mouth twitched. "Much."

Sunnëva forgot her next retort when Jökull crouched down in front of her. Not kneeling, yet lowering himself to her level.

"My Gate won't open until you and I are in harmony," he said. "Help me, Sunnëva. Help me open my Gate, and you will not only rid the Everfrost of winter's misery, but I will also drag my brother back with me."

They fell silent again as he waited for her reaction to his plea. She had no answer when her tongue was tied up in knots by her thoughts and by the way he looked at her. Truly looking at her as if she was more valuable than anything in the world.

"Is this your attempt to woo me?"

"Woo?" Jökull arched an eyebrow. "I am a *God*. I do *not* woo."

Sunnëva couldn't help but smirk at that. As if he could. He was wilder than she was. "Then are you being kind and giving me gifts in hopes I would agree?"

He chuckled. "No, the sword is because you need it, and I am attempting to not be a beast, as you say. I don't need to buy your help when all that you see—" He waved at the castle and the land. "All of my coffers and wealth will already be yours once I'm gone. You will still be Queen."

Sunnëva's mouth parted. He was serious. She would be left to inherit his kingdom and its holdings. That meant she would be able to protect Ansa and Fenrin. Her people.

"Will the land be green again?" she asked faintly.

He nodded, and her heart swelled with emotion. That's what Freya had dreamed of. The feel of grass beneath their feet, and the sun's warmth on their faces. Knowing it was possible made Sunnëva want to cry. If she did this, the land would finally be at peace.

"But what about the demons?" She frowned, coming out of her daze. "Will they go, too?"

A look crossed Jökull's face that she didn't like. "Unfortunately, not all of them. Whatever the Shadow God made from pure magic will vanish when he does, but the demons sired with flesh will remain."

Her happiness deflated. "Once you're gone, they would no longer be confined to the south and would run rampant. The snow would no longer shield the clans."

She hated to admit it, but they needed the winter.

"The demons left behind would be greatly weakened once my brother is gone." Jökull sat next to her. "And you will be here to teach your people how to defend themselves. I will make sure you have a full armory of Nightstone for the clans and every new demon slayer you train."

Demon slayer...

The image of Rune's easy smile and his warm amber eyes flashed through Sunnëva's mind. She ached with pain and horror at how easily she had forgotten his death when she considered helping Jökull.

No matter what he had done for the land, he was still responsible for their hard life and so much death. He almost convinced her with his words like honey in her ear.

Jökull sensed her change in mood and frowned at her questioningly. Sunnëva leaped up, stepping away with a hiss as he stood. Energy stirred in the atmosphere and cracked like glass. The wind howled, rattling the trees. Fenrin rose to his feet, growling deep.

153

"Sunnëva," Jökull breathed her name when tears gathered on her lashes, turning to frost.

"We already had the best demon slayer," she said through her teeth. "And you took him from me."

"What? What do you mean?"

"Rune," she said, clenching her fists and energy hummed on her skin. The air crackled again. Frost was forming on the ground, spreading from her feet. Shards broke away and rose into their surroundings. "You killed Rune!"

The shards shot out at her scream. The sharp ice sliced past Jökull's cheek, neck, and arms, but he continued staring at her. Sunnëva gasped, stumbling back as she looked down at her hands. How did she do that? She shook at the sight of her white talons. Her palms bled where they had pierced her skin. "I—I'm sorry ... I don't know how I—"

"It's all right. You're all right." Jökull took her shoulders. She flinched and looked up at him. The cuts had already healed, leaving dried streaks on his cheeks. "Who is Rune?"

"He was my..." Sunnëva shook her head and closed her eyes. "He was with me the night I came to steal the rose. But I couldn't get past the gargoyles. He stayed behind so I could escape ... and I watched you fall upon him." She inhaled a soft cry. "I don't want to know what you did to him, but please tell me where ... where did you bury him?"

Jökull was so still she opened her eyes to find his were glowing a menacing blue like chipped ice. His expression hardened, and he let go of her, stepping away. The atmosphere crackled once more, but this time, it was him.

She recoiled at Jökull's laugh. It was dark and angry. Cold.

"Oh, right when I think you could not be any more depraved, I am always proven wrong," he said, his voice a low snarl. She withdrew further away from him. "Instiller of lies, schemes, and hatred. I really have been a fool, haven't I..." His icy gaze slid from her face to the woods, where the receding light didn't reach. "*Rumiel?*"

A second voice laughed, and the hair rose on her arms. Sunnëva stiffened when a form solidified in the dark trees. Jökull moved in front of her. Ren and Riona drew their swords, running to them as Fenrin came to her side defensively, baring his teeth at the shadowy figure.

"How sweet you are to her," the God of Shadows said, voice warping as it came from all around them. "Speaking to her so intimately. I may be the instiller of lies, but you wear them deftly. Do tell her what she will become if she remains by your side. Show her your true face, Jökull."

"Show her *yours!*" He swiped his arm, and blue magic cleaved through the canopy of the trees, dissolving the shadows.

Sunnëva's entire body went cold. She squeezed her eyes shut. "No."

"Look at him," Jökull growled. "*Look* at him, Sunnëva."

She forced herself to open her eyes, taking in the man standing in the trees.

Except he was no man.

His once tan skin was now pallid, like the color of river stones. His irises were molten red with flame and pointed ears poked out of his ebony hair. He was dressed finely, all in black, his tunic partly undone, exposing the tattoos that traveled the width of his firm chest to his neck. Sunnëva inhaled shaky breaths at how otherworldly he was. His features had sharpened with a fierce beauty that could only belong to a God. A few black scales dusted his cheekbones and the back of his clawed hands. He was an entity of smoke and embers, shadows wafting off the edges of his face and silhouette.

One end of Rune's mouth lifted in an easy smile, and she found that part of him had not changed. It was the playful smiles he had only for her ... for the moments they were alone, kissing in the shade.

"I have missed you, Su."

Sound dulled, her mind fogging, struggling to clear. Emotions lodged in her throat, stealing her words. Sunnëva couldn't make sense of them, but it couldn't be fear, because her feet moved toward him. She stumbled into the trees, and he appeared in front of her in a wisp of smoke, catching her.

A gasp shot out of her mouth at the rapid movement because he had moved like that before ... in the Black Woods.

Beyond the crimson hue, she saw the man who had been by her side for the past three years.

It was him.

Her Rune.

"It's really you," Sunnëva murmured. "You're alive..."

He brushed her cheek with the back of a clawed finger. "Did I not promise I would find my way back to you again?"

"But I ... I saw you die." Her thoughts cleared with a sudden sharpness.

She had always thought he moved like a demon with the violence and ruthlessness to match. His speed and strength. And now it all made sense. He was a God. A divine being with dark power who had roamed the world for a millennium, too.

The horror must be plain on her face because his shadows warped the air, and he returned to the form he had always been. Warm, human Rune, in his usual leather armor, fur pelt, and axes at his belt. His aloof expression wavered a bit.

Sunnëva shook her head. "You were never human."

He took her arm when she tried to step back into the light. "Su, listen."

"Let go—"

Jökull's savage growl rumbled through the courtyard. *"Get your hands off my wife."*

A blast of ice hit Rune, ripping him away from her so fast it threw him across the courtyard into the last rays of the setting sun.

She fell from the force, immediately caught in Jökull's arms. He pulled her behind him, backing her away. Rune flipped before he hit the ground to land in a crouch. He vanished in a burst of black mist and reappeared in the shelter of the shadowed trees. He was unscathed, other than a burn on his cheek.

He snarled at Jökull as it healed, baring his fangs. "Low blow."

"I hope it stung."

"You ... have always hated the sun..." Sunnëva said blankly, thinking of all the times he kept up his hood and avoided going outside when he could. Avoided stepping in patches of sunlight within the trees.

She couldn't believe Rune was standing there.

No, not Rune. *Rumiel.*

Her mind was spinning, words tumbling out of her mouth as the realizations kept hitting her like slaps to her face. "You're the reason demons are migrating north. Like the wargs." Fenrin growled beside her, and her next breath halted. They had been together during the raids. "You got Fen bit ... didn't you?"

Fenrin's growls faltered.

Rune hesitated.

"THE TRUTH!" Sunnëva shouted. "Did you have my brother bitten by a warg?"

Rune sighed and leaned up against a tree, crossing his arms. "To be fair, I intended it to be Bjorn. He was your least favorite and a little shite. But Fenrin, being the hero that he is, got in the way." He tsked and frowned at Jökull. "Really, brother? A century ago, you would have killed the boy without hesitation. You have grown sentimental in your old age."

Jökull's fists clenched. "In so ensuring her hatred for me, causing me to never open my Gate. You targeted her."

But how did he know about her? How did he know she was going to become Jökull's bride?

If he knew I was touching you like this, he would be furious...

Pain lanced through Sunnëva's heart. "Was it all planned?" she asked, her voice catching with dismay.

Rune didn't answer, but the look on his face was enough. None of their interactions had happened naturally. Every kiss and affection ... all lies. She flinched from the invisible blow that landed in her gut.

"Don't hold it against me, Su." He canted his head, his brow creasing. "It was a minor necessity to prevent him from opening that door. I'm *not* going back."

"You don't have a choice," Jökull told him. "We are not meant to stay in this world. You will come with me or—"

"Or what?" Rune's eyes flamed with red wisps. He prowled along the edge of the forest, his shadows whipping restlessly around him. "You cannot kill me, and I cannot kill you. Stupid law of the Heavens Father put in place, but that does not mean another can't lift the spear—"

Sunnëva flipped up her Nightstone dagger and threw it at him. Rune vanished in a swirl of smoke and the knife lodged into the tree where he'd been standing. He reappeared beneath another shaded pocket in the trees.

"Su—"

She snatched the knives strapped to Jökull's thighs and tossed them, each one zipping through a cloud of smoke and shadow, missing him by inches.

"You used me!" she shouted.

"I did," Rune said placatingly as he inched closer to her. "But those moments we had, every moment I held you and kissed every inch of you..."

Jökull released a biting growl.

"They were real to me." Rune stopped at the edge of the shade. He wouldn't cross it, but nightfall was quickly approaching.

"Why are you here now?" Sunnëva demanded. "You could have come the first night. Why wait and appear to me still disguising what you were?"

"The castle is warded against me. I could not get to you the first night." His jaw worked with irritation. That hadn't been part of his plan. "The only reason I could enter your room was because you called out to me with your thoughts."

Sunnëva stilled. She had been thinking about him in her chambers and then now.

"I didn't get a chance to explain myself before you attacked." Rune smirked, impressed. "That really hurt, sweetling. But I broke through his wards again and risked the light for you. I am here because I came to take you back." He held out a clawed hand to her.

She searched his face, not sure if she could believe him anymore.

Be with me, Sunnëva. His voice wove through her mind. *Choose me, and there will be no more ice. Nothing but what we make it.*

The courtyard faded away, and she found herself in a black castle set upon a peak. She stood by Rune's side, terrible and fierce, with a crown of shadows on her head. The whole world bowed at her feet with fear and despair. Thunder spanned the black skies, flashing in her wake. A beautiful nightmare. Her pulse raced, her thoughts darkening with that power.

Why be the Winter Queen when you can be the Dark Queen?

"Get out of her head!" A force shoved into her mind and banished the vision. Sunnëva fell against Jökull, gasping for air.

"I refuse to let you keep her," Rune growled. "She *will* come with me, Jökull."

Jökull's fingers tightened on her shoulders, his mouth curving with a cold sneer. He grabbed her neck and kissed her, claiming her mouth. Claiming her. She squeaked in shock, inviting more of him in. The kiss devoured her whole. It stirred something in her being, like magic weaving into her soul. When he released her, her lips followed, her mind whirling in a daze to even react. A current swept over her skin, making it briefly glow.

And both Gods had noticed.

What was that?

Jökull nodded. "I dare you to try and take her."

Rune bared his fangs at him with a hiss.

"What is that other law we Gods have?" Jökull said. "Oh, right. The bride must *choose.*"

He had always given her the choice.

When she was on her knees in the snow, then during the marriage ceremony, Jökull offered her the choice to be his bride. She had chosen to be his without knowing what it meant.

The day in the forest when Rune had returned from the raids, he also asked her to choose.

"You can still choose me," he said, his tone insistent. "Be my bride, Sunnëva. He cannot stop you."

In agreement, Jökull's hold fell away from her. He didn't speak, though his expression was grim. Hard. He clutched his hands into tight fists as if to restrain himself. Regardless of that kiss, he was again giving her the choice.

"Su..." Rune called. That soft sound of her name was music to her heart's dance, responding to the memory of the man she knew. "I *will* fight him for you."

The warning made her meet his crimson gaze. It only reminded her that every time they had been together, he had kept a part of himself hidden away. And he had tried to trick her into going with him.

She couldn't believe what they had was real, even if she wanted to. She had seen what would become of the world if she went with him.

And that wickedness she so despised would be her crown.

All she had wanted was a world without Gods, and now she found herself stuck between two. Yet, in some strange irony, the lesser of two evils was the last person she expected.

Sunnëva took a breath and moved to stand with Jökull. "Leave," she said faintly. "I won't ever choose you again."

Rune's expression flickered with disappointment before it switched to cold resignation. "How unfortunate."

Then he vanished in a plume of smoke.

19

The sunset fell beyond the trees and sank into the horizon, draping the courtyard in the veil of twilight. She glanced up at Jökull, and they looked at each other silently. They were both surprised she had chosen to stay. If he asked her why, she wouldn't have been able to form an answer.

Horns blared from the battlements, sounding an alarm.

Jökull cursed. "Take the Queen to her chambers," he barked at her guards. "Don't let anyone in, and arm yourselves with Nightstone."

"Yes, sire." Riona motioned for her to follow. "Come, my lady."

"No. What's wrong?"

"We are under siege. Demons are at the front gates," Jökull said tightly. "I need you inside. Now." He waved his hand. All the knives she had thrown at Rune appeared in his hold, and he returned hers. "While I would greatly enjoy throwing you over my shoulder and carrying you to your room, I would rather you not fight me on this."

Sunnëva ignored the way that image made her stomach flip.

"I don't care what you need," she said, crossing her arms. "I will not cower in my room like some princess in a tower. I can fight. You know I can, so let me."

Fenrin growled in agreement.

Jökull heaved a sharp exhale as he regarded her and the sword at her hip. "If I allow this, you will do exactly as I say. Agreed?"

She nodded, trying not to show her surprise.

He pointed at Ren and Riona, each word biting. "Stay by her side, no matter what befalls tonight. If she dies, it's because you died first."

A very clear threat lined his order, promising what would happen to them if they failed. The knights bowed, clanking a fist over their hearts.

Jökull marched to the castle with a swift stride. "Fenrin, I could use you on the front lines." He opened a portal, revealing the castle gates where soldiers were already gathering, and her brother went in. "Can you shoot a bow?" he said next as they continued.

"Do you have to ask?"

He smirked. "I suppose I don't. Then you will stay on the battlement with the archers. *Far away* from the battle." Jökull took her arm and rushed her inside. "That is not up for debate, vicious thorn. I don't want you on the front lines. Say it."

Sunnëva fluttered her eyelashes daintily and clasped her hands together. "I will behave like a perfect little lady."

He was still glaring ahead, but his fangs flashed in a feral smile. "Now that is one thing I don't think is possible."

Tally came running around the corner. "My lady!"

"Take this." Sunnëva handed her one of his Nightstone daggers. "Go to my room and bar the doors."

Her handmaiden nodded and ran through another hallway as they continued on.

"This way." Jökull opened a portal to the armory teeming with his riders, snatching up weapons and shields. "You will need armor."

"Can you open a portal anywhere?" Sunnëva asked as she quickly slipped on some chain mail.

"Benefits of being a God." He helped her strap on a chest plate and buckled on her grieves.

She tugged on a pair of archery gloves next. Once she grabbed a bow and quiver of Nightstone arrows, Jökull opened another portal that led outside onto the battlement of the castle's defensive wall. The wind whipped her hair away from her face.

Voices and movement swarmed around her as the Castle Guards got into positions. Aero and Garr were at the balustrade, looking out.

"Aero, report." Jökull marched on. She followed with Ren and Riona on her heels.

"About fifteen hundred wargs, sire," the mage said. "Amongst other beasts."

Sunnëva came to his other side, and her eyes widened. Gauging the distance from the ground, they were at least a hundred feet high. Wargs charged across the land for the castle, along with goblins, trolls, and giants. Rune wasn't among them.

Below, Jökull's soldiers and riders were falling into formation. They were armed with Nightstone swords and shields embossed with the white Ice Phoenix emblem. From the way it caught the light, the emblem had to be made of Moonstone.

But she saw a significant difference in their numbers.

"They outnumber us nearly three to one," Aero said.

A dark smirk edged Jökull's mouth. "I like those odds."

Garr grunted. "I am more worried about the Drakon."

Creatures screeched in the sky. They were a smaller species of dragon but with long, eel-like necks.

Sunnëva whipped her head around to Jökull. "He has Drakon? But Jökull, you hardly have five hundred men down there. I thought you had an army of twenty thousand."

"I do. When I've called on all the lords and clans to serve. It's too late to call on them now." He didn't look worried, though.

Garr nodded to the horned male beside him. "Call it, Quill."

"You heard the general," Quill barked. "Ready the archers. I want those mirrors on the wall. Move your arses!"

The men rolled out several round reflective plates on wheeled tripods made of wood. They weren't mirrors but polished saucers of pure Moonstone.

Aero shook his head. "But why this sudden attack? It's not enough to overthrow the castle. Perhaps to barricade us here."

"No," Jökull said, his tone hard. "This is merely to spill blood out of spite. Rumiel was able to breach my wards. He was in the courtyard. He tried to take her." The mage and orc stared at Sunnëva. "I will take care of the Drakon. Garr will lead the ground assault with coverage from the battlement. You will stay here with her, Aero." His sharp eyes turned to him. "On your life."

Aero bowed his head. "Of course, sire."

Jökull looked at her, and his brow pinched. It wasn't only the hesitation on his face. She sensed his worry.

Sunnëva nodded. "Go. I'll be fine."

He leaped off the battlement and shifted into the Ice Phoenix midair. Sunnëva inhaled a soft breath as he soared amongst the clouds. The rising moonlight shone over his translucent feathers like glass. There was something about it that looked so majestic in the night. The gargoyles on the castle roofs came to life with a roar and they flew after their King.

She silently wished him well.

Garr climbed onto the balustrade and bellowed out to their army. "No quarter. No prisoners. No mercy!"

Their voices rose in a wave of cheer. The large orc leaped off and Aero's magic softened his landing below. Someone blew on a horn. The soldiers charged for the wargs. The Castle Guards took the large mirrors and aimed them to catch the moonlight, sending the light beams across the land. The wargs they hit instantly dissolved into black ash.

"Archers," Quill called. "Nock!"

The men loaded their bows with arrows tipped in Nightstone. Sunnëva nocked her bow. Ren winked as he and Riona did the same.

"How is your first day going?" she asked them.

KING'S BRIDE

He grinned. "Absolutely marvelous. What better way to face death than with honor and duty?"

Riona frowned flatly. "I'd rather not face it at all."

The Ice Phoenix's screech echoed across the sky as he fought with the Drakon. He caught the neck of one in his beak and ripped off the head.

The wargs cut through the left unit of soldiers below. Some managed to get past them and loped toward the castle. Sunnëva inhaled a low breath, bracing herself.

They were coming.

Purple light edged her vision at the flare of magic in Aero's hands. "Ready!" he warned.

They all aimed. Wargs scaled the walls, tearing out bricks with their claws.

Quill motioned. "Loose!"

Arrows fell like rain.

Each one they hit burst apart in smoke. The soldiers fired at will as they took them down. Sunnëva was beginning to hope they would win without heavy casualties.

A Drakon released a piercing scream, and they all covered their ears. A shadowed rider was on its back, and she instantly knew who it was. Rune flew down on his Drakon and lit the dugout trenches on fire. The flames caught and flared high. Black smoke spiraled into the sky, veiling the moon.

Aero cursed. "He took away our ability to use the mirrors."

And their support for the army below.

The loss of that advantage rallied the wargs. They overtook the battlefield, and the cries of their riders filled the air. More wargs scaled up the walls, and they kept shooting. Aero cast out a wave of electricity, spearing the creatures. He stayed by her side until some started making it over the balustrade.

"Hold your positions!" Quill shouted, drawing out a wickedly large blade.

165

Wargs descended on the Castle Guard, tearing off heads and throwing bodies over the walls.

Sunnëva whipped out her sword and fought with Ren and Riona covering her back. Blood and ash misted the air. She tasted it on her tongue.

"Get them over the wall!" Quill hollered, hacking away at the horde. "Don't let them—"

His voice cut off when three wargs took him down.

"Help him," Sunnëva ordered. Her guards hesitated. "Go, I command it!"

Ren and Riona shot into the air with their colorful wings.

"The men below need support, Aero," she shouted at the mage as she beheaded another demon. "If they fall, the wargs will swarm us and make it inside. Go down there and help them."

Aero blasted a warg leaping through the air for him, and his griffin tackled another that almost got his neck. "I can't. My orders are to stay with you."

Fenrin's sharp whine reached her ears. He was in the middle of a standoff with a troll and wargs biting into his heels. Rune was cleaving his way through the front lines with his shadows. No one could fight against his blades of smoke. Jökull dove to defend the lines, but the Drakon swarmed him. The gargoyles quickly came to his aid, ripping into them.

Sunnëva fought off a Nightwalker that climbed over the wall, spearing his heart with the end of her iron dagger. He screamed, clawing at his burning chest until Riona finished him off. She backed away and bumped into Aero's back. Fighting continued all around them, smoke obscuring the sky.

They couldn't go much longer this way. They had to change tactics.

Something stirred deep in her chest, and Sunnëva's ring pulsed on her finger, sending soft currents of power through her veins. She knew what she had to do.

"Wind is part of your element, right?" Sunnëva said to Aero over her shoulder. "We need to clear the smoke and bring out the moonlight."

He nodded, throwing another blast of magic. "I'll get it done."

"Also, how much weight can you levitate?"

"What? I can lift quite a bit—" He frowned a second, then his eyes widened. "No—"

"Don't let me fall to my death." She sheathed her sword and ran for the balustrade.

The shouts of her guards and Aero followed behind. No time to think. Boots pushing off the edge, she leaped, and the wind ripped her away. A full view of the teeming battlefield and fire rushed to meet her. Purple light blazed around her body, and Aero's Essence slowed her fall.

Sunnëva braced her legs and dropped with a roll. Ren and Riona landed behind her. Drawing out her sword, she sprinted for Fenrin. She slid across the slush, slashing through the wargs attacking him.

A furious roar had her spinning around. Blood and sinew spurted through the air as the body of a rider landed at her feet. Rune was in his God form, tearing their army to shreds. She searched for Jökull and found him moving on a sheet of ice as he cleaved through Drakon with his scythe. His eyes were brighter than she had seen them, white instead of ice blue and filling the entire orb, blood smeared on his mouth.

He was too busy fighting to notice the troll charging right for him.

She whipped out a blade and hurled it. The edge flashed with firelight as it spun through the air and speared through its eye. It crashed heavily behind Jökull. He saw the creature, then searched the area until he spotted her.

His face contorted with fury. He slashed a Drakon in half and stormed for her. "I told you to stay up on the battlement. What are you doing here?"

"Saving you."

"I don't need saving," Jökull growled and pointed a threatening finger at Ren and Riona behind her. "I'm going to pluck off your fucking wings."

"No, you won't." Sunnëva ducked under a warg and slashed through its stomach. It burst into ash. Up on the battlement, Aero's glowing hands were pointed toward the sky, and the wind picked up. "You may be immortal, but your men are not. You don't have the numbers to hold for long. If you want to make sure they survive tonight, do as I say."

Jökull glowered at her, but his mouth curved. "What's your plan?"

"Have you heard of a shield wall?"

His scythe slashed past her, decapitating a troll. "Aye, clan tactics."

It was a standard maneuver, but they were going to need more than that.

"Then get your men ready." Sheathing her weapon, Sunnëva took one of his knives and winced as she drew the blade across her palm.

Jökull snarled and grabbed her wrist, inspecting the cut. "That is the only wound I will permit. You better return without so much as a scratch."

Sunnëva smirked. *Bossy beast.*

He let her go, and she sprinted for Rune.

Smoke permeated the air, the clash of battle raging all around. She was halfway across the battlefield when the scent of her blood caught the attention of the enemy. Snarls and hungry howls rang out. The ground rumbled as wargs, Nightwalkers, and trolls chased after her in a frenzy. Her heart pounded as she ran.

Her guards shadowed her, cutting down anyone who got too close. But a warg knocked Ren down, and Riona was hit. A troll was on Sunnëva's tail. Jökull's spear of ice whipped past her, impaling the creature through its skull.

"Rune!" Sunnëva screamed.

Rune ripped his axes out of another soldier and turned around. Shock crossed his face at seeing his creatures chase after her. He waved his hand, and his shadows halted them in place, much to her relief. It had been a gamble if he could stop them, or if he would. She slowed her run until she stopped halfway between them.

He smiled at her casually, his face speckled with blood. "Have you changed your mind, sweetling? Or shall I let them continue tearing these poor mortals to shreds?"

Sunnëva leaned on her knees, panting to catch her breath as she took in the many bodies piled around him. How did she not see his real brutality until now?

The reason Jökull's land was full of bones stood in front of her.

"He isn't prepared for this fight, Sunnëva. But I have been preparing a long time for this."

Nevertheless, the one thing he hadn't prepared for was her.

Sunnëva straightened. "You caught him by surprise."

"I am full of surprises." Rune grinned, flashing his fangs. "Now, will you be a good girl and come for me?"

She sneered at his teasing tone. "I have to say Rune, we've known each other for some time, but you don't know me that well. What was it you said when you returned from the raids? Oh, yes. I always seem to surprise you as well."

Moonlight streamed in through the parting clouds, bathing the battlefield in silvery light. Rune's eyes flared red with flame, and he hissed.

"Shield wall!" came Jökull's distant bellow.

He had his men in formation, and the soldiers crouched to form a wall of three rows of shields, glinting with the symbol of the Ice Phoenix.

Rune released his hold on his army and vanished in a burst of shadows. The wargs came charging for her. Sunnëva faced the oncoming horde of demons and beasts as her ring began to glow and power surged in her veins.

Like before, instinct came to life in her chest. She raised her fist in the air toward the moon with a cry and a blaze of white magic shot out like a wave. It reflected off the shield wall and blasted across the land, disintegrating the wargs on impact.

The remaining creatures not burned to ash screeched as they fled with Rune. His retreating form flew away on a Drakon into the night.

The sound of Sunnëva's heart pounded in her ears. It worked? Her plan really worked.

The hum of a chant rose from the riders, voices rising with each other like a roar. It took her a second to realize everyone was staring at her as they recited one word. Every single one of them fell to their knees and bowed their heads.

The highest deference they have ever shown.

Jökull marched toward her, his black cloak fluttering in the wind. He looked like a vision of war covered in blood and dirt, the last wisps of smoke curling in the moonlight around him. The way he was looking at her ... no other man had done so with such intensity. Like he could see her, truly see.

Shock spasmed through her chest when he reached her and lowered to one knee.

"My Queen." He took her bloodied hand and pressed his cool lips on the back of her fingers.

The chant rose higher, shooting goosebumps down her arms. She didn't understand. They were speaking in a language before her time.

"What are they saying?" Sunnëva asked faintly.

"Reigani," Jökull repeated, one end of his mouth curving as he gazed up at her in a way that made her next breath catch. "Goddess."

20

"You would leave all of this?" Sunnëva asked. They stood on Jökull's balcony looking out at the land bathed in moonlight. The air was sweet with the scent of enchanted roses, vanishing all traces of fire and smoke. The blooms glowed on the trellises climbing up the castle walls.

"I would leave it to you," Jökull said. "As Queen, you have the right to rule once I'm gone. After today, I know the court will serve you loyally."

That should have made her feel overwhelmed. Nervous or maybe happy that the kingdom would be hers. But she felt ... numb.

Now that the battle was over, she hid behind a wall because she wasn't ready to acknowledge Rune's betrayal. And her decision not to follow him. It hurt, she knew it did, but she wasn't letting herself feel it yet. She hadn't fully let herself mourn his death the first time. Now it was as if something else had died.

She looked down below, but there was no sign of the battle. Jökull had already buried the dead far beneath the snow.

"Many were lost today. I'm sorry I couldn't save more..." She couldn't help feeling at fault. Rune attacked because she chose to stay. "Maybe I should have—"

"No." Jökull turned to face her. "You did more than enough. Don't lessen what you accomplished. They would be slighted to think the Queen they died fighting to protect deemed it worthless."

"Of course, I don't think that."

"Good." His eyes narrowed. "But if you risk your life like that again, it will not be forgiven."

Sunnëva had gone to the front lines because power brewed inside of her, calling to her blood.

"The Moonstone." She looked down at her ring. "I didn't know what to expect with my plan, but I am relieved it worked."

"It was marvelous," Jökull said. "The Moonstone has never shone that brightly before. Not even for me."

"Then how did I do that?"

He observed her for a moment, and his mouth curved on one end. "When we wed, you chose to bind yourself to me, and therefore, to my power."

Will you bind yourself to me by accepting this ring?

Now the strange question made sense.

"We have been standing outside for a while now, yet you have not complained about the cold."

Sunnëva looked down at her armor, realizing she didn't wear a cloak. "I'm hardly cold ... Does this mean I can use your power?"

She felt it moving through her now as if it were becoming her own.

"Yes, you will begin to."

"Can I turn into an ice bird?"

He chuckled, brushing a stray lock of hair that caught on her lashes. She stilled under the stroke of his fingers. "I don't think so, vicious thorn. There is only one God of Death."

Heat rushed to her cheeks. His touches were becoming more frequent, and she fought them less and less.

Sunnëva exhaled a low breath. "When you're gone ... will the ring still work?"

"I couldn't say for certain," Jökull said. "My brother's brides could use their magic as well, each in their own way. But I don't know what happened once they crossed."

She looked down at her pale hands where her ring glinted. Her claws were gone, but his magic had left behind an impression in her veins. Like it had marked her soul. Even when Jökull left, she guessed some of his power would be permanently a part of her. And by the look on his face, he suspected the same.

"But is it possible for two Gods to go through a Gate?" Sunnëva asked as she strolled among the rose bushes.

"Yes..." He sounded hesitant, though.

She raised her eyebrows.

Jökull frowned and rubbed the back of his neck. "I hope so," he amended. "The Gods left with their brides but through their respective Gates. I am not certain if Rumiel can cross mine."

Sunnëva couldn't help smiling at how vexed he looked at the prospect of his plan not working. She leaned down to inhale the sweet scent of the roses and brushed her fingers over a petal. "Hmm ... can that be considered wishful thinking?"

At Jökull's silence, she turned to find his stare fixed unwaveringly on her hand, cupping the rose. Her pulse sped as his softly glowing gaze lifted to her face, his white lashes stark like threads of starlight.

Sunnëva caressed the silky petals coated in frost. Jökull watched her intently, his eyes dilating as she stroked the rose. "Do you feel this?" she asked faintly.

His jaw flexed. "Yes."

"And this?" She ripped the stem from the bush, thorns biting into her skin.

He snarled and snatched her wrist, glaring at the red droplets of glistening blood. The blue rose lay cradled in her palm, beautiful and glimmering beneath the moonlight.

"I feel everything, Sunnëva. I gave these roses life, thus they are tied to me." He brought her hand to his mouth, and his cool tongue slid against her finger, licking her blood away. "And now, so are you."

Heat rose to her face, but she didn't pull away. Her pulse thrummed to a new dance as they observed each other in the brisk night.

"Does that mean you ... can feel me, too?"

Cradling her palm, his thumb brushed her ring. "I feel your fear, your anger, the flush rising to your cheeks. The way your heart races when I cross every line..." He turned over her palm, and she held her breath, quivering as his lips brushed over the pulse at her wrist. The soft touch made her lashes lower at the sensation that sank through her body.

Sunnëva held his gaze a moment before letting her eyes fall to his mouth. An inexplicable feeling surfaced that she couldn't give words to, but she didn't have to. Jökull stepped closer and his soft hair brushed her cheek, his cool breath sending shivers down her neck. He was inches away, and she could nearly feel him on her lips. All of her burned with anticipation and indecision. She swallowed as he leaned in, her heart beating so fast he had to hear it.

"If I had chosen him?" Sunnëva whispered.

Perhaps it was the wrong question or the sudden gust knocking into her senses, but the mood changed with the soft flurries drifting down.

She stepped back, and Jökull straightened. He remained near, but that small gap allowed a muddle of thoughts to wedge between them.

"I would like to say I would have been gracious about it," Jökull said, dragging his thumb across his bottom lip, as though to wipe away what they had almost done. "If you had chosen him, it would have taken every ounce of my will to let you go. Gods are jealous beings, and I do *not* like to share. Knowing he touched you filled me with the urge to hack off his limbs and feed them to Fenrin, even if he can grow them back."

Sunnëva laughed. "Barbaric fiend."

Jökull's expression faltered, his mouth parting.

"What?"

He shook his head, and starlight played across the wonderment on his face. "Nothing."

"What is it?" She frowned. "Tell me."

His fingertip faintly brushed along the edge of her bottom lip like the flutter of butterfly wings. "No, or you may not do it again."

Sunnëva flushed at the touch, not sure what he was talking about. "And if he had taken me against my will?"

The air chilled at the chipped ice in Jökull's eyes. "Then it would have been my army breaking down his walls."

He would go that far to get her back? The intensity of his expression and the pull of his power in the air attested nothing would stop him.

But this wasn't merely about her.

"Forcing Rune through the Gates isn't the only reason why you two are at odds, is it?" Sunnëva asked. Because she had sensed abhorrence in Rune.

Enough to want to sabotage him.

Jökull looked out at the land. "We were once close a century ago, but I ... denied him something, and our friendship could not withstand it."

Sunnëva searched his face and found regret there. If she had a chance to have Freya back, she would have done anything.

"I think you should try to reconcile," Sunnëva murmured.

"Do you still care about him?" Jökull asked after a pause.

"I..." She looked down at the rose she held, sensing Jökull's stare as he waited patiently for her to answer.

What hurt her the most about Rune was knowing he was the one who pulled her out of the woods five years ago. She couldn't stand the touch of anyone for a long time, but he had been the one she trusted with her body. The friendship they shared had been her only treasure, and now she mourned that loss. Because the part of him she fell in love with had been good.

"He was my first love. It's difficult to forget those feelings."

"I see..." Jökull didn't look angry. If anything, he seemed ... Her thoughts stalled when he closed the distance between them, his next

175

words landing on her lips like winter's kiss. "I will help you forget him, Sunnëva."

His tone had fallen into a velvet pitch that did strange things to her. She told herself it was only the rare occurrence of him saying her name that curled warmth through her stomach. Not because its cadence was different with him.

Her breath halted when Jökull traced the line of her cheekbones, as though he couldn't help himself. The faint touch left behind cool prickles, like blooms of frost on her skin.

"When I saw you fight today, I was made to understand why it had to be you, why no other could ever be my bride. You were created to be mine." He slowly traced his fingers along her collarbone, sparking every nerve to life where his touch landed. His next words came out low, rough. "Every fragile, soft part of you allures me. I cannot deny that something in me wishes to claim you in every which way possible. All over this castle."

Her pulse danced with each contact of his fingers, and her breath shuddered. Every look and touch spoke of desire. Of *want*. Yet it was the last thing she expected him to say. They were supposed to be enemies.

Jökull's eyes rose to hers, his lashes catching with frost. His body pressed closer, stirring feelings she shouldn't have. "I will be patient." He delicately cupped the side of her neck, tracing her racing pulse at the hollow of her throat. "One day, the only thing you will ever crave is my touch. However long it takes."

With the way her heart was thundering now, she didn't think she would ever be accustomed to it. Jökull lowered his hand, and his fingers came away with a dusting of snowflakes.

"Can that be possible while being your prisoner?" Sunnëva asked.

"Fair enough." A translucent ripple pulsed in the air at the flick of his hand. "The magic containing you to the castle is lifted."

How easily he allowed it. He was truly giving her the choice to choose him. Both were very aware she had yet to answer whether she would help him.

"If I run?" she asked.

"That will depend."

"On what?"

A sly edge curved his lips. "Whether you want to be hunted. Run from me, winter rose, and I will punish you when I find you."

She was struck by the new name, and the heat in his eyes. The statement should have been a threat, but by his tone, it didn't sound like one. Whatever he meant, her punishment wouldn't be pain. Heat flooded her face, pooling in her stomach.

Sunnëva couldn't speak. His glowing gaze held her in a trance. The very thought … she could picture it clearly—his shadow descending on her as he ravaged her whole. Kissing her the way he had in the foyer, touching every part of her. Instead of fear, her pulse thudded with something else she tried to ignore.

A spiral of blue light opened a portal next to them, revealing her chambers.

"It's getting late," Jökull said softly.

She was infinitely grateful for the chance to escape the heated tension growing between them.

"Yes." Sunnëva held out the plucked rose.

"Keep it. My gift to you." His smile came true then. They were both thinking of how this all started with a rose. With another wave of Jökull's hand, a beautiful decorative dome of crystal appeared on her table. "To preserve it so that you may have it always."

For a menacing beast, he had it in him to be kind, at least toward her. But before she could appreciate the gesture, the Druid's voice crossed her mind.

When your hatred begins to thaw...

"Thank you." Sunnëva stepped backward into her chambers.

Jökull regally bowed his head, and the portal closed. Sunnëva stood there, staring at the spot where he had been. When had she stopped hating him?

She made herself go to the table and placed the enchanted rose inside the dome. It shone softly in the dark, illuminating her room in a pretty blue hue. So many rampant emotions flooded her chest that she had to take her ring off out of embarrassment.

They weren't enemies anymore, nor friends. Whatever this was, it made her feel vulnerable. She didn't like it.

Damn it.

Sunnëva couldn't make herself move yet. She stayed there, staring at the rose, waiting for her heart to stop its stupid fluttering.

It didn't.

Jökull had perfect penmanship. Sunnëva watched as he dipped the quill in a well of ink and wrote elegant black letters across the scroll. The library was silent save for the soft scratching of the quill and the crackle of the fire in the hearth. He had set their table close enough for her to feel its warmth. If he was uncomfortable, he didn't show it.

It had been a week since the battle. There were no more signs of Rune after his failure to recover her, and no more mentions of the Gates. Jökull was waiting for her answer, but he didn't pressure her for it. Which was just as well, because she still didn't know what to do.

Logically, it made sense to join his mission, but she had her sister to think about. Their father still held Ansa over her head.

She was building up the courage to ask Jökull for help, but she had to word it properly without revealing her father's plan. If he discovered the rebellion, it might end with the execution of her entire clan. Yet as she looked at the God of Death, his expression at ease, she didn't want to believe he would do that, even after the violence she'd seen.

Jökull slid the scroll across the table to her. "Can you read this?"

Sunnëva squinted at the letters and slowly read aloud, stumbling over the words. "Mur-der*ous* Queen, so pre-tty and mean, w-will rip out your *sp*-leen." She snorted. "Write another sentence like that, and I might."

He grinned. "I suppose your instructor taught you well enough."

"If so, why did you dismiss him?" She took the quill and carefully copied the sentence below his.

"You were not enjoying it." Jökull's hand wrapped around her small one and corrected a letter. "Learning should be something you appreciate and absorb with excitement, the way you do with science."

His fingers slipped away, leaving a trickle of energy on her skin. He recovered the scroll as he wrote something else down.

She supposed there had been a difference in how she regarded both sessions. She enjoyed science because she found it interesting, and she was working toward something.

"Henceforth, I will see to your education." Jökull passed her the scroll again.

"S-select a subject," she read with less trouble. "How about the Seven Gates?"

He paused and straightened in his chair. "What would you like to know?"

"Well, all the clans know is that there are Seven Gods and we pass through their Gates when we die."

"At the beginning and at the end," Jökull clarified. "Souls are created within the Heavens. They cross each Gate to the Mortal Realm, and they return the same way when it's their time." He began writing down each Gate, and she read them aloud.

"Heaven's Gate. Life's Gate. Spatial Gate. Time Gate. Mortal Gate. Netherworld Gate. Death's Gate. They go through yours last and first?"

"Death is the only path to life."

She could agree with nothing more. "Are their Gates like yours?"

"Each one is unique, but they are gone now. Their Gates vanished when they did. I keep mine glamored. It must remain hidden."

"Why?"

"The power of the Gates is only meant for Gods. A mortal cannot cross it and live."

That explained why they only passed through at the beginning and end of their life.

"What are the Gods called, if I may ask? What do they do?"

179

Jökull's quill dipped in the inkwell again. He drew a circle on the scroll and began writing strange symbols on the circumference. "Elyōn, or the God of Urn, as humans call him, is the God of Life and our Maker. We regard him as a father, but we were not born, nor do we share blood with each other as true brothers. He created us from the matter of stars. Gavriel, Goddess of the Heavens, is considered our mother. She is the overseer of souls."

Sunnëva's heart dipped in wonder, and her mind whirled as he formed more odd shapes. It was the language of the Heavens, she realized.

"Hiram, the God of Time, deals with the past, the present, and the future. Zohar, the God of Space and Dimension, oversees the bridges between realms. Eitan, the God of Mortals, fills the worlds with animals, mountains, and the seas. As the God of Shadows, Rumiel oversees the Netherworld, where the wicked are sent to repent or be punished. Then there is I, the God of Death."

Seven names, equally spaced.

Jökull didn't elaborate on his duty, though she assumed it had to do with souls. She wanted to ask him about it, but he suddenly seemed uncomfortable.

"Over time, they have written down their sacred knowledge about the makings of the universe. However, I feel such knowledge is not suited in the hands of mortals."

He nodded to a plated chest on one of the shelves filled with artifacts. It was sealed with a brass lock. She imagined inside were stacks of rolled-up parchments filled with dire secrets.

"Too much of any God's power can cause a disruption in the world," Jökull murmured, and she thought of what became of her homeland, forever frozen and filled with demons. He drew a dot a few inches above each name. "The Gods are split by darkness and light. Elyōn, Gavriel, Zohar, and Eitan are light. Rumiel, Hiram, and I are dark." He drew a continuous, curving line from each dot that connected the circle to the next dot. Each one attached a light God to a dark one until the diagram formed an interwoven, seven-pointed star. He finished by drawing a larger circle around it. "And we are all held in balance together."

But could the Heavens be stable with Jökull and Rune not there to fulfill their duties? His brow furrowed, and he rubbed his jaw. He was worried about that, too.

"How long have you been away from your Realm?" she asked.

"Longer than I care to admit."

Why did their father leave them behind in the first place? It didn't make sense.

Jökull glanced down to where she'd been absentmindedly scratching the small scar on her wrist. She could nearly see his thoughts churning.

"Sometimes my scars itch," Sunnëva said, tugging her sleeve over it. "Thank you ... for not asking about them."

"It's not my place to ask about your pain. But if you wish to speak of it one day, I will listen."

The offer left her speechless. No one had asked to speak about her past, not that she could bring herself to. It was too ugly to speak about.

His expression was open, kind. She looked away, letting the curtain of her blonde hair cut the sight of it away. Sympathy was the evidence of ruin.

She didn't want that reminder.

Sunnëva tore off a tiny corner of the scroll, rolling it between her fingers. "Could an immortal God even understand pain? Consider it a gift to not suffer what humans do."

Jökull grabbed the armrest of her heavy wingback chair and jerked it around to face him, the legs screeching over the floor. She stilled under his frown. "Immortality is not a gift," he said. "I have lived through endless ages watching everyone around me die. I have lost count of how many pyres I have burned and graves I've buried. So many friends I have seen fall. Their tombs have long vanished beneath the sands of time while I am unchanging. For centuries, I chose to be alone so as not to suffer the inevitable loss of seeing another I cared for perish ... or to endure the sting of their betrayal." His brow creased, and he exhaled a low breath. "Don't presume I have not felt pain. Most of my existence is filled with it."

Maybe that was her problem.

She had assumed him a bloodthirsty beast without considering there might be more beyond the talons and fangs.

"I envy you," Jökull admitted with a soft mutter. "Of the mortality of your kind." He curled a lock of her hair behind her ear, his fingers trailing down her jaw to lift her chin. "So delicate, like glass. Every breath you take, every sunrise and sunset, leads to an inescapable end. That makes every moment of life all the more beautiful. What I would give to know what it feels like to be human. What it means to truly live."

Sunnëva stilled under the way he was looking at her, and the soft tone of his words. She could only observe him under the sunlight streaming in through the windows, feeling as if she was seeing the hidden depths of a God's heart.

Sunnëva's eyes fell to his chest, where it surely lay. She had wanted to carve it out of him before, but now the thought of it crumbling away strangely bothered her. "You would choose to be mortal even if it means dying one day?" she asked.

His reply was a soft murmur. "Sometimes, the most significant thing you can do is die."

Their eyes met and held.

A knock came at the heavy double doors. Ren and Riona opened them to allow Aero inside. The cautious look on his face had them both immediately standing.

"Sire." The mage bowed. "My Queen."

"What is it?" Jökull asked.

Aero straightened. "Bjorn Morkhàn has arrived at the front gates."

21

Her brother was here. Sunnëva immediately assumed the worst. Was her sister hurt? Did Rune attack her clan? Or had her father finally decided he was finished waiting?

"...along with three other clan warriors," Aero continued.

Sunnëva blinked at him, coming out of her thoughts. "Why is he here?"

"He seeks an audience with you. He assured me it's a social visit and not a matter of concern. Except he did ask to speak with you alone."

Sunnëva released all the trapped air in her lungs. That meant Ansa was all right. The one who was truly summoning her wasn't her older brother, but her father.

He wanted results, but she had none.

After Sunnëva had learned the truth about Fen and Rune, her vendetta had lost its purpose.

Fenrin lounged in the hallway with her guards. Tally sat in a chair beside him as she tended to her sewing. All were watching her, waiting for her answer.

Jökull took her shoulders. "What do you wish to do, Sunnëva?"

She closed her eyes at the rumble of his voice speaking her name. When had he started calling her that?

"Aero will send him away. Simply say the word."

Hearing that made her find her bearings. He didn't know why she froze, but he must have sensed her panic because she could feel it on her sweaty face. But things were different now. As she looked at all of them, waiting to do whatever she asked, she didn't feel so alone.

"I ... I will see him," Sunnëva said, looking up at Jökull. "Will you come with me?"

"Of course."

She glanced down at her leather armor. "But I need to change first."

Jökull opened a portal to her room, and Tally sprang up to go with her. She helped her peel off the armor and greaves, and she tossed her weapons on the bed. There was no time to bathe. A quick swipe of a soaked cloth from the water basin took care of the sweat. Tally helped her into a long-sleeved blue gown with silver embroidery that shimmered in the light.

"Should we be concerned, my lady?" Tally asked worriedly as she brushed out her hair.

"I don't know," she lied.

"Then why do you seem so frightened?"

Sunnëva stared at her wide eyes in the mirror and forced herself to take a breath. It helped to compose her expression. A knock came at the door. Tally opened it and bowed at Jökull's entrance. He had also changed into clean black clothes with a gray fur pelt on his shoulders. Sunlight edged one side of his face, gleaming off him like gold. Why did he always look so handsome?

He held out his arm, and Sunnëva took it. They walked together, taking the long way instead of a portal. As if he knew she needed time to collect herself.

"You won't ask me what is wrong?" she said after a few minutes of silence.

"If you wanted me to know, you would tell me," Jökull replied.

Why couldn't he be the despicable, growling man he had been when they first met? It would make this much easier if he wasn't so considerate.

"I ... can't explain it yet," she said. "But while we are in there, can you follow my lead?"

He dipped his head in a nod. "As you wish."

They entered the empty throne room with only Aero and Fenrin on opposite sides of the steps and her Queen's Guard waiting by the doors. Jökull opened a portal to the dais so they could skip the climb.

Sunnëva halted in place.

The dais had changed. Instead of one throne, there were now two. Both were equally sized, but hers was softer, with no jagged edges to poke her, and enchanted rose petals lay frozen within the ice. It glinted beautifully beneath the light.

She struggled to speak. "When did you...?"

"The night you won the battle. What is a Queen without her throne?"

You, he said. *Not us*. He had given her all the credit and made sure others knew her place. Not behind him, but at his side.

A lump tightened in her throat. "Can you remove it?" she asked faintly.

He frowned. "Why?"

"Please?"

With a wave of his hand, her throne dissolved away, leaving a scatter of petals at their feet.

"It was perfect." Sunnëva took his cool hand in hers. "You can make me another once he is gone."

His brow relaxed.

"For now, sit." She pushed him into his throne, and she sat down at his feet, between his legs. She placed his large hand on her throat. "Hold here. Treat me as your plaything. I will perform the silent, submissive wife."

Jökull chuckled quietly and grinned. "Well, I am beginning to like where this is going."

She glowered. "Put those fangs away."

185

"Why? I don't bite. Not unless you want me to."

A blush crept up her face, and she tried to ignore the implication behind his offer. "Stop looking at me like that."

His grin grew sly. "Like what?"

"Demented beast." Sunnëva smirked, but her smile faded as she sighed. "I know this situation is strange. I need to know what my brother has come to say first."

"Whatever it is, the truth cannot be hidden while in this room." Jökull motioned to the ceiling. Within the sill of the open windows were carved runes visible only from their vantage point. He pointed to one that was an infinity symbol on its side, like an hourglass. "The rune for truth and lies will glow if your brother speaks either."

That made her feel better, but not as much as knowing he would be here as a barrier between her and whatever her brother had to say. It was best for Jökull to be as frightening as her people knew him to be, and for her to be a glorified prisoner. That way, demands could be rejected if needed.

She forced herself to take a breath.

"Sunnëva." Jökull's eyes met hers. "Don't be afraid."

The softness of that assurance soothed her. He would be here, and that was enough to calm her down. She inhaled another deep breath and nodded. They were a team, even if it hadn't been said aloud.

Petals floated around her, seeming to rise on their own. Roses sprouted from the ice and climbed up the pillars and walls, filling the throne room with their scent.

He looked at her with a soft smile. "Ready?"

She nodded.

Jökull straightened in his seat, and the softness faded from his expression. It was hard and cold as ice. Even among the flowered pillars, he looked menacing without even trying.

Her knights pulled open the colossal doors embellished with the phoenix crest. Bjorn and three clansmen from her village marched in. Their heavy cloaks fluttered around their booted feet wrapped in fur. They wore her father's colors and were well-armed. It had been a month since they had seen each other last. Bjorn's blond hair was a little longer, and he had a short beard, but something else was different. He looked healthy, someone well sheltered and fed.

Her brother's jaw dropped at the sight of the enormous room and the skeletal chandeliers. They halted when Fenrin stood, nervousness crossing their faces. Then they noticed her and the King and immediately bowed.

Straightening, Bjorn's eyes shot to Jökull's hand, casually wrapped around her throat. It struck Sunnëva how oddly comforting it was. Even when black talons extended from his fingers, possessively pressing against her skin, visibly staking his claim over her. His thumb stroked her pulse, assuring her nothing else would ever get near. Her breathing evened out, and her body relaxed against him.

Jökull's hand drew away. In its place was a delicate necklace of ice around her neck, and he wrapped the end of the long chain around his fist like a leash.

Several twitches crossed her brother's face, going from disturbed to startled.

"Bjorn, son of Thorstein," Jökull's dark, gravelly voice rumbled in the throne room. "What brings you to my castle?"

He nervously cleared his throat. "Your Majesty, I have come to see my sister. I would like to speak to her in private, if I may."

"You may not," Jökull replied. His fingers traveled to the nape of her neck and he snatched a handful of her hair in his fist, tugging only enough to make her softly whimper. The odd sensation flooded warmth through her body, sinking into her stomach. "My wife does not do anything unless I allow it. Is that not right, *dearest*?"

Sunnëva glared up at him. She hoped Bjorn took her hiss as pain and not annoyance. Jökull's mouth curved ever so slightly. She dug her nails into his knee, out of sight from the others.

He didn't need to make it *this* believable.

Loosening his hold, Jökull sat back on his throne and pulled her up. Sunnëva's next breath halted when he seated her on his lap, and her heart jolted behind her ribs. Her stiffness was completely genuine.

His glowing eyes danced with brief mischief before they coolly fixed on Bjorn again. "Now, what do you want?"

Bjorn squirmed. She could see him trying to devise a proper response. He hadn't prepared for the possibility he wouldn't be permitted to get her alone.

"Ah, well, I—" Bjorn lost his train of thought when Jökull's hand landed on her thigh and began tracing the embroidered patterns of her dress.

Every touch shot explosive currents through her body, making it hard to breathe. This man ... he had a way of making her feel things.

Bjorn cleared his throat again and looked away. "I am here on behalf of my father. He wants my sister—"

"*Queen.*" Jökull interrupted. "And Thorstein will not send his son to make demands."

He bowed his head. "Pardon. The Earl asks if the Queen may come home to visit her family."

She was hardly listening. Her attention was on the track of Jökull's finger. Whatever her worries, they were quickly becoming a distant memory. She tried not to look as he traced the spiral leading to her inner thigh.

Sunnëva's toes curled in her slippers, electricity shooting up her legs to a spot that had been neglected for some time. Jökull brushed her hair aside as he skated his nose along her throat to the shell of her ear. A heated pulse sparked all over her body at the intimate touch.

It was only a show, she told herself. He was going along with her plan.

This was madness. His touch was maddening. Yet she allowed it to continue. Heat surged at the apex of her thighs when his finger faintly brushed the crease of her legs. Her core throbbed with a building need. Her breath quickened as his fingers traveled up ... and up.

"Might she come to stay for a few days?"

Jökull's hand stopped, and her mind cleared with the stark disappointment it struck her with.

"What?" he growled. The air grew frosty. "I've hardly had her long enough to be satiated, yet your father expects me to dispatch my newlywed bride to him for a *few days?*"

"For however many you would be kind enough to allow," Bjorn amended quickly.

Jökull looked at her, perhaps giving her the chance to answer, but she needed more time to think. "Hmm..." He brushed her hair, curling a lock around his finger. "I don't think I am quite ready to part ways with her yet. She provides me with long hours of rigid ... amusement."

A blush flooded her face.

Sunnëva aimed to pinch his leg, but Jökull pinned her hand on his lap. It landed on something firm, and she was almost certain it wasn't his dagger. If he wanted to play games, so would she. Sunnëva grabbed his collar and pulled him to her, kissing him angrily, wildly.

This was retaliation, she told herself. He deserved it. Or she was merely out of her mind and didn't care.

Sunnëva fisted the hair at his neck, threading the silken locks through her fingers. His presence filled her awareness, the form of his powerful body, the softness of his lips, his large hand on her waist. She wanted to sink her teeth into him. To lose herself in the planes of his skin. She was gratified by the shudder that went through him when her fingers traced the pointed edge of his ear.

When they pulled apart, his eyes were dilated, nearly black. The desire between them was a taut strand, ready to snap.

A sly turn curled Jökull's flushed lips, and he said aloud, "Yes, I think we are finished here, dearest. I want you upstairs now."

She glared. Oh, he was really enjoying this.

"Wait," Bjorn insisted. He looked up at her earnestly. "We miss Sunnëva terribly, our younger sister most of all. Please reconsider, if only for Ansa's sake, who has fallen ill."

All the growing heat in Sunnëva's body instantly cooled. The truth rune glowed blue, and her heart sank. But those words could mean anything and still be true. Was Ansa truly ill or made to be ill to lure her home?

"I will take it into consideration," Jökull said on seeing her reaction. "You and your clansmen may stay for the night." His tone sharpened. "Do *stay* in your rooms lest you wish to become someone's meal."

The men paled and quickly nodded in agreement.

"You'll have my answer by the morning. That will be all."

As soon as they were escorted out, and the throne room emptied, Sunnëva exhaled a shaky breath. "Thank you."

Jökull smirked, and at the snap of his fingers, the ice chain melted away. "My pleasure."

She arched a brow at his lap. "I'm sure it was."

"Don't deny you didn't enjoy it..." He leaned on the armrest, looking at her in a way that made her pulse do that weird dance. "You felt something."

She rolled her eyes. "Oh yes, *loathing.*"

"Ah, but see, I wouldn't have it any other way." He stood, his height towering over her. Little currents of electricity danced over her skin at his nearness. "There is no other stronger feeling than hate."

Sunnëva had no reply to that. Her thoughts were trapped by the intensity of his gaze. She broke the spell by shoving him back. He budged perhaps half an inch and only because he allowed it.

His pale eyes swept the room. "That was a nice touch, what you did with the roses."

"I didn't do that." She frowned. "I thought you did."

He shook his head. "You remade your brother. Maybe you're making these, too."

"But I don't have magic."

"Mine seems to like you."

"Gods." She cursed, then winced at his chuckle. "Sorry."

"What do you want to do, Sunnëva?"

She wrung her hands as she paced. "Would you allow me to go?"

"If that is what you wish." Jökull caught her shoulders, making her look at him. "I will deny you nothing except going alone."

Inexplicably, that filled her with instant relief. When before his presence was a deplorable thing, now she found it reassuring.

"I have decided." Sunnëva inhaled a steady breath. He stilled, seeming to hold his. "I will help you open your Gate, Jökull. But please, I need your help first."

22

By the next morning, Sunnëva and Jökull were ready to travel to the Morkhàn clan. They were joined by an entourage of his riders and servants on crystal horses, Fenrin included. Bjorn wasn't happy about it, but he had no place to dispute the King's decision, and she was glad.

They had much to gain if they worked together and much to lose if they didn't. But she had a plan now and would see it through.

Sunnëva looked out the carriage window at the white planes. Tally sat beside her with Aero and Jökull across from them. They decided to travel around the Black Woods, even if it added an extra day to their journey.

"Will we camp soon?" she asked.

"Not yet, my Queen," Aero replied.

Jökull frowned at the view of the Hermon River beyond his window. "I don't plan on stopping tonight. We are too exposed out here."

Because Rune was still a threat.

She sighed. It was going to be a long ride.

Jökull rapped his knuckles on the ceiling, and the wheels creaked as they rolled to a stop. "Come."

He stepped outside, and she followed. Moonstone and Tanzanite layered the outside of the carriage, making it glitter.

"Where are we going?"

"I sensed you getting restless. We can fly part of the way." Jökull shut the carriage door and removed his cloak. "Unless you prefer to stay seated."

Sunnëva stretched her cramped legs and stiff shoulders. "I wouldn't, but I also don't want to be carried off by my arms again."

Ice wings sprouted from his back. "How about I carry you off in mine?"

"Oh, um..." She studied his impressive build, and her throat dried. The thought of having his large body wrapped around hers stirred something low in her belly. She needed to get a hold of herself and stop swooning. They were only muscles. "All right."

One end of Jökull's mouth curved in that half-smile of his. He drew her to him, and her hands landed on his chest, completely by accident. She ignored how firm he felt beneath her palms as he placed his heavy cloak around her shoulders.

Once Jökull pinned it in place, he said, "Try not to be so nervous."

"Nervous about what?"

He flashed her a grin. The next second she was swooped into his arms, and they shot into the frigid sky. She gasped and held onto his neck. The wind whipped against them as the frozen land fell away. The Hermon River snaked below into the forest in the southeast. Everything was bathed in gold by the setting sun.

When they were high above the world, Jökull asked, "Do you trust me?"

She arched an eyebrow warily at his sly expression. "I don't trust anyone until they earn it."

"Then merely trust that I won't let you fall to your death."

"What—?"

Jökull tossed her high into the air. A scream tore from Sunnëva's throat as she came down. The Ice Phoenix swooped under her, and she landed on his back with an *oomph*. She clutched his feathers and wrapped her thighs tightly around him.

"Oh, you will pay for that, barbaric bird."

Jökull made an odd chirping sound that could only be laughter. *I would never let you fall.*

She jumped at the sound of his voice in her head. *Have I gone mad, or did I hear you speak to me?*

His chuckle rang clear in her mind.

One of your many talents, I assume. She smiled. He flew steadily with her into the horizon. She shifted back and stretched out her arms. For the first time in her life, Sunnëva felt on top of the world. *I have a question.*

Pray tell.

Why a phoenix? Sunnëva asked as they rose above the clouds. Mist coated her face, and she found herself in another plane of endless orange sky.

Elyōn gave the Gods a true form and a beast form, along with an element we possess. All to serve our purpose.

It made her wonder what Rune's beast form was.

Now that I've agreed to join you, how do you plan to make Rune cross your Gate? she asked. *Once it's open...*

He will most likely stay in the Waste Lands. It's warded, so I cannot open a portal there. I suspect this will result in another battle before the end. Jökull sounded indifferent, but Sunnëva could feel his concern.

Rune nearly defeated them on Jökull's land. If they came to his territory, the disadvantage would be worse. She prayed it didn't come to that.

When night fell and the temperature grew too cold for her, Jökull flew to the ground. She didn't want to ride in the carriage, though,

and she didn't want to stop the procession to sleep either. He conjured a crystal horse from the frost, and they rode together.

He moved further up the road until the sounds of the riders faded, giving the impression it was only them in the woods. Faint moonlight streamed over the ground and frosted branches. Sunnëva's breath fogged in the air, but she was warm under Jökull's cloak and in his arms. He held the reins in one hand.

The day's weight must have finally reached its peak because Sunnëva was physically exhausted, but her mind wouldn't quiet.

"Sleep," Jökull murmured.

"I can't," Sunnëva sighed. "Too much burdens my mind. I keep thinking..." About what she would find when she returned to the village.

And about his faint breath drifting down her neck.

"You're worried about your sister."

"If she is unwell, I hope it's true because the alternative would be worse."

"I already warned your father."

"You don't know him." Sunnëva shook her head. "I'd rather not discuss it."

"Shall I ramble on about the Gates until I bore you to sleep?"

She sighed, managing a weak smile. "Perhaps another time."

"Then may I ask you a question?"

That drew her curiosity. "Only if I can ask you anything in return."

"Agreed," he replied, and Sunnëva could hear the smile in his voice. She braced herself, waiting. "What were you thinking about yesterday in the throne room?"

When she was on his lap.

She assumed that's what he meant, or because that was the first thing that came to her mind. Heat swirled in her veins at remembering the currents of electricity his fingers had created.

Sunnëva glanced at this hand holding the reins and visually traced the veins running through them. "I was thinking ... what an uncomfortable chair." His quiet laugh tickled her ear, and she shivered. "What were *you* thinking about?"

"Hmm, many things. That I needed to destroy whatever frightened you. And ... I was pleased you depended on me to help you."

The last part was said hesitantly, as though Jökull wasn't sure if he should admit it, but wanted to. For some reason, she had relied on him without a second thought, somehow knowing she could.

Jökull leaned close, and his head dipped, sending a flutter through her chest. "I liked that you no longer shied away from me and didn't flinch when I touched you." His free hand circled a slow pattern over her abdomen and it tightened beneath the stroke of his fingers. The fabric of her dress suddenly felt too thin. "When I had you on my lap, all I could think about was how much I wanted you. I could hardly remember what we were there for. Then your lips were on mine, and for a moment, I forgot all else."

It didn't seem real to hear his soft words in the night, yet her heart did a little flip. Sunnëva didn't know what to do with his honesty, but to offer the same.

"I..." She swallowed. "When I saw the throne you had made for me ... I felt more equal at your side than anywhere else in the world. I wondered when your talons wrapped around my throat had become reassuring instead of a threat. And when your hand was on my thigh, I also wished ... to forget everything else."

Why was she telling him this? Her confession filled the void between them. It was stupid. Risky. She should have taken it back, but she didn't.

Because it was all true.

Jökull was quiet for a pause. Something stilled in the air that made her hold her breath.

Sunnëva nearly leaped out of her skin at the sensation of his cool lips brushing her ear. It shot a current through every corner of her being.

"Allow me to grant your wish."

"What do you mean?" But she knew. She did because her pulse instantly thrummed.

His fingertips traced around her navel, circling the pearl buttons. It awakened little sparks all over her body, sinking heat into her core.

"I think you know, winter rose." Jökull's nose skated down her neck, and she instinctively leaned back to give him more access. She quivered as his fingers traveled to her thigh and traced the dress's embroidery again. Every touch made her heart beat faster.

"What are you doing?" she asked breathlessly. Pointlessly.

"Continuing what we started in the throne room."

"That ... that was only..." Sunnëva couldn't concentrate enough to argue. All of her attention was on his fingers.

"It was meant to be only a ruse we put on display, yet I felt how your heart raced as I caressed you," he said, his fingers tracing the length of her thigh. "Heat colored your cheeks a lovely pink as you bit your lip the way you are now."

She quickly released her lip.

Jökull traced the patterns up higher, rumbling in her ear. "I was so focused on you, I wasn't paying attention to anything else. I was drunk with your emotions and your need. We both wanted the same thing. My touch on your skin ... past every damn layer of fabric between us."

His heated confession made her heart beat quicker. She could sense his want, too. A burning craving to feel her skin against his. Something in her chest thrummed, yearning for it. And damn her if she didn't want it, too.

His cool tongue flicked against her pulse. It struck such a wild sensation between her legs she inhaled sharply. It grew in intensity at the gentle scrape of his fangs. They traveled up her sensitive ear, tracing the shell. Sunnëva squirmed, and something hard pressed against her lower back. It sent little sparks of fire to all the delicate places all over her body. She gasped and grabbed his arm. He immediately removed his hand.

"Shall I stop?" His tone was soft.

Sunnëva shook her head. She trembled, but not in distress. It was with overwhelming desire, coiled through her so tightly she could hardly breathe. Every reason why she shouldn't do this faded beneath her pounding heart. She wanted him to continue stroking her. To hold her as delicately as he did now.

This was such a terrible idea.

Jökull's breath swept over her throat as he inhaled her scent. "Can I keep touching you, Sunnëva?" She quivered at the question, tingles shooting to her throbbing center. "Can I explore the softest part of you? Feel how warm you are inside as you moan so sweetly for me?"

His palm rested on her thigh but moved no further, awaiting her permission.

Sunnëva turned her head toward him, her mouth trembling against his jaw. "Yes," she whispered, shocked the words slipped past her lips before she thought better of it. "Touch me."

Jökull's mouth descended on hers, consuming her in a devouring kiss. He led the horse off the road, and they stopped in a small glade filled with moonlight. Her dress inched up as he bunched it in his fist, exposing her thigh to the night, but she didn't feel cold. She was flooded with heat at the fiery stroke of his fingers exploring her bare skin.

"This is what I wanted to do to you in the library that night." His velvety voice purred in her ear. "I wanted to feel every delicate part of you as you came undone in my fingers."

Sunnëva's body hummed with his every caress, leaving her slick with need. Out here in the wilderness, they seemed to be in another realm where nothing else existed but them.

Jökull gathered her dress and moved it aside over her other thigh, above her hips. He slid a talon underneath her undergarments and snipped it, completely exposing her. She gasped.

He inhaled a rough breath, and a low sound rumbled in his chest. "You smell like warm honey."

Heat rushed into her cheeks. He could smell her arousal?

Jökull's talons retracted, and he said, "Look at how beautiful you are."

Sunnëva made herself look down as the first stroke of his fingers slid along her folds. Her entire body spasmed with a soft moan.

Jökull growled low at how sleek she was. He slid to her entrance and gathered her lust, spreading it up to her clit. Every touch was delicate and precise. Her breaths sharpened and her head fell against his chest as more shocking heat flooded her body.

"Does that feel good?"

She dug her nails into his arm. He knew it did.

Jökull chuckled. His fingers moved teasingly toward the apex of her thighs. Goosebumps prickled down her shoulders with electric currents. Her toes curled in her boots, and her stomach tightened. He created a need within her, drawing out her whimpers.

The hitch in his voice was pure roguishness. "Do you want to come, winter rose? Let me hear you ask for it."

She might have been mad with desire, but she wouldn't beg.

"No." Her breath hitched with disappointment when he pulled away.

"So stubborn." His mouth slipped over her earlobe. The way his tongue licked it heightened the lack of attention between her thighs. He ran his fingers through her folds, avoiding where she wanted him. Sunnëva bit her tongue so she wouldn't pitifully moan.

Jökull gently nipped her neck, making her shiver all over. "Ask, and I will make you see stars."

A sigh dragged out of her in defeat.

"Please." She looked up at him, shuddering with trapped release. "I need it."

His eyes were bright with hunger as he smiled down at her. "Good girl."

He rolled his thumb over her clit, and she let out a cry. Her core throbbed with pleasure. Sunnëva panted, opening her legs wider for his reach.

He growled, his chest heaving with sharp breaths. Jökull's erection pressed against her, and the considerable length made her body squirm with the need to feel it. To have him *in*.

"Having you like this, I want to seat myself in you so deep until your thighs are drenched with me."

Such filthy words scandalized her, and she loved it.

"Can you imagine it, Sunnëva? How it would feel to have me sink inside of you? How fast I would take you? Because I have." Jökull plunged his fingers into her and he silenced her cry by crashing his mouth into hers.

His fingers were so long and thick. So perfectly snug against her walls. When he started moving them, Sunnëva's eyes rolled. She began to shiver and shake. His tongue fucked her mouth with the same pace as his fingers, his other hand skimming her waist to clutch her breast. The squelching between her legs sounded so lewd, revealing how drenched she was, and how much lust he drew out of her.

If he was to have his way with her, so would she.

She grabbed his arm and dug in her nails, held him there as she rocked into his hand brazenly, seeking more friction, demanding more.

"That's right. Hold on to me. I'm not afraid of your thorns." Jökull thrust his fingers into her in a rhythm that made her picture exactly what it would feel like to have him inside of her.

"Oh Gods," she moaned.

"No, winter rose. The only God you should plead to is me." He tugged on her hair, making her look at him through her hazy vision. "Who is touching you?" His fingers curled, hitting a spot that made her jerk off the saddle. "Whose fingers are inside of you?"

She couldn't refuse to answer when he rendered her molten and mindless. All of her was weakened by the delicious friction in her core.

"Yours," she said in a breathless whimper.

Her reward was him stroking her bundle of nerves, and she let out a mewling cry. He pumped faster, harder. Her body melted into him, yielding completely.

Jökull swore. "You're so wet."

Her entrance dripped with every thrust. All of her throbbed, begging for more and more, her body starved for him.

"Only I can touch you." His eyes glowed bright, erotic, and sinful. His body supported her as she rocked against him. "This belongs to me."

A gasp burst from her when he slipped a third finger in. She bit back a cry that was part sob, and she quaked violently with pleasure. But she was so full and tight she tensed.

"It's all right," he crooned. His soft lips pressed against her temple. "You can take it."

Jökull waited until she completely relaxed and adjusted to him before he gradually picked up the pace again. "This is only a hint at how it would feel to have me inside you."

Gods, was he that large?

He would fill her to the brim. The thought only pushed her further.

Sunnëva undulated faster, so she could feel his fingers come in harder and deeper inside. He growled in satisfaction and rubbed directly over her most sensitive spot. She let out a shrill cry against his cold lips. Every time his fingers thrust in, she arched. Her inner walls clenched around his fingers, and Jökull gutturally cursed. A current swept across her skin as he brought her closer to the edge.

Yes, right there. Don't stop, she internally pleaded with desperation. *Please, don't stop.*

Her thoughts blanked, and she let go, bucking obscenely and lustfully into his fingers. The God of Death had his hand buried between her thighs. The savage growls he emitted were because he was a beast the world cowered to.

But Sunnëva didn't give a damn.

Her body pulsed, throbbed, and quivered. She was so wet that she could feel the smooth slide of his fingers that moved faster as her entire being tensed. Sunnëva chased it. She was about to split, and she didn't care about anything else.

"Right there," Sunnëva rasped as she uncontrollably rocked into him. "Please."

"Sunnëva," Jökull groaned low against her neck, sounding so unhinged, so mindless, all of her vibrated.

His thumb stroked her clit, and she crashed. He captured her mouth, swallowing her scream. Ecstasy hurtled into her body as she was overtaken by tremors of pleasure. If Jökull hadn't been holding her against his chest, her spine would have bowed from the force. He continued stroking her through her release until she went limp. Her heart pounded wildly, her body shuddering. Her blurry sight misted and white sparks danced in her vision.

He really made her see stars.

After a minute of calm between them, the embarrassment finally set in. She must be insane to have allowed this. To want this. So much that she pleaded for his touch until she dissolved into nothing.

The breeze blew against her hot face, but Sunnëva didn't regret it.

Jökull's nose brushed hers with surprising affection. "Are you all right?"

She nodded, unable to speak yet.

"There. That should ease your mind for the night."

Sunnëva clenched around his fingers, and he swore.

"Naughty thing. Hold still for me." Jökull gently slipped out of her body, leaving her unbearably hollow.

From some pocket, he drew out a handkerchief, and another blush sank into her cheeks when he carefully cleaned up her mess, then put it away. Jökull reached around and adjusted her dress again. He was tented in his trousers but shook his head before she could do anything about it.

"Another time." He tucked a loose strand behind her ear. "Sleep now. I have you."

After what they had done, how could she?

Jökull eased her legs to one side of the saddle and laid her head on his chest, his arm cradling her close. He wrapped his heavy cloak around them, covering her completely.

The sweetness behind that action was like the spark of an ember in her chest. He stroked her hair softly, lulling her with each soothing touch. She couldn't remember when anyone had touched her this delicately before. Every caress was done with care, as if she were as cherished as his roses.

Jökull led the crystal horse onto the road again. Her eyes drifted closed as she listened to his steady heartbeat and breathed in the scent of frost and cedar that only belonged to him. There was a comforting familiarity to him that soothed her being, and she didn't know why.

Sunnëva was so confused by that she didn't notice when she fell asleep.

23

They arrived on a rocky bluff overlooking the valley below. In the distance appeared the village of the Morkhàn Clan. Sunnëva's spirit wilted a little in part to dread and a combination of nostalgia.

Frigid winds blew across the open plains once the procession reached the bottom. It whipped against the carriage so hard that she half expected it to knock over. It was late afternoon, with snowflakes scattering in the air like dust. Oddly, she found it colder here than in the castle. Jökull had her bundled up in a heavy fur cloak and thick trousers under her dress. The chill found its way into her clothing as soon as they stepped outside, but it was bearable.

Bjorn had sent one from his party ahead to announce their arrival, no doubt, to prepare their father. Thorstein was waiting at the entrance of the village with a handful of her people. The sight of him made her chest tighten again, but she was pleasantly surprised to find them all healthy and well-fed.

Jökull had kept his word about providing for her village.

Sunnëva almost smiled and waved to them but reminded herself she was to play the submissive wife to the frightening King of the

Everfrost. She moved a step behind Jökull. He frowned, but she subtly indicated he should go ahead of her. She walked after him with Aero and her handmaiden.

"King Jökull," Thorstein greeted with a short bow of his head. "Welcome. Forgive me, but I had not expected to receive so many guests. I would have prepared for better accommodations. I will have my servants add more hay to the barns for your men."

"That won't be necessary," Jökull replied. "We won't be staying long."

Her father's mouth pursed slightly. Though to his credit, he didn't look at her yet. "Surely you can stay awhile."

"As much as I would like to, I have a kingdom to oversee and cannot waste time frolicking in the muck." Jökull swept past him. "Show us to your hall, Thorstein. My wife is tired, and her condition is much too delicate for this weather."

Her father's wide eyes shot to her face at the implication. His expression was visibly shocked and angry. She flushed and inwardly cursed that beast. She would pinch his arse for that one.

"My lady." Aero motioned for her to follow.

Sunnëva nodded and ducked her head, Tally staying close by her side. When Fenrin came around the carriage, her father cursed and reached for his sword. The villagers scrambled out of the way, gaping up at his massive form.

"I trust you will not be opposed to our warg coming along," Jökull said without looking back. "No need to worry. It's tame, but very protective of Sunnëva and isn't fond of others getting too close. My beauty goes nowhere without her beast."

She sensed Jökull wasn't speaking about Fenrin, but he couldn't mean her. What part of her was beautiful?

Nonetheless, her brother played the part and growled, startling everyone into giving him a wide berth. She hid a smile. Fenrin must be enjoying all the attention.

"I will walk with my daughter," Thorstein said to Aero. He wasn't asking.

The mage only looked at her, awaiting her decision. Sunnëva nodded. Tally and Aero walked a few paces behind but stayed near, as did Fenrin. Their presence wouldn't allow her father to speak as freely as he wished.

Thorstein peered at her stomach, wondering if it was true. "Are you treated well?"

"Yes," she answered faintly.

"I suppose you must be preoccupied since I have not received another word from you."

Aside from the message he had already ignored.

But Sunnëva read the true meaning behind his words. *Since the King is still alive...*

If only he knew how preoccupied she had been last night. A flush of heat warmed her face at the reminder of Jökull's touch and his breath on her neck.

"Forgive me if my lack of thoughtfulness wounded you, Father," she said carefully, keeping her attention fixed ahead. "My duties as the wife of the King are many. I spend quite a bit of time ... learning."

This piqued his interest. "Yes, I am quite sure. Have you come to learn anything useful?"

"Perhaps."

He gave her a rare smile, though it was harsh. "Then you must indulge my curiosity and tell me of your new life in the castle. The Morkhàn clan is very proud."

She tilted her head in a slight nod. When the longhouse came into view, she smiled and hurried onward. But it vanished when they entered. It was the same as she left, warm with a crackling fire in the large pit, servants moving about as they set up the tables with food.

"Where's Ansa?" Sunnëva asked as she removed her cloak. "I heard she was ill."

"That is not a matter you should concern yourself with," her father told her, his tone sharpening slightly enough.

She stepped back, bowing her head. Best not to anger him.

Jökull climbed up the steps to the Earl's chair and sat facing the great hall. "My wife asked you a question, Thorstein. Do give an adequate reply." His cool eyes locked on a servant. "Bring another chair for the Queen."

Thorstein noticed where Jökull had chosen to sit, and a vein pulsed in his temple. He stiffly turned to her. "Your sister is with Gyda. Her illness left her bedridden for a couple of days, but I expect her to recover soon."

Sunnëva finally allowed herself to feel some relief. She would visit Ansa next.

When she sat beside Jökull, he jerked her chair close and leaned toward her. "Don't do that again," he said, a growl in the back of his throat.

She blinked at the frosty look on his face. "Do what?"

"Retreat." He bit out the word as if it offended him. "You bow to *no one*. The kingdom kneels to you. And if it doesn't, you make it."

The words made something shake inside of her. Even when he called her his Queen and his subjects bowed, Sunnëva hadn't seen herself as one. She'd come from nothing, where not even her father acknowledged her.

She looked away from the force of his gaze.

Soon, the hall was filled with villagers and Jökull's riders as they feasted on the meal the servants prepared. Their voices and the smell of cooking meat permeated the air. The familiar sounds and scents she grew up with made her a little sentimental.

"How are you feeling?" Jökull asked her. He lounged comfortably in her father's chair, with his arm propped up on the armrest.

Sunnëva dramatically sighed and placed a hand on her stomach. "Oh, much too tired, my King. How did I make such a journey in my *delicate* condition?" She shot him a side glare. "I owe you for that one."

He hid a smile behind his fist. "I think I have lost count of how many you owe me. Thought it might be a good distraction."

Well, it worked. Her father, standing across the great hall, glowered at her hand's placement. She quickly moved it to the armrest.

"Pregnancy is not a jest, Jökull. You shouldn't make such insinuations lightly."

"If Thorstein made his assumptions, that's his doing." He leaned closer to her, his hand curling over her stomach. The touch made her insides leap and the coolness of his palm seeped through her dress, his pinky so close to her navel. "If ever the day came, I planted my seed in you, I would never leave you out of my sight, Sunnëva. Let alone allow you to step foot out of the castle."

Her pulse climbed at the low possessive growl in his voice, her eyes catching on his with his face so close. Her mind was barely able to form a coherent thought.

"Why?" she asked, her voice a faint whisper. It would be lost to anyone but his sharp ears. They hadn't even consummated their marriage yet, but the thought of the actions that would lead to such a thing had delicious heat stirring through her being.

His fingers lightly grazed up her arm. "You have become too precious to me. Too important," Jökull said softly, mystifying her and subduing her at all once. He brushed the hair from her cheek and tucked it behind her ear. "With my child in your belly, I imagine this savage instinct I already have to claim what is mine would become maddening, for you would be my weakness ... and a target for my every enemy. My only recourse would be to keep you under me, where no one can reach you."

Even when he flirted so openly and touched her freely as he was now, Sunnëva couldn't let herself acknowledge what had been growing between them. Because she was too aware of what would become of this marriage once they opened his Gate. Yet her pulse thrummed to hear him murmur those words to her, stirring desire in her lower stomach again. Sunnëva couldn't deny that after last night, she did want to know what it would feel like to be with him.

What if that did result in a baby? Could she fall pregnant by a God? Or was he merely teasing a fantasy?

"It's very possible." He slyly grinned.

She narrowed her eyes. "Are you reading my thoughts?"

"I don't need to when your thoughts are on your face."

Sunnëva shifted in her seat, ignoring her blush. "I didn't know Gods could reproduce..."

"You would be surprised how *highly* effective we are at that." He chuckled darkly, and she flushed at the insinuation. Gods were creators, so naturally, they would be fertile as well. "Though carrying our offspring is not the same as it is for your kind."

"What do you mean?"

"The term is much shorter, for one. And demigod children are very different from human children. There is a great deal of magic involved."

Her mind reeled with these revelations. "Would it change me?"

Why was she asking this?

"No. If anything, giving birth to my heir would secure your position as Queen once I am gone," Jökull said. "However, it is a considerable decision to make. The choice is always yours."

When he put it like that, she couldn't help feeling enticed, not merely due to her standing, but having a piece of him left behind oddly made her happy. It had to be infatuation, because she knew how dangerous this world was. That didn't stop her mind from imagining what it would be like to hold a child who looked like him.

But sleeping with the King meant he would want to see and touch every part of her. The thought made her heart shrivel. She was well aware of the scars on her body, and how ugly and useless they made her feel. He had yet to know how worthless she was.

"Why have me birth your heir when you could have any woman in the world with a better standing than me?"

Jökull's brow furrowed, sensing her mood again. "There is no other who could ever be more suitable to carry my blood than you."

There was a meaning behind his tone she didn't understand, but he was looking at her again in a way that made her feel seen.

Sunnëva noticed her father's sharp focus on her. What a view they must paint for him, sitting so intimately close. She got to her feet abruptly, forcing Jökull to sit back.

"I'm going to find my sister. Alone," she added when he moved to stand.

Jökull searched her eyes, and she saw the conflict there. He didn't want to let her go alone, but her reddening face gave away how much their conversation had left her flustered. "Ren, Riona, accompany the Queen."

Her guards bowed. Aero and Tally also stood where they had been sitting at the table closest to them.

"No, I will be all right." Sunnëva waved them back and gathered her fur-lined cloak. "Gyda's hut isn't far."

Jökull caught her wrist. "Take Fenrin with you. It's not a suggestion."

Sighing, she nodded and hurried away before he could mention anything else. The brisk air was a relief against her hot face. Why did he have to say such things that always left her mind in confused knots?

Fenrin rose from where he had been laying outside the longhouse.

"Let's go see Ansa." She threw on her cloak over her cream-colored dress and they took the path up a short hill.

Since the battle, things had changed between her and Jökull.

But Sunnëva couldn't allow it to continue, because their partnership was based on the fact that it wouldn't be forever. He had to go home to a Realm she couldn't reach. Letting herself get lost in him would only end up hurting her in the end.

When Sunnëva reached Gyda's hut, she found the healer sitting outside by her campfire.

"I wondered when I would see you again..." Gyda's milky eyes lifted to the large warg lurking in her wake. "Fenrin."

Sunnëva gaped at her. "You knew?"

She used her staff to poke at the firewood. "In so giving him the rose, he would become a product of the magic lent by the Shadow God and the Death God. I knew not what he would become, only that his curse would change."

"How do I fix him?"

"Fix? There is no fixing him, girl. He is forever changed."

Sunnëva's heart sank. "You mean he will remain this creature for the rest of his life?"

Fenrin whined and sat on his haunches.

Gyda hobbled to him, studying his skull face up close. "Hmm..." She patted his bony snout. "Perhaps not, if you can change his curse. But who he was will never be again. I am sorry, dear boy."

A sad sound hummed in her brother's throat, and he lowered his ears.

"We won't give up, Fen." Sunnëva sighed. "And Ansa? Is she all right?"

"I am perfectly fine," Ansa said from the entry to the hut. But her sister had lost weight, and her pale face was gaunt.

"Gods." Sunnëva rushed forward and hugged her tight. "What happened to you?"

"Nothing at all," Ansa said tiredly. She tried to smile, but her thin body betrayed the slightest tremble.

"That lout father of yours didn't allow her to eat for a few days," Gyda grunted with disgust. "I assume to bring you back here."

It was as she feared. Her father was beyond cruel.

Sunnëva gritted her teeth so she wouldn't shout a curse. Fenrin certainly did with the snarl that ripped out of him.

Ansa gasped, and her face lit up when she saw him. "Fen! When Gyda mentioned a warg had come into the village, I dared to hope." She went to him and hugged his large body without any hesitation at all. He licked her cheek. "I am so happy that you and Sunnëva are safe."

"But you're not safe," Sunnëva said. "Father will continue to find ways to hurt you merely to control me. I need to take you away from here."

"But how?"

"Jökull will help me."

Ansa and Gyda wore twin expressions of shock. When she had asked him for help, Jökull didn't deliberate for a second.

"He and I ... well, let's say we have come to an understanding."

Gyda tsked. "It seems more than that, girl." She eyed her suspiciously. "His magic certainly becomes you."

"What do you mean?"

Ansa was studying her, too. "You look different. Your hair and eyes ... your face..."

Sunnëva touched her cheek. What was wrong with her face?

"Not in a bad way." Ansa pulled her hand down. "Your features are lighter. Otherworldly. You feel ... different..."

"She's changing," Gyda said. "It happens to every bride who marries a God. If you continue to stay with him, if you take him unto your heart, his magic will evolve you, Sunnëva."

The Moonstone ring glinted on her finger, reminding her of the power she wielded during the battle. Then in the throne room with the roses.

She was suddenly conscious of the wind blowing against them, and it hardly having any effect on her. When had she grown accustomed to the cold?

Do tell her what she will become if she remains by your side.

"Into what, Gyda?" Sunnëva asked faintly. "What will I evolve into?"

"Into *whatever* he is."

24

Sunnëva followed the path in the receding evening light as she headed toward the village. Her thoughts were as complicated as the lines of a snowflake. But she pushed it out of her mind and focused on her purpose here. She left Fenrin behind to guard Ansa in case her father tried anything again. They wouldn't leave without her sister.

But Ansa wasn't his current target.

Bjorn appeared between the pit houses with a grim expression. "Come."

He led her to the growing shadows beneath the canopy of the Azure Tree where her father waited.

Thorstein didn't waste time on idle conversation. "Why is he still alive?"

Sunnëva folded her hands at her waist. "You sent me to kill a *God*. Did you assume it would be an easy task?"

"I assumed you had proper motivation."

Sunnëva glowered at him with angry disbelief. "You starved her," she hissed. "That's how far you're willing to go?"

"Don't assume missing a meal is the depth of my persuasion."

Her chest tightened painfully, her lungs struggling for air at how vile her father truly was. He didn't care as long as he got what he wanted.

"How could you?" She jerked a step forward, but Bjorn cut her off. "How can you stand this?" she snapped at him, her voice breaking. "She is your sister, Bjorn. As am I. You're supposed to protect your family. When will you be a man and start doing that?"

But he merely lowered his eyes. He was too spineless to say anything to their father. It had always been that way. Living all their lives under his thumb.

"What is wrong with you?" Sunnëva shouted at Thorstein, her voice catching with a sob. "How could you mistreat us this way? All I have ever done was try to earn your love, but it was never enough for you. I may have married the beast in the castle, but you are the monster."

He sneered. "Yes ... a beast you seem very taken with. One who treats you like a common whore rather than a wife."

Sunnëva gritted her teeth. Bjorn was doing well not to meet her gaze. Well, she shouldn't be surprised after the spectacle they made in the throne room.

"Are you with child?" her father demanded.

"I am not."

"Good. Otherwise, I'd cut it out of you myself."

She stared at him, horrified by this new level of cruelty.

He stabbed a finger at her stomach. "Your womb must not be filled with his spawn. I have another in mind for you."

"What?" Sunnëva flinched back. "Who?"

"That is none of your concern."

Something like panic was building in her throat, squeezing her lungs with helplessness at the thought of being removed from the place that had somehow become her sanctuary. "I am already married."

"Not for long." Thorstein got in her face, nearly spitting. "I saw the way you looked at him, Sunnëva. Do not forget the reason why you were sent there in the first place. This is not a real marriage. Once he is dead and we have seized the kingdom, you will be married to another wealthy lord. One who assures me the land will look much different during my reign."

Sunnëva's throat caught with a sharp breath, her mind spinning over his meaning. He would sell her off again for his gain ... and planned to make himself king. There was no end to his ambition.

"Now tell me what you learned. You said you learned something."

"I did," she said tightly. "I learned how to read and write. Valuable knowledge."

A vein pulsed in his temple. "Are you mocking me, daughter?"

"I wouldn't dream of it."

"You have been in that castle with him this whole time. I find it hard to believe you haven't discovered something of use," Thorstein said, watching her very closely. She tensed, and he noticed. "You have."

As the sunlight faded into dusk, Sunnëva decided at that moment whose side she was on. She didn't know exactly what Jökull's weakness was, but she would never reveal the clue about the Skellings. Even if she mentioned he would eventually leave through his Gate, only death would satisfy her father.

Bring me his heart.

"You give me too much credit," she said. "I am kept up in a tower, nowhere near his secrets."

Thorstein studied her, but she remained perfectly indifferent. "Then I suggest you find what I need if you want Ansa to be well."

He strode away with Bjorn, leaving her with that warning. Her chest compressed under the familiar weight of his scorn. Again, that helplessness balled in her throat. All her life, he made her feel small. He was doing it now, but she refused to be a stone for him to step on.

"No."

They halted and turned around.

"I won't help you kill him or marry anyone else you try to sell me to," Sunnëva said. "I'm finished withstanding your threats."

215

Her father's mouth curled, furious. Magic pulsed in the air with the churning of the wind, and it fell over her like a veil. Inhaling a breath, she composed herself, steeling her expression as she had seen her husband do.

"Your dominion over my life has ended. *I* am Queen of the Everfrost. This is *my* kingdom, and you are my subject. So you will *kneel.*"

His eyes widened incredulously at the crown of ice that had formed on her head. He snatched her wrist. "Wretched witch. You dare speak—"

"Remove your hand before I carve out your fucking skull." That deep, male voice drifted through the night, coursing a shiver down Sunnëva's spine.

Thorstein immediately let her go.

Jökull stalked out of the shadowed trees. With the darkness coating his cold features, he truly looked like the God of Death. It reminded her of the first time she'd seen him. Back then, she feared what he had symbolized.

Sunnëva wasn't afraid anymore.

Jökull came to her side, his frosty presence like a fortress of stone, and the Nightstone scythe materialized in his hand. "My Queen has given you a command. Either your knees hit the ground, or your head will."

Thorstein held out his hands in surrender and quickly lowered. So did Bjorn. "Sire, I don't know what you heard—"

"I heard plenty." The wind picked up with the rumble of Jökull's voice. "You're not the first to try assassinating me, Thorstein. Though you are the first coward to use his daughters to do it."

Her father kept his head down, his fingers digging into the snow.

"Therefore, Ansa will come to the castle, where she will be Sunnëva's lady-in-waiting. I will pay her wages and ensure she is properly *fed* and provided for. Should you wish to dispute this, I will remind you of our agreement." Jökull's mouth sharpened into a menacing smile. "You remember what we discussed, don't you?"

Thorstein blanched.

Sunnëva glanced back and forth between them. Not sure what they were talking about. Did he mean his promise of protection for Ansa? He had threatened to take her father's hands if she was hurt.

"I never touched her."

"I believe *harm* was the word I used." Jökull used the tip of his scythe to lift Thorstein's chin. His eyes were two icy orbs glowing in the twilight. Her father's throat bobbed, sweat shining on his forehead. "Her emotional well-being was included in that."

"Take her," he blurted. "Take Ansa."

"As if you had a choice." Jökull turned to her. It took her a moment to realize he was silently asking for her verdict. If Sunnëva decided she wanted her father dead, he would do it. Instantly and swiftly.

At times, death is the kindest gift fate has to offer.

Perhaps she should have ordered his execution, if not for their suffering, then for his treachery. But she couldn't. No matter how cruel Thorstein was, they were still family. That earned her mercy this once, but any affection she had for her father ended tonight.

"Be grateful that I am leaving you with your life," Sunnëva told him. "I am taking Ansa away from you. She is in my care now. If you touch my sister again, I will bury my dagger in your gullet so deep you will taste nothing but steel and blood."

Thorstein's jaw clenched with indignation, but he bowed his head to her.

Jökull looked behind him. "Come. We are leaving."

Fenrin and Ansa had been watching from a distance. She held out a hand and her sister rushed forward to take it. Sunnëva covered Ansa with her cloak, then they left the village without looking back.

Jökull's riders were already mounted on their crystal horses, and Tally was seated with Aero on his.

Once they got Ansa in the carriage, the reins snapped, and they were on the road. Sunnëva caressed her sister's hair as tears rolled down her hollowed cheeks. Ansa silently cried until she fell asleep in her arms.

The soft moonlight danced along one side of Jökull's face, where he sat across from her. They observed each other for a few minutes as the land passed them by.

"Thank you," she murmured.

He nodded. The heavy silence proved he was leaving her to continue. May as well get it over with.

"When did you follow me?"

"I was always there." His eyes held hers. "I'm never far behind when it comes to you. Nor did I plan on leaving you out of my sight today."

That meant he had heard everything. Did he notice her hesitation when asked if she had discovered something? Jökull didn't look angry, but the space between them was muddled.

Cautious.

"You already knew, didn't you? About my father's plan."

"I am not a fool, Sunnëva. Thorstein has never been among those I deemed loyal. I suspected what he was after when he offered your hand," Jökull scoffed softly with a shrug. "And you weren't exactly subtle."

"You married me, nevertheless."

"I am all-powerful, remember? A little thorn can't harm me."

She shook her head at his light tone. "Don't tempt me."

His mouth edged on a smile that made hers grow. "Oh, but that's exactly what I intend to do."

"I cut you before."

"Yes. You certainly did." He canted his head as he observed her. "It's been a long time since another has drawn my blood."

Only because she had used his magic against him that day in the courtyard.

Sunnëva looked at her reflection in the carriage windows, finally seeing all the subtle differences in her features. She hadn't noticed at first because it was gradual. Beneath the crown of ice, her hair was a light shade of blonde, her irises more vibrantly blue than ever. She even seemed … beautiful.

She was turning into the Winter Queen.

Tonight, she had accepted that role.

With her sister safe beside her, Fenrin alive, and the land protected from the Shadow God, Sunnëva had stopped caring to know what Jökull's weakness was anymore.

Because she had run out of reasons to want her husband dead.

25

"Sunnëva? Where have you gone?"

She was pulled from her thoughts by her sister's voice. She blinked at Ansa. "Sorry, what?"

"It's your turn, my lady," Tally said beside her as she poured her another cup of tea. Steam swirled from the spout as she set the pot down on the outdoor table they were seated at.

Ren and Riona stood guard at the entryway of the courtyard. Fenrin leaped among the trees with Cael, both making a game out of trying to catch a crow. Other fae wandered the gardens, enjoying the rare clear skies and the warm sun.

"Oh." Sunnëva frowned at the game pieces set in front of them. Glass figurines of all creatures and chips of carved stone with symbols. But she had already forgotten the rules.

"Are you feeling all right?" Ansa asked across from her, her face softening with concern.

Her sister looked much improved in the three weeks since they had rescued her. Ansa's cheeks were filled and rosy, her complexion and hair much healthier. Happier, too. She had taken to their new environment with ease. The many creatures wandering the halls hardly frightened her. She was more curious than wary of Sunnëva's new world.

It was odd how much her life had changed.

Since knowing Jökull's magic would change her, it had been a pressing thought in the back of her mind. What would she change into? Did she want that? She wanted to ask him, but he hadn't been around lately. Aero had taken over her morning lessons, saying the King had left due to a report that arrived from his northern garrison.

A Skelling had been spotted flying near their territory lines.

Sunnëva was torn between worrying whether the Skellings were truly preparing to attack the Everfrost for more land, or if this was merely Jökull's excuse to avoid her.

Maybe she was overthinking it, but he had been distant since they had returned.

Ansa came to sit beside her. "Are you feeling sad because of today? I should have known playing a game wouldn't be enough to distract you."

"Today?" Sunnëva frowned.

Ansa's face fell. "It's the anniversary ... of Freya's death."

Gloom settled over her head. Gods, with everything that had happened, it slipped her mind.

Her eyes widened. That meant today was the lunar eclipse.

There was a sudden shout and a vicious snarl. Sunnëva whipped around to see Fenrin attacking Cael. He caught the griffin's wing in its jaws, and Cael screamed, clawing at the ground to get away.

"Fenrin!" Sunnëva ran to them.

Her brother spun around, but all she saw was a hungry warg. His eyes were flaming, no recognition in him at all. She retreated slowly. He snarled and lunged at her. Sunnëva rolled out of the way, his sharp teeth missing her by inches.

A burst of light blinded her as a portal opened into the courtyard. Jökull strode out in front of her, his black coat flaring around his legs. He conjured his scythe as Fenrin attacked, and he slashed him. The blow threw her brother across the courtyard.

"No, stop!" Sunnëva screamed. "What are you doing?"

Jökull didn't look at her. He leaped into the air, landing on Fenrin's back. Another portal opened beneath them, and they dropped through it.

"Sunnëva!" Ansa and Tally ran to her.

"What happened?" Sunnëva asked, staring at the spot they vanished. Her hands shook. Fenrin had tried to bite her.

"My Queen." Aero was there suddenly, helping her up. He must have come out of the first portal. "Are you all right?"

"Y-yes." She blinked up at him. "What happened to Fenrin? Why did he..."

The mage sighed grimly at his griffin. Cael screeched weakly, his bloodied wing hanging at an odd angle.

"Forgive me." Aero laid his glowing hands on the wound, and Cael settled as the magic took away his pain. "I was off my charts by one day," he told her. "The lunar eclipse will rise tonight. Unfortunately, it affects some of the fae and monsters, reverting them to their vile natures. Some more than most when the moon is linked to their power and weakness."

The moon was linked to Fenrin?

Gods, why had she not thought of that? The day she gave him the rose, there had been a full moon in the sky.

"But the moon didn't affect him last month," she said.

The mage nodded. "The eclipse awakened something in him. Well, I suppose this gives us another clue about his physiology. Tonight, he will need to remain in confinement. As will you, Tally, and Lady Ansa. The castle is no longer safe for humans. Not that it was in the first place. Please come with me." He motioned at four Castle Guards. "Take Cael to my workroom. Be careful."

"Yes, my lord."

As they took care of the griffin, Aero escorted her and the others promptly through the castle, with Ren and Riona guarding the rear. Now that Sunnëva was paying attention, she felt the danger in the air. She drew out her dagger as Ansa clutched her arm. Aero kept Tally close.

There were more creatures than usual swarming the halls. Their eyes reflected in the shadowy corners. Purple Essence blazed in Aero's hands as he commanded them to stay back. The creatures hissed, their claws curling.

They made it to her chambers without confrontation. Ren and Riona took their posts at the door inside.

"Please, *stay* here." Aero looked only at her. None of the others were inclined to disobey him. "Once the moon is shrouded, we are under threat of Rumiel making an appearance."

Of course. Tonight was perfect for him to wreak havoc. None of their light spells would work. That added another thing to her list of concerns.

"Nothing will detain the demons from coming out tonight," Aero continued. "It's my responsibility to maintain the wards on the castle while Garr remains on watch from the battlements. The Queen's Guard will be on duty, with more posted outside your door, should anyone decide to come hunting."

Sunnëva swallowed. Her pulse was climbing.

During the eclipse, the clans always poured a ring of salt around the villages to deter demons and monsters. Now she understood the dire extent of it all.

"And Jökull? Why hasn't he come to speak to me about this?"

Aero cleared his throat, looking away. "His Majesty is preoccupied. It's a demanding day for him most of all." He motioned behind her. "However, the King assumed you would not like to sit here while others protected you, so he made the necessary arrangements."

On the bed, full armor was laid out for her. Chain mail, chest plate, pauldrons, and gauntlets secured with hidden Nightstone blades. Weapons of every kind: Moonstone, iron, and steel daggers. Her sword was beside it, along with a quiver of Nightstone arrows. The room had already been lined with salt. Her table had also been set with a small feast to keep them fed through the night.

Sunnëva exhaled. "He assumed correctly. Thank you."

Aero nodded and turned to Tally. "You will stay here with—"

"No." Tally clutched his sleeve. "I'm coming with you."

"Tal, you can't be out there."

Her eyes welled, and she shook her head.

Aero's expression softened with a sigh. "I suppose now would be a good time to give this to you." From his robes, he drew out a dark blue pouch made of velvet and handed it to her. She blinked at it in surprise and reached in to pull out a medallion. It was made of silver, encrusted with diamonds. In the center rested an indecent Moonstone.

Tally gaped at him. "This is too fine for the likes of me."

"I made it specifically for you." Aero slipped it over her head, and it rested over her heart. They gazed at each other for a moment, then he cleared his throat and reached into his robe again. "This is for you, Lady Ansa." He handed her a Tanzstone crystal. It was a pretty light blue, about three inches long, and shaped into an ice drop. "It's spelled to shield you. To use it, hold it, and speak the word *scutum*."

"Thank you, Lord Aero." Ansa clutched the crystal to her chest.

He nodded, but the mage hesitated to leave.

Sunnëva straightened her shoulders. "We will be fine. Go protect the castle."

Aero and Tally bowed, then they walked out together. He slipped his fingers through hers, holding her hand with a familiarity that surprised Sunnëva, but only a little. He pulled Tally protectively to him again before the door closed.

Sunnëva changed out of her dress into trousers and a leather corset over her tunic. Then she strapped on her armor.

"Will Fenrin be safe?" Ansa asked as she helped her buckle it into place. "He's locked up. What if something tries to attack him, and he can't get away?"

That was one of her worries, too. She had to trust he would be all right.

Sunnëva sheathed the last of the knives in her thigh holster and buckled on her scabbard. "He should be secure in the dungeons."

It was still early afternoon, so there wasn't much to do but wait.

"Go on and eat something," Sunnëva told them. "It's going to be a long night."

Ren and Riona came forward to serve themselves.

Sunnëva brought her sister a plate to the bed and sat next to her. As they ate, she studied the sun's position in the sky.

"Who is Rumiel?" Ansa asked.

Sunnëva stiffened. "No one."

The subject of Rune was still a sore spot.

"I saw your face when Aero mentioned him." Her sister picked apart a roll of bread. "So I know that isn't true. Why don't you talk to me anymore?"

She frowned at her. "What do you mean?"

Ansa ducked her head. "Since we arrived, you have been quiet and distracted. I can see there is a lot on your mind, but you don't confide in me like you used to. Is it ... because of the King?"

Ren exchanged a look with Riona, and they got to their feet. "We will stand guard outside, my lady."

They promptly left without waiting for her response. He was her favorite Knight. Pleasant and perceptive.

Ansa searched her face. "What's wrong?"

Sunnëva sighed. "Nothing's wrong. I am merely..."

Having to explain that she had been sleeping with the God of Shadows, and fell for all of his lies as he used her, was humiliating. Then she would need to mention she aligned herself with the God of Death to defeat the ex-lover she had come to avenge in the first place. Yet now she was fighting confusing feelings for him, too.

All of it left her mind reeling.

"I only caught part of what Father said to you in the village," Ansa said. "But I heard you say you weren't going to kill the King anymore. Is it ... because you're in love with him?"

A piece of bread lodged in Sunnëva's throat. She coughed, ignoring her flush. "Don't be ridiculous."

"Then are you going to kill him?"

She furrowed her brow at the question. "He saved you, Ansa."

Her sister frowned. "No, *you* did that. If it wasn't for you, he wouldn't care. I wonder if you have forgotten what kind of King he is. The clans have suffered under his rule. You have lived it. But I wonder if..." Ansa pursed her mouth and looked away. "I wonder if you have chosen to ignore that while living in this lavish castle."

A shocked exhale slipped out of Sunnëva's lips. She stood, taking a step back. "I can't believe you said that to me."

"I feel like you have forgotten about us."

"What do you mean?"

"Sunnëva, you forgot Freya died today five years ago!" Ansa snapped. Her expression contorted, and the tears gathered on her lashes.

She shook her head. "That's not fair, and you know it."

"The entire time we were apart, I gladly endured everything Father did to me because I thought you were here trying to save us from the King. Only to realize you had changed your mind. His magic is changing you. Gyda said that is happening because you are accepting him. I see how well you fit in with the others. How they bow to you. You're protected here. Provided for. Why would you want to give that up?"

Sunnëva faced the hearth. She waited until the lump in her throat dissolved before she spoke. "My whole life, there was no one to protect me, Ansa. But you have always had me. I would face any monster, man, or beast for you without a second thought." She turned around. "You're right. I did change my mind about Jökull for reasons I don't need to justify. But I have always cared about you and our people. When I came here, I was ready to die whether I succeeded or not. Don't you dare insinuate I'm a traitor."

She inhaled a shaky breath and rubbed her face, feeling the scar on her temple. "The day we lost Freya, it dragged me down into the darkness and it shredded me apart. But I picked myself up and crawled out of that pit so I could make sure it *never* happened to you." Her throat constricted, emotion catching in her voice. "I have relieved that moment in my nightmares every day since ... until I came here."

They stopped coming the night she slept in Jökull's arms. It was when she finally believed what he declared in the courtyard. That he wouldn't allow anything to hurt her.

Sunnëva blinked away the sting in her eyes. "I didn't have someone there for me then, but I do now. I forgot what today was because I finally feel *safe*. Is that wrong? Would you begrudge me that?"

Ansa covered her mouth with a sob, shaking her head.

Sunnëva wrapped her arms around her. "I was there when you were pulled out of Mother's belly. You were born unto a hardened father with a hollow heart, but I decided you would have more than me. I made sure to give you all the love that I never had. You and Fenrin are what I live for. I will never forget about either of you."

Ansa balled up into her like she used to when she was a child. "I'm sorry."

She brushed her hair aside. "I think that was the first time you yelled at me. Where is this coming from?"

"I think ... when I saw all the ways you've changed ... I felt left behind. You *belong*. I wish I had that, too."

Sunnëva sighed. "No matter what, you will always belong here." She tapped her heart.

Ansa laughed wetly. "Liar. You pushed me aside for that husband of yours."

She blushed. "I don't know what you're talking about."

"Yes, you do, and you're going to tell me all about him, right? Because I must know what he did to change your mind about sticking your dagger down his gullet."

At that, Sunnëva smiled and told her everything.

26

When the day slipped into night, the sounds of the castle grew frightening. Ansa stayed on the bed with the blankets wrapped around her. Sunnëva stood by the balcony doors to watch the sky. The moon's energy hummed against her being. Wispy clouds veiled the dark sky for a moment before it began to change color. A ghostly crimson hue gradually crawled over the full moon's surface until it was as vivid as blood.

Howls broke outside below, and gargoyles snarled on the roof. The entire castle came alive with the beasts within, and her pulse drummed with dread. One night. They had to survive only one night.

Ansa looked at her frightfully.

Sunnëva nodded. "It's all right—"

"Stay back!" Ren ordered outside her door.

"This is the Queen's hall!" Riona shouted. "You cannot—"

The sounds of a fight broke out in the hall with the clash of swords, the hiss of a beast, and cries of pain. Sunnëva put herself between the bed and the door. Drawing her sword, she braced her legs. A body hit the frame so hard, the salt ward broke, and she cursed. Blood began leaking out from under the door.

"Activate your crystal, Ansa," Sunnëva said. "More lives will end tonight. Follow my instructions, and it will not be yours."

"But what about you?"

"Do it!"

Ansa clutched the crystal in her shaking hands. "*Scutum!*"

Golden light flared and formed around her in a glowing dome, encasing her inside. Then everything outside of the hall fell deathly silent. Sunnëva's heart pounded loudly in her skull. Taking a moment to calm her breathing first, she inched toward the door. She pressed her ear against it, listening. Nothing. Did it leave?

Sunnëva glanced at her ring. If she was in danger, Jökull would have come.

Her shaking hand reached for the handle, and it creaked as she slowly pulled it open. The hallway was bathed red. Bodies were strewn everywhere. Some were crushed, their limbs and bodies twisted, like they'd been snapped in half. Riona lay at her feet, her empty eyes staring at the ground. All of her guards were dead, their blood and entrails painting the hall.

Ren was seated against the wall, his bleeding head lolled against his chest. One of his beautiful wings floated in a puddle of blood on the floor.

"Ren!" Sunnëva leaped over bodies to get to him. She kneeled beside him and shook him.

"Rio..." He moaned, his lashes flickering. "She ... she..."

"She's gone, Ren. I'm so sorry."

His brow pinched with pain before his eyes rolled shut, and he slumped over. She needed to find help.

Sunnëva grabbed Ren's legs and dragged his heavy body into her room.

"Gods." Ansa leaped up from the bed, rushing to them. "What happened?"

"Something attacked them," Sunnëva grunted, heaving him to the rug by the fireplace. "All the guards are down. I need to inform Aero. Stay here."

"What? Alone?"

"I can't take you out there." Sunnëva dumped more salt across the threshold. "Whatever killed them is still wandering the halls." She handed her a dagger. "Lock the door behind me and keep your crystal activated. Nothing can get past it. I will be right back."

After Sunnëva shut the door behind her, she waited until the sound of the lock fell into place before leaving. Keeping her sword out, she listened carefully to the sounds of the castle. She ducked behind pillars whenever a form lumbered past. Growls, snarls, and faint screams rose from every corner.

Her heart hammered with her labored breaths. Sunnëva forced herself to keep calm. Once she reached the high alcove overlooking the throne room, her stomach roiled with the scene below. It was full of monsters of every kind, and they were feasting. On humans. On each other. The ice was drenched in red.

The Castle Guards weren't around to maintain control. They probably hiding, too.

A deep, feral growl rumbled behind her. Sunnëva whipped around to see a dear-horned wendigo coming her way. But in the next second, its head was ripped off. It landed with a splat across the hall.

Rune walked by as the body dropped, licking the dark blood from his talons. "I love it when this night comes around."

Her stomach rolled, and she stumbled away with a sharp breath.

"What? Last I checked, you liked that I was ruthless." Rune stopped by the banister and looked down below, watching the carnage ensue like it was a play for his entertainment. Shadows spiraled around his silhouette.

"How do you keep coming in here?" Sunnëva said. "I wasn't thinking about you. Jökull's magic should have kept you out."

"I have my ways." Rune shrugged. His tattoos writhed up around his neck, glowing a faint red. "I thought you would be happier to see me, given I saved your life. Odd to find you so *unprotected*." His garnet eyes rose to hers with a sly turn of his mouth.

Did he know her Queen's Guard was dead?

Rune leaned against the balustrade with his elbows casually supporting him. He was dressed in all black, his godly form on display. Now that the truth was out, Rune didn't bother to hide himself any longer.

Sunnëva reached for her Moonstone dagger, but the moon wasn't on her side tonight. She drew out her Nightstone dagger instead.

Rune frowned. "That won't work on me, sweetling."

With a flick of his finger, shadows knocked away her sword and dagger.

She gritted her teeth. "If you came to take me away…"

"Not tonight." He played with a tangle of shadows in his palm. "Unless that is what you desire. We can go now. No one will stop you."

Sunnëva eyed him suspiciously. Other than his appearance, he seemed like her old Rune. Relaxed, casual. As if they were having one of their idle conversations outside of the village. Completely the opposite, as he had been in the courtyard around Jökull.

"Why have you come?"

"Perhaps I came merely to make sure you would be all right." Rune searched her face and his expression softened. He knew what this day meant for her.

What it meant for both of them.

It made her eyes sting, and Sunnëva curled her lip.

"Why do you look at me that way?" Rune asked. "Stop it."

"Look at you like what?"

"Like I disgust you."

Maybe another might have found him frightening, but it wasn't his appearance that disturbed her. It was the lie their entire relationship was founded on. He played with her heart, and she felt so stupid for it.

He was not her Rune. Not anymore.

"You do." Her vision welled. "You disgust me."

His brow furrowed, and he sighed. He was quiet before saying, "It wasn't all lies, Sunnëva."

She wanted so badly to believe him. The time they shared together had been good. Rune saved her in more ways that she could ever explain. It had been so easy to fall in love with the part of him she knew. But those memories were now tainted by the truth.

"You used me. That will never change."

"And did you not use me, too?" Rune asked softly as he drew closer. "You wanted to be touched and desired. Loved." His fingers caressed her cheek, leaving little smoke trails behind. "That is how we began until it grew into something more."

He cupped the back of her head and pulled her mouth to his. But instead of sweet, he kissed her dominatingly, trying to reclaim something he once had. His kisses used to spark a fire in her, but there was none now.

This didn't feel like love. It felt like hate.

But not for her.

Sunnëva bit Rune's lip, and he tore away with a snarl, his pupils dilating wide. She could taste the divinity of his blood on her tongue.

He gave her a heated chuckle and wiped the red smudge from his lip. "Well, if I knew you liked it rough..."

"You hate him," she blurted.

Rune's smile fell away.

"Why?"

His eyes glowed with ire, and he looked away. Something crossed Rune's face. Something dark and cold that was shadowed by despair.

"What has he done to make you want him dead?" Sunnëva asked faintly.

"Why does it matter?" He stuck his hands in his pockets, leaning against the balustrade again. "Several weeks ago, you wanted the same."

"I want to know, Rune. I can't trust you when I don't know the whole story."

He sighed and looked at her. "Jökull explained why he needs you."

"He needs my help to open his Gate."

"No, Sunnëva. You are the *only one* who can open his Gate. Because you're his bride. Why do you think mine hasn't opened?"

Her mouth parted in a shallow gasp.

All the Gods had a bride, which meant so did Rune. Sunnëva waited for jealousy to sprout, maybe some possessiveness to surge over her once lover, but there was only dismay—for *him*.

She held her breath. "Where is she? Have you found her?"

Shadows flickered in his gaze before it was hidden by rage. "My bride is gone, and so is any kinship I had with him." He held out his clawed hand. "The only one I care for now is you."

Maybe if Rune had told her the truth of who he was from the beginning, or revealed himself on the first night she came here, she might have gone with him.

It didn't matter that he looked like a demon.

Rune was still fiercely handsome, and she knew he wouldn't harm her. Looking at him now in his full power, his body corded with muscle, he could have easily crushed her bones, slash her to ribbons with his talons or his magic. Yet when he held her, whenever he took her wildly in the woods, he had always been gentle. She realized now he had been holding monumental control over his strength.

He did care for her, but that didn't change the purpose of his scheme. Something happened that caused Rune to lose his bride, and he blamed Jökull for it.

What better revenge than to take away his bride, too?

"If I go with you, what will you do?" she asked.

His expression hardened, and his eyes flamed. *"Rule."*

His mind connected with hers for a moment, and Sunnëva saw the world draped in darkness and fire.

"I can't go," she whispered.

"I can easily cut through his wards."

Sunnëva shook her head and changed her answer. "I don't want to go with you, Rune."

His jaw clenched. "You don't love him."

Her heart dipped, and she glared. "I'm his wife."

"Already so *loyal*," Rune gritted out, his voice harsh. Embers wove through the black smoke spiraling at his feet. "Yet where is your husband now, Su? Have you asked yourself what Jökull is doing at this moment? Have you not wondered why he won't see you?"

Her pulse raced as her stomach twisted. Sunnëva had wondered. A part of her suspected why, but she didn't want to consider it.

"He is the God of *Death*." Rune grinned at the poor lives being ravaged below, giving her a glimpse of his fangs. An awful shudder crept down her spine. "And the lunar eclipse brings out the depravity in us all."

Sunnëva backed away from Rune, watching him until she reached the hallway. Then she spun around and sprinted away. His laughter echoed through the halls in her wake. She didn't stop until she reached Jökull's chambers. Swallowing, she took a moment to catch her breath, working the nerve to dare reach for the door handle. Before she could talk herself out of it, Sunnëva pushed it open and went inside.

Her heart stopped when she saw him.

Jökull stood on his balcony with his clawed hands held out to the sky, his long white hair blowing in the wind. His ice wings arched behind him. Every part of his body was completely covered in transparent feathers. They grew on the edges of his cheeks and neck, along his arms, down his back, and around his torso, continuing down his legs to his clawed feet. His skin was the dark of night, glittering with stars. Frost coated his cheekbones and beneath his vivid white eyes, half his face encased in a skull.

Show her your true face...

Yet his beastly form wasn't what horrified her. It was the hundreds of souls soaring in on a constant wave, wailing. Cold horror sank into her stomach. She felt their pain and fear. Each one helplessly plunged into him, making his tattoos pulse blue.

Jökull consumed them all.

But then suddenly their pain faded and in its place was ... peace.

He turned and fixed his glowing eyes on her. She stumbled back with a gasp. There was no recognition in his blank face, and she instinctively knew she shouldn't be here.

Sunnëva spun around and ran for the door, but a force crashed into her. It tossed her across the room and she landed on the bed with Jökull on top of her. He pinned her wrists above her head, and his mouth crashed into hers. It was such an invading kiss, Sunnëva found herself sinking into it with fear and excitement tangling all through her being. His hips ground into her with a feral sound she had never heard from him before. His power cleaved into her, and he was swimming through her very soul.

His claws seemed to sink into her being as he grasped her possessively. He devoured her mouth in a consuming kiss. His icy tongue slid past her lips, forcing his way in. She squirmed, feeling his erection grinding against her center. That ignited him further. He pulled at her armor and the metal screeched as it shredded in his claws like paper. Sunnëva's heart hammered, and she tried to push against his feathered chest, but it was like trying to move a mountain.

He had her restrained under him, but heat pooled between her legs. She whimpered and clung to him, striving for friction. His power's hold, the touch of his kiss, tugged at her being, diving into it. But then her body glowed as her soul came to the surface, and she had a horrid thought.

He's going to peel it out.

Sunnëva screamed against his mouth. Conjuring a dagger made of ice, she drove it into his thigh.

Jökull jerked back. He sat on his heels, staring at the icy hilt sticking out of him in confusion. Slowly, he came to and stared at her, his mouth glistening. He noticed their positions and her shredded armor.

"Sunnëva..." Jökull lifted a hand, and she recoiled. Seeing that, he quickly moved off her, backing away from the bed. "I..." His chest heaved with wild breaths, his eyes wide and devastated. "Get out..."

She stared at him. "What?"

"GET OUT!" Jökull roared so loud the castle shook.

The harsh words were a blow against her chest.

Sunnëva scrambled off the bed and bolted out of the room. She sprinted away, so many emotions bombarding her at once. Above all, she felt like an idiot. She didn't belong here.

Staying would be the end of her.

Sunnëva ran and ran until she came to her room and banged on the door. A yelp responded from the other side. "Ansa, let me in!"

The latch lifted a second later, and Sunnëva rushed inside, locking the door behind her. Ren was still unconscious, but Ansa had bandaged his head and covered him with a blanket.

"Put on your boots and gloves. We're leaving." Sunnëva yanked off her useless chest plate and traded it for leather armor.

"What? Why? What happened?"

"We have to go, Ansa. Hurry." After throwing on a furred cloak, she pulled out a bag next and started stuffing clothes in it. Her heart sped wildly, feeling as if Jökull or something else would come for them any second.

"But what about Fenrin and Ren?" her sister said anxiously. "We can't leave them here."

Sunnëva threw a second cloak at Ansa and wrapped food in a cloth before stuffing it into another bag. "Once they let him out, Fen will find us. Aero will find Ren in the morning."

Ansa took her arms. "What happened, Sunnëva? You're scaring me."

"I will tell you later. But we have to leave. *Now!*"

Throwing open the balcony doors, Sunnëva rapidly tied a line of rope to the balustrade and motioned for Ansa to come. She spared one last glance at the castle, then yanked off her ring and threw it into the bedroom. It clattered to the stone floors and rolled away.

Ansa looked at her questioningly, but she ignored it.

"Hurry. And don't look down," Sunnëva warned. "I'll go first."

She climbed over the balustrade, and her feet caught against the stone. They were several floors up high. Her heart raced, and she forced herself to breathe as she scaled down the side of the castle. Ansa started coming down next. Howls were loud in the night, the blood moon gleaming in the sky. She prayed no one would spot them and that they wouldn't fall to their deaths.

Maybe it was her fear or desperation to escape, but soon her boots landed in the courtyard. She led her sister to a section secluded by shrubs and pushed them aside to reveal the hole in the wall. Sunnёva went in and helped Ansa climb through.

They tightly held hands and ran into the night. Her heart jolted when a horn blared into the sky.

The Castle Guard had spotted them.

"Don't look back," Sunnёva said. "Keep running!"

Jökull's voice echoed over the land, bellowing her name. The misery in his cry made her eyes water. But she couldn't go back.

The calls of a hunt went up from the castle battlements, and the ground rumbled with the chase of riders. Ansa tripped, nearly taking her down.

Sunnёva yanked her up. "Run, Ansa! Run!"

The sky rumbled with thunder, and storm clouds appeared out of nowhere. The flutter of wings soared overhead, and a shadow passed over the moon. Oh, Gods, he caught up to them.

They dashed across the landscape for the rise to the top of the hill. But they never got a chance to climb down the other end. The powerful gust of wings nearly knocked them over. Sunnёva looked up at the enormous bird-like creature diving for them. It was too fast and too dark to see, but she knew one thing with an ice-cold certainty.

Whatever that creature was, it wasn't Jökull.

Sunnёva and Ansa screamed as talons snatched them off the ground and hauled them into the night.

27

The nightmare returned. For nothing kept her safe anymore. Yet there were no screams this time. No pain. Sunnëva only felt so cold. She curled into a ball as she waited for those hands. Pleaded for them to come. As soon as they scooped her up, she sagged against him and silently wept. They carried her away from the darkness. Away from the blood.

Simply away.

Sunnëva woke to the sound of soft voices. She blinked through her blurry vision, finding herself lying face down on the icy stone ground. Searching for Ansa, she spotted her kneeling by the entrance of a cave. Crouched in front of her was a young man in a long, dark brown cloak. He said something that made Ansa quietly laugh.

Sunnëva sat up, realizing the one her sister spoke to wasn't a man at all. Not a *human* one. She had mistaken a cloak for his very large wings.

"Ansa, get away from him!"

"Oh, you're awake," Ansa said happily and went to her. "It's all right. Kerro won't hurt you."

Sunnëva pushed her sister behind her and reached for a knife, but they were missing from the scabbard on her hip.

Kerro, or whatever he was, rose to his full height. He was *tall*. At least eight feet. He had handsome angular features and tawny skin, but that was where his human likeness ended. Dark brown feathers grew from his head and went down the back of it like hair. More layered the edge of his bare chest and the outside of his arms, attached to his wings. He wore leather pants with the woven sides bare, so more feathers poked through. He wore no other clothing besides a fur pelt on his broad shoulders and a necklace of black claws and beads. A baldric made of woven material crossed his left shoulder to his waist with a curved knife strapped to it. Though it may not have been needed when he had wickedly sharp talons.

Sunnëva was struck by how much he reminded her of Jökull.

Kerro cocked his head curiously and blinked his strange eyes at her. They were light gray, the black pupil wide and large.

Like a bird.

Even without all the feathers, it was clear he was strong. He was pure muscle. The strength was needed to walk around with those wings. They were so big they dragged on the floor.

Kerro watched her warily, his talons curling. He glanced at Ansa as if he wanted to snatch her away.

His clawed feet moved closer and Sunnëva shouted, "Stay away!"

Kerro hissed. "You do not command me, woman."

Sunnëva's mouth fell open at the sound of his gravelly voice. She hadn't expected him to speak so clearly.

"It's all right, Kerro." Ansa went to him and patted his large forearm, much to Sunnëva's shock. "My sister is only a little startled. But you aren't going to hurt her, right? Because we are friends."

Ansa looked so tiny next to him, barely reaching his chest. She smiled up at Kerro sweetly, and that seemed to put him at ease. Now that she was at his side, Kerro crouched again and extended a wing around her, shielding her from the wind blowing into the cave.

Kerro smiled, holding out his lethal hand to her. Ansa placed her small palm in it. "Friends," he echoed in a soft rumble.

He tried to lean toward her, but Ansa lightly smacked his cheek and pointed at him. "No. I said no kiss."

Kerro gave her a roguish smile.

Sunnëva gawked at them. How long had she been unconscious? Was she even awake?

"Ansa..." Sunnëva looked past them finally to the land beyond the cave. There was only snow for miles. She inched closer, giving Kerro a wide berth to look outside. They ... they were on the side of a mountain. "How did we get here? Where are we?"

Kerro stood, startling her into backing away. "This is the Frost Lands. My father's territory. He wanted you brought here."

"What?" Sunnëva shook her head, still not understanding. "Why? Who are you people?"

Ansa giggled. "Can't you tell? He's a Skelling."

Once Sunnëva stopped gawking, Kerro leaped out of the cave and shifted midair into the bird they had seen last night. His black beak was curved and sharp, his dark brown feathers catching the light. He resembled a hawk, but he was enormous. Perhaps even bigger than Jökull.

The bird cawed at them and flattened himself on the side of the mountain.

"I think he wants us to go with him," Ansa said.

She took a step, but Sunnëva grabbed her arm. "What are you doing? Why are you so at ease with him?"

Ansa looked at Kerro thoughtfully and shrugged. "I don't feel unsafe around him. I don't think he means any harm."

"We're clearly hostages. The Skellings are Jökull's enemy, remember?"

Ansa searched her face. "And you're worried that he may come looking for you."

Sunnëva sighed, realizing she *was* worried about that. The Skellings were dangerous to him somehow, but Jökull couldn't find her without the Moonstone ring. Still, she left one bird to fall into the talons of another.

"Well, they must have brought us here for something," Ansa said. "Let's go find out."

Sunnëva helped her out of the cave, and they climbed up Kerro's wing onto his back. Once they were seated, he took off and flew them across the frozen land. Sunnëva held Ansa close, trying to shield her from the bitter cold. Soon, they came upon a colossal Azure Tree with lush blue leaves the color of sapphires. He turned sharply and flew into a gap in the leaves. Huts made of woven sticks hung from the branches like raindrops.

Nests.

Curious feathered faces peered at them as they flew by. They were like Kerro, with winged arms, and feathers in all shades of dark gray to brown, some patterned with stripes. Some of the branches coiled around the tree like a spiraling bridge, with rows and rows of homes. The thick leaves did well to keep out most of the wind.

Kerro landed in the center of the tree where more Skellings waited. Hundreds of bird-like beings blinked down at Sunnëva from within the canopy.

She picked out the Chief by his presence alone.

He was older than the others, wearing a dark cloak and eyes bright yellow. He was seated on a chair of woven sticks and leaves, lined with fur pelts. It rested on a thick branch above them like a dais. His chest was adorned with a necklace of long black talons. Beside him stood a pretty female Skelling with white feathers tipped blue.

Once Sunnëva and Ansa climbed off him, Kerro shifted to his other form and stepped back a few paces, but remained close to her sister.

"Welcome," said the elder. "I am Kyrr, Tribe Chief of the Skelling." He arched an eyebrow at Kerro. "We expected one bride, son. Yet you have brought two."

Kerro glowered at the titters falling from the branches. "They were attached, Father. Running together across the Death God's lands." He spat on the ground, and so did all the Skellings. "It was too dark to tell them apart. I had to bring both."

Kyrr studied them. "Which one is Sunnëva?"

She took a breath and stepped forward. "I am."

Kerro made a sound of distaste, and the chief grunted.

"Well, Lady Sunnëva, your hand was promised to my son. At least, that was the agreement I had with Earl Thorstein when he sent word of desiring to form an alliance. I agreed, but he did not send you. I suppose it was to honor our traditions, for in our tribe, the males capture their mates. Which is why I had Kerro bring you here himself. I trust he has been a gentleman."

"Yes ... he has been cordial," Sunnëva said, eyeing him. "But I think there has been a misunder—"

"I don't want to mate with her," Kerro blurted. "I have chosen another."

"Oh?" His father raised his eyebrows.

Kerro wrapped a large wing around Ansa. "She attacked me. Here." He pointed a sharp claw at the red mark above his navel. "She is a little thing, but fierce and beautiful. I will mate with her."

Ansa turned bright red. "I told you I was sorry. And don't say that word, please?" She cringed sheepishly at Sunnëva and whispered. "Once we landed, I tried to stab him with your knife when he got close. Apparently, attempting to kill a male who has captured them is how females choose their mates here."

No wonder he was so taken with her. Having an inclination toward murderous women reminded her of another beast.

"There will be no mating," Sunnëva announced aloud. "My sister is under my care, and I don't intend to marry her off. Nor am *I* available to be wed. I have a husband."

It was nice to say it, but she didn't know if it was true anymore after leaving him like that. Her heart tumbled into her stomach.

The Skellings fluttered their wings, making rough chirping sounds. They sounded displeased by her refusal. Kerro pulled Ansa closer to him.

Sunnëva frowned. "My father should have told you I was married to another instead. I am sorry to disappoint you, Chief Kyrr, and for wasting your time. I know we have only arrived, but I would like to go home, please."

"Home." He canted his head like a bird and his pupils narrowed. "To your mate, I assume."

She tensed.

"What were you doing in Jökull's territory on such a dangerous night?"

Sunnëva worked to keep her expression neutral. "I should not have been there," she said carefully. "I was attempting to return to my clan."

"And yet, why would a human be there in the first place when the castle is full of savage beasts?" Kyrr pressed. A quietness settled over the Skellings, and she sensed the tension rise. "Do you serve the God of Death, Lady Sunnëva? Or are you married to him?"

She froze under the question. This could only go one of two ways. If she answered, they would either use her or let her go out of fear. She could lie and try to talk herself out of this, but that put her sister at risk.

Sunnëva chose to gamble.

"Yes," she said, straightening her shoulders. "I am the Winter Queen."

The Skellings hissed at her, baring their teeth.

"I see." Kyrr's expression settled on indifference. "I was unaware he was capable of such a thing, as cruel as he is. Did you know he banished us here, forcing us to try to survive in such horrid conditions not meant for my kind?"

"No..."

"And did you know for the past twenty years, we have been requesting for him to extend our territory past the mountain so we may have a modicum of reprieve from the harsh winters? It is painful for us to fly when our wings are half-frozen. We fly less and less and our younglings are not able to learn or some are born with their wings deformed. *Did you know?*"

She started to shake her head, but stopped because it wasn't fully true. "I ... I heard there was a request."

"And?"

She wrung her hands, not able to make herself lie.

Kyrr scoffed. "He has denied us time and again. I think it is time we *stop* asking."

Her blood ran cold at his meaning. He was angry, but collected. He had the aura of someone who knew he had the advantage.

Jökull's weakness.

"Once I return, I will speak to him about your conditions," she said. "I will make him see reason."

The Tribe Chief laughed, and it sounded bitter. "Reason? These are the depths of your husband's reason." Kyrr let his cloak fall. His wings were sheared from his arms, leaving only stems of tattered feathers. And his hands ... they had been cut off at the wrist, left to heal into stumps. "Perhaps I should send Jökull your hands in a pretty box to persuade him. And if that doesn't work, your legs next."

She backed away. "What—"

The Skelling guards closing in on her seized her arms before she could run.

"Sunnëva!" Ansa tried to go to her, but Kerro grabbed her.

Sunnëva's mind spun, failing to devise a plan of escape. She cursed herself for leaving her ring. Now she had no magic to defend herself.

"Chief Kyrr, please," Sunnëva said, trying to remain calm. "You know the King, therefore you know you shouldn't do this."

Kyrr didn't look concerned.

"Do you know why he took my hands?" He frowned down at his stumps. "Jökull never intended to give me the means to take his life. My talons were the only thing that could cut him, you see. An unforeseen fruition by fate when he made me with a drop of his blood and a handful of ice feathers."

She sucked in a breath. Jökull made him?

That's why they looked like him.

"While I had the power to turn others into Skellings, they didn't have my poisonous talons. He thought taking my hands would be enough." Kyrr looked at his son. "Yet he did not consider others could be *born* with that gift."

Then Sunnëva noticed the Skellings had white claws, but Kerro's were black. Exactly like Jökull's. She recalled their first night together when he had cut his throat with his talons.

The Chief and his son wore a necklace of those deadly claws. Their spears and daggers were bladed with the same.

They had made weapons to fight him.

"Yes," Kyrr said. "I think this world is finished being ruled by a cruel God who cares for no one but himself."

He was too angry to listen. Not after what they endured.

Sunnëva clenched her shaking hands. She didn't know where to run, but to the one she left. She squeezed her eyes shut, wishing with all of her might to be with that infuriating beast now.

"This does not have to end in bloodshed," she said. "Please, let us go. If you hurt me, he will come here and kill you all."

"It's far too late for that."

Her heart thrummed at the sound of that voice.

A portal flared open behind her, and Jökull stepped through with a whirl of frost and a burst of blue magic. But Sunnëva's relief at seeing him quickly vanished. He looked furious. A force of blue magic tore away the Skellings holding her back.

"How dare you take my wife!" Jökull thundered.

245

A tempest of frost and wind spiraled in the air, tossing the Skellings. They screeched and flew for cover, some thrown against the branches violently. The force knocked Sunnëva to the ground. No, he was truly going to kill them.

Kyrr was shocked to see him, and he searched wildly among the chaos, shouting for Kerro.

"Jökull, stop!" she shouted at him.

He ignored her and tossed out lances of ice that pierced the branches and Skelling wings.

Behind him, Kerro stood from where he fell with Ansa and ran at him, raising his clawed hand.

Sunnëva threw herself in the way, and Kerro's talons ripped into her shoulder. She fell at Jökull's feet. Her heart raced so hard, she hardly felt the pain.

His icy eyes blazed. He snatched Kerro's neck and his hand glowed as he began to rip the soul out of him.

"Not my son!" Kyrr cried.

That revelation startled Jökull. His head whipped around to the Chief, halting his attack.

That one second gave Kerro an opening, and he drove his talons into Jökull's stomach. He jerked and looked down at himself.

Sunnëva cried out.

Jökull blinked in a daze at Kyrr as blood leaked from his mouth. All of his magic vanished from the air, his scythe dissolving away.

"I suppose this means the prophecy came true after all, master," Kyrr said grimly.

Kerro jerked his talons out of him, and blood sprayed out. He stepped away, forcing Ansa behind him.

"Jökull." Sunnëva supported him against her.

"I need to get to the castle," he rasped, his complexion quickly losing color.

"The portal."

"I can't—" Jökull grunted in pain and stumbled.

Skellings were all watching them, curling their claws.

"We need to go." Sunnëva looked around for her sister. "Ansa!"

But Jökull yanked her with him and tossed her off the Azure Tree. Sunnëva's scream cut off when she landed on the Ice Phoenix's back. He flew away from the tree, speeding across the landscape.

"Wait! My sister!" Sunnëva shouted above the roaring wind. "We have to go back!"

He didn't listen. His wings worked hard to climb the air. Thunder boomed, dark clouds spanning overhead. The whip of a rainstorm knocked into them violently. This was Skelling magic.

Sunnëva couldn't see a thing. "Jökull!" she called, frightened.

Without warning, a spear ruptured through his wing.

The Ice Phoenix's screech pierced the sky. They nosedived into the clouds. The wind whipped away the scream from her mouth. Sunnëva buried her face in the icy feathers, hanging on for dear life. They hit the ground, and the collision threw her into the snow, knocking the breath out of her lungs. The Ice Phoenix collapsed beside her.

Sunnëva's entire body ached, and her shoulder throbbed. So much blood leaked from her wound, but nothing seemed broken. Her vision keeled when she forced herself off the ground and stumbled to the phoenix on shaking legs. The spear was still in his wing.

Taking the shaft, she worked on pulling it free from the muscle. She finally got it out and tossed it aside. The phoenix shifted, leaving Jökull unconscious in the snow. Red spilled endlessly from his arm. She'd never seen him like this, so near death.

Her fault. Her fault...

She ignored the incoming Skellings flying down as she dropped to her knees beside him.

"Jökull?" Sunnëva took his face in her trembling hands. "Jökull, wake up," she begged. Her mind fogged, and weakness overcame her, leaving her to slump against him. At his still silence, her vision welled. "Wake up, you stupid oaf. You're supposed to be an all-powerful God." She hugged him and closed her wet eyes. "Please ... please wake up..."

28

Rattling chains and growling curses pulled Sunnëva to consciousness. She sat up and blinked blearily at their surroundings. The dark chamber was damp and smelled like turned-up dirt. A soft blue light glowed above her head like stars. But it wasn't the night sky. There were glowworms on the ceiling.

"Sunnëva." Jökull's eyes reflected in the darkness.

Relief immediately flooded through her when she saw him. He was seated on the ground, with his hands chained to the wall above his head. His torn tunic hung open, exposing his wounded arm and stomach. They no longer bled, but dark veins spread from both injuries like webs.

"How badly are you hurt?"

"Me?" Sunnëva's shoulder was bandaged, but it had no webbing like him. Other than the faint pain, her only discomfort was her damp clothes. "You're the one who was impaled."

He licked at the dried blood staining his lips. "I'm fine."

Her boots scraped over the hard earth as she rushed to his side to inspect the wounds. They were swollen and warm to the touch. Though the one on his arm looked better.

Jökull winced. "They missed my heart. I'll live." Standing loosened the chains but still pinned his arms behind him.

"Where is Ansa?"

He sighed. "They kept her."

Sunnëva rubbed her face and tried to keep calm. Ansa was probably with Kerro, and he seemed protective enough to keep her safe.

"We need to get out of here." She found the entrance. It was covered by something rough and coated with more dirt. "Where are we?"

"Inside of their Azure Tree, deep in the roots. The chains must be woven with talon fragments. I can't break them."

Her shoulders slumped. She got him captured and nearly killed. "How did you find me?"

"Because you're mine, Sunnëva," he said ardently. "There is no corner in this world where I wouldn't find you."

Her treacherous heart squeezed. She told herself the same things because it was easier. He didn't mean it that way. She was a means to cross his Gate. He had to keep her alive.

"I said I would hunt you, and I meant it."

Scoffing, she crossed her arms. "You also told me to go, Jökull. You practically screamed it at me."

"I had not meant—" He cursed and heaved a breath, lowering his gaze to the ground. "I couldn't bear to have you see me that way. My true form is monstrous ... and I nearly—" He raised his eyes to her, and his expression softened. "I shouldn't have spoken to you that way ... or held you down. I must have frightened you."

Sunnëva folded her hands together, feeling the scarred skin. "That was not my first time..."

Jökull fell still, the silence suddenly heavy.

She cringed and rubbed her face. "I'm sorry ... I ... I don't know why I said that."

"You can tell me anything, Sunnëva. No matter what it is," he murmured. "I will always listen."

No one had ever said that to her before, offered to listen to her pain. Not even Ansa.

Those sorts of things were too revolting and personal. It was better left in the past, long forgotten. Because if she peeled away her shell, it would expose the rottenness beneath. And anyone who saw those decaying parts would be tainted by it.

But Jökull watched her with an open expression, waiting for her to show it to him because he didn't care about that rot.

It suddenly made her feel so vulnerable.

Sunnëva turned around. That made it easier. To pretend she was alone, speaking her secrets to the dark.

"I remember being happy that night." She traced the scar on her hand as the memories came to her in flashes. "I felt so pretty in my stupid dress, dancing around the fire and laughing with my sister, Freya. I was drunk and foolish, teasing all the clansmen. I even dared to ask one for a kiss." She laughed wetly, feeling like such an idiot for being so brazen. "But we had offended their pride." Her throat tightened. "Four clansmen ... dragged me and my elder sister to the woods. I fought so hard. They beat me half to death and took turns cutting me merely to hear me scream."

Her mouth trembled, and she brushed the scars over her heart, hidden beneath her clothing. She hesitated but decided if she was peeling off her shell, let him see it all. Her shaking fingers yanked off her leather armor, letting it fall to her feet. She loosened her corset and then let her tunic slide down her shoulders. The moment she bared her back, a jagged inhale cut through Jökull's lips, and the sound made her fists shake.

"Freya ... I had to listen to what they did to her as I bled out," Sunnëva said. "She begged me to help her, so I stopped fighting. I let them have their way with me. I would have let the whole clan rut me, if it meant saving my sister. But they still hurt her, and they didn't stop. Not until she went quiet."

Sunnëva looked up at the ceiling to keep the tears welling on her lashes from falling. "I wish I had been the beautiful one, so I could have taken her place. I wish I could have thanked the beast that killed them, but there are days I wished it had killed me, too." Her voice caught. "I wish ... it had been my teeth and my claws that tore into them, over and over, until I could taste their blood on my skin. I'm so angry I lived instead of her. It was my fault. I should have died, not her. Now her screams will haunt me for the rest of my life. That night ruined me."

This was all that remained of who she used to be. Hardened by her father's abhorrence and her own. She had nothing to live for but to make sure she never failed her siblings again.

"No."

At his rough reply, Sunnëva adjusted her tunic and turned around.

Jökull's jaw was clenched tight, his mouth pressed into a tight line. Even in the dark, she could tell every line of his chest was taut, his arms bulging with the clenched fists she couldn't see. "I won't say that night made you stronger because that is shite. But it was not your fault. They broke you, yet you put those pieces back together and chose to live. I saw the scars when I held your soul, and I saw how well you stitched it back together. I have never seen a more beautiful soul than yours. So don't you ever say you are ruined."

The tears Sunnëva had been fighting spilled. She quickly wiped them away, not able to stand letting him see.

"I will say whatever I want. It's my story, not yours." She leaned up against the wall beside him. "Thank you ... for listening."

They fell silent for a moment, watching the glowworms twinkle. Finding herself in this place reminded her of last night and what led her to Jökull's chambers.

"Speaking of the past, why does Rune hate you?" she asked.

Jökull stiffened.

"What did you do to his bride?"

He gave her a surly frown. "What did *I* do?"

"He said she's gone, and he implied it was your doing."

"I did not *do* anything," Jökull said. "Rumiel lost his bride due to his own actions."

Sunnëva searched his face. "How?"

He exhaled a low breath and rested his head against the wall. "Our brothers met their brides first, and they struggled to find harmony with them. It's inevitable, I think. An intended trial we are forced to endure as a diamond must go through fire. Humans are frightened of us naturally, and their first reaction is either to flee or attack." There was a somber thoughtfulness in his voice. "Rumiel found his bride a century ago. She was a kind girl, but he believed her too soft-hearted to know the truth of what he was. So he disguised himself as human."

Sunnëva sighed heavily, sensing that lie was his downfall.

"But he cannot hide what he truly is. None of us can." Jökull shook his head. "Our purpose calls on us to fulfill it. His bride saw him for what he was one night. In his true form, creating demons and shadows. She fled. Rumiel chased her through the woods in a panic. By the time he cornered her, she was so frightened of him ... her heart stopped."

Sunnëva covered her mouth, and her own heart sank into the pit of her stomach.

"He brought her to me, but it was too late. Her soul was already gone."

Sunnëva briefly closed her eyes in solemn sympathy. "He must have known there was nothing you could do to bring her back."

Jökull was quiet for a pause, then said, "We have immense powers within our purpose that can make us invincible. There are many things I can do with the dead, but we have laws we're not supposed to cross. Forcing a soul into a body long gone cold disrupts the law of fate. He wanted me to break this law and bring her back."

"Is it possible to bring someone back ... ?" Sunnëva dared to ask.

"Yes."

A creeping sensation washed over her skin.

"Everything has a balance. You cannot give without taking. To resurrect her, there would need to be a sacrifice to take her place, for only death pays for life. That goes against what the Heavens deem sacred. I refused him, and he could not forgive me." Jökull's brow furrowed, and she saw his remorse. "I suppose it is partly my doing that he does not have a bride."

That grief turned Rune against his brother, his family, and the world.

If it was fate that his bride died, she could understand why he was angry with the Gods for denying him what should have been his happiness. But he was blaming all of them and not his own negligence.

"No," Sunnëva said. "It wasn't your fault. I shouldn't have assumed without knowing the truth."

"Hmm. That might be the first time you haven't blamed the God of Death for someone's death."

She awkwardly nudged his arm, making him wince. "I'm sorry."

Jökull searched her face. "I am, too. For what it's worth."

It went unspoken, but they both acknowledged their apology covered more than what brought them here.

"I didn't know you were capable of saying that word."

He grunted, his mouth lifting at one end. "I am capable of many things, Sunnëva. Some may pleasantly surprise you one day."

There was an implication in his tone that made her glower. "Do you mean like cutting off Kyrr's hands and wings?"

Jökull's amused expression dropped. "I don't want to talk about that."

She crossed her arms. "Oh, and when would you like to talk about it? Because at the moment, we are imprisoned in his tree while we await to be executed. I think now is the *perfect* time."

There was enough light to see the hard scowl on his face.

"You made him, Jökull. You gave him life as you did your roses. He is, in some terms, your son, and you maimed him. Then you banished him here to suffer."

"Kyrr is not my son," he growled.

Sunnëva frowned at him.

Sighing heavily, Jökull's gaze fell to the ground. He let the silence lingerer between them before he finally spoke. "I spent many centuries alone in this world after my brothers left. I grew to resent the quiet days. The world was big. We filled it, but it felt … empty."

He'd been lonely, Sunnëva realized. His sadness stirred in her chest, somehow connecting with him.

"Thus, when I came across a dying hawk, I gave him a new life. My mistake was that I remade him with my blood," Jökull said, looking at her. "Our blood holds a great power to make and unmake things. And only a God can create their own undoing. I sensed I had given him the power to unmake me, but I couldn't bring myself to end him. I kept it secret instead. I gave Kyrr his name and taught him everything he knew…" Jökull fell quiet again, staring blankly ahead, reliving that time.

"You raised him," Sunnëva gently pressed. "Yet…"

"I trusted him." Jökull's expression hardened. "And he betrayed me."

Sunnëva turned his cheek. "What happened?"

"Kyrr walked in on me during the lunar eclipse. He witnessed me reaping souls, and he called me a demon. Like you … he fled."

Her heart sank into her stomach. No wonder he shouted at her to leave. He thought she had felt the same.

"I can't blame him for thinking it," Jökull murmured. "But Kyrr went to Rumiel, and my brother told him I would consume every soul in the world. There is truth to that. It's my purpose as the God of Death to guide each soul through the Seven Gates. Rumiel twisted that fact to convince him I needed to be destroyed. He took him to the Druid, who prophesied a Skelling talon would take my life. Then Kyrr believed that to be his purpose."

Sunnëva sighed. "Did you try speaking to him?"

"No … I was too enraged. I punished him instead."

Perhaps too prideful, as well.

"But the punishment was brutal …" she murmured. "You cut off his *hands*."

Jökull's eyes flared brightly, reminding her exactly who she was speaking to. "As opposed to being stabbed in the back? He is fortunate I did not cut off his head instead."

She recalled the jagged scar below Jökull's shoulder blade, inches from his heart. His own making nearly killed him.

"Now he has begotten a son to finish the task."

But as angry as Jökull was, all Sunnëva mostly saw was unhappiness. "I think his betrayal hurt you more than you care to admit. I have seen you kill for less, but you let Kyrr live. Why?"

Jökull leaned against the wall and looked up at the glowworms, the faint blue light illuminating his features. "At the dawn of my creation, I reveled in death. Reaping souls and ending lives as I pleased until I was repulsed by the taste." His eyes closed, chuckling dryly. "My days are filled with death, and I am sick of it."

It finally occurred to her why he made enchanted roses that never perished. He needed at least one thing in his life to stay.

The world feared him for his violence, but that wasn't who he was anymore. His tattoos were frequently glowing, because he was always gathering souls, even when he didn't want to. She knew what that felt like. To be sick of constantly seeing loss and wishing it would end.

People died every day. But Jökull didn't want Kyrr to be another, no matter how much he had hurt him.

"It's not too late," she said. "If he truly wanted you dead, you would be. Otherwise, why leave you alive? Talk to him. Reconcile and come to an agreement of some kind."

"It's not that easy."

"It can be. Invite him and the Skellings to the castle for a banquet. Invite all the clans, and we can hold a ball. Make him feel welcome again."

Jökull frowned. "A *ball*?"

"I think somewhere in his heart, Kyrr knows you're not the evil Rune made you out to be."

His white lashes lifted, and his pale blue eyes studied her silently.

"I don't think you're evil..." Sunnëva admitted faintly, her gaze falling to the markings on his bare chest. "It startled me at first to see all those souls, but I felt the peace you gave them. I was not afraid of your true form ... I thought you looked..." She flushed, not daring to say aloud how captivating he was.

255

"You do not think I'm a monster?" he asked, his voice a soft rumble.

"I find true monsters rarely look like monsters." She met his eyes. "I stopped being afraid of you a long time ago."

Because the beast she had always been most afraid of was herself. It lurked inside of her, beneath her own darkness.

"But then you pounced on me, and I sensed your hunger. How much you wanted to consume me, too. I think I ran because ... I realized ..." Sunnëva swallowed, looking at his lips. "That I wanted..."

All of him, too.

She wanted his mouth on hers, the weight of his body, the hidden thoughts of his mind, the idle days when they were together. She wanted to feel him in her soul again.

But she shouldn't want those things. These feelings were too overwhelming and startling. They were breaking past her shell to a place where she couldn't defend herself. She didn't dare say it aloud, but he had to know because the way he looked at her made her stop breathing.

The chains clinked as Jökull shifted closer. His cool breath coasted her cheek, and his nose brushed hers. One of his braids fell past his pointed ear. It glinted with her small blue bead that he had kept.

"Sunnëva..." Hearing the soft tone of his voice speak her name sent a rush down her spine. It was low, barely a whisper. Yet she understood what he asked without saying it.

They would probably die today, so why not?

Laying her hand on his chest, she brushed her mouth against his cold lips. Lightly. Tentatively. Not aggressive and lustful like their other kisses. It was slow. *Gentle*. This was a real kiss that cracked her open, leaving her raw and bare.

Jökull's lips completely enveloped hers, taking her into him. Her palms slid up his chest, tracing the ridges of hard muscle, her body arching toward him. This kiss tasted of frost and blood. His blood, but it was sweet and divine, like impossible magic.

Everything that mattered, her troubles and worries, always vanished in these pockets of time. Because her focus was on him and how he felt when he touched her. She wanted to keep kissing him like this, and all the other ways he could kiss her.

"It's strange, isn't it?" Sunnëva asked between kisses.

"What is?" He muttered, his lips skimming against hers.

"That we no longer hate each other."

She started to weave her fingers into his white hair, but Jökull drew back.

"Oh, but I do hate you, Sunnëva." He dipped his head again, tongue darting out to take her earlobe in his mouth. She inhaled a soft gasp. His mouth found hers again, speaking gravelly words against her lips. "You have no idea how much I *loathe* you." His voice was ragged, his body warmer than it had ever been. He kissed along her throat, purring words against her pulse. "I hate the way you have invaded my mind, haunting me every damn waking hour. You have truly cursed me, vicious thorn. Because I hate the way I crave the very essence of you that I can nearly taste you on my tongue. And I undeniably hate that I am restrained right now. If it weren't for these chains, I would throw you up against this wall and punish you for running away from me."

His heated admission sank a delicious shudder down her spine and sparked a throb between her legs.

"How would you punish me?"

Jökull tried to kiss her again, but she stepped away. He jerked against his shackles and cursed, making her slyly smile.

"I can think of plenty of ways." Feral hunger filled his glowing eyes, sending goosebumps down her arms. "Come here and let me show you."

Sunnëva was very tempted.

But her answer was interrupted when tree began to groan.

29

The large tree root covering the entrance of the chamber rumbled as it withdrew. Sunnëva was hit with monumental relief when she saw Ansa standing there. She ran to her, and they embraced.

"Are you all right?" Sunnëva asked, looking her over. "Did they hurt you?"

A derisive sound came from the hallway, and she spotted Kerro lurking in the shadows, his feathered arms crossed.

"No one will harm her," he growled. "She's mine."

Sunnëva glared at him. "You listen here. She's not—"

"Sunnëva," Ansa cut her off. "Look at me. Sunnëva, *look* at me." She took her face, forcing her attention. "I am perfectly fine. Now I need you to listen carefully. For the last few hours, I spoke with Chief Kyrr on your behalf. I convinced him to give you and Jökull another chance to renegotiate peacefully and come to new terms."

She gaped at her incredulously. "How did you convince him of that?"

"By agreeing to become Kerro's mate."

"You what!"

Ansa smiled sheepishly. "His son needs a wife, and you need a bargaining piece."

Sunnëva shook her head. "No, Ansa. I can't let you do that."

Guards slipped past them to unchain Jökull from the wall.

"It's my choice. Kerro likes me and I like him, too." Ansa smiled at her shakily. "Don't ask me to explain because I can't find the right words. But while I was with the Skellings, I saw how they lived, how they value each other, and fiercely protect the ones they love. They have already accepted me as part of their tribe, and I finally understand what you mean by feeling safe. My whole life, I have waited to find where I belong. I think I have found it. This feels right." Her eyes welled at the same time Sunnëva's did. "Now, both of you need to meet with the Chief. You will discuss new territory lines and my hand in marriage with his son. This will seal your alliance with them."

Sunnëva didn't want to accept it, even if what Ansa said made sense. She hugged her tight. "I am the elder. It's me who is supposed to protect you, not the other way around."

Ansa smiled at her wetly. "I think it's time I start protecting those I love, too, don't you?" She slipped away and took Kerro's waiting hand. "I will see you in the quad."

They vanished down the hall together. Jökull's chains rattled as he came to stand beside her. The Skelling guards kept their talon spears out, watching him warily.

He was visibly annoyed. "That decision was not your sister's to make."

"Be grateful," Sunnëva said under her breath as the guards led them into the narrow hall. "She may have saved our lives."

A dismissive sound rumbled in his throat. Their footsteps shuffled across the dirt, glow worms lighting the way overhead.

"They only want the mountain," Sunnëva whispered as they climbed a set of steps carved into the tree. "It would cost you nothing,"

"It would cost a fourth of my land," Jökull growled behind her.

"You don't need the mountain, greedy god. Why not let them live there? Agree to it, and you would gain an ally."

"Or an enemy within my borders. You expect me to see him as an ally again?"

"Kyrr will be in your debt. Things have to change so there can be peace. This will avoid war, and he won't try to kill you. The decision is logical." At his silence, she sighed and turned around. "I am thinking about what's best for you."

"No..." Jökull stopped, his eyes lifting to hers. "You are thinking like a Queen."

Her heart warmed at that, but she couldn't quite smile. After hours of lessons on governing a kingdom, she had to learn something. For treaties to be made, both sides had to give up something.

They resumed their walk, and her feet dragged, knowing the outcome of today.

"You're wrong," Jökull murmured. "About this agreement costing nothing. The price is your sister. That is worth more to you than any chart of land."

Sunnëva briefly closed her eyes and fought the ache in her chest. Why did she have to keep losing her family?

They were led up a series of tunnels until they reached cold air and were brought to what must be the quad. It was the same place as before. A large wooden platform in the center of the Azure tree. The Skellings were seated on the branches, chatting and eating amongst themselves.

They were led before a long table where the Chief waited. Kerro and Ansa were seated on his left. The white-feathered female sat on his right, who Sunnëva now realized was Kyrr's mate. She gave Sunnëva a small, kind smile.

The constant chirp and fluttering wings of the gathered Skellings fell quiet at their arrival. Kyrr and Jökull shared a long stare.

The Tribe Chief broke the silence first. "Can I trust you not to attack me or my people if I release your bonds?"

"The trust between us was broken a long time ago, Kyrr," Jökull said coolly.

Sunnëva shot him a look.

He glowered at the canopy of leaves. "You have my word. I will not harm you or your kin this day."

An iridescent sheen swept through the air.

Kyrr glanced at her, and a slight hitch tugged at the end of his mouth. He nodded at the guards to remove his chains. Once freed, Jökull rubbed his raw wrists.

"We have not seen each other in quite some time," Kyrr said. "I admit, I was not expecting to greet you here."

Jökull's eyes narrowed, and he said through his teeth, "What did you expect my reaction would be when you abducted my wife?"

He reached for her without looking, and Sunnëva slid her fingers through his.

Kyrr's eyebrows inched up at this, staring at their linked hands. "In all honesty, we didn't take Lady Sunnëva to spite you. She was promised to my son first."

Jökull snarled, baring his fangs. The possessive sound vibrated through her being, and she inwardly shivered with a thrill.

Kyrr smirked. "Aye, she's yours. You've made that quite clear. Which is in our favor, seeing as Kerro is taken with Lady Ansa. I am pleased with his choice."

"I am not," Sunnëva said.

He frowned. "Lady Ansa has served as your emissary while negotiating in your stead. She has proposed a marriage between herself and my son. This would join our Houses and bring amity."

Sunnëva stepped forward. "Ansa claims she has chosen this, but in doing so, she would be kept here, and I would lose a sister." Her chest constricted, and she took a breath. "She is the dearest part of my heart. So I will not approve of this union until I am assured of two things. You must swear on your life that she will always be happy and protected while in your care. Second, thus formalizing our alliance, you will relinquish *all* talons and any weapon or means that can be used to harm my husband. Agree to it, and you will have your mountain, Chief Kyrr. In so guaranteeing the survival of your people. Those are my terms as Queen of the Everfrost."

The Skellings chirped in response, flapping their wings. Jökull stared at her. Not with shock, but with pride.

Kyrr stood, and the Skellings quieted. "No harm will ever come to your sister, Winter Queen. Mates are our most valued treasure." He reached for his mate and she took his arm. They looked at each other for a moment and seemed to communicate something, then Kyrr said to them, "I may consider relinquishing the talons if no harm will come to my people by your hand now or ever, for as long as we live. What say you, King of the Everfrost?"

Jökull glanced at her. It took her a moment to realize he again sought her opinion. They would be taking a monumental risk with that promise, but so was the Chief to give up their only weapon against him. One could not take without giving.

She gently squeezed his hand.

"Sunnëva believes this is within reason," Jökull replied. "What husband would think it wise to argue with his wife?"

Kyrr exhaled a short scoff that was almost a laugh. "Not I."

A cheer went up throughout the Azure Tree. One by one, the guards began piling all of their weapons and talons into a pile at their feet.

Kyrr came down with Kerro and dumped their taloned necklaces on top. "That is what we have, save for what is natural of my son."

Jökull waved his hand, and the talons dissolved away to dust, left to blow away in the next breeze. "The Skellings will never again be harmed by my doing now or ever." His pale gaze fixed on Kyrr as the magic of his divine promise fell over the tribe. "I banished you here not only out of ire, but for the wound you dealt me with your betrayal. I have come to accept that if you could believe Rumiel's lies, you and I were never friends."

Kyrr lowered his head.

"I can't say I forgive you yet, but after a hundred years, I am finished bearing the weight of my resentment."

The air stirred with a sheen of magic once more, and frost spiraled around them. Kyrr tensed until a cerulean light emitted from his wrist and arms. Sunnëva gasped softly as beautiful auburn feathers unfurled and wings grew to brush the floor at his feet. His hands were remade with white talons. Kerro's talons had changed, too.

Now nothing was left to harm Jökull.

Kyrr stared down at his new hands and wings, his eyes misting. He couldn't bring his head up, and Sunnëva knew how guilty he must secretly feel.

"Your banishment is lifted," Jökull said. "For the sake of my wife, so she may visit her sister as she wishes. Likewise, Ansa is welcome anytime. The mountain is yours."

Sunnëva swallowed back the tightening in her throat.

He put aside his pride for her.

"Thank you," Kyrr said faintly, his voice hoarse. "You ... are welcome to stay with us tonight ... if you wish."

"I do not." Jökull turned away, and Kyrr's shoulders sank. "But Sunnëva and I will hold a ball at the castle within a fortnight to celebrate our union and reaffirm alliances. You and your kin are welcome."

The Tribe Chief watched him go, his brow creasing with remorse. It may take some time before they could repair a fragment of the friendship they once had, but Sunnëva hoped they would one day. Before following, she exchanged a watery smile with Ansa.

It was hard to let go, but it was time for her sister to fly, too.

Sunnëva followed after Jökull. "I'm proud of you."

He grunted.

Sunnëva laughed. "I must admit, I half expected you wouldn't listen to me."

He slowed and stared at her again with that same look. The one where he was astonished, like he had seen a great wonder of the world. "I value your input, Sunnëva," he finally said. "You have the makings of a fine Queen."

She looked away so he wouldn't see how much it affected her. He was the first to say she was valuable. "How are we going to get home? Can you fly?"

Jökull paused, and a faint smile hovered on his lips.

"What?" Sunnëva touched her cheek. Was her face stained with dirt?

"You called the castle your home." He brushed her matted hair aside, letting his hand slide down her arm. "I liked hearing that. I also liked hearing you set the terms of negotiation."

She flushed, looking down at where his fingers brushed hers. The black ribbon she had tied to her ring finger as a symbol of her mourning was still there, worn and fraying.

He cradled her palm in his, and from his pocket, he drew out her Moonstone ring. "You left this behind."

"Would you believe me if I said I regretted it?"

Jökull's eyes held hers as he slipped the ring on her finger, and the chill on her bones was banished by the magic it contained. Sunnëva took one end of the ribbon and tugged it off. The wind stole it away, and they watched it go.

"As for our route of travel, I am afraid I'm not fully recovered yet," he said. "Took quite a bit of power to dissolve the talons and remake Kyrr. Traveling by air or portal is out of the question, at least until tomorrow."

"Oh, then what are we to do, all-powerful God?"

"I think I have enough magic for a horse. We can ride part of the way to the mountain until I recover."

"Not without supplies and proper shelter," Ansa called from behind them. She rushed forward and threw her arms around Sunnëva. "I couldn't let you go without saying goodbye."

Kerro, her constant shadow, grunted at Jökull. "Come. My mother told me to give you food and pelts for your female. She is featherless and frail, like mine. You must keep her warm."

He motioned for him to follow. To her surprise, Jökull went with the gruff Skelling, giving them some space.

Ansa checked no one was near before she pulled her into a shadowed groove within the tree. Small enough for only them to fit and for a sliver of privacy.

"You never told me why you ran from the castle," she said under her breath. "You were white with fear. Either you were afraid of something, or you were afraid of him. If you are ever afraid again, I want you to have these." Ansa gave her a package wrapped in cloth. Inside were two large black talons nearly the size of her forearm.

Sunnëva gasped and quickly covered them. "Where did you get that?"

"Kerro gave them to me last night as a gift for my hand, but it's best if they don't stay here. You should have them, in case you may need them one day."

"I won't." Sunnëva frowned. "He would never harm me."

Ansa searched her face. "Are you happy with him?"

She flushed. "I ... want to be."

"Then I want that for you."

They hugged each other for a long minute before Sunnëva could make herself let go. "I'm going to miss you." She kissed her cheek. "If you change your mind, if you ever need me, I will come."

"I know." Ansa smiled, squeezing her hand. "And I will always be there for you, too."

After Kerro and Jökull returned, they were flown to the base of the tree and went on their way. She tried not to think about the lethal cargo in her pack, or what Jökull might do if he discovered talons had been kept from him. It would destroy the delicate alliance he struggled to accept with the Skellings ... and with her.

All Sunnëva could do was wait for the right moment to dispose of the talons before anyone found out.

30

The sharp airstream blew mercilessly against them as they rode a crystal horse across the frozen planes of the north. The Azure Tree had long fallen out of sight hours ago, and the sun was beginning to descend. Sunnëva's face was numb, and her lashes were coated with frost. She huddled under the thick fur pelt.

It was so cold, the sharp airstream stabbed her like a thousand needles. Even the ring struggled to keep her from freezing. She could have relied on Jökull's magic, but he needed all his strength. His large body leaned on her heavily, sheltering her from the sharp gust, but she couldn't go on like this much longer.

Sunnëva pulled down the thick shawl she'd wrapped around the bottom half of her face. "Jökull?" she called, the howling wind stealing her voice from the air. "We need to stop for the day and get warm. I can't feel my legs."

He didn't answer.

"Jökull?" When she turned, his full weight slumped against her and he began to slide off the saddle. "Jökull!"

She grabbed his coat, but he was too heavy. The fabric tore from her grip, and he dropped to the snow. She leaped off, and the horse dissolved into flurries. Sunnëva flipped Jökull over. His face was flushed, and he was breathing heavily. Purple veins webbed up his throat.

His eyes rolled. "Out..." he rasped. "Get it out..."

She jerked up his coat and saw his stomach wound was inflamed. It hadn't healed like his arm. Something was wrong.

"What do I do?" She shook him. "Jökull?"

He had fallen unconscious. The color drained from his complexion by the second. Was he going to die? Her heart spasmed with panic, and she prayed to the Gods once more.

Please, please don't let him die.

The arctic wind snapped her to her senses. They had to get out of the cold.

Sunnëva looked around for shelter, but the endless snowy landscape stretched on for miles. Putting up a tent was useless when it would be blown away. She would have to risk using a little of his magic.

Sunnëva pictured a small cave for shelter, and the ground shifted beneath her. The snow grew and reformed to come around them like a Skelling nest. Yanking out the blankets from their pack, she made a bed and rolled Jökull onto it. She started a small fire with some kindling from their supplies. Then she removed his coat. His wound looked worse in the firelight.

Why wasn't it healing? Jökull said it missed his heart and that he was fine, but he clearly wasn't. Sunnëva regretted leaving the Azure Tree. They should have stayed until he fully recovered. Now they were miles away from help in either direction.

She wasn't a healer, but she had seen Gyda treat various injuries. *Maybe...*

If her guess was right, it would only get worse if she didn't do something. Taking a deep breath, Sunnëva stuck two fingers in the wound. She tried not to cringe as she rooted around the soft tissue until something small and sharp poked her forefinger. She grabbed the splinter and carefully pulled it out. It glistened black and red in the light. She tossed it in the fire.

267

No sooner had she done it, Jökull's injury healed into a scar. She was cleaning the blood away when his lashes flickered open.

"Back from the dead," she teased. "Again. For a God, you're not that hard to kill."

He pressed on the site where he'd been struck. "What happened?"

"There was still a piece of the talon left inside of you. I got it out. Lucky for you, I didn't have to cauterize the wound."

His mouth hitched tiredly. "Put me to fire, and you would have risen me from the ash."

"What does that mean? Is fire another one of your weaknesses?" She eyed him with playful suspicion. "If I douse you in flame, will you melt?"

"Elyōn, help me. She still wants to kill me..." Jökull mumbled tiredly, and she laughed. He fell still, and he looked at her the same way he had after she'd won the battle.

"What?"

"I really like that sound."

"What sound?"

"Your laughter," he murmured. "You don't do it enough."

Warmth fluttered in her stomach. Why did he have to say things that always left her speechless?

He frowned at the domed snow cave. "Where are we now?"

"We're still in the Frost Lands. I had to use a little of your magic to put this together." Sunnëva covered him with the blanket. "We will stay here for the night. I'll take out some food. You need to eat to regain your strength."

"I'm fine. Keep whatever we have. I already feel my strength growing." His voice did sound better, and the color was returning to his face.

"You're not hungry?" Her stomach had been hollow since last night. If she was starving, he had to be.

"Gods do not feel hunger the way humans do. At least not for food." His eyes glinted in the firelight as he turned his head toward her. "Eating is merely a ... *pleasure*."

By the way he was looking at her, she wasn't sure if they were still talking about food.

Ignoring her blush, Sunnëva sorted through their pack of supplies and pulled out a bag of dehydrated fruit, seeds, and dried meat. She chose what looked to be some purple fruit and quickly scarfed it down. It was sweet and tangy.

Jökull watched as she ate a handful of the seeds and another piece of fruit. The silence made her aware of how alone they were inside the snow cave. Her nerves tightened her stomach, and suddenly she couldn't eat more.

"Are you cold?" Jökull asked. "You're trembling."

Sunnëva flushed to find her hands were shaking, but it wasn't from the cold.

"Come here. You were injured, too. Let me see."

She hesitated before removing her pelt to lay it on the snow beside him and sat on top. Not looking at him, Sunnëva unfastened her damp tunic and slid the sleeve down her shoulder. She grimaced in pain as she peeled the bandage away from the dried blood sticking to her skin.

Jökull hissed at the three gashes. They were swollen and angry. "I should have taken his head for that."

Sunnëva sighed. "That would have served nothing but more bloodshed."

Her breath caught when he leaned forward and pressed his cold lips on her wounded shoulder. He blew on the lacerations, making her shiver and clutch the pelt. They shimmered with radiating magic, shining so brightly it enthralled her. Within seconds, her pain vanished, and her wounds seamlessly healed.

No scar left behind.

Jökull melted a bit of snow in his palm and used it to wipe away the blood from her arm.

Her throat knotted. "You shouldn't use magic when you haven't recovered."

His pale eyes lifted to hers. "Even if I had a mere drop of power left, I wouldn't hesitate to give it to you."

There were a thousand things she wanted to say but could give voice to none. He treated her so well, it sometimes triggered her damaged heart. It quivered as if it was shaking awake, starved for more of the tenderness he offered. She had never been cared for in that manner, and she didn't know how to react.

"Why?" she whispered.

"Why did you jump in the way to save me?" he asked in turn.

Sunnëva lowered her head and hid behind her blonde hair. "I thought ... after today ... you knew." She didn't want him dead anymore. Somewhere among their time together, she'd grown fond of him and his gruff ways. Dare she admit it, she wanted him in her life. At his silence, her face grew hot. "Do I need to say it?"

"No, winter rose," Jökull replied. He took her chin and lifted her face. His head dipped, his nose gliding over her cheek, breathing her in.

"Why do you call me winter rose?" she asked faintly.

"Because you are as cold and beautiful as those silky petals. Sweet as its scent and sharp as its thorns," Jökull murmured, his lips coursing up her shoulder to her neck. Her pulse leaped and danced with every press of his mouth. His fingers played with the loose strings of her corset. "I think you have forgotten I can feel everything you do, Sunnëva. I feel you right now. The way your heart is wildly beating in anticipation of what I am going to do next."

"You want to do this now?" she panted as his cool tongue licked the hollow of her throat. "Here?"

"What do you think will happen here?"

"I don't know."

"Oh, but you have already imagined it," Jökull said, and she felt his cocky smile against her throat. His fingers threaded through her hair and exposed more of her neck to him. His grip was firm but never painful, as though he knew she secretly liked it when he took control. "Tell me all of your filthy desires."

Sunnëva trailed her nails along his muscular arms as heat gathered between her legs. "Where's the fun in that?"

He chuckled darkly. Sitting back, Jökull pulled her onto his lap and she straddled him. "Indeed."

"But you were unconscious not a short moment ago."

It was a weak protest. From his complexion, he was growing stronger by the minute.

"Now I aim to do the same to you." Jökull removed her corset, and his cool hand slid underneath her tunic. She flinched at the first contact of his touch. His fingers trailed over her abdomen in gentle circles. When he traced the scars near her breast, she stiffened, and he paused.

"If you want to end it now, it will, Sunnëva," he said, pressing a kiss to her temple.

Always so caring, her thoughtful beast.

"I don't want it to end," Sunnëva whispered. "But ... but what does this mean?"

Jökull's mouth grazed her fluttering pulse. "It will mean whatever you want it to."

Her heart beat wildly with want and indecision. She wanted him, wanted so much, but a part of her was still hesitant to open her heart again, knowing in the end it couldn't last. There were so many loose ends to this marriage, which she first accepted out of hatred. Now, she wasn't fully sure what she felt for her husband. Only that she wanted to explore all of him and simply *feel* something that wasn't fear or anger.

She wanted to dive deep into him, regardless if this only made it worse for her. Because even if she was falling, it took courage to leap.

"Then it doesn't mean anything," Sunnëva said. "We are merely acting on impulses, and we'll be over it come morning."

It was such a big lie.

But she was fine with it as long as he believed it.

Jökull didn't respond for a breath. Sunnëva tensed, thinking her answer ruined the moment, until he said, "I have many impulses when it comes to you." His frosted breath fell against her skin as he faintly traced his fangs over her collarbones. His hand trailed up her waist to her ribs, sending her heart thundering as he continued upward. Inch by torturous inch. "I wonder if you can handle all of them."

His nose skated up her neck to her cheek, his breath falling over her exposed chest as her tunic slid further down. Her nipples pebbled with the cold. They were tight and desperate for his touch.

Jökull growled at the sight of her bare chest. "Can I say how much I adore these?" His fingertips grazed her faintly, so light, like a tickle of snowfall. It struck her with such a wild course of sensations, Sunnëva shuddered.

"So soft." Jökull hovered over her mouth. She waited for him to kiss her with a wild longing, but he hummed as he continued to the other cheek. He cupped her breasts in his palms, his talons faintly prodding the plump curve of her cleavage. "So delicate."

He pinched her nipple, making her whimper. Sunnëva squirmed and rocked against him, needing friction. She aimed for a kiss, but he drew away.

"Not yet," he tsked. "Don't think I have forgotten. You ran away from me, and I truly..." His fangs lightly grazed her shoulder. "Absolutely." He retook a handful of her hair with the perfect amount of pressure that sent waves of pleasure through her aching core when he pulled her close. "*Detested* it."

Jökull's lips traveled along the column of her throat. "Your skin..." His tongue licked up the shell of her ear, and she shuddered with a breathy sigh. "It tastes as sweet as the dew on a winter morning. How does the rest of you taste, Sunnëva?"

She moaned as he continued to massage her breasts. Liquid warmth soaked her undergarments. Her core throbbed, begging for attention. She continued rolling against his waist and whimpered at finding no reprieve. There were too many layers between them.

"So needy," he rumbled. "Do you have any idea how beautiful you are? It's maddening. You are the tide that I am helpless against. I am out of my depths with you."

His lashes brushed against the soft curves of her cleavage, his cool breath making her break out in goosebumps. A sharp moan suddenly cut its way past her lips when his tongue twirled over a nipple, sending a quake throughout her entire body, shooting straight to her center.

"I love how you taste," he murmured before doing the same with the other.

Her toes curled and heat liquified inside of her like a pool of fire. Her body only reacted like this with him. He stirred a wild want with the simplest caress because he was being so gentle with her.

He wrapped his arm around her waist, rocking her against the length of his erection. She sulked at the barrier of fabric, muting the friction. She wanted to feel more of him. To explore every plane of his smooth, hard skin.

As if reading her mind, he stripped off his cloak and jerkin. Immediately, she ran her hands over his sculpted chest. He was so *warm* and vibrating beneath her. She arched back as his mouth went to her throat again, his hands replacing where his lips had been. His thumbs kneaded her nipples, leaving her panting. She was hot all over. Her hips bucked against him, but it wasn't enough.

"Jökull," she whined.

"Yes, love? I want to hear you say it. Tell me what you want."

Sunnëva quivered to hear him call her that. All of her dissolved into him. She wanted his touch, his mouth, all over her. In her. "Please," she begged. "Kiss me. I want you to touch me."

Jökull traced his finger along her jaw, tipping her face to his. He devoured her mouth. Ravenously. Claiming. Hungry. She wrapped her arms around his neck, bringing her chest flush against his. A wild growl rolled through his throat as she ground herself on him. He kissed her like he was asserting his claim. She was more than eager to let him.

The light skim of his talons traveled up her nape to cup her head, holding her to him. The cool touch sent shivers down her spine. Having him kiss her this way felt almost familiar. It stole away all her thoughts, her worries, and her fears until they sank into the ice of the cave. Her body hummed with every meeting of their lips because she wanted more. She *needed* more.

She parted her lips in invitation, and his tongue slipped inside, her fingers threading in his hair. His cool hand stroked her stomach again, and her body sparked wildly as his fingers slid past her navel. Feeling him tug at the stays of her trousers, she shifted to her knees between his legs. He helped pull them down past her hips. Her soaked undergarments came away in his talons.

Jökull rumbled a pleased sound, and his nostrils flared at the scent of her arousal. "You smell so sweet. Are you already wet for me?"

He cupped her between her spread thighs. His talons retracted, and she whimpered at the stroke of his fingers, finding her sleek and pulsating.

He groaned against her throat. "You're drenched."

Her breath came in soft pants as he stroked her. She clutched onto his shoulders, waiting for him to touch that spot that throbbed for him. But he merely continued circling where she wanted him.

Sunnëva moaned. "Please."

She wanted him *in*. She gripped his arm, rocking against his hand.

"If I will be inside of you, Goddess, it won't only be with my fingers."

She whimpered in protest when Jökull's hand pulled away, his fingers glistening with her lust. To her shock, he brought them to his mouth and sucked. A rush of heat flooded her face.

That was so filthy it drove her wild.

"Fuck," Jökull let out a low groan that bordered on a growl. "I've been craving another taste of you since that night."

He meant when he first touched her. Sunnëva stared at him.

When she fell asleep, did he...?

His fangs flashed in the dark at his wicked grin. Oh, good Gods, he was a lewd beast.

"This isn't enough," Jökull said. He rolled her onto the bedding, his eyes flaring in the firelight. His erection strained against the seam of his pants. "I need more. I need to taste you on my tongue. I will take every fucking drop ... if you'll let me."

Sunnëva's heart thudded against her ribs. She'd never done that before. Rune had tried, but she thought it too exposing. They had never had sex without her clothes on, either. But with Jökull, she didn't feel the need to hide. She wanted him there, close to her in every way.

Holding his gaze, Sunnëva kicked off her boots, and he helped slip her trousers completely off. Instinctively, Sunnëva shut her legs, suddenly embarrassed to reveal every intimate part. Jökull lightly placed his hands on her knees as he searched her face. The desire was there, the hunger, but he rose past it and waited for her. Silently asking for permission without pressuring her. Sunnëva knew if she changed her mind now, he wouldn't be angry. He would end it as quickly as it started. That alone had her legs relaxing and spreading open for him.

At the sight of her, Jökull's chest hitched with a harsh breath, and he let out a low, guttural curse that pulsed in her stomach. "You're riveting, Sunnëva."

She yelped when he pulled her up toward him, forcing her to lie flat on her back.

"Why are you my perfect form of torment?" His frosted breath coasted over her exposed center, making her shiver. "Each moment you tried to kill me, I wanted you so much I could barely contain myself. Several times I imagined sinking into you so deep until you were screaming with release. I am a God, yet you had me so mindlessly aroused. I was utterly obsessed with you and I despised it."

Jökull kneeled and kissed the inside of her thigh. "You don't know how long I've desired this." He kissed the other thigh, so close to her folds. "I dreamed of your taste, so much your scent haunted me in every damn room." He spread her open further, cupping her ass, and groaned another curse as he gazed at her wet entrance. "I went to bed every night hard as a rock, fighting every urge to hunt you down and plunge into you. I hated myself for craving you so much, I was half mad. Now I have you before me, spread open for my own pleasure, and I don't think I can control myself."

Hearing him confess it all in such a hoarse voice was doing things to her. Sunnëva focused on his words and the raw honesty in them. Her entire body was quivering while she hung on every admission he spoke. Her heart was slamming so hard against her spine, her bones were shaking. He had to feel her reaction to him.

She lightly trailed her nails along his thigh. "You dreamed of being on your knees?"

His glowing eyes softened. "Love, you've had me on my knees a long time ago."

He lowered between her thighs, and she cried out at the quick swipe of his cool tongue sliding from her entrance to her clit. Jökull shuddered, and his fingers dug into her thighs.

"Fuck. It's even better than I imagined," he moaned against her sensitive core. She was so completely exposed. She squirmed instinctively, but he gripped her hips tight. "Where do you think you're going? I'm only getting started."

He lifted himself over her, and his mouth was on hers, carrying her taste. He pressed gentle bites along her throat, stopping only to whisper in her ear. "I haven't even begun to tease you yet. By the time I am done, you will only remember the feel of my lips on you and no one else's."

Each word sent skitters of desire through her. He kissed down her chest, licking her nipples on the way. He nipped her hipbone, scraping his fangs across her skin. Sunnëva moaned, shivering from every touch.

His voice vibrated against her navel. "I have been starving for you, winter rose."

The devotion in his tone left her trembling with a need so overwhelming she fought to breathe.

Jökull's head settled between her thighs. She held her breath, and it burst out of her at the touch of his lips. His mouth learned her shape with reverent kisses. His tongue traced her slowly, delicately. She moaned as he switched between circling her throbbing bud of nerves and avoiding it completely. Right as her climax climbed, he would pull away, keeping her constantly on the edge. Sunnëva whimpered and clutched the blankets in her fists. It was torture.

He said when he got on his knees, she would beg, and she did. She begged with each whimper, lifting her hips pleadingly against his face, with her fingers digging into his hair. She was on the brink of insanity.

"Jökull, please."

He chuckled against her folds. "As you wish."

His lips clamped over her, and she cried out in delight. Her body heated with every stroke of his mouth, his fangs lightly teasing her flesh. He slipped his fingers into her as he sucked on her clit, and her back lifted off the ground. Her legs dripped with her lust, and he licked it all away. He was ravenous.

Jökull cursed. "You taste so good," he said with a ragged breath. "I feel you quivering on my tongue."

He devoured her whole. Sunnëva pleaded for more, for his lips, for his kiss, for everything he would give her.

She yelped when Jökull flipped her over. He was suddenly on his back with her legs straddling his head. "What are you doing?" she gasped.

"I've imagined this moment exactly like this," he said, his voice dark with hunger. "With you sitting on my mouth and your warm thighs wrapped around my face."

Jökull plunged his tongue inside of her.

Sunnëva screamed, practically lifting off the ground. His tongue filled the very depths of her. Her body liquefied. Her mind completely lost. A tremor shook her being to the point everything tingled, everything clenched—her toes, her core, and her clit. All of her *throbbed*.

She bucked against his mouth wildly, her entire body was careening. She couldn't contain it and couldn't think straight. He stroked her with his thumb, making her moan so loud it filled the cave. She was getting close, her legs trembling. Her heart raced, a hot rush washing over her skin as he carried her to the edge.

"Oh please," Sunnëva said, the words a gasping cry. "Please don't stop, oh please."

She begged and begged *shamelessly* as she rode his face, and he granted it.

And when his lips clamped over her clit, she was gone.

Her back arched, and she shuddered with a gasping scream as an orgasm swept through her. Sunnëva's legs clamped around his head, fisting his hair in her fingers. He was trapped against her while she rode out her release. Jökull kept licking her, making her plunge with another orgasm.

As promised, he swallowed every drop hungrily, his moans of pleasure rippling through her.

His tongue continued slowly gliding through her folds, bringing her down until she stopped shuddering. A long sigh slipped out of her, leaving her floating on a wave of ecstasy. She looked down at Jökull lazily and smiled at the pleased look on his face. His lips were swollen and glistening with her, his piercing eyes nearly black as his head lolled.

Jökull groaned in satisfaction. "You taste like a dream."

Sunnëva was floating on a high, and she wanted him to have the same. She slid off him and reached for the stays of his trousers, but he caught her wrist.

"Rest," he said, pressing his mouth to her fingers. "After the day you've had, I will be the one to put you to sleep."

Sunnëva tried not to show her disappointment. Once Jökull hung up her clothes to dry above the fire, he wrapped her in a thick blanket and hooked an arm around her waist, pulling her flush against his chest. She nestled into him, her butt pressed against his groin. Sunnëva frowned at the dying fire. He was still aroused. Why didn't he want to continue? This was the second time he passed up her offer.

Jökull must have sensed her thoughts because he murmured in her ear, "I don't think you're ready for more yet." His voice was gentle, in a way that made her petulant at first until she realized he was right. He stroked her hair slowly, and whatever was in his touch made her sleepily sigh. "When I claim you, it won't be in some snow cave in the middle of nowhere. It will happen where you feel safe and because you want it to. When that day comes, I will have you in every way possible."

She huffed, residual heat stirring in her core. "Will you, now? This may be your only chance, and you're passing it up to hold to some shred of nobility. What makes you think I will want you tomorrow?"

Jökull chuckled quietly, and she heard the mischief in his sultry voice. "My sweet *apricity*, you will sleep tonight with the memory of my mouth between your legs and crave more. When you're begging for it, I will be inside of you so deep, you won't know where you end and I begin."

A flush washed through her cheeks at imagining it. Sunnëva ground herself into his erection, and he cursed.

"Behave, woman."

Sunnëva grinned to herself, wondering what apricity meant.

Jökull continued caressing her hair, and sleep began sinking into her spent body. She was so warm cuddling up into him, she could almost forget they were in a globe of snow.

31

When morning arrived, Jökull had fully recovered. He opened a portal, and they entered the castle library. Sunnëva was ragged, tired, and filthy, but she was happy to be home. They took two steps but then spotted Aero and Tally around the corner. The mage had her petite frame pinned against the bookshelves with her legs wrapped around his torso, kissing each other so passionately it made Sunnëva blush.

Tally gasped at the sight of them, and they broke apart. Aero quickly set her down and adjusted himself before standing at attention with his arms folded behind his back.

Sunnëva stifled a giggle and said under her breath to Jökull, "Who knew? My handmaiden and your Advisor."

Smirking at their reddening faces, Jökull lounged in a chair by the fire. He kicked up his feet and closed his eyes. "Aero, I trust you have kept the castle in order while I have been gone."

He cleared his throat and bowed. "Of course, sire."

Tally dipped in a low curtsey. "My lady, I am glad you have returned safely."

"Is that blood?" Aero frowned worriedly at the red stains on their clothes. "Are you injured? What happened?"

"A minor encounter. We're fine now." Sunnëva smiled tiredly. "I need to wash up. I will leave you and His Majesty to discuss our latest venture ... along with preparations for the arrival of Kyrr and his Skellings."

Aero's jaw dropped open. "What?"

"Sunnëva." Jökull peered at her through his white lashes. "I had your things moved to my chambers. I want you in my bed from now on."

A blush crept up her face. For him to say such a blatant thing in front of others, even if he was her husband.

Even if he did have his face buried between her thighs last night...

The thought sent a tingle to her core, and she swore Jökull's mouth twitched.

"Ah, yes. Your chambers were destroyed during the eclipse, I'm afraid," Aero explained. "The tower will need reconstruction."

"And more knights must be retained to replace your Queen's Guard," Jökull added. "Until then, I am not leaving you out of my sight. Go on ahead. I will join you shortly, *sweetness*."

Sunnëva glowered at him. She knew what he was referring to by calling her that. *Vulgar beast.*

Turning away, she nodded for Tally to follow her, and they went on their way.

"I see you have been well," Sunnëva said teasingly once they were in the hall.

Tally flushed bright red. "Forgive me. I know I had no right. Please don't punish him. I will stop—"

"No, no, it's all right." She hugged her shoulders and chuckled. "You're not a slave anymore, Tally. Kiss whoever you like. You have nothing to fear from me or the King. But I am curious. How long has this been going on?"

Tally's face turned impossibly redder, and she fidgeted with her skirts. "Not long. I thought ... perhaps there might have been something there when we spent our days together, but I was sure it was merely infatuation on my part. I didn't dare act on it, knowing my station. And Aero is so..."

"Stiff as frozen mud?"

"Reserved." Her handmaiden huffed, smiling shyly. "He was always proper with me. Never forward. During the lunar eclipse, he held me while we hid and I sensed he wanted to kiss me. So I decided to stop being a coward and do it myself."

"Tally, you little minx." Sunnëva laughed. "He must have been thrilled."

She covered her mouth, giggling. "When I kissed him, he said 'Thank the Gods.' And then, he was no longer ... reserved."

Sunnëva's cackle filled the hallway. "I must tease him about this later. I'm pleased you two are together. It seems my sister has found someone as well."

"Is that why she has not returned with you?"

Sunnëva smiled, feeling a little wistful and forlorn. She already missed Ansa. Her father would be angry when he found out, but for once, she didn't give a damn what he thought.

"That is life, I suppose. One never knows where it will lead us..." Warmth sank through her body as she reminisced about last night, and the lingering impression of Jökull's mouth on her skin. She cleared her throat. "How was the castle after I left? Were there many losses?"

Tally sighed. "The smaller fae and beasts fell quickly if they weren't in hiding. Aero found Ren in your room shortly after your departure. He is in a deep sleep now, recovering in the infirmary. I am sorry to say Riona and the rest of your guard didn't survive."

A twinge swept through Sunnëva's chest. She hadn't known the knights for long, but they did their best to protect her and each other. Ren would be devastated when he woke.

"And Fenrin?" As soon as she asked, her brother scampered around the corner like an excited puppy. Fen crashed into her, and she laughed as he licked her cheek. "I suppose this means you're all right now."

Whatever aggression came over him during the lunar eclipse had passed. She was relieved to see him out of his cage, too.

He keened softly, searching the hallway and sniffing the air.

"Ansa isn't here." Sunnëva stroked his furry chest. "Don't worry. She's safe. I will tell you about it at dinner. First, I must remove these soiled clothes and take a long bath."

"I will head to the kitchen and have some water heated for you, my lady," Tally said. "Fen, could you help me carry it up?"

His paws clicked on the floor as he followed after Tally, his tail wagging.

Sunnëva took the stairs, already knowing which direction to go. They would be sharing rooms now. Maybe it should have bothered her, but she didn't feel anything other than nervous excitement.

That vanished the moment she entered Jökull's chambers and found Donelle naked in his bed.

The dainty fae languidly stretched across the bedding on her stomach, her hair adorned with delicate chains and red gems. Every part of her body was bare and perfectly flawless. Sunnëva halted in place. Shock splashed across her face faster than she could hide it.

Donelle simpered and brushed her black hair over her shoulder. "Oh, dear. Were you dragged through the mud? You look awful."

"And you were leaving," Sunnëva replied tightly, opening the door wider. "Get out."

Donelle laughed. A glimpse of her dark tongue flashed behind her fangs. It was long and forked. Sunnëva inwardly shuddered. What kind of fae was she?

"Be called queen enough, and you start believing it," Donelle retorted as she rolled over, exposing her breasts, not a blemish or freckle in sight. She trailed her long decorative fingernail guards up her knees. "Yet you have no idea what happens in the castle. Like how often I am in this bed, *filled* with his—"

Sunnëva let out an exasperated groan. She went to take a seat at the round table in the corner and dropped her pack on the floor. She kicked it under the table and started removing her boots.

"Look, Donny—can I call you Donny?" She smiled sweetly. "I am sure whatever territorial game you're playing has worked in the past, but I am too exhausted to care. As of today, these chambers are mine, and I would appreciate not having your secretions all over my sheets. Now leave before the only thing you're *full* of is so much iron you won't be able to see straight."

Donelle hissed and curled her fingers. "Try it, human. See how well it goes for you."

A low chuckle from the doorway had them both whipping around.

Jökull leaned against the doorframe with his arms in his pockets. "What's all this then?"

Donelle sat up and pouted at him. "I missed you, Jo. I wanted to see you."

He regarded her indifferently. "I thought I made it clear to you the last time we spoke. You are here as a court emissary only. Come to my chambers again, and my wife will do with you as she wishes."

Red washed through Donelle's pretty features. She picked up the sheer black dress off the ground with her ass exposed to him, slipped it on, and strode for the door with a seductive sway to her hips.

"You know where to find me if you change your mind," Donelle murmured as she passed Jökull. She reached for his arm, but he stepped into the room without looking at her.

Sunnëva might have gloated at the stunned look on Donelle's face when he shut the door on her. Turning around, she continued removing the rest of her armor and cloak.

"Sunnëva."

"What?" she said a tad too sharply.

It had taken everything to keep her composure when Donelle had been present. Now the wall on her emotions crumbled, and she was hit with anger so strong it made her stomach roil. If it had not been empty, she might have had more than bile lodged in her throat.

Jökull turned her around, and his mouth curved with a half-smile. "If you care to know, I have not touched her."

He pulled her toward him and kissed her. Sunnëva hardly put up a fight. How effortlessly he tamed her. It was so easy to drown in him, but she couldn't allow that. What Donelle said only reminded her that they weren't in any real relationship to claim.

Sunnëva jerked her mouth away. "That's not what she implied, *Jo*."

He frowned. "She lied."

"Fae can't lie."

"No, but they are deft at twisting their words. I told you I only have eyes for you, my vicious thorn. No need to be jealous."

She hissed. "Who said I'm jealous?"

Yet the thought of someone touching him was making her veins frost over. She shouldn't care. She shouldn't.

"Even if you did not look as though you wish to murder me again, I feel everything you do." Jökull lifted her hand with the Moonstone ring. She tried to yank it off, but he stopped her, his jaw clenching. "Sunnëva."

She stilled at the way he said her name. He sensed her emotions, even if he couldn't read her thoughts. She was too embarrassed to speak about them. Expectations would only bring her pain.

Sunnëva looked away. "I merely want to wash the filth off me and lie down. I don't care if you want to continue bedding Donelle. With that flawless body, who would fault you?" Her throat tightened, and she rolled her eyes to mask the way they stung. What a stupid thing to be insecure about, but she was. Every part of her was always aware of her horrid scars. "We already said last night would mean nothing. So fill her all you wish. I only ask that you don't do it in front of me."

The touch of his gaze stayed on her face a moment, then his hold fell away with a sigh. "The bathing chamber is on the left."

She didn't realize how much she wanted Jökull to protest her approval until he didn't. In the end, there was no point. Why pursue a doomed thing that could never last? Once the Gate opened, it would be over.

Sunnëva walked away, pretending her heart didn't shrivel up on the floor at his feet. The bathing room was constructed of polished stone, with a series of small windows near the ceiling to let in soft light. The large bath was built into the floor and already filled with steaming water.

"When was..."

"Portal." Jökull came up behind her. "I let Tally and Fen in while you were busy threatening Donelle." He slipped past her as he pulled off his jerkin and let it fall to the floor. "I would have enjoyed seeing that, by the way."

He tugged on the stays of his pants next, and Sunnëva balked. "What are you doing?"

"You are not the only one who needs to bathe." He smirked at the startled expression on her face. "My dear winter rose. I thought we were past being shy. I have already seen all of you."

But she hadn't seen *him*.

He tugged on his waistband, and Sunnëva quickly looked away. Her stomach flipped at the splash of water. With a bated breath, she took a peek, unable to resist anymore.

Jökull stood in the large bath. The steam curled off the surface, concealing the lower half of him. He brushed his long, white hair out of his face, making his arms flex in remarkable ways. Intricate tattoos curved over the lower part of his neck, continuing down his chest and arms. He wore leather cuffs that covered his wrist, but more tattoos continued over the top of his hand. She visually traced the honed muscular ridges of his abdomen, and the path of hair trailing down into the water. Her throat dried. She didn't need to see to know he was stunning there, too.

His piercing gaze was on her, his mouth curving at her heated stare.

She swallowed. Might as well.

Taking the strands of her tunic, Sunnëva stripped and took her time doing it, well aware he watched every move. The fabric slid off her shoulders and floated to her feet. She took her trousers and slowly pulled them off, making sure he had a view of everything.

With another breath, Sunnëva climbed into the bath and moaned at the heat sinking into her bones. She sighed and leaned her head against the bath's edge.

The water lapped around her with Jökull's movements. Her eyes flew open when he took her arm and pulled her onto his lap.

"Jökull!" She squealed and tried to move, but he held on. "What are you doing?"

"Me? Oh, I am taking the pleasure of washing my *wife*," he said gruffly. "The one who I have been stubbornly faithful to since the night I laid eyes on her, even when she tried to murder me quite a few times."

Sunnëva blinked at him. He hadn't been with anyone since then?

"And if I remember clearly, *I* did not say last night would mean nothing." He tucked a curl behind her ear. "Only that it would mean what you wanted it to. If you want me, I'm yours. If you don't, I will wait around like a fool until you do. I meant what I said. No part of you is ruined. Every scar and mark, the cracked shards left behind by the pain of life, are the most beautiful parts of you. They shaped your soul and made you who you are. It means you survived. Never, for a single moment, should you believe I don't find that fucking perfect."

Emotion surged in her throat, and her eyes stung. As easy as that, all the anger melted out of her.

"Now, hold still. You're the first woman I have ever cared to wash, and I want to do it right," Jökull grunted. "If you tell anyone I said something so soppy, there will be violence."

Sunnëva giggled and fell still, completely melting into him. He was remarkably gentle and focused on what he was doing. He poured something on her hair and massaged her scalp into a lather. It felt so nice. His touch soothed the tension from her body. A low groan sank out of her, and she rested her head on his shoulder.

His soapy hands moved on to rub over her body, getting close but never touching the sensitive areas. Her breasts were perked, craving his attention. A secret smile hovered on the edges of his mouth as he transferred her to the bath's ledge, then lifted one of her legs on his shoulder and dragged a washcloth up it torturously slow. He lifted the other, spreading her wide as he worked. Getting close to her center, but still avoiding it completely.

She narrowed her eyes. "I know what you're doing."

He chuckled. "And what is that?"

"My turn." Sunnëva sank into the water and pushed him to sit. She straddled him. Pouring soap in her hands, she massaged it into his scalp and long hair. His bright gaze stayed on her as she worked, his hands resting on her waist. The silver locks ran through her fingers until the water came away clear. She took the cloth and worked on washing him.

She ran her fingers along the many veins in his toned arms, feeling all of the corded muscle. Gods, he was a vision. A godly beast who might be hers, if she let herself fall into him completely. Half of her had already claimed him with such possessiveness, and she wouldn't hesitate to cut down anyone who attempted to take him from her.

"Do these markings mean something?" She traced one of the weaving tattoos marking his shoulder. Rune had them, too. Though his were slightly different.

"They did, at the beginning of all things."

"And now?"

"Now they are merely a reminder of where we came from and a purpose I hardly maintain." Jökull leaned back. His brow creased slightly, and she wondered what he was thinking about. He seemed troubled, and she wanted to take that feeling away.

Sunnëva kissed his neck. A low rumble rolled in his throat in response. His wet, spiky lashes lifted, his piercing eyes glowing softly. She glided her hands over his chest, memorizing the firmness of his smooth skin. His abs constricted when she reached his stomach, and she felt him grow harder beneath her. Her fingers lightly traced the shaft, and she inhaled a low breath at finding it impressively bigger than she imagined.

Jökull caught her wrist. "Don't play with me, vicious thorn."

"Maybe I want to play," she said.

He brushed his nose along her shoulder, nipping her skin. "I play too rough for all of your soft curves." He cupped her face, his thumb dragging over her bottom lip. "This pouty mouth. It makes me want to do bad things to you."

She smiled slyly, her body heating. Whatever he meant, she didn't care as long as it left her screaming like last night. "What things?"

"If I take you now, I will flip you around in this bath and fuck you senseless until you're quivering and begging. But I barely got you clean."

"It's a good thing we are still in the bath." She rolled against his erection. A low growl rumbled in his chest. His fangs lightly dragged over her throat, and she rocked against him, feeling him slide between her folds.

Jökull hissed a curse. He yanked her face to him and demolished her mouth. Her lips parted, meeting the stroke of his tongue. His soapy hands slid to her breasts and teased her nipples. She whimpered against his lips, grinding herself on him.

He groaned as if it was torture, his breath sharpening. Some veil had lifted because she felt his craving for her. His boundless *need* to make her his. She wanted him too, and she wasn't going to let him dither anymore.

Sunnëva moved back and motioned him to stand. Jökull rose to his feet, the water falling away. His cock was as devastatingly stunning as the rest of him. She took him in both of her hands, awed by his girth and length. Imagining taking it inside of her. Would it even fit?

"Winter rose." Jökull sighed and cupped her face with a tenderness that didn't match his earlier words. "I am trying to go slow with you, but you're making it difficult."

She frowned. "Stop being so good. You said you take what you want. So, take it. I am not resisting."

"You want me now, but you're merely in your lust."

"Why should that stop you, lewd beast?"

The idea of giving herself to a God made her heart pound either from need or wracking nerves. His gaze held hers as he stroked her cheek. There was something ethereal about Jökull she couldn't help but stare at him.

The way he made her feel last night, she desired that again. Not only how he touched her, but everything he said. She wanted to discover what it meant to be accepted as she was, to be adored and cherished. She wanted him to sink into her very soul.

His pupils dilated further at whatever he must be feeling from her. She pumped his shaft once, earning his guttural curse.

Jökull yanked her up to her feet and hauled her onto his shoulder, climbing out of the bath. "Damn you for making me crave you, woman." He struck her wet ass, and Sunnëva yelped, breaking out into laughter.

He carried her into their chambers and promptly laid her on his large bed. The sheets had already been replaced with new ones. She smiled up at him indulgently as the rain beat on the windows behind him. The room darkened with thickening storm clouds.

Jökull leaned over her, water dripping from his hair onto her chest. "Tell me you want this, for I am finished fighting what you do to me." He pressed a kiss to her temple, moving down her cheek. "I want all of you, Sunnëva. And once this starts, you're not leaving my bed."

A shiver of delight scattered through her body.

"Well, I didn't plan on leaving," she whispered.

His mouth came over hers, stealing her next breath. She wrapped her arms around his neck, feeling his pulse against hers. His breath fell over her skin, every touch of his lips branding her soul. She was finished fighting what he did to her, too.

Jökull kissed down her chest to her stomach. He lifted her leg to part her open, but he paused and his nostrils flared with her scent. "I smell blood. Are you hurt?"

Oh no.

Sunnëva shot up. All the heat coursing through her body immediately cooled. She yanked a sheet over herself and covered her face, groaning. After everything that happened, she lost track of her menses.

"It's nothing. Merely the curse of being a woman." That would certainly stop their intended actions. She winced at the surprised look on his face. "Please don't say you don't know what that is."

She would decease from embarrassment if she had to explain menstruation to a god.

He chuckled. "Yes, I know about the monthly endeavor of women. You bleed, yet it is not fatal enough to die."

"Sometimes the pain feels like I will."

He brushed her cheek. "Well, I don't mind a little blood."

Did that mean ... he wanted to continue? She smiled, and he lifted her chin, taking her lips in his.

A hesitant knock came at the door.

Jökull's mouth broke away, and he glowered at it. "If you value your life, Aero, leave now."

The mage cleared his voice. "Forgive me, sire. I don't mean to disturb you, but I'm afraid I must. We have ... a guest in the castle."

"Why did you allow them inside? You know the protocol."

"Sire, I would have gladly shut the door in his face—if he had used the door."

They both stilled, coming to the same conclusion. There was only one other person they knew who didn't use doors.

The God of Shadows was here.

32

They found Rune lounging on Jökull's throne with his feet kicked up, looking rather comfortable. A black crown rested atop his head, each point as sharp as a blade. Shadows pooled on the floors beneath him like fog. How did he keep coming inside?

"Ah, pardon me if I interrupted something," Rune said shrewdly. From the look on his face, Sunnëva suspected he knew *exactly* what he had interrupted. "I thought I should give my family a visit."

Rune had returned to his mocking, indifferent self. A guise, she realized, he only presented in front of his brother.

"What do you want, Rumiel?" Jökull said. He stood beside her, tall and imposing, his expression matching the frost on the walls.

"I want many things." Rune's gaze remained on her, the meaning clear. He plucked a rose and began tearing the blue petals to pieces. Jökull bared his fangs, snarling. "In truth, I came to inquire about your trip to the Frost Lands. Was the heartwarming reunion everything you secretly hoped for, brother?"

Sunnëva sucked in a low breath, surprised he knew.

He chuckled at the look on their faces. "Oh, you can hardly think I wouldn't find out about that." His shadows thickened and writhed over him, sparking with embers. "I know every secret spoken in the dark."

His shadows, she realized. He only needed the darkness to spy on them.

Jökull growled. "Get out before I spear your head to my wall."

Rune twirled a dark wisp around his finger. "How uncouth of you. It is common courtesy to at least offer your guests a meal at your table."

"You presume too much if you think you're welcome here," Sunnëva said, taking Jökull's hand.

That action made Rune's mouth curl scornfully. "You have seen him for what he is. A devourer of souls. *That* does not disgust you, but I do?"

"Maintain a modicum of your dignity and let her go," Jökull said.

"What he is has nothing to do with how I feel about you," Sunnëva added. "You broke my trust."

Rune scoffed, tucking his scaled hands in his pockets as he climbed down the steps. "*Trust.* Interesting that you should say that. How much *do* you trust each other?"

Sunnëva tensed at the sharpened edge of his smile. This was why he came.

Rune snapped his fingers, and her pack materialized from the shadows in the air. It dropped on the floor with a heavy thud.

Her blood ran cold. "How did you get that?"

Rune merely winked. She tried to grab it, but he tsked. "Oh no, that's not for you, sweetling." He flicked a clawed finger, and it skated across the icy floor, bumping into Jökull's boots.

He glanced at her, and he slowly bent to retrieve the bag.

"Wait." She rushed to him. "Don't."

Jökull opened it and fell still as he stared at the contents inside.

"I am very impressed, Su." Rune grinned. "Vicious little thing, indeed."

Jökull didn't speak. He didn't move.

"It's not what you think," Sunnëva said shakily. She took a step, but he backed away and the action stung. "I can explain."

He reached into the bag. A cold sensation washed over her at the sight of the sharp black talon in his hand. "Well ... when you say you are going to do something, you truly commit," he said faintly.

The bag and talons dissolved away.

"No." Sunnëva took Jökull's face and made him look at her. "If I wanted you dead, why did I save you? Why did I panic and pray to any Gods listening that I would find that shard and pull it out? Why did the thought of you touching anyone who wasn't me hurt so much?" Her vision blurred. "Yes, I wanted you dead before, but you can feel me now, can't you? Does my heart still hate you? Because it feels things I can't admit yet, but they cannot hide from you."

Jökull searched her face. She saw he wanted to believe her, but he'd been betrayed too many times. "The talons were in your pack. You brought them here. Do you deny it?"

Sunnëva closed her eyes and let him go. "No."

"Where did you get them?"

"My sister ... she thought I should have them ... if..."

"If you changed your mind," he said dryly.

She clenched her fists, digging her nails into her palms to ground herself in pain. She was trembling. "I never intended to keep them."

"Then why didn't you tell me?"

"Because ... I didn't want to unravel..." What they were beginning to build. "I couldn't ruin your reconciliation with Kyrr."

Jökull's jaw set. He didn't believe her excuse because it was only partly true.

She glared up at Rune where he loitered by the steps, grinning. "Are you so despicable you can't help causing contention in the world?"

"Pardon. I was feeling a little nauseous over the repugnant miasma of elation and lust floating around you both. I remember when you used to look at me like that. Like you couldn't have enough of me." He smirked at Jökull. "And she really couldn't."

Sunnëva flushed, grinding her teeth. She threw a knife, and it cleaved through the black mist in his wake. His laughter floated in the shadowed corners of the room.

This wasn't only because of jealousy.

"I know why you're doing this," Sunnëva called out. "You're afraid." She turned to where Rune materialized in the gallery across the throne room. "The closer we grow to each other, the closer we are to opening the Gate and getting rid of you."

"Sweet Su, is that what he told you?" Rune cackled. "Oh, how delightful. I hardly even have to try."

Jökull's jaw clenched. "Get out of my castle."

"What is he talking about?" Sunnëva asked him.

Rune strolled around the throne room, playing with his shadows. "There is something my dear brother has conveniently forgotten to mention about the Gates in particular." He dragged his talons along the wall covered in roses as he passed. They all withered and blackened in his wake. Jökull growled. "His Gate won't open merely because you two have *grown close*. It will only open when his bride *falls in love* with him."

She stared at him, her thoughts halting.

Rune misted away and reappeared on the dais. "Why do you think Jökull has been so attentive? Did you think every sweet nothing he said, every care he provided, his protection over you, didn't have a purpose behind it?"

Sunnëva's next inhale caught in her lungs, and her heart pathetically dropped into her stomach.

"Don't listen to him," Jökull said. "This is what he wants." He bared his fangs at Rune. "You put people up against each other. Maker against creation. Husband against wife."

She couldn't do more than stand there, blinking at the desiccated rose petals on the floor as she recalled every moment they had together.

There is no one else in the world for me but you.

Oh, she had been so stupid.

They had agreed to work together, but that didn't mean he wasn't actively working to guarantee he accomplished his goal. All his touches, his seductive flirtations, his care—it was all to gain her trust. To make her *love* him.

Her eyes burned with bitter tears.

How nice it had been to be called his. He had known exactly where to lure her when she had been longing for that type of affection. He saw right through her need to be craved. To feel like she wasn't a useless disappointment.

Jökull tried to take her arm, but she slapped his hand away. His brow creased. "Don't let him do this."

"Yes, yes, ignore the *villain*." Rune chuckled, looking up at the runes on the ceiling. "Yet we are standing in your throne room where no lies can be spoken."

Jökull snarled and shot spears of ice at him.

He teleported across the room with his shadows. "Well, it seems I have overstayed my welcome. As for the ball, I do expect an invitation. I'll be the one in black."

Rune winked at her, then he vanished in a cloud of smoke.

33

Moonlight, roses, and wolfsbane. What did those three things have in common? Sunnëva frowned at the items on the table in Aero's workroom. Bowls of enchanted blue rose petals, a bowl of purple wolfsbane petals, and every ore Jökull created. She frowned at the gems of Moonstone, Nightstone, Bloodstone, and Tanzstone.

"Something is missing here," she said. "Something that will fix Fenrin, but I don't know what it is." Sunnëva kneaded her temples and groaned. "I feel as if the answer is obvious, but I cannot get my thoughts in order."

"Perhaps you cannot concentrate because you have other things on your mind," Gyda mused.

Sunnëva glowered at the old healer seated across the table from her. She had invited Gyda to come stay in the castle and help her work on a cure for Fenrin. Aero had been stretched thin lately with his duties, among other things.

"Which God preoccupies your mind today?" Gyda asked.

Sighing, she sank into her chair.

Rune came to separate them, and he succeeded.

For the next two weeks, Sunnëva hardly spoke to Jökull. He attempted to discuss what had happened in the throne room, but she asked for space instead. He complied by avoiding her when he could leave her under the watch of her new Queen's Guard. At night, they shared his bed with their backs to each other. He didn't bring up the subject again, even when she sensed he wanted to.

Was Jökull truly this patient, or was it also part of the ruse?

Sunnëva didn't know what to think or what to do with the feelings she smothered in her chest. So she didn't think about them at all.

They were still cordial. Any time they had together was spent planning the ball and safety measures of the castle against Rune.

Nothing more.

"Both, it seems."

Sunnëva eyed her narrowly. "Did you know Rune was the God of Shadows?"

When she had explained everything, the old healer barely batted an eye.

"I merely suspected he wasn't human." Gyda shrugged, looking small under her heavy gray cloak. "He moved swiftly and strangely, and he liked to lurk in the shadows. I thought perhaps he was an exiled fae of the Night Court."

More like an exiled God.

Sighing, Sunnëva rolled a Moonstone gem in her fingers.

They were on opposite sides of this war, and she had to find a way to stop him. But it weighed on her.

"Rune ... he saved me in more ways than I can count," Sunnëva murmured. "He was my friend. It pains me to turn my back on him, but I have to for the sake of the world. Except to do what I must, it means opening my heart to the God of Death ... but I can't."

Gyda studied her changed features and shook her head. "My dear girl, I'm afraid there's no stopping that."

She closed her eyes to hide from that fact a little longer. As much as she wanted to deny her feelings, they were showing on the outside.

Maybe there had never been a way out of this. And it scared her. Not that accepting him would change her into something new, but because she would give up her heart.

Could she do that? Could she let him have it?

Did he even want it?

The thing in her chest was battered and ruined, destroyed a long time ago. What if giving it away ended up ruining her further?

"I believe the real reason you called me here is because you need someone to speak some sense into you," Gyda said as she ground some herbs in a mortar. "Ignore your heart, and you break the world. Follow it, and you break yourself when your godly husband leaves. Either way, you lose. But I will say this. Life is too short to live it in fear. I have already seen you broken, girl. If you survived that, you can survive love."

What did Sunnëva know about love?

If this was love, it was frightening and overwhelming, and it made her feel helpless. It felt the same way as when she was plummeting through the storm. Those feelings were impossible to fathom when she hadn't forgiven Jökull for hiding the truth. He must have sensed her falling for him too, which made it more mortifying.

Yet what disturbed her the most was the question if any of it had been genuine. Had she been made a fool by two Gods?

"You certainly have a knack for choosing lovers," Gyda continued. "One who devours souls and the other who thrives in darkness."

Sunnëva played with the gems. *Thrives in darkness...*

She leaped to her feet with a gasp, startling the healer. "Seven Hells, that's it."

Her guards opened the door to the workroom as Aero and Tally entered. "Ah, here you are, my Queen—"

"Aero, I got it!" Sunnëva held out a red gem to him. "Rune only comes out at night, so we have relied on the moon for defense. But we should also consider the sun."

The mage paused at her blurted statement. "With the Bloodstones?"

"Yes! They repel sunlight, but maybe they can be made to harness the power of sunlight instead. At any time of day."

Aero cradled the gem in his palm, his expression thoughtful. "Bloodstones don't repel sunlight. They create a barrier around the wearer to contain them from outside forces."

She frowned. "Then, it's not possible?"

"Perhaps not with these. The concept you're suggesting sounds plausible. However, solar magic is outside of the King's abilities. He created the Bloodstones in collaboration with mages. Therefore, I will reach out to the Head of the Sun Guild and inquire about his thoughts on a new ore." He crossed his arms behind his back. "Meanwhile, we have more pressing matters."

They shared a look and glanced at Tally.

Her handmaiden smiled, but it didn't fully reach her green eyes. She had dark circles and her face was pallid from exhaustion.

Tally curtsied. "It's time, my lady."

The last rays of the sun slipped through the window with the approaching evening, reminding her of tonight's event.

"I must go prepare," Sunnëva said. "I have a ball to attend."

"Yes, you must. And no, I have no desire to attend such frilly events." Gyda waved her off before she could invite her again. "I will continue to test more theories here among the wizards' findings," she said, without looking up from her work.

"He is a mage," Sunnëva whispered, shooting Aero an apologetic look.

"Same thing, girl."

They left the workroom together, with her guards following in their wake. Aero's deep purple robes swayed around his feet as he strode steadily onward, the sunlight catching on his silvery hair.

"Our first guests should arrive soon," he said. "The ball is ready to begin at sundown."

"The guest rooms are made?"

"Yes, my Queen."

"And we have enough food?"

"Of course. The kitchens have prepared more than enough, and the dining hall is already set. Everything is in order."

Sunnëva sighed in relief. "Thank you, Aero. With the Skellings and the Clan Lords coming together in one place, tensions may be high."

They had sent out invitations to every clan in the Everfrost, including the major kingdoms in Urn. The King of the United Crown sent a politely worded letter that he regretfully couldn't attend, and they received no reply from the Argyle Kingdom. But the Emperor of Xián Jīng assured his daughter would be delighted to attend in his stead.

Sunnëva looked forward to meeting the Dragon Princess.

Now the day of the ball had arrived, and she was a jumble of nerves and excitement. But Tally stared blankly ahead, hardly there at all.

Aero noticed, too. "The Castle Guards are prepared. I believe tonight will go peacefully."

"There is a saying among the Morkhàn clan," Sunnëva said as they reached her chambers. "Peace is fleeting."

"I suppose that's true." The mage bowed, excusing himself to get dressed. As he passed, he squeezed Tally's hand, giving her an encouraging smile. Hers was feeble in response.

Tally remained quiet as she helped Sunnëva bathe, fix her hair, and change into an opulent gold gown laid out for her on the bed. The bodice was made of decorative gilded armor, with translucent sleeves and delicate chains that flowed down her arms to her wrists. The skirts moved around her like liquid gold, shimmering as if the fabric was woven with stars. It was the finest thing she had ever worn. Sunnëva looked at her reflection in the mirror, not sure what she thought of herself. Her vivid blue eyes stood out on her pale complexion, her hair flowing around her shoulders in silky streams.

"The King had it made for you, my lady," Tally said next to her, a small smile finally rising to her face. "You look absolutely lovely."

Jökull had it made for her? That formed a knot in her throat, but she pushed the feeling aside.

Sunnëva took her small hands. "How are you feeling, Tally? You haven't seemed well, and I can't help but think it's due to the Rulem clan being in attendance today."

Tally lowered her head. Her lip started to tremble. "Forgive me. When I came here, I was glad to never see the Earl again. But when I heard of the ball, all I could imagine was him stalking me in these halls." She inhaled a deep breath and straightened her shoulders. "But I will be brave and be here to serve you."

Sunnëva hugged her. "He cannot hurt you anymore."

"I know, my lady. Thank you." Tally turned away, wiping her cheek, before picking out some shoes.

Her new Queen's Guard stood by the door. More fae knights, but from another court this time. They were quiet, stoic males. It made her miss Ren and Riona.

"Has there been any change in Ren's condition?" Sunnëva asked as she sat at the vanity and slipped on a pair of gold heels with Tally's help. Aero had put the knight under what he called a healing sleep to extract the poison from him. Whatever killed her guards had a venomous bite and was large enough to crush their bones.

Tally shook her head somberly. "I am afraid not, my lady. Aero thinks he might have extracted the poison too late, or..."

"Or?"

"Ren doesn't wish to wake."

Sunnëva sighed. Because when he woke, it would only be to find his sister dead. That would be too much for his kind heart.

"But Aero is working on a new type of magic," Tally said as she opened an ornate box of jewels. "He says there are energies within us that are the source of life. Channels that carry Essence through our bodies. Aero has a theory that if he can connect with them to see within the body, he could access a deeper form of healing by seeing what ails Ren."

Sunnëva raised her eyebrows. "Do you think it's possible?"

"It's still a working theory. Aero does not want to harm Ren. He will attempt an experiment of sorts on Fenrin, which your brother approved, my lady," she added quickly at Sunnëva's frown. "Seeing as he is quite durable."

"Speaking of Fenrin, where has he gone?"

"I believe he is outside on the battlements. He wanted to see the gentry arrive."

Trumpets echoed from outside. She and Tally exchanged an excited smile.

The blue light of a portal swirled in the chamber, and Jökull strode in as he adjusted the sleeves of his elegant blue jacket, a fine white pelt on his shoulders.

Jökull paused at the sight of her, his piercing gaze slowly taking her in. Her pulse thrummed when it warmed. He took a shallow breath and said, "Ready?"

She nodded.

He crossed the room in swift strides, hand outstretched. She had no choice but to take it. His large fingers close around hers, cool and smooth. His touch elicited little shocks of energy over her skin. She met those eyes that always seemed to make her thoughts pause. They were fractured with shards of ice, like cracked Celestine. His thumb stroked softly over her palm, a shockingly intimate gesture that elicited a current of energy through her body.

Sunnëva looked away merely to remind herself she was angry with him.

Jökull placed her hand on his arm and opened another portal. They came out on a wide landing platform high up in the castle, with a view of the land. The road to the main gates was full of people on horseback and in carriages, with the clans displaying their flag colors. From the north flew in a flock of Skellings with Kyrr in the lead and Kerro carrying Ansa on his back.

Sunnëva's mouth fell open when she spotted three dragons in the sky. They were *enormous*. One had dark green scales, nearly black. Another was deep crimson, like wine. The largest of them had silver scales that glinted in the sunlight. Riding it was a woman, the hem of her long red robes flaring in her wake. Bellowing out a roar, the dragon flew straight for them. Jökull moved Sunnëva back. Wind whipped around them, and the castle shook as it landed on the platform. Its rider dismounted from the saddle and climbed down the creature's body.

The Dragon Princess possessed a divine beauty.

She seemed to glow in the setting sun, light catching on her soft, heart-shaped face and delicate red lips. Her black hair was done up in an elaborate knot, adorned with plum blossoms and gold jewelry, that danced with each of her movements. On her forehead dangled a golden pendant with a red gem glinting in the evening light.

She beamed brightly at Jökull. "I could not believe it when I received a letter of invitation to a ball in the castle of ice. A ball, of all things!" The tone of her country accented her voice, but she spoke Urnian perfectly.

Her red Xián Jīng robes fluttered in the wind as she strode to them. It was elegant, made of many layers, adorned with gold trimming and embroidered lotus flowers. Her silver dragon soared into the air and circled the sky with the others.

Jökull inclined his head. "Princess Daiyu, I am pleased you were able to join us. You've come far."

"I was more than happy to make the journey. It is not every day that I have an excuse to leave the palace and travel across the country."

"You have come alone?"

She gasped dramatically. "My parents would never. You know how they are. The Emperor and Empress trust that you would never let anything happen to their precious daughter, Jökull, but they insisted that my ladies-in-waiting and a handful of guards accompany me. Including my dragon riders. They are arriving by carriage and horseback on the road."

Jökull's mouth hitched in an easy half-smile, showing how comfortable they were with each other. They must be long-time friends, evident by her informal greeting.

The princess's honeyed brown eyes fell on Sunnëva, and her smile widened. "And this must be your..."

"Yes, this is my Queen." His gaze glided to hers a moment, and he held out a hand in introduction. "Sunnëva, this is Princess Daiyu Long of the Xián Jīng Dynasty."

She lowered into a curtsey. "Welcome, Princess. It's an honor to meet you."

"Pretty and so polite." Daiyu chuckled, hooking an arm through hers as they strode for the castle. "Let us skip the formalities. Call me Daiyu."

She smiled, instantly liking her. "This is my handmaiden, Tally."

Tally curtseyed low.

"Oh, look at how small she is! Another darling. Come here." Daiyu pulled her close, like they were old friends. "I have a penchant for pretty things, so don't mind me. Let's get out of this dreadful cold. Sunnëva, tell me how you managed to snare this icicle of a man while we go spy on the parade of fine gentry coming to your banquet."

"Icicle?" Jökull grunted behind them.

"I am taking all her attention away from you while I'm here, Winter King." She winked at her as they walked down the hall. "I simply must learn more about your wife. Since you declined my marriage proposal, I'm convinced you're madly in love with her."

Sunnëva grimaced, suddenly embarrassed by the assumption. She was also curious why he would turn down such a charming woman.

"I owe you a great debt, Sunnëva," Daiyu whispered loudly. "My parents constantly pressure me to find a husband. I want to discover the world and live my life, not fatten in a castle while spending my days serving some king only interested in his coffers and land."

"I am right here," Jökull reminded them.

Princess Daiyu snickered. "Not you. You're perfect." Then she continued telling her, "But my parents wanted their dear daughter to marry the best, and they had their minds set on a God. The only way they would stop trying to marry me off to Jökull was for him to be taken by another. Therefore, you are my new best friend."

Sunnëva grinned. "You know, there is another God—"

"Oh no, please! I convinced them he was a demon. If they discover another prospect for my hand exists, I will never hear the end of it."

Sunnëva threw back her head and laughed. "I think you and I are going to get along fine, Daiyu."

"My thoughts exactly."

34

They strode into the dining hall where their guests were waiting. The women arrived in their finest gowns in every color, with the men in their livery. The fae were easy to differentiate.

The Sea Queen was the splendor of the sea. She wore a crown of coral and pearls, with a river of teal blue hair moving on invisible waves, and a gown that glittered like the ocean. Her court had insipid skin tinted gray to sea green. Some glistened with scales and webbed ears, others had translucent teeth and kelp in their pale hair.

Prince Dagden arrived, surrounded by his court of wild fae and knights with red-scaled armor. He was dressed elaborately in a coat designed to look like autumn leaves that matched his garnet eyes. A crown of gilded antlers rested on his head, accentuating his long, blond hair.

They were all beautiful, as most fae were.

Princess Daiyu recognized a Lord and excused herself to greet him. Sunnëva and Jökull fell back as people streamed in a constant wave. All nine clans were present, proven by the colors of their clothing and sigils.

Sunnëva was glad to see the mystical King and Queen of the Vale of the Elves were present. Even the mages had arrived, each Guild distinguished by the color of their elegant robes.

Aero spoke to an older woman with silvery hair and white robes. When he noticed them, he excused himself to join them.

"Who is that?" Tally asked him.

"That is Lady Selene. She is the Head of the Lunar Guild and my grandmother," he said. "Shall I introduce you?"

She flushed. "Oh, um ... maybe another time."

"Your grandmother?" Sunnëva said, watching the mages with awe. It pleased her to know women could have a prominent position in the Magos Empire. She hoped it always remained that way. "You must have learned a lot from her."

"Everything I know." Aero looked proud of it, too. He turned to Jökull. "Chief Kyrr and the Skellings have all arrived, sire."

Their tall forms lingered on the other end of the dining hall, sticking together in a cluster of feathers. Ansa was among them. Sunnëva raised a hand to wave, but Tally recoiled abruptly and bumped into her.

Her wide eyes were fixed on Bram, Earl of the Rulem clan. He was a large, ruffian of a man. He'd been conversing with the other Earls when he noticed Tally. His greasy mouth sneered.

"Pardon me, my lady." She ran away through the servants' doors. Aero went after her.

Bram chortled with his clansmen and continued chugging down ale. It took everything in Sunnëva not to draw out her hidden knife and shove it into the man's kidney. But she took a deep breath, calming herself. He would get his.

"Well, what is your plan of attack?" Jökull asked beside her, holding out his arm.

"Divide and conquer," Sunnëva replied evenly as she took it. "We mingle and fortify alliances. The kingdom certainly needs it."

They went to stand at the front of the room together.

"Lords and ladies of the land," Jökull called out, and the room quieted. "Thank you for joining us this evening. We have guests from every corner of the Everfrost, even special arrivals from the west."

Princess Daiyu lifted her glass in greeting.

"Introduce yourselves to one another, and we will have dinner shortly."

The crowd slowly resumed their conversations.

Earl Lazar approached Jökull to thank him for the recent reserves sent to his clan. He was a tall man with dark skin and braids. When he excused himself, the Earl of the Tanner clan came eagerly forward with his clansmen. Each had bright red hair and thick beards. They kneeled and lowered their heads to the ground with reverence.

"My liege," the Earl said. "It's an honor to be here tonight in your divine presence. Exalted are the Seven."

"Exalted are the Seven," his clansmen recited.

"Markus Tanner, you honor me," Jökull said, his mouth twitching when Sunnëva gave him a look. "Please rise. Allow me to introduce you to my Queen."

There was no need. Markus already knew her and her father. But they immediately returned to their knees and bowed before her as if she was true royalty.

"Blessed be the Winter Queen," the Earl said humbly and his clansmen echoed it.

"Please stand, Earl Tanner. Go enjoy yourselves tonight." Sunnëva tipped her head, smiling politely, though inwardly she cringed. It seemed not all the clans feared the Death God. "I must greet Kyrr and my sister," she murmured to Jökull.

She made her escape as the Earl mentioned they were building a temple in honor of him.

The Skellings hovered in the corner, watching the crowd as warily as the others watched them. They stood out with their feathered bodies and noticeable height, their clothing mostly crude leather and decorative beads.

The crowd parted enough for her to see Ansa. Kerro had seated himself on the ground, holding her in his lap. He leaned his head down to hear something Ansa said, and she gave his cheek an affectionate nuzzle. Her sister looked so happy she glowed with it. She wore a dress woven with leather like the clothing of the Skellings, making her look like a wild princess of the forest. They smiled at each other.

But Ansa shrank back when Bjorn tried to approach her. He quickly learned that was a terrible idea. Kerro bared his fangs menacingly, wrapping his wing around his little mate. The Skellings hissed in warning.

Bjorn retreated, stumbling over himself.

Sunnëva tried not to laugh as she strode for them. She might not have wanted their union, but she had no doubt Kerro would keep Ansa safe. No one could harm her sister now.

When Sunnëva passed him, Bjorn grabbed her arm and pulled her aside. "Father is angry that you married off Ansa without his permission. Now they keep her from her family."

"I don't need his permission, and you have no reason to go near her," Sunnëva said sharply, glancing down at his grip. "Release me unless you wish to lose that hand."

Blades were drawn as the Queen's Guard surrounded him, and Fenrin loomed up behind her, snarling. The dining room quieted, everyone's attention falling on them, including Jökull's. His piercing eyes glowed from where he sat at the head of his table.

Bjorn paled and immediately let go. "I am her brother, Sunnëva. And yours."

"When have you acted like one?" she asked. "When have you ever cared? You stood by as Father constantly harmed us, turning a blind eye to our pain. Better us than you, right?"

Bjorn's brow creased, and he looked away. Exhaling a heavy breath, he tugged down the edge of his collar, exposing his chest. He bore an old, horrible scar where he had been branded with the Morkhàn sigil like cattle. "You're wrong if you believe Father didn't hurt me, too..." he muttered. "Maybe I am a coward, but I did try to help."

Sunnëva stared at him with wide eyes. Bjorn left before she could say more. He had tried, she realized. He had attempted to keep her from disobeying their father by warning her with a look or word. When he had arrived at the castle before, he mentioned Ansa's illness because he knew she would find a way to stop it.

Sunnëva met her father's dark stare where he stood with Earl Bram, nursing a horn of ale. None of them had been spared.

She continued, and when she reached the Skellings, Sunnëva looked up at Ansa's mate placatingly. "May I greet my sister, Kerro?"

He grunted, pursing his mouth.

Ansa lowered his brown wing with a soft laugh. Sunnëva gathered her skirts, and they rushed to each other, embracing. Out of everything that would happen tonight, this was what she cared about the most.

Once they caught up, Jökull approached Kyrr. "Come dine with us at our table. You are amongst friends."

Things were still awkward between them, but the request seemed to please the Skelling Chief. Their guests soon began to fill the seats.

Princess Daiyu came up beside Sunnëva as she headed to the table. She gaped up at the warg accompanying her in wonder. "Well, hello."

"Princess, this is my brother Fenrin."

"Your *brother*?"

"He is under a curse of sorts. I am in the midst of trying to undo it."

"Oh my. I have seen many curses, but this one is certainly new." Daiyu smiled at him teasingly. "Are you handsome under all that fur?"

He bared his teeth in a feral grin.

Daiyu laughed behind her fan. "I bet you are. You know, I heard true love's kiss is an effective way of breaking curses."

Donelle chose that moment to saunter on by in a silky crimson gown. She gagged at the suggestion, looking at Fenrin in disgust. "Kiss that one, and you may end up cursing yourself."

"He will overcome his condition, but the same cannot be said of you," Sunnëva retorted.

Donelle tittered to herself as she sauntered away.

"Snake." Daiyu curled her lip. "I hate snakes."

They took their seats at the dining table as everyone got settled. Dinner was uncomfortable, to say the least. Old feuds were apparent in the way the Lords jabbed at each other. Many were guarded against the Skellings and questioned what their lifted exile would mean for the land. Sunnëva sighed, letting their voices drone on.

She perked up when Earl Bram drunkenly ambled away from the dining room with two of his clansmen. Probably to relieve himself of all the ale he'd been drinking. She looked at Aero. The mage's jaw set. Rising from the table, he excused himself and went down another hall.

Jökull arched an eyebrow at the exchange and took a drink. "What was that about?"

She picked at her meal, replying quietly enough for only him to hear. "Nothing you wouldn't approve of."

"Hmm." His mouth curved. "Have I mentioned how beautiful you look tonight?"

She smirked. "No."

"Sunnëva, you are radiant. More so when you're murderous."

She simpered playfully, twirling her fork. "It will cost you an alliance with Rulem."

When she approached Aero with her plan last week, he agreed because he already intended to deal with the Earl. Neither of them asked permission. This was happening whether her husband agreed or not.

"They were never loyal, regardless. I trust your judgment, and if this is the verdict, there is a reason." His eyes held hers, and her heart did that stupid dance thing again. This was the most they had spoken in a while. Jökull laid his hand over hers. "I despise this distance between us. I want to be patient, but I hate being parted from you in any way." The soft confession made her pulse flicker. "I would rather have your anger than your silence."

She sighed. "You lied."

"I didn't lie, Sunnëva."

"Withholding the truth is still a lie by omission."

Jökull frowned. "Then shall we agree that both of us withheld the truth? Yours far more dire than mine."

"How so?"

He growled. "Really?"

She looked away. "I already said I didn't intend to hurt you."

"I didn't intend to hurt you either."

"Who said I was?" Sunnëva meant to sound indifferent, but the tightness in her voice betrayed her. She pulled away.

Jökull frowned. He leaned over, his head dipping to her ear. "You can act as cold as you want, winter rose, but I have already felt how warm you are from the inside."

Her cheeks flamed, and she clenched her teeth. Those intimate moments only made her feel more used. "All you have proven to me is that you're as cold as they say you are."

A raw expression crossed his face, one she had never seen before. "If you believe what we had in our time together was false—"

She shook her head. "Please, I don't wish to speak of this."

It was too hard to share the truth and show him more of the darkness inside. That to want something so much made her feel weak and afraid.

"You think I am not afraid, too?"

Sunnëva stilled in her seat at his question. How did he always know the state of her heart when she couldn't make sense of it?

"You don't know how long I—" Jökull heaved a breath, and his fist clenched on the table. "I understand wanting something so much you fear taking it, even when it stands before you."

She lowered her gaze because she couldn't bring herself to look at him.

With a low exhale, he got to his feet. "When you're ready for me to say what you cannot hear, I will be around."

Sunnëva blinked away her wet vision as he left the table. It was easier to lash out at him. It was safer to push him away than to acknowledge what she couldn't hide from anymore.

Tally came in through the servant doors and rushed to her side. "My lady, please forgive me for my earlier outburst. I thought I would be prepared to see him here, but—"

Sunnëva stood. "Come with me."

Tally ducked her head and followed.

"I used to blame the Gods for my misfortunes," Sunnëva said as they left the dining room. "Until I realized they gave us free will to do right and wrong. Unfortunately, that means there are people out there who are more monstrous than beasts. There are laws in place, but sometimes that is not enough to protect us from those in power. From those who got away with all the horrible things they did to others because they could. There are times when justice must be what we make it."

They went through the kitchens to a darker part of the castle and took the narrow steps to the dungeons. Passing through the door, Sunnëva's heels clacked on the ground, meshing among the sounds of wails and growls coming from the dark cells. Tally clutched her arm, keeping close. They followed the torchlights until they reached a cell that glowed purple, where the sounds of muffled screams grew louder and the air was ripe with the stench of burning flesh.

Tally gasped.

Lord Bram was inside, stripped to his undergarments and pinned to the wall with bindings of magic. He sweated profusely, his body blistered with burns. His clansmen lay unconscious in the corner.

The Earl screamed against his bindings as Aero struck him with volt of electricity, searing another mark into his belly.

"Aero," Sunnëva called idly.

The mage's blazing purple eyes fell on them, and he stepped away from the bleeding man.

"What you do with him is your choice." She held out a knife to her handmaiden. "Nothing will befall you for taking your justice, and no one will judge you if you choose to let him live. But when you leave this cell, you will no longer allow him to burden your life. Tonight, you free yourself of him, Tally."

Tears streamed down Tally's cheeks. She accepted the knife with shaking hands and faced Lord Bram. She was so small, yet she looked like a giant at that moment, standing before the man who violated her. He writhed with panic, screaming at Sunnëva, curses or pleadings, she didn't know. Nor did she care.

Maybe this was wrong. Maybe it made her evil.

But no one could argue that he didn't deserve it.

Sunnëva's gold gown swished over the dirty cobblestones as she turned away. Perhaps she was also letting go of another piece of that night in the woods. This was for that robbed innocence.

For Freya.

And for all the other women who had their lives stolen from them.

Their attackers threatened pain or humiliation if they fought back, but they still hurt them. Better to hurt them, too. To leave their own mark and make sure it cost them the same.

Tally's light voice echoed in the dungeon as Sunnëva strode for the door. "Why do you look so afraid?" she asked. "Don't you remember what you used to tell me when I was a little girl? We shouldn't fear love."

Sunnëva smiled to herself when she heard the first strangled scream. If luck was on the Earl's side, his suffering would end quickly. As some infuriatingly handsome beast once told her, there were worse things than dying.

The heavy door shut behind her, silencing all else.

Sunnëva made her way to the ballroom. It was brightly lit with golden chandeliers above, reflecting off the frosted walls adorned with enchanted roses. Their sweet scent and the sound of music filled the air. Fae musicians played on a short platform in the corner as their guests swayed with their partners in a dance.

Her father idled with a group of clansmen in a corner. Noticing her, he strode in her direction. Well, she knew it was coming. May as well get it over with. She watched the dance as he came to stand beside her.

"Father," she greeted. "I trust you have enjoyed yourself."

"I have," Thorstein admitted. "You called forth this farce to reaffirm alliances, but you know the clans don't honor him."

"Some do."

"Not the ones that count. We were supposed to remove him from power, Sunnëva. You betrayed your clan and brought shame upon yourself and your House."

"The only thing I am ashamed of is how much I tried to make you love me," Sunnëva said, turning to face him. "Nothing I did was enough ... because you could not stop blaming me."

Pain and anger lined his face. "I lost my child that night."

Sunnëva smiled wryly, if only not to cry. "I am your child, too."

Finally, she could admit to herself that she had longed for a father who doted on her, who praised and held her, instead of the one who cut her with his words. But he had only given that to Freya.

If he could love his eldest daughter, that meant he was capable of loving all his children. She merely wasn't worth being loved.

"I'm sorry." Sunnëva's voice caught. "I'm sorry she died. I'm sorry I couldn't protect her. I'm sorry I couldn't be what you wanted me to be. But even before then, you weren't a father. Whatever pain made you, you carved it into us. I bear those scars in addition to my own. I tried to earn your affection. Tried to please you. But I stopped when I wondered if you even acknowledged the pain you fed us on a broken spoon."

She searched his face for remorse or regret. There was none.

"If you await an apology, I have none to offer," Thorstein said. "I raised you as needed to survive. Do not forget. Everything you have accomplished is because of *me*."

Sunnëva shook her head at the ceiling, waiting for her misty eyes to dry. It was useless to argue with him or to expect a sliver of an apology. He only saw his way.

Maybe he was never capable of loving them, or he never cared. Maybe it was due to his own upbringing, with a father who was equally cruel, and enduring the hardships of life that rendered him this cold man. Maybe she was right, and the shred of affection he ever had died with her sister. Her father had closed himself off from caring about anyone else because it was safer.

He broke them because he was broken, too.

Sometimes it was family who caused the most damage. She bore that pain all her life, but she was done allowing him to hurt her.

"Yes, thank you for selling me for your benefit. In that, you have my gratitude." Sunnëva tipped her head. "Goodbye, Father."

"You may have turned on your people, but the land is shifting into the era of humans," Thorstein said before she could leave. "Jökull is not of this world. As much as you wish to live here in this extravagant castle with him, you cannot dispute that. Therefore, I will find a way to remove him, Sunnëva. With or without you."

She sighed heavily, tired of this conversation. "You can't beat him. You don't have the power or the army."

Thorstein wasn't offended. He almost smiled, and the look on his face made her still.

"I will." He looked around the ballroom and nodded. "The time has come for new alliances to be made."

He turned to go.

"Why do you hate him?" Sunnëva blurted. Because she finally saw it there, plainly on his face.

Pure loathing.

His back remained to her for a moment, then he said, "Because all he returned with was you."

She frowned, confused by his meaning, but he didn't elaborate.

Thorstein walked away as the song ended, and whatever bound them as father and daughter broke apart like two glaciers at sea. That constant pressure in her chest vanished too, allowing her lungs to expand with a full breath. At her next exhale, she let go of all the guilt she had carried for the past five years.

Bjorn and the rest of the Morkhàn clansmen followed their Earl out of the ballroom.

Sunnëva watched them go, so lost in thought she didn't notice the shadows gathering around her until it was too late.

35

The shadows whisked Sunnëva away and brought her to a vacant gallery overseeing the ballroom from above. It was small, with a few empty seats. And away from the bright lights.

Rune's voice slinked out from the dark. "Your father has always been the worst end of an arse. There were several times when I had to restrain myself from cracking his spine in half."

He leaned up against a column outside of the vestibule, his arms crossed. He appeared as the version of him she remembered. Warm skin. Amber eyes. His human form that she had fallen for. It shook her to see it as if seeing a ghost.

Sunnëva glowered. "What are you doing here?"

"I came to the ball," Rune said, holding a hand to his chest with mock pain. "I am wounded you didn't invite me, but I will forgive you if you join me in a dance." He had dressed up in a fine black coat trimmed in gold and brushed his hair. "I give you my word. I mean no one in this castle harm tonight."

Magic rippled around her with his divine promise.

She eyed him warily. "Then you will leave?"

"If that is what you want."

Sunnëva sighed. Might as well indulge him. She took his offered hand, and Rune pulled her into a dance. He moved her with ease, each step perfectly timed with the soft music below.

"I miss you," Rune murmured, drawing closer.

Sunnëva put space between them. "What scheme are you planning now?"

"No scheme. I came to see you out of my genuine will."

So he only pretended to be a conniving prick when Jökull was present. Or was he trying a different tactic now that they were alone?

"You don't love him, Sunnëva. If you did, his Gate would already be open." Rune spoke softly, his touch gentle as she remembered it. "I admit, the last time I came was out of jealousy ... I sensed you drifting away. It hurt when you didn't take my hand and chose to fight at his side." His expression creased, his mouth softening with a wounded frown. "Despite everything, I still want you with me. Why won't you choose me?"

This was as vulnerable as she had ever seen him.

"Have you forgotten all that we shared?"

Sunnëva's wariness softened. "No..."

She would never forget the hand that reached out to her that night. Never forget that he carried her out of those woods. But that bond between them was lost, and with it her affections.

"If you had been my bride, my Gate would have opened long ago." Rune brushed her cheek.

Did he mean because he loved her or because he believed she still did?

Where would she have fallen in his plan for domination? If none of this had happened, if Rune had changed his mind about using her, if they had gotten married instead, would he have ever revealed the truth about who he was?

"I don't think so," Sunnëva said faintly.

She let him go and stepped back. There was no point in asking herself these questions when the answer was irrelevant. Her heart might have been his in the past, but it didn't thrum for him anymore.

It was silent in her chest.

"Su—"

"You can't stop lying, Rune. You've lied to me the entire time we knew each other, and you continue to lie to yourself." She folded her hands together over her golden gown and sat in an empty seat. "Even if your Gate did open, you would never go through it, would you?"

"Why would I return to the Heavens to be commanded? The day my brothers left me behind, a weight lifted off my shoulders. In the dawning of that new age, I was ... free." His mouth lifted in a faint smile. "You know exactly what I speak of. You felt that same freedom when you were cast out of the home you suffocated in. All I want is to preserve that with you in our future."

The view of the ballroom vanished. Sunnëva found herself seated on a throne of black marble, an ebony tiara on her head as the world bowed before them. The sky was shrouded in darkness, rumbling with fire. Rune stood beside her in his true form, a crown of shadows on his brow, black mist moving around him.

"This is the future you've envisioned," she said. "All I have ever known—destroyed."

"Is the land not already destroyed under the ice? Those bones outside the castle were not put there by me alone. Death or shadow, the wickedness remains." Rune lifted her chin, making her meet his crimson gaze. "But as you have stayed his hand, you would stay mine. By my side, you would have everything you deserve. I would bestow upon you the grace of night and the beauty of the stars, with a power far greater than the foundation of the universe."

How seductive the words sounded, but they tasted like ash on her tongue.

"You chose me first. I am asking you to choose me again, Su." Rune's expression was earnest. Brittle. "I can't lose you to him."

He already had.

Jökull had wormed his way into her veins, wedged in so deep, fitting so perfectly she had no way of pulling him out. He had done it not with promises of power, but by simply helping her regain her value. He saw her for who she was, rotten and ruined, and found it beautiful.

"Rune."

He dropped his hand at her pacifying tone. "No."

The ballroom gallery reappeared. Rune's eyes smoldered with flames, and she saw the dejection behind his anger. He did care, in his own way.

She stood. "Sometimes ... we can't help the things we lose."

"You know nothing of what I have lost," he said sharply.

"I'm not her," Sunnëva whispered. "I'm not your lost bride."

Rune's feet rocked a step back as though her words had been a blow deep in the pit of his stomach. His face. He looked devastated. Shattered.

"Rumiel—"

He hissed, shadows whipping around him wildly. "Don't call me that."

"Calling yourself by a different name doesn't change who you are," she said gently. "Maybe ... if you had accepted that, she might still be alive."

Pain overtook the anger on his features. He rubbed his face as if to get rid of the feeling or to hide it from her. His grief was so strong it thickened the air. As much as Rune had blamed Jökull, she saw the truth. He carried the weight of her death.

Sunnëva looked away, regretting speaking about his bride because she could feel it. How much he had experienced a pure, everlasting love for her. "I'm sorry."

"I don't want your sympathy, Sunnëva."

"I know what you want, but I can't give it to you."

Rune's expression pinched, and he shook his head. "You were meant to be on my side of things. Don't force me to be your villain. Don't do that to me."

"There is a fine line between villain and monster." She looked at him solemnly. "The world is a cruel place, and it's never fair. There is darkness everywhere, but there is good, too, if we look for it. That's worth protecting. If that means I have to defend it from you, I will. With everything I have."

The anger melted away from his features, along with every previous emotion. His stillness was unsettling. Leaving only the shadows to darken around him as he regarded her indifferently.

Because he finally accepted the end of what they had.

"If you think I'm a monster," Rune said, his voice dropping low. "Then I will be the vilest one."

Shadows crawled up his face, his eyes becoming hearths of flame. A shudder crept over her. He turned away and strode for the vestibule of the gallery, where the candlelight didn't reach.

"Don't do this," she called after him. "Simply go home. You don't belong here."

He paused and cast a smirk over his shoulder. "Neither does Jökull. He has to return with me, Sunnëva. Have you thought of that? Are you prepared to be left behind?"

No, she wasn't prepared for that, but it was unavoidable. She had always known where she stood in this. Jökull never offered to take her across not only because she was mortal, but because only two Gods could cross a Gate and he intended it to be him and Rune.

She was going to lose him.

That's what truly held her back all this time, but her heart had already made up its mind. Rune had to live with his regrets, but she didn't want those regrets to be hers, too. She didn't want to hide from her heart anymore.

Sunnëva exhaled a soft breath. "I would rather be with Jökull in the time we have left than not be with him at all."

Shock crossed his face.

She touched her lips at the admission they spoke aloud. But it was true, proven by the fact that the past two weeks had been torture.

All she wanted was him.

Rune glanced past her shoulder, then strode away into the shadows. She didn't turn, sensing who stood behind her now. Jökull never left her side, even when he had walked away.

"Sunnëva…"

Her heart shook at his presence, and she lowered her lashes. The way he said her name confirmed he had heard her confession.

Jökull's arm came around her waist, pulling her close against his chest. His mere touch ignited her being. His cool breath fell against her neck as he whispered three words against her fluttering pulse.

"Dance with me."

He led her backward into the portal he came through, bringing her to the rose garden. Their sweet scent carried in the night air, and the clear sky was lit with a scatter of stars. Music drifted to them from the ballroom. The tones wove in a gentle, sweet melody, as though to recount the tale of the way she slowly but surely fell in love with this God.

They danced together beneath the night sky, flurries drifting down around them. Moonlight gleamed over the courtyard, catching on his long white hair. He looked very striking in his elegant blue jacket, so different outside of his usual heavy armor. There was a sweet tension between them, filling up the mere inches of space between their bodies. She wanted him and only him, and she didn't care anymore about anything else.

Lowering her into a dip, Jökull pulled her back up to him with ease. He looked at her as though she were everything he could ever want. The wind picked up, and glowing rose petals drifted past them, but she didn't feel the cold. Right now, she was so full of warmth that she couldn't give words to it. Still, the feeling made her heart tremble because she finally accepted what it meant and how much trouble she was in. He spun her around, and her back flattened against his chest.

"I didn't tell you the truth about the Gate," Jökull said. "Because I feared you would never accept me."

Sunnëva shook her head, smiling. She had accepted him a long time ago.

The music led them into another turn, and she faced him again, their hands linking together. Jökull pulled her closer, and his cool palm slowly drifted up her spine. As though he wished to memorize the feel of her.

"I have seen your eyes filled with every emotion. But the way they shine tonight ... I want you to always look at me the way you're looking at me now."

"How am I looking at you?" she asked, snowflakes catching on her lashes.

"Like you trust me ... and want me to kiss you."

"Traitorous eyes," Sunněva whispered as Jökull leaned in closer. He took her mouth in his, gentle and sweet. She fell freely into the embrace of winter's kiss. His arms wrapped around her, holding her close, and she sighed against his cool lips that moved so gently over hers.

"I have decided something," he murmured between kisses. "I will spend the rest of my days living only for you."

"I thought I was a vicious little thorn..." Sunněva murmured, and he smiled against her lips.

"Oh, you are." His nose skated her cheek. "My prickly..." His tongue darted against her earlobe. "Sweet..." His mouth trailed over her throat. "Winter rose."

She focused on him and how he felt around her, on his scent of frost, cedar, and roses. She fought tears at the thought of not having it for long.

"Does this mean your Gate will open now?"

His soft sigh drifted over her cheeks. "Would you laugh if I told you I no longer want it to?"

She did, though the sound caught in her throat with the sob she held back.

"I have been searching for a way to open my Gate for so very long," he said. "I roamed the whole world, looking for signs, hoping my brothers had left some clue behind. Then I recalled Hiram made Seers who saw beyond time and thought perhaps they may have the knowledge I need. So I sought out the one they call the Druid."

Sunněva's eyes flew open. "What?"

"That's how desperate I was." The wind blew against them, and Jökull brushed the loose strands of hair catching on her lashes. His jacket sleeve dropped enough to reveal the tattoo on his wrist.

She had seen that before.

Taking his arm, Sunnëva yanked back his sleeve, exposing his pale skin to the air. One end of his tattoo was a spiral that looped up into a circle and crossed down into another spiral to level with the first.

"This..."

"It's a God's Mark," Jökull said. "We all have it."

She blinked up at him, her next breath halting in her lungs. "What did ... the Druid say?"

"That to open my Gate, I would need to find the bride fated to be mine. It would only open once she loved me, but in doing so, I would lose all of my power to her." His face softened, sheepish. "I was infuriated by that. I refused to let some human take everything from me. Then all I had was hate for my bride. I decided I would find another way to get what I needed. I had him reveal where you were so I could destroy you." Jökull took her face gently in his hands, his lips brushing away the tears gathering on her lashes. "He instructed me to attend a clan wedding on the night of the lunar eclipse, and the woman who asked me for a kiss was my fate. So I disguised myself as a human, and I went there with every intention of killing you."

"Disguise?" she whispered.

Magic rippled around Jökull, and his appearance changed. His hair became black and his ears rounded. His pale skin warmed, but those pretty eyes remained the same. Looking at him like this, she was struck by how much he resembled Rune.

His glamor returned to how he had previously looked. "When I saw you, all I could do was watch you dance." He smiled faintly. "And you most certainly did look very beautiful in your dress."

Sunnëva's throat tightened, and her vision blurred, her pulse swaying to a new tempo.

"You asked me for a kiss with such a sweet smile that if I'm being honest, I probably would have given you anything at that moment," he said, his voice catching. "I was holding you in my arms, my hand on your back so close to your heart, but I had no desire to take your life. At the first touch of your lips ... I couldn't. Finding you was like my soul coming alive. That connection filled me with so much light, I was sure the world could see it. My entire existence was filled with death, but you—you were life. I was so taken aback, I could hardly speak."

Sunnëva inhaled a shaky breath, knowing she had felt the same.

And what had happened next.

Jökull's brow creased. "But I left you out of my sight for one moment and ... they ripped out your light." His jaw clenched and his hands fell away, wickedly sharp talons extending from his fingers. "Then I became who I was always meant to be. The bringer of death."

"It was you..." Her mouth trembled. "*You* killed them."

He had been the beast in the dark.

An icy expression crossed his face. "Yes."

She recalled something Aero once said about Jökull's ability to instill fear and the utter terror the men expelled in their screams. "You lost control..."

"Oh, I was very in control," Jökull said, his voice a near snarl. "I *eviscerated* those men one by one. I wanted that fear to perpetually mark their souls as I shredded them apart until they were reduced to bone and carnage."

He searched her face, waiting to see how she would react to the gruesome confession. She started to cry. Not because of what he had done, but because she thought it had been Rune who saved her that night. That last strand of gratitude that had clung to her old feelings so stubbornly was snipped at that moment.

"Your sister had already passed, but you were still clinging on by a thread. I healed your greatest wounds, assuring your soul stayed."

She finally understood why Thorstein hated him. Jökull had only saved one daughter.

Her father made her feel like her survival had not mattered, but it did matter to someone.

It did to *him*.

"We don't ever truly die," she whispered.

"We only change worlds," Jökull replied. "And I need you in this one."

Her tears freely spilled.

Sunnëva pressed a light kiss over his God's Mark. "Thank you..." she said, cupping his cool hand to her cheek. "Thank you."

At last, she could say it.

Jökull sighed, and his forefinger fell over the scar above her brow. "Whenever I see your scars, I fight the urge to bring them back to life merely to slaughter them again."

Sunnëva almost wished he would.

Nothing about her was pure anymore. She'd been shredded and shorn. Her edges were now sharp and jagged, like rusted blades. Her heart was violent, with a need to hurt those who hurt others. If those men hadn't died that night, she would have dedicated her life to hunting them down one by one. Each of their deaths would have been brutally and *torturously* slow.

"I have made and unmade many things," Jökull said, stroking her cheek. "But I could not put your pieces together. For all my power, I could not undo the damage done to your soul. That was not my place. I had to accept I lost my bride. For how would you allow anyone to be close to you after what you endured? Before I left, I warned Thorstein I would break open his ribcage and rip the lungs out of his back to lay them on his chest if he or anyone else ever harmed you again."

Her father never struck her after that night. Now his fearful reaction to Jökull's threat in the village made sense.

"Knowing you were safe was the only way I could leave, but for the past five years, you were always there in my mind. And when I saw you again, it took all my will not to reveal the shock on my face." Jökull's mouth curved faintly, and she thought his eyes looked wet. His low voice was a tender brush against her cheek. "You threw that sword at me with all of your might and released that fierce scream, so full of rage. It burned inside of you like fire, and I saw that you were *alive*. Whatever you did, your light returned. The scars were there, but you repaired yourself with such defiance. I heard it in that cry. I think that was the moment I was completely done for." He tucked her hair behind her ear and softly smirked. "Or it may have been when I woke to you on top of me, half naked, with your dagger at my throat."

She laughed wetly.

He lifted her chin. "I love you, Sunnëva."

Her face crumbled at the confession.

"I love you," he said again with such ache she felt it in her bones. "Every single damn part of you. Even the parts you believe are ruined. Every scar. Every imperfection. From the first moment I kissed you, and every moment you tried to kill me, even when you hated me—I *loved* you." His expression softened, and he wiped away one of her tears. It turned to ice on his fingertip. "I was merely waiting ... and hoping for you to want that."

She had many wants, but only one was thrumming in her right now. This was it for her. She could no longer hold back, no matter what came after. In the end, she couldn't keep him, but tonight he would be hers.

"Take me," Sunnëva murmured. "To our room."

Jökull paused, understanding what she meant. He trailed his fingers slowly down her arms. "I didn't tell you this to get you in my bed."

"I know." She pressed her lips to his jaw. "I am merely tired of pretending as if you don't already have my heart. It's scarred and broken, but it's yours."

36

Jökull picked her up in his arms and kissed her as they flew through the night sky. He tasted like winter dreams and sweet promises. Sunnëva breathed him in, losing herself in the beat of his heart and the brush of his lips. They landed on the balcony of his chambers, and he carried her inside.

He let her slide to her feet, and the back of her legs bumped into the edge of the bed. His fingers wove through her hair, holding her closer, tighter, and she felt him tremble. As though he doubted this was real or she might disappear. Sunnëva clung to him and kissed him harder because this right here was inevitable.

The shape of him, the mold of his mouth, the cadence of his voice, and the softness of his words were all hers.

Sunnëva sat on the bed and looked up at him. The wind blowing in through the glass doors ruffled Jökull's hair around his face, starlight catching on his lashes. Her heartbeat fluttered under his gaze as he loosened his collar and removed his fur pelt. The veins shifted in his hands with each button he loosened on his jacket. He tossed it on the chair, then his shirt fell away, leaving her to admire his form in the moonlight.

Glancing at her legs, Jökull made a come-hither motion. Warmth rose to her cheeks when she understood what he wanted. Sunnëva lifted her foot, and he rested it against his thigh. His cool fingers supported her calf as he unfastened the clasp at her ankle and slipped off her shoe. Then he removed the other.

Her skin tingled as his fingers glided up her arm. After this, there was no going back. Her heart would be ripped from her chest and placed in his hands to hold.

She stood up, trembling in her golden dress. Her body thrummed as his lips coursed up her jaw in featherlight kisses. She was afraid of what would come after, but as he looked at her in the candlelight with pure adoration, Sunnëva decided to face that future with him.

Jökull paused, searching her welling eyes. He kissed each tear away, like wishes on his lips. His hand drifted to her bodice. "May I?"

She wordlessly nodded.

He took his time. The silk laces slowly slid through his fingers and tickled against her spine as he undid each one. Once he got it free, Jökull gently tugged the sleeves down her shoulders, watching as her skin slowly unveiled. The dress slipped away and pooled at her feet, exposing her lacy undergarments.

Her nipples pebbled under his heated stare, and he hissed, his fists curling at his sides. She could see the visceral beast side of himself surfacing, but he restrained it ... because he was afraid.

Afraid of frightening her and making her run away again.

"No part of you scares me anymore," Sunnëva said, her voice faint. Her fingers landed over his scars, tracing them. "You have touched my soul and marked me as yours."

Jökull looked at her as if she handed him the moon and all the stars in the sky. As if she held all the answers. "Sunnëva..."

Her name was a whisper. Syllables on a breath. A granted wish he never thought to have. Ever since he had spoken her name, it never sounded the same.

"I dreamed of you…" she whispered. "Since that night, an echo of you stayed behind. I didn't know it was you in the darkness when I was scared and alone, but you were always there."

A brokenness fractured the ice in his eyes. They melted like water welling on his white lashes.

Gripping her waist, he pulled her close, his mouth on hers with a soft kiss that drew her in.

"Several times, I wanted to hold you and tell you everything," he murmured against her lips. "There is so much I wished for, and I would give it all up for you. But I believed you would never want me, for why would the beauty ever choose the beast?"

Beauty. It was only with him that she truly felt beautiful.

"I'm sorry you had to wait so long for me to stop being stupid."

His lips left cool imprints of his mouth on her throat, and he said softly in her ear, "I have waited a thousand years for you. I would have waited a thousand more. You are my end and my beginning."

Sunnëva couldn't take it. His tenderness. His devotion. They were splitting her open again.

His nose brushed hers. "Can I touch you? All of you?"

She smiled. "You never have to ask."

There would never be a time when she wouldn't want his touch. Because there would never be anyone else for her but him.

Jökull sighed against her cheek, breathing her in. He turned her around to face the floor-length mirror across the bed. His hands roamed her body, every touch and kiss lingering. He cradled her breast, kneading her nipple. At his gentle squeeze, she swallowed back a whimper. His other hand grazed her stomach, slowly circling her sensitive flesh. She grew hot all over with every caress. His talons retracted, and his hand glided down to cup her between her legs. He tugged her undergarments aside, and she inhaled sharply at the first stroke of his fingers.

Jökull groaned out a curse. "Do you feel how wet you are?" he purred in her ear. "I can smell that melted honey already heating."

He sat on the edge of the bed and kept her facing the mirror. Taking the ends of her undergarments, he glided them down her hips to her feet. Once she stepped out of them, he seated her on his lap. "Open up for me."

In the reflection, Sunnëva's face flushed with lust and desire. Jökull's hungry gaze grew darker as she spread open one leg, and he hooked it over his knee. He did the same with the other, exposing her fully. An approving growl rumbled in his chest at the sight of her, pink and glistening. Heat flared throughout her entire body as his two fingers stroked the needy bud at the apex of her thighs and slid down to tease her entrance. She moaned and her eyes drifted shut.

"Keep your eyes open, winter rose," he rumbled. "Look at yourself."

She did.

His hand moved between her thighs, her folds spread around his fingers. There was something so filthy and erotic to watch him move through the very center of her. All of her was thrumming. Every touch stole her thoughts, rendering her his supplicant.

"I have never seen such a perfect sight," Jökull said, unable to look away from their reflection.

Her breathing grew sharper and her hips bucked.

"Does that feel good? Let me make it better."

Sunnëva cried out when he sank those thick fingers inside her. She bit her lip, her walls clenching around him as his thumb stroked her clit.

"Focus on me and how this makes you feel," Jökull said against her cheek and he started slowly moving them. "If you need to hold on to something, hold on to me."

He picked up the pace. The switch in rhythm sent a blaze of fire across her skin. She whimpered and moaned, clinging to his neck with one hand. Completely spread open, she was powerless as he had his way with her.

"Continue watching, Sunnëva. Look at what I'm doing to you."

Her hazy eyes stayed on the mirror as he bade, watching his long fingers pump inside of her. He curled them toward the tender spot that made her see stars. Her legs stiffened around his, and her stomach tightened, her core pulsing wildly. She was about to—

"Please, I need you," she begged, her voice nearly shrill.

She ached for him to plunge that thick girth deep inside of her. Jökull caught her wrist when she tried to reach for him, and he kissed her hand.

"Not yet, love. Not until you come for me like this. I have to prepare your body to take me first."

Oh, Gods. That's what he had been doing since that night he first touched her. Slowly easing her to fit him. More heat pooled at her entrance.

He slipped a third finger inside and her mouth fell open with a whimpering cry. An electric current zapped through her entire body, curling her toes. She was stretched and taut. It felt so good. So full. Her body was flushed, her face and breasts rosy with color. He started thrusting, leaving her panting, quivering, and nearly sobbing.

"Almost there. You're so close," he said as she undulated into his hand. "I love it when you're so needy. Look at how well you take me."

She was helpless against what he was doing to her. Entirely submitting to him. She gripped his neck, needing to hold on to something as his fingers moved faster. Her stomach tightened and her heart sped. She rocked into him, her walls constricting and trembling.

With his free hand, he turned her face toward him, swallowing her up in those icy blue orbs. "Tell me it's mine. Your body. Your heart. Your soul. All of it."

"Yours," she gasped, right before he locked her in a deep kiss, his tongue forcing her mouth to part and take him in deep.

"Now give it to me, Sunnëva," he said against her mouth. "Scream for me."

His fingers stroked exactly where she needed him, with the perfect amount of pressure. Her orgasm came swift and crashing. Her back arched sharply as she let out a high-pitched scream. Pleasure crashed in like a blissful wave, expanding through her insides. When her spasms slowed, her body sagged against him limply.

Jökull pressed his lips to her temple, and she whimpered at the pressure of his fingers slipping out of her, leaving her empty. He flipped her around onto the bed, laying her in the center of it. Holding her gaze, he stood and lowered his trousers, freeing his cock. All of her vibrated wildly at the length of him. She scooted toward the headboard as Jökull climbed over her. His fangs nipped her hipbone as he made his way up, tracing the scars over her heart with his lips.

"Nothing could ever compare to you." The rough sound of his reverent voice made her chest rise and fall with uneven breaths. "My beautiful rose. You have no idea how much I have wanted to bury myself inside of you." His icy tongue flicked her nipple, and she let out a panting whimper. "How much I craved to hear that sound."

He kissed her deeply, so devotedly, there was no doubt he was as much hers as she was his. His hands took hers, linking their fingers.

Jökull moved between her thighs and watched himself tease her wet, heated slit and he cursed. "I have desired you for so long, I don't think I will last. But I must be gentle."

"Don't be." She didn't want gentle right now. She hooked her arms around his neck and pulled him to her for a kiss, lifting her hips to guide him in.

"Sunnëva." He drew back, making her look at him. "I *need* to be careful, and you need that from me, too."

Not only due to his size, but because of how precious she was to him. He could easily crush her if he lost control. And they both knew it was partly because of what she had been through. Jökull was conscious of all of it. He was vibrating with need, but his every touch was tender and careful. Always putting her above himself.

Sunnëva relaxed into the bedding, never feeling more loved than right now. She kissed him languidly, tangling her fingers in his hair. He stroked his cock along her wet folds and it sent tingling currents through her core with anticipation. He had her thrumming, eliciting sweet shivers down her spine.

"I'm going to take my time with you," Jökull said, every word strained. "Claiming you. Loving you. Until you take all of me."

And she would.

Every part of her yearned for him terribly.

She didn't know exactly when the lines between hatred and desire had started to blur. Only that she needed him in every way possible. In her life. In her body. In her soul. She wanted them so completely interlaced, there was no way she could ever erase his imprint from her being.

Her hips rocked against him, gliding him along the very center of her. But the friction wasn't enough, and it was leaving her on the verge of madness.

"Jökull, please."

He chuckled against her neck.

"If you don't stop teasing me, I will take care of it myself." Sunnëva reached down, but he caught her arm.

"Oh, I don't think so. That honor is only mine." He gathered both of her wrists in his large hand and pinned them above her head. "You're mine to ravish and fill. By the end of the night, you will be spilling with me, so you know exactly who you belong to." She flushed at his crass words, and her core clenched with a yearning for him to do exactly that. "Now take a deep breath for me, love."

Sunnëva expanded her lungs with a breath, and he slowly eased himself into her. Her head fell back and her lips parted in a silent cry at the twinge of pain mixed with deep carnal pleasure. Her chest heaved and her legs quivered from the way he felt inside her. Jökull groaned low, panting into her throat.

But he was so big. Too big.

He stretched her so much it hurt. She peered between them and saw he wasn't even halfway in yet. He held that position for a few seconds, letting her adjust to what he'd given her. She spread her legs wider for him. He inhaled a ragged breath, and he sank another delicious inch. She whimpered, clinging to his shoulders as her core stretched to take that incredible girth.

"You're doing so well, love," Jökull coaxed, and she relaxed. "Yes ... that's it."

His magic glowed around them, soothing her pain. She eased more of him into her body, and her walls tightened around him greedily. He was trembling, or maybe it was her. He was so warm. She shifted her hips and moaned when she finally slipped him in to the hilt. His length stuffed her to the brim, reaching places she never imagined. He may very well blissfully snap her in two.

Jökull stifled a strangled groan, and his entire body shuddered above her. "Fuck. You feel so good. So fucking tight." His voice was hoarse. Shaky.

Every part of her body was quivering in utter bliss.

He kissed his way up her neck to her jaw. "From the night I saw you dance around the fire, you were constantly in my thoughts. I dreamed of your voice. Of how you felt in my hands. I had time to think of how I would have you. Every which way I would love you. I longed to map every inch of your body with mine. But this is nothing like—" He broke off in a curse when she clenched and he looked down at where they were joined. "You're far better than any dream I could create."

The words made her eyes water. This moment was a dream they were living in, but she didn't want it to be forgotten.

Sunnëva brushed his cheek. "Let's create something new together," she murmured and rolled her hips. She whimpered at the tightness and fill.

"Sunnëva," Jökull moaned brokenly. "Sunnëva, wait." He pulled back a bit to search her face. "Do you mean..."

She'd been thinking about it since he first mentioned it. One day, he would be gone. If a child was what he left her with, then it would be the last gift he ever gave her. The state of the world suddenly didn't matter anymore, because that dream she had of green and life, she would hold a little piece of it.

"Yes," Sunnëva said. "Give me a future."

A shudder plunged through his body, and Jökull took her lips in his. She succumbed to the sweetness of his mouth as he left a rain of kisses on her skin, each one making her feel cherished. "Sunnëva, my Sunnëva. You're breathtaking."

Her heart hummed with his affections.

Jökull supported himself on his arms, and his abs constricted with the first, gentle thrust. All of her dissolved.

He filled her everywhere. Heat washed through her body. His hips rolled again, a little firmer, giving her a taste of what was coming. She clung to him, wanting to be even closer than they already were. His weight pressed her into the bed, keeping her body locked in place against his hips. She moved with the current of his thrusts. Something fluttered in her chest, so light and carefree, while her body vibrated with pleasure. He fit her perfectly. As though her body was made to have him there. Like he had always belonged there.

Sunnëva pulsed with the beat of Jökull's heart that she could feel at the very center of her being. He was gentle, and continued that pace, helping her body adjust to taking him.

His soft moans merged with hers as they moved together. She relished in every meeting of their hips and the warmth of his body. His heated groans made her skin tingle, every thrust done with care. She was tightening, trembling, soaring. Light glowed around them, lifting off their bodies.

Jökull's white lashes closed. "I've waited so long for you," he breathed against the side of her cheek. "I've longed to hold you. To have you. To worship you. I was dying before this."

He picked up the momentum, sending a pleasure like a bolt of lightning through her body. His arms flexed with every thrust, his fingers weaving with hers. She lived off his deep moans and faint whimpers, knowing it was because he was inside of her. His cock was pulsing, her walls throbbing as they climbed together. Her stomach clenched, and his body stiffened. One pump of Jökull's hips and she cried out, quivering as the orgasm shook her very being. He let out a deep groan as he tumbled after her.

He pressed his forehead against hers, partially collapsing on her chest. His long white hair curtained around her face. "Are you all right?" he asked roughly, still catching his breath.

She smiled at him lazily. "Perfect."

"Good." Jökull sat on his heels. "Lift your legs, love." She blinked at him in a daze, surprised he was ready to go again. He gave her a roguish smile and his eyes glowed, reminding her again he wasn't like any other man. "Don't think it will end here," Jökull rumbled. "I plan to ravage you all night." She smiled back and lifted her legs. Setting them on his shoulders, his cool lips pressed a kiss to her ankle. "Hold on to me."

She heeded the dark warning and grabbed the ends of his knees.

Jökull thrust into her and they both cried out.

"Look." He turned her face toward the mirror. She whimpered at the sight of his cock sliding in and out of her. "Watch as I take you over and over again until I have claimed every single part of you entirely."

He pumped into her, taking her harder. Her body quaked with each thrust. She wanted him deeper and faster, and that's what he gave. Jökull's groans deepened, panting as he took his pleasure from her. Sunnëva dug her nails into his knees, her moans filling the room.

"You are mine," he growled. "Say it."

"Yours!" Sunnëva let out a broken cry the moment she finally reached her impending orgasm. It tore through her with a divine swiftness only he could achieve. She sagged into the bed, feeling herself go limp as ecstasy flooded her body.

Jökull let her ride it out, slowing his thrusts. Rose petals floated in from the open balcony, filling the air with a sweet scent, mingling with their release.

"Can you smell that?" he rumbled above her, his fangs nipping her shoulder. "That's my scent marking you. I want it all over you, in you, until you're permanently soaked in it."

He was so filthy.

When she finished shuddering, he lowered her legs and lifted her to him so she was straddling his waist. She gasped when he plunged into her again.

"I am not done with you," Jökull growled against her mouth.

She moaned in pleased shock. How much longer would he continue? No man could keep up with this, yet he was harder than ever. His eyes glowed bright, spelled by the magic they created. And she knew he wouldn't stop anytime soon. His power wove into her again, soothing her ache and revitalizing her energy.

Jökull chuckled darkly. "I said all night." He wrapped her hair in his fist, planting lingering kisses on her lips. "Do you know how good you feel? You look so beautiful like this. It makes me insane." He licked her pulse, telling her every filthy thing he was about to do to her. "I want to fuck you all night until I tear into your soul. Until I sink so far deep into you, there's no breaking us apart. I want it all."

Every word was branded on her skin. Sunnëva held him to her, cradling his head against her racing heart, because by all the fates, she never wanted this to end. She rolled her hips into him desperately, meeting his thrusts with wave after wave. As she began to climb, Jökull pulled out of her and she whimpered in protest until he flipped her over. She readily rose on her hands and knees, exposing herself to him.

He let out a low curse. "You're so ... I can't..." His frosty tongue traced her spine, and he pressed cool kisses on her neck and her shoulders, murmuring short incoherent sentences against her skin. *So beautiful. My Sunnëva. I can't get enough of you.*

Jökull's weight pressed against her back as he wedged his legs between hers, spreading her open. He slid into her in one deep thrust, and her spine arched with a wild cry.

The angle of his cock reached a new spot that made her spasm. Her toes curled as he drove into her. She molded perfectly around him, taking everything he gave. She was so tight, so full. There wasn't an inch he didn't reach. They were glowing again with a light that made her feel connected to him in a way she'd never been before.

Jökull's feral growls rumbled in her ear, and there was nothing human about them. His hands clutching her waist hardened, talons pricking her flesh. Goosebumps sprouted throughout her body when the flap of wings fluttered at the edge of her vision, and she swore he *enlarged* inside of her.

Sunnëva whimpered, shuddering from the sheer euphoria of it.

He was fucking her in his god form.

That alarming fact had her screaming for more, screaming his name, begging him not to stop. Her cries drove him into a frenzy. Her core vibrated with pleasure as she was completely devoured by the God of Death.

She was so insanely aroused, she constantly spilled down her thighs. Her body convulsed, clenching. She attempted to turn her head to see him, but Jökull thrust harder, forcing her down into the bed. Taking a handful of her hair in his fist, he tugged enough to give her that blissful sting. All of her was dancing, elevated on the high of his control.

Jökull started erratically thrusting, spearing her repeatedly. He shoved hard, rammed deep. He snarled her name and held her firmly against him so she couldn't slip away. The room filled with the erotic sound of his snarls melding with her moans. She clutched his arm, digging her fingers into his ice feathers to feel the real him. He rolled his hips in a way that stole all of her thoughts, leaving behind only the craving for release.

Yes, yes, right there. Don't stop! Her cries were sharp, gasping, begging. He groaned out a ragged curse, panting to the point he was breathless.

His voice was dark and rough, revealing how little control he had over himself. "Come for me, Goddess. Give me one more."

Her walls clenched around him again, and Jökull snarled in satisfaction. She was so close, chasing exhilaration to the edge. One last thrust and she ripped a few feathers as she screamed.

Sunnëva came so hard, her vision darkened and blurred. Jökull let out a bellowing roar. She could feel every throb of his cock against her walls as he filled her again, pumping into her through his release until he slowed.

Completely spent, she flopped onto the bed, shuddering. Jökull dropped next to her and panted to catch his breath. His gentle hands flipped her over to face him. He was in his glamored form again.

Jökull tucked her against his side, his large body curling around hers. Soft moonlight gleamed over the planes of his face and the gratified smile on his lips. Sunnëva rested her head on his arm, nestling into him. His scent of roses and crisp nights was now permanently engraved in her mind. She would treasure it in her memories as much as this moment.

"My winter rose." Jökull brushed the sweaty strands from her forehead and held her closer. "I'm never letting you go…"

A ghost of a smile touched her lips as her eyes drifted close. Absurd beast.

Longing squeezed her heart, and it crackled with frost, bracing for the pain to come when he inevitably returned to his Realm. He would have to let her go one day, but for now, she would stay right here.

37

Sunlight filtered through Sunnëva's closed eyelids, but she didn't want to open them yet. Her body ached with the pleasure it drowned in last night and craved now in the present morning. She felt different. Fuller. Buzzing, like she teemed with divine energy. As if her very being had changed after joining herself with Jökull.

She curled in bed and hugged his pillow, exhaling a happy sigh. It smelled like him.

"You're awake." Jökull's amused, velvet voice washed over her. It was so pleasant a sleepy smile played on her lips.

"Good morrow," she murmured. It was such a simple thing to say. Not once had she said it before to anyone. Not friends or enemies, because there had been nothing good about waking each morning in this world. She found it wasn't true anymore.

There was a smile in Jökull's voice as he said, "It is indeed."

Sunnëva laughed lightly as she nuzzled into the soft sheets, simply feeling too blissful to do anything else.

"I had food and water brought up for you," he said, still speaking in that velvety tone. "I need you to eat, love."

The last time he spoke so quietly to her, with such a gentle trickle of emotion, was in the garden when he said he loved her.

Sunnёva finally made her eyes open so she could see him. Jökull leaned against the balcony door frame. The open doors streamed bright sunlight behind him. His corded chest was bare and so were his feet, his ankles crossed one over the other. There was a faint sheen to his skin, like glimmering frost. She took in the long length of his legs to the dark trousers slung low on his hips.

"You took a bath without me," Sunnёva said at noticing his wet and rumpled hair.

"I've been up before dawn." One end of his mouth lifted. "I didn't want to wander the castle with your scent on me for others to smell. That is only for me to enjoy."

Flushing, Sunnёva sat on the edge of the bed with the sheets pulled up around her as she admired her husband.

He couldn't be anything more than a God.

The sunrise drew out his divine light. It highlighted him in a ring of gold, making his hair glow like liquid amber. Her graze roved over his torso, fascinated by the view of every delightful crease in his muscled chest and stomach. The angled ridges of his hips pointed to the trail of hair disappearing beneath the waistband.

If she had to eat something...

Jökull's smirk deepened. "Later. Food first."

He went to the table that already had a tray of fruit, cheese, salted ham, and eggs. He picked up a plate beside it with sliced bread, drizzled with honey, and brought it to her. She tried to take it, but he moved his hand, giving her a look.

Smiling, she let him feed a piece of bread to her. As soon as the flavors hit her mouth, her stomach clenched with surprising hunger. Sunnёva swallowed down the bite and ate more. He had her drink water, which she gulped down before scarfing down some fruit.

"I'm famished." Sunnёva laughed, wiping her mouth. Well, she hadn't eaten much at the banquet, and they were indeed up all night making love in every corner of the room until she couldn't move. "You wore me out."

"I certainly did." The word was said softly, but it held heat to it. He made her another plate and watched her eat, but there was a crease in his brow.

"What?"

He sighed. "I am merely glad to see you fed. You were so thin when you came here."

She looked down at herself. Her body did look fuller, and her complexion was more rosy.

Jökull sat on the bed next to her. "I know the rations distributed to the clans were never enough. Farming land was not possible here. Grain had to be shipped in from overseas, and that led to high taxes to cover the cost. I kept the castle's reserves at a minimum, so I could send additional rations to your clan when I could."

Sunnëva never knew that. She thought of all the times she hated him for leaving them to forage for scraps, and how the people called him a tyrant for taking half their bounty. "I ... hunted your crows for food," she confessed.

A despondent smile hovered on the edges of his mouth. "I know. Who do you think sent them?"

That's why they always appeared during the worst part of the season. Even then, he had been caring for her.

She smiled back, if only not to cry. "I thought they were a bad omen. I only hunted them if I was very desperate, and I always secretly feared you would slaughter me for it."

Jökull shook his head. "Several times I had to restrain myself from bringing you here to feed you. I knew you would never come willingly."

The platter of food on the table was a small feast. The castle may be on short reserves, but her meals hadn't been limited or small. And they held a banquet for the ball she suggested. She finally understood how much he had done for her.

"You will never go hungry again," Jökull said, following her stare.

"I can't eat all of that."

"I know. I wasn't sure what you would like, so I brought a little of everything."

She fought the lump in her throat. He was ridiculous.

Jökull fed her another piece of fruit dipped in honey, and her tongue swiped the nectar from her lips. He observed the action steadily, the intensity of his glowing stare focusing all of his attention on her.

She grinned and did it again.

He took her chin, his talon skimming the edge of her mouth. "You're treading on thin ice, love." His voice dropped to a deeper bass that made her skin prickle. He wiped a dollop of honey from the end of her chin. "Open that pretty mouth for me," he said, pressing a slice of pear to her lips.

She did as he said, and he groaned when she sucked his finger into her mouth. She rolled her tongue over it, cleaning off the sweetness, and he inhaled sharply through his nose, teeth grinding together. He visibly shuddered, and she sailed on the high on the power she got from it.

"Fuck, Sunnëva," he whispered, and the bulge in his pants visibly grew. Her body flushed with the memory of last night, and her core ached for a repeat. "The things I want to do."

He took the plate and set it on the table.

"What things?" she teased.

His hand lifted to her face, and the talons retracted as he traced her jaw. "I want to shove my cock in your mouth and watch you gag on it until I'm spilling from your pretty lips. I am not a nice man. I am a worse king." His face softened as he took her chin. "But I have too much respect for you to do those things."

The crassness of his confession layered in the regard for her, pooled more heat between her already wet thighs. Her body throbbed to do exactly as he desired. She shifted on the bed, folding her legs beneath her. She let the sheet drop and looked up at him with a docile pout. His breath caught, expression heating.

"It's not disrespectful if I also want those things," Sunnëva murmured. She desired nothing more than to savor him on her tongue. To hear him moan her name while losing control.

His jaw clenched when she lightly stroked his contained erection. "I want to taste you, Jökull. And I want to see you. The real you."

He stared at her for a moment, perhaps shocked or not sure if she meant it.

"Show me."

Jökull's hesitation was thick before magic warped the air and his glamor fell away like a veil.

She inhaled a soft breath at the sight of him. His dark blue skin swirled with stars, the translucent feathered wings shimmering at his back. Her gaze slowly roamed to his pointed ears, over the feathers layering his arms and edges of his chest, to his long white hair. No bone mask this time. She admired the planes of his face and his firm mouth. His glowing white eyes were cautious, reading her reaction to him.

"You're beautiful," Sunnëva breathed.

And the stiffness from his shoulders melted away with a low exhale. She took Jökull's long fingers, tipped with lethal claws, and kissed the soft, cool feathers on his hand. His wings shuddered, clinking softly like glass. She tugged at the stays of his leather pants. It slid off his hips and her eyes fell on his cock. The glistening rod was the darkest shade of blue and she swallowed at the size. It seemed larger than in his glamored form.

Sunnëva ran her finger along the sensitive length and he let out a hiss.

"Careful, Goddess."

Sunnëva did feel like a Goddess, and it was her turn to make him beg.

Smiling up at him, she lightly stroked him as he watched, groaning. The warm flesh was heavy in her palms. He was thick and hard, like smooth stone wrapped in silk. She traced the many veins that were throbbing so heavily. Other than the unusual color of him, his size and feel, he wasn't much different from a man. And he looked mouthwatering. She licked her lips, and his nostrils flared as his attention fell to her mouth.

"Seven Hells, you are mesmerizing," he breathed. "I've been waiting for you. For someone to challenge me."

Oh, she would give him a challenge.

Sunnëva brought her face closer to him, letting her breath fall over his sensitive flesh. He let out a strangled groan and his head fell back as she caressed the thick vein underneath the length of him. His body gave a deep tremor, like her touch was too much to endure.

"Does it feel good when I touch you?" she asked.

"Yes," he growled thickly. A bead of cum dripped from the opening.

"Do you want to come in my mouth, Jökull?"

He bucked when she reached the rim of the head. "You enjoy torturing me, don't you?"

"Say it."

"I want your mouth, winter rose."

Sunnëva flicked her tongue out, licking away his musk, and he shuddered. The moment his taste coated her tongue, her lashes fluttered shut, and she moaned. The musky sweetness made her crave more. She licked him again and an abrupt pant burst out of him right before he swelled, enlarging in her palms.

She swiped her tongue over the head. Jökull jerked, and he let out a ragged groan. He was tense, his entire body rigid, and his talons lightly skimmed her neck.

Sunnëva lightly smacked his hand away. "No touching."

He clenched his teeth and he fisted his hands at his sides. His glowing eyes darkened as the tip of his cock sank into her lips. It was the only thing allowed to touch her. She worked her tongue over him. He snarled a curse, his chest heaving with sharp breaths. He gripped the bedpost and his talons dug into the wood.

"Sunnëva." Her name was a growl. A plea. A warning. He was a breath away from snapping and shoving his way into her.

She smiled.

Pressing her lips together, she slipped him further into her mouth. A searing moan dragged out of him. It was impossible to take all of his length, so she worked the rest of him with her hands.

He brushed her cheek with the back of his fingers. "My stunning little rose. I adore this pretty mouth."

Sunnëva stroked her nails up his thigh and cupped the warm sack at the base of him. A growl ripped out of Jökull and his control snapped. His grip clamped on the back of her head as he thrust into her, hitting the end of her throat. She gasped, choking on him. Jökull growled savagely and his free hand dug into the bedpost, the wood cracked under the force of his grip. He was so lost, his soft whimpers and moans humming in her ears. Seeing him in his true form, so unhinged, she absolutely loved it.

"Fuck, I'm going to break you," Jökull grated, forcing himself to slow. Arousal pooled between her legs, and his nostrils flared with the scent of it. A rough sound rumbled in his throat. "You're going to be the death of me."

He pumped into her with every word.

She was entranced by him, by the thrusting of his hips and the glint of the sunlight on his white hair, the straight lines of his tattoos that pulsed white against his midnight skin. He tightened his grip on her hair as his abdomen constricted. She could feel him pulsing against her tongue.

Yes, give it to me. She wanted to be the one to make him fall off the edge.

He thrust firmly into her mouth, groaning deep in his chest. He was panting, shuddering, and he went taut with a wild groan. Her mind glazed over, and her body vibrated as the strong spurt of his release spilled down her throat, coating divinely on her tongue. It was unlike anything she had ever tasted.

Jökull clenched his teeth as he slowed with his release. His entire body quivered. Sunnëva slipped her lips off of him, giving the tip a kiss. He leaned against the bedpost as he panted.

He gazed down at her hazily, and his thumb brushed over her lips. "Why are you so perfect?"

Sunnëva sighed, cupping his hand to her cheek. It was so large it cradled her face. "I am not perfect, Jökull. Far from it."

He lifted her chin and said with a soft snarl, "You are to me."

She supposed she couldn't argue with that, because as she looked at the God of Death, as otherworldly and frightening as he appeared, he was perfect to her, too.

When she stood, Jökull lifted her by her thighs and wrapped her legs around his waist. "Are you sore, my winter rose?"

She smiled, and her core throbbed with a distant ache. "A little. But I don't give a damn."

"Good." He carried her to the wall and thrust into her. Her gasping cry filled the room.

Sunnëva wrapped her arms around his neck as he drove into her wildly. His magic wove around them, frost spreading across her skin. Jökull must have used magic again because all her soreness vanished, leaving the rising tide of ecstasy he created. Moans heaved out of her with every meeting of their hips. Wave after wave of pleasure beat against her body. His gruff breath panted against her neck, and he nipped her skin with his fangs. She wanted this every day. To have him within her so deep, it felt like he was weaving through her being.

They came together, and his roar seemed to shake the castle. His release dripped down her thighs. Jökull laid her on the bed, and spread her legs. He growled in satisfaction at the evidence of his spend.

"I love the sight of your cunt drenched with me."

She flushed and tried to shut her legs. "Perverted beast."

"But yours all the same." He kissed her forehead.

Yours. She liked the way the word hummed through her veins, and she pulled his mouth to hers. "Mine."

A knock came at the door.

Jökull looked at the door with murder in his white eyes. "I said no one is to come down this hall lest they wish to forfeit their life. You better have a good reason for standing there."

With an awkward clearing of his voice, Aero said, "Sire, there has been an occurrence."

There was something in his tone that put both Sunnëva and Jökull on alert. Her mind rushed with several possibilities. Had something

349

happened to their guests? Had Rune pulled another scheme? Was it her father? Were her brother and sister safe?

"Is it the Rulem Clan?" Jökull asked. "Demanding vengeance for their Earl, I imagine."

They had attacked Bram in their castle while he was an invited guest. That was bad form and probably would ruin everything they worked for. Sunnëva bit her lip.

"The Earl lives," Aero said coolly. "He departed last night with his clansmen. A pound of flesh lighter."

Sunnëva stifled a laugh. Tally let him live, which was more than she was capable of. But at least Bram paid for what he had done to her.

"Then what happened?" Jökull asked warily, his glamor falling into place. "Good or bad?"

Another pause.

"Good?" Aero said uncertainly. Then more affirmatively. "Yes, definitely good."

Jökull sighed in relief and partial annoyance. He quickly dressed and slipped on his coat, covering his fine body from her sight. "Wait for me."

She smiled. "I'm not going anywhere."

"Your guards are at the end of the hall. I'll be back shortly." He pecked her lips quickly and stepped away from the bed. She headed for the bathing chamber, but he grabbed her wrist and spun her around to kiss her again.

Sunnëva laughed. "Go. I will wash meanwhile."

"The bath is already filled. If I return in time, I'll join you." He stole another kiss and stepped out.

38

Blue rose petals floated on the steamy surface of the water. Sunnëva smiled to herself. *A poet and a romantic.* Stepping into the bath, she filled it with soap. She scrubbed her arms and neck, sighing happily as she thought of every way Jökull touched her. She hummed the song they danced to last night as she ran the cloth exactly where he had been.

Surprisingly, she sustained no bruises unless he had healed them while she slept. It may have been the lighting in the room, but her skin looked unusually pale. She must need to eat. But even her hair looked shades lighter than it had ever been. Maybe it was her body changing again with Jökull's power.

Sunnëva ran her fingers through her hair and her ring snagged on the wet strands. Sighing, she removed it from her finger to untangle it. Once she freed the ring, Sunnëva left it to clatter on the bench of oils. Her cloud of euphoria vanished at the sight of her geas mark, reminding her of the Druid she had made a deal with.

What is not a God but gives life? What bleeds but doesn't die? And is as unpredictable as the rising tide?

Even now, she never figured out what the riddle meant.

And you won't know, scheming mortal. Until the day comes, you'll wish you didn't.

A fear like no other sank through her very being. She had the sudden sense Jökull was in danger.

Sunnëva quickly clambered out of the tub and rushed to the room to get dressed. Her hands shook as she threw on a dress, along with a leather chest plate and her gauntlets. But ... there was no need to worry. She no longer wanted him dead, so there was no point to the riddle now. He was fine. She exhaled a breath, easing the tension from her body. But this was something else they needed to discuss. She had to tell him everything.

The sound of shouts and clashing swords in the hall startled Sunnëva out of her thoughts. Her Queen's Guard was fighting. The sounds grew more violent—and closer. Her eyes widened as she listened, frozen because it sounded exactly the same as the night of the lunar eclipse.

Then came silence.

Sunnëva ran for her sword propped up against the table. The door ripped open behind her, blasting out splinters of wood. She hit the ground from the force.

Donelle slithered into their chambers with a malicious cackle. Sunnëva gaped at her.

The emissary didn't look like a beautiful fae anymore. Her features were sharpened and gaunt, two holes replacing where her perfect nose had once been. Her torso led to a scaled black tail that coiled behind her. The hallway was bathed red with the bodies of her fallen guards. They were broken at odd angles and crushed, twisted like dough.

"What—"

Donelle's long tail slashed out, and Sunnëva rolled out of the way. It hit the table, knocking over the dishes and food with a loud crash. Sunnëva leaped up and pulled out her iron dagger. Dammit, her ring. Without it, she couldn't use magic.

Nor could Sunnëva get to it with Donelle in the way.

Sunnëva studied her narrowly. "What are you?"

"Take a guess," Donelle hissed, her long tongue forking out.

Snakes ... I hate snakes.

"I really thought you would get yourself killed by now." Donelle slithered around her. "I opened the door for you on your first day here. Then I sent the beasts after you in the hall when you ran from him. I even left you defenseless on the night of the eclipse. You simply *wouldn't* die."

Rage spewed up Sunnëva's throat. "It was you?"

She killed Riona and hurt Ren. For what? To see her dead out of spite?

Donelle clenched her teeth, baring her glistening fangs. "They both had to love the pathetic human. I was told not to touch you, but I am tired of watching you ruin everything. My lord will thank me later."

Before she could ask who she served, Donelle lunged.

Sunnëva threw herself out of the way. "It must gripe you," she said, gripping her dagger. "To pine after him for so long, only to be cast aside for a human."

Donelle hissed and curled her clawed hands. "Do you know what my favorite thing is about your kind?" She smiled sharply. "How much you bleed."

A growl rumbled from the doorway as Fenrin stalked in.

He leaped at Donelle, but she stabbed him in the shoulder with her fingernail guards. They lodged into the muscle and sizzled and smoked, where they punctured him. He keened sharply and tried to pull them out with his teeth, but it burned him.

Silver. They were made of silver.

His movements slowed, the flame in his eyes fading away. He collapsed, his chest heaving. Black blood leaked from his mouth and ears.

"Fenrin!" Sunnëva ran to him, but Donelle cut her off. Sunnëva thrust her iron knife deep into Donelle's gut. Yet the wound didn't burn. It didn't even bleed.

"Wrong choice." Donelle pealed with laughter. Her tail coiled around Sunnëva, constricting so tight, she gasped for air.

"Jökull will tear you apart," she wheezed, struggling to break free.

Donelle squeezed harder and something snapped inside of her chest, wrenching out Sunnëva's scream. For a second, she couldn't breathe.

"Oh, he's gone from the castle, fragile human. Why do you think he was called away the morning you both woke up together so *madly* in love? What would be the one thing that would get him to leave you unprotected for a single moment?"

Sunnëva stilled. "The Gate."

It must have opened.

And Donelle was here to close it—by killing her. The only reason she had to do that...

Sunnëva's fogged mind started turning. The reason Rune always knew their movements and could evade the castle wards was hissing in her face. The hairpin Donelle wore glinted with crimson gems in the sunlight.

She was never fae.

Sunnëva punched the lock on her gauntlet and drove the Nightstone blade into her tail. The Naga demon shrieked and threw her off. The force snapped off the blade as Sunnëva hit the ground. She scrambled to her feet and ran for her sword. Donelle descended on her and raked her claws across her entire back. Sunnëva screamed, falling to the ground.

Her sword was inches away, but she struggled to move. Her body went heavy as a searing pain immobilized her. It felt as if her flesh was flayed open, leaving her blood to seep through her clothing.

"Do you feel that?" Donelle cackled as she rose above her. "That is my venom sinking into you. It will burn as it slowly kills you, but I don't have the time to watch you die—"

A sword burst out of Donelle's chest and dark blood rained down over Sunnëva's face.

Ren stood on shaking legs behind her, his complexion ashen, but his mouth twisted in fury. "That's for killing my sister, bitch."

He twisted his sword and ripped it out. That blow had cut through the demon's heart. It should have killed her ... if his blade had not been made of steel.

Donelle lunged around with a feral snarl and sank her fangs into Ren's throat. His eyes stretched wide, a gurgle of blood spilling from his mouth. His dull wings twitched behind him.

"No..." Sunnëva cried out weakly.

The demon threw him across the room. Ren smashed into the wall and collapsed, his body spasming as he bled out.

She bit back a sob. *Damn her.*

Sunnëva pushed herself up and quietly grabbed her sword. Donelle hissed down at Ren, raising her clawed hand for the final blow.

"Hey, Donny."

She whipped around, and Sunnëva swung. The Nightstone blade caught the light as it sliced through Donelle's slender neck. Her expression froze, her body going lax. The head slid off and hit the ground with a wet plop. Then her body dissolved away into black ash, leaving the Bloodstone hairpin to clink on the floor.

Sunnëva stumbled to Fenrin and pulled out the nail guards from his shoulder. Her brother was unconscious, but his pulse was strong. She turned to her loyal knight.

Ren stared past her, shallow gasps shuddering on his bloodied lips. "No ... not yet ... not ... my face..."

"Gods, please." Sunnëva staggered toward him, but the venom won, and she collapsed. His gasping breaths grew fainter until they halted and the light from his eyes faded. Her vision dimmed, blurring with tears. "Ren..."

The voice of another tsked behind her as their footsteps approached. "His time has come."

That voice. She knew that voice.

A ragged black hem dragged past her, the frayed ends smearing the blood on the floor. Sunnëva hazily looked up at the Druid. His gold eyes idly regarded her from behind a golden fox mask, the hood of his cloak pulled up. He continued on and crouched by Ren with his back to her.

"Why...?" She couldn't get her tongue to move. She wanted to ask why he was there.

"I've come to collect a debt. Everyone pays in time."

The geas of the oak tree on Ren's hand faded away.

"He bargained for his blade to always aim true. Faulty wording to those who bleed for honor. Better to ask for a blade that vanquishes everything it cuts." The Druid removed his mask and set it down at his feet.

Sunnëva could only see his gnarled hand reaching out, and he curled his fingers over the dead knight's cheek. When he stood and turned around again, the rest of her body went cold.

It was now Ren who looked at her ... with golden eyes.

He took his face! Why his face?

"There are privileges reserved for the pretty," he said, and she shuddered at the sound of him speaking from Ren's mouth.

Did that mean the Druid was ugly before?

"Get up, Sunnëva, or you will die here." His irises glowed as he peered at her. "And so will the ones you now carry in your womb."

"What...?" Her mouth trembled with the words she couldn't form. He couldn't possibly know that.

"I've seen it, as I have seen how this story ends." He canted his head with a simpering smile, green hair falling around his pointed ears. "I am still waiting for you to figure out the riddle, scheming mortal. When you do, I'll be waiting."

When Sunnëva blinked again, he was gone.

The riddle ... Jökull...

The pain swallowed her whole. She could barely stay conscious. Every breath fought to fill her lungs. Her ribs were broken. Pain spasmed through her body, and her sight darkened more. She was losing too much blood. It pooled around her, filling the cracks in the floor, slicking her skin, and soaking her dress. She lifted a shaking

356

hand to her stomach. Maybe it was her mind hallucinating, but there were ... three pulses of energy within her, *living*.

So soon? How?

That didn't matter. She had to get up.

Blood loss and shock made her head spin. With a scream, Sunnëva forced herself to stagger to her feet and think past the pain.

Find help.

She stumbled for the door, pushing her feet to move one before the other, fighting to keep her blurred vision from darkening. She tripped into the hallway and her blood-soaked hands slid against the frost covered surface. Sweat beaded on her face and her pulse pounded in her temples. The ground seemed to shake as a ringing filled her ears.

She limped onward, calling to Jökull in her heart.

Sunnëva! His voice flared in her head, and her vision welled. She must be on her last stretch of life to hear him so clearly. Her heartbeats slowed, and the world became dull.

Jökull ... I think I'm dying...

The sword she still held slipped from her trembling fingers and clattered dully at her feet. The world tilted, and she fell into a bed of shadows.

They carried her away to the vestibule where the sun shone bright. The open coldness of the space fell over her, or it was her body at last going numb.

She looked up at Rune's grim face. He gently laid her on a chaise, even as the light burned his skin. "You came..."

"Anything for you, sweetling," he said with a faint smile, reminding her of who they used to be. He stepped backward into the dim corridor.

"I thought ... we were ... enemies..." she rasped.

"After this, we are." Rune vanished into the shadows as Tally and Daiyu came running up the stairs with more guards.

A flash of blue light and a roar ripped through the air. Jökull's scent came first above the blood, and his wide eyes crossed her blurred vision. He called her name. The unsteady shake in his voice was unmistakable. He sounded so scared, and so far away.

There was a rush of movement around her, a muddle of alarmed voices, and a spark of purple magic. She had the distinct feeling of being lifted and cradled against a solid chest. It rumbled against her cheek with vicious words and a snarl that she couldn't clearly hear.

But she was safe.

Even if she bled out here, Sunnëva let it all go because, in the arms of her beast, she was...

...safe.

Sunnëva was floating, without form. Her aura was a pale wisp, slowly fading. She felt cold and scared as the world seemed to sink away. But a glowing tether snatched her, and she clung to it desperately. She didn't want to go.

Please...

The tether wrapped around her with a possessiveness that refused to let go. Her soul cried with gratitude. *Hold on to me. Don't let me go.*

Her soul slammed into her body, and she was hit with excruciating pain that sunk deep into her bones. It was worse than claws raking into her back. Worse than the blades that etched scars on her skin. It felt like threads of fire were stitching her soul through her spine, tearing through the very fabric of what made her. She was being squeezed so tight, constricted under the vice hold of a snake.

A scream tore from her throat, and she thrashed, desperate to get free.

"Shhh, love, it's me." That voice was like a balm. It was Jökull's arms around her. The bed sunk beneath his weight as he shifted himself into a more comfortable position, nestling her against him. "You're safe, Sunnëva. I am here with you, holding you while we remove the venom. It's going to hurt, but you don't have to go through this alone. You will be all right. I won't let go. Not until you tell me to."

Her ear was pressed against his chest. She grounded herself in the steady thrum of his heart. She'd never felt so protected as she did at this moment, and it made her want to sob.

Simply knowing he was there, that she wasn't alone, put an end to her cries. He would hold on for as long as she allowed it, and the feeling of helplessness ebbed away.

A long, heavy sigh left her, and she went limp in his arms.

She drifted in and out. The room was dark and cool and it smelled like him, like a winter garden surrounded by trees. Candles flickered hazily in her vision. Her back was scorching hot, but her front was freezing. There was pain, but it was dulled behind a wall that didn't reach her senses, protecting her from fully feeling it.

Jökull's rumbling voice floated around her, vibrating against her ear. Her naked torso was pressed against his, her breasts flush with his icy chest. He was sitting up in bed with her legs wrapped around his waist, cradling her firmly but gently.

He snarled steadily in her ear, cupping her head to his shoulder. There was a tugging against her flesh below her shoulder blades as bindings of hot magic wove into her being. Blood spilled down her spine and the soaked fabric of her dress pooled at her waist.

It should have hurt, but she hardly felt it.

Only fire and ice.

"Don't look at me that way," Aero said quietly behind her. "I'm being careful and working with the utmost respect. If this bothers you, step out. I can lay her on a bed of snow to control her temperature."

Jökull snapped a vile word, and Sunnëva inwardly smiled. She closed her eyes, letting herself drift away.

39

When Sunnëva woke again, she was laying completely on top of her husband in bed, her head resting on his heart. Afternoon sunlight streamed in over them in a soft glow. Jökull's chest rose and fell with even breaths, his exhales fanning her hair. Something hard pressed against her stomach and she wiggled to adjust herself. Jökull's cool hand clamped on her waist. His lashes parted as he sleepily peered at her.

"I was defending myself," Sunnëva said abruptly.

"You could kill the lot of them, and I wouldn't care." Jökull brushed the matted hair from her temple, tucking it behind her ear. "As long as you keep breathing."

He wasn't angry that she killed one of his emissaries?

"Even if you hadn't, I was enraged enough that if there had been a body, I would have peeled her flesh apart and hung it from the battlement along with her head. No one touches you save for me."

Her heart did that flip again whenever he said such things. "How long was I unconscious?"

His cool fingers brushed down her jaw. "Three days."

Was he here with her the whole time? She tried to move to look behind her, but he held her to him.

"Don't move, Goddess. I am not finished holding you."

How could he say that when she had to reek? She couldn't feel any discomfort, but she must be sticky and gross. She flexed her back. Instead of the expected sting, she felt nothing. His magic had to be numbing her pain.

"Fenrin, is he all right?"

"Yes, he is fine," Jökull said, and his brow pinched.

"How bad is it?" Sunnëva whispered. She could already imagine the horrid scars.

"There is not a single mark on you, Sunnëva."

"What? How is that possible?" She reached over her shoulder where Donelle's claws had sliced into her flesh, only to find her skin flawless. "How? Aero's magic can't do this."

"It's not his magic. It's mine," Jökull murmured. "I realized I have left you defenseless. No more."

Sunnëva blinked down at her hands resting on his chest. Her skin was pale, which she thought had been due to her blood loss, but she seemed to almost shimmer with frost. And she had *claws*. Gasping, she jerked and her hair slid like silk down her shoulders. No longer blonde, but white as snow.

"You gave me your magic?" she asked in a shaky voice.

"I gave you my immortality."

She balked. "What? Why?"

"So nothing could ever hurt you again." His brows softened and his thumb traced her jaw. "Rune managed to plant a spy here, and she nearly killed you. I should have known it was her. I should have known you weren't safe simply for being in my castle. You nearly died. I have never experienced the fear I did when I felt your heart stop. Against every law of life, I forced your soul to stay in your body ... because I couldn't let you go. My life is already endless. I don't need my immortality. All I need is you."

Her vision watered. "But what does this mean for you?"

Jökull's eyes no longer glowed as vivid and, while his tremendous power hovered off him, a part of it was missing.

"Are you no longer a God?"

"That has not changed. I am merely less indestructible."

She stared at him. "If I were to stick a knife in you right now, would you bleed?"

"You and your vicious tendencies," he scoffed, but she read through his evasive expression.

"Answer me."

Jökull sighed. "Aye ... I would bleed."

She inhaled a sharp breath. He didn't say it, but she knew what this meant.

"Take it back. I don't want it. You made yourself easier to kill—" Sunnëva covered her mouth and searched for any lurking shadows. The sun shone brightly in the room. "The talons are gone, but you're more vulnerable than ever, Jökull. If anyone knew—we have so many enemies. I need you alive, too."

His mouth curved on one end. "You're worried about me? The God of Death?"

Sunnëva glared at him. This was serious, and he was acting as if it was inconsequential. Icy energy built in her veins, crackling in her like frost. "Jökull."

He frowned. "Sunnëva."

Gritting her teeth, she sat up, and the stiff bulge pressing against her stomach grazed her bare center. She was completely unclothed. His gaze heated.

"Really? You find this arousing?"

He arched an eyebrow. "You're asking me why I am aroused by this beautiful, fierce creature who is glaring at me with murderous eyes while straddling me with her breasts in my face? I am still a man, love."

She pulled the sheets up to cover herself. "Did I need to be naked?"

His cool hand slid up to her waist. "You were burning from the poison, cooking from the inside. It was the best option to cool you down the fastest and to take your pain." The glide of his fingers continued up her ribcage, grazing her breast. "And maintaining you covered kept me from attacking Aero for touching you."

She glared and rocked her hips against his erection sharply. "Selfish beast."

He hissed. "Cruel, insidious creature."

"I mean it, Jökull. *Take it back.*"

His jaw set, and her anger grew. "No."

"Take it back!" Frost shot out of her and covered him with jagged pieces of ice. Sunnëva stilled in place, trembling. Jökull didn't move, careful so the sharp pieces didn't puncture his throat, but he didn't look startled. "I-I'm sorry. How did I...?" Power thrummed inside of her. She was hit with another wave of shock when she noticed the frosted wings fluttering over her shoulders. "You gave me wings?"

He smiled. "This is all you, love. Calm yourself and call your magic."

Your magic ...

At her deep breath, the ice melted away, leaving water droplets to leak down the ridges of his chest. That didn't come from the ring. The magic came out of *her.*

What will I evolve into?

Into whatever he is.

She touched her cheek, half expecting to feel feathers. But it was silky smooth. She looked down at her bare body and found the scars were gone. Every single one. Something about her mouth was strange. She touched her lips, feeling the small fangs, and poked them with a clawed fingernail. Eyes the pale blue of winter looked at her from the mirror in the corner. Her features were refined with an otherworldly beauty, framed by snowy hair.

"You're the Winter Queen, Sunnëva. My equal balance." Jökull ran fingers through her silken locks. "The Goddess of Death."

She struggled to speak. "Equal...?"

"You're as powerful as I am now." He smiled, the edges of his fangs flashing. "And I might like that you have the ability to kill me at any given moment."

Sunnëva shook her head. "But ... but I thought it was the ring that connected me to your power. You said I was drawing from you."

"In a sense." Jökull took her hand where her ring was missing, and his thumb traced the geas on her finger. His gaze lifted to hers. She held her breath, but he continued. "The ring was merely a conduit, but you could have used my magic without it. I didn't want to frighten you ... or let you know you had the means to delve into me." He joked lightheartedly. "But your powers are due to our mate bond."

A bond? She had heard of such things, but they didn't happen to humans.

"I told you already, you're my fated bride," Jökull said. "The first strand of our connection formed the night we first touched. Another strand formed when we were wed. The longer we spent time around each other, the more strands began to weave us together."

"This was the reason you could feel my emotions..."

"Yes. I could feel your anger. Your hate." He trailed his hands up her pale legs, shooting currents to her center. He sighed, his mouth curving slyly. "I felt everything you tried to hide. Like your arousal. I could smell it on you every time we were together. The indescribable need you felt when I kissed you in the foyer was the bond urging us to complete it. That tie connects us. It's how I found you in the Frost Lands." He cupped her cheek. "When you called out to me in your heart, the bond led me to you."

The breath was knocked out of her when she felt it. A current of energy in the center of her soul that tethered her to him.

"I also sensed your doubts and indecision. Occasionally, I heard snippets of your thoughts."

Then it wasn't a coincidence that he somehow reacted to her thoughts and answered her unsaid questions.

"When did *that* start?"

"It started the night we were wed. Far away fragments." He grinned. "*Sleep. Sleep. Sleep.* I must admit, I was very curious about what you planned to do, so I indulged you."

She groaned, covering her face, and he laughed.

"Even then, it was faint."

"But it grew stronger," she guessed.

"It did. Beginning on the night when you let me touch you." Jökull's fingers traced an invisible pattern on her thighs, and her face warmed. He knew exactly how to touch her because she had screamed it in her head. "Your voice grew clearer after you confronted your father."

That day in the village was when she took back her life. He had given her the courage to do that. Thereafter, she started to feel closer to Jökull.

But it was still embarrassing.

Jökull sat up with her on his lap. "I didn't invade your mind, love. I only heard the thoughts that slipped through, but you did well to hide most of yourself from me as you grew stronger with your magic. Nonetheless, I could never predict what you would do next, no matter how much I tried." He cupped her face, his thumb brushing her lip. "When you accepted me and we joined our bodies, the last strand fell in place and our bond was complete."

"The light..." she said faintly. "I thought ... that was you taking my pain away. That was our bond forming?"

He brushed his mouth against hers. *You're my fated bride. My mate. The other half of me.*

She gasped. His voice rang clear in her head, as the day she had flown with the phoenix.

"From the moment I met you, I decided to protect you for the rest of your life. And it's not because I see you as a helpless woman. It's because you are *my* woman. I am the God of Death. I fear nothing..." His eyes grew pained, misting. "Except losing you."

Sunnëva's eyes stung with unshed tears, and she kissed him. His fingers slipped up the back of her head, holding her to him. His mouth was tender and loving. Fortifying everything he said.

Her body responded, and she ground against his erection. He groaned, low and deep.

Jökull's hand clamped on her waist to stop her from moving. "I sense where your thoughts are going, Goddess. But I want to take care of you first."

She rocked against him again, sliding his delicious length through her folds. He looked down and gutturally swore.

"You will pay for that later." He rose from the bed with her, setting her on her feet. A portal opened next to them, revealing a cave with a hot spring. From it drifted the scent of wet stone and sulfur. Jökull grabbed a lantern and led her inside. It was quiet and completely private, away from interruptions.

Sunnëva smiled and climbed in with his help. A long, contented sigh slipped out of her as she sank into the steaming waters. She leaned against the rim of the pool.

"I am still angry with you," she murmured.

"Oh, I am sure you will prick me with your thorns later," Jökull replied.

There was something in his tone that made her sit up. "Why did we come here?"

"I figured it would be a nice place to relax before dinner."

"Why?" she frowned. "What's special about dinner?"

"Nothing in of itself. There is a conversation we must have."

"What do you mean?"

"Later." Jökull shifted away to sort through a basket of glass bottles beside a basket of folded towels, proving he'd come here before. His shoulders were stiff, and the air suddenly tense.

"I know your Gate opened," she blurted.

He stilled. Sunnëva regretted bringing it up. She regretted getting in this spring.

"Can I wash your hair?" he asked quietly.

She nodded.

Jökull returned and pulled her onto his lap again with her facing him, and she let him do as he wished. He poured soap into her hair, his deft fingers massaging her scalp as he worked it into a lather. The stiffness soon melted from her shoulders.

White bubbles frothed down their bodies, and she ran her soapy hands over his chest, glancing at her geas. "You're not going to ask me about it?"

"You would tell me if you wanted me to know," Jökull said, wiping a washcloth down her arms. He never pushed even when he could.

"I also ... went to see the Druid," she admitted quietly. There was no pause as he continued washing her. No doubt he already knew what the geas meant. "On the day we married, I asked him to tell me how to kill you."

A soft smirk hovered on the edges of his mouth, though it didn't fully surface.

"He didn't give me a clear answer. Only a useless riddle I never deciphered. And I have no interest in doing so." She searched his face, waiting for his reaction.

Jökull took a wooden bowl and water trickled gently as he washed out her hair. "I am not angry if that is your concern. Don't forget, I also asked him for the same." He sighed as he looked at her. "It's a foul thing to trade with Seers, for you never get what you truly desire, and the cost is always painful."

He had found her only to lose her to the depravity of others. She found her way back to him, and now it was her turn to lose him.

Jökull's hands fell away. Her dread climbed at his hesitation. The air thickened with words he didn't want to say. But she already knew.

He had to leave the Mortal Realm.

Silent tears streamed down her face to join the steam. She knew this was going to happen and that it would hurt. But not how much. There was no way around it, but she already felt left behind. Sunnëva's hands flitted to her stomach protectively under the water.

They would be left behind.

Closing her eyes, Sunnëva decided not to tell him. The tension was taut between them. She didn't want this to be something else they argued over. He had a mission to complete, and she swore to help him.

"I know what you're going to say," Sunnëva murmured. "Let's not make it awkward or wait until dinner to discuss the inevitable. It's all

367

right, Jökull." She forced a smile and spoke lightly. "We both knew this would not be forever."

He was watching her, though she couldn't meet his gaze.

"I-I think it's about time we discuss how we are going to get Rune through the Gate." She slid off him and turned around, running her palms over the water's surface. "You don't have to form an apology or bother with goodbye. I will see you again when it's my time to cross over."

"Sunnëva..." By the tone of his voice, the pain wracking through her heart reached him. The delicate pretense she tried to build dissolved.

She sucked in a shaky breath and wiped her cheek. "I'm sorry. I was hoping for more time with you. It was foolish, I know. I always knew this would happen, and I accepted it. Don't feel guilty. Let me be sad, it's only natural."

Jökull flipped her around. "I'm not leaving."

"What?" She gaped at him. "Did something happen to the Gate?"

"No. It's open. I can feel it now, calling to me. Aero placed a cloaking spell over it, and I have guards in place."

"I don't understand."

He took her face. "I am not leaving you."

Her eyes widened. "I beg your pardon?"

"Only two Gods can cross a Gate. It was always supposed to be *you* and *me*."

A God and his Goddess. That was how his brothers had crossed with their brides, she realized. They had also been made immortal.

"One way or another, Rune must go through that Gate," Jökull said. "But thereafter, it will only allow one God to cross. I can't do it, Sunnëva. I refuse to go if you're not with me."

Her vision welled, and her heart squeezed, but Sunnëva shook her head. She moved away from him. "I can't believe you."

He sighed. "We're going to fight over this, aren't we?"

"Yes, we are," she exclaimed. "What are you doing, Jökull? You're supposed to leave!"

"Do you want me to?"

"Of course not! But I—" Her voice broke. "I knew going into this that I couldn't keep you. I fell into you anyway because I couldn't stop myself. I could withstand letting you go in the end if I got to have you, even if it was only once. But you said it yourself. This world was not meant for Gods. You have to go home."

He crossed the pool and pulled her into the cradle of his arms, holding her against his chest. He held her so gently, his next words falling against her cheek. "My home is right here."

She stifled a sob because she wanted that. She wanted so much for that to be true. But she had to put her feelings aside because the land needed balance, and it couldn't be with two Gods roaming it.

It took everything Sunnëva had to make herself step away. "Not anymore."

Jökull stared at her, his brows curling. "What are you saying?"

It was impossible to answer that question without unraveling in front of him. She turned away so he wouldn't see her cry. At the show of her back, his agony shook their bond like a quake.

"Our souls are meant to exist together, not apart," Jökull said, his voice catching in a way that made her throat clamp. "Can you do that? Can you live an endless existence without me? Because when I cross that Gate, there is no turning back." He turned her around and forced her to meet his fractured eyes, pleading with her. His hands trembled on her shoulders, and her heart sank into her stomach. "You will never see me again. Is that what you want?"

Her vision blurred.

Sunnëva waited to speak until she was sure her voice wouldn't quiver. "Please don't ask me that. It isn't easy saying goodbye."

His lashes closed, and his hold slipped away. "Yes, it is. You just did."

40

Jökull brought her to their bedroom in stony silence and vanished through another portal without looking back. He closed himself off from the bond, and she did the same. Sunnëva didn't want him to feel her as she sobbed into her pillow. Tally knocked on the door, but she didn't want to see anyone. Sunnëva stifled her cries as her heart inevitably broke. At night, he didn't return. She drank water simply to cry it out again, and the room frosted with her ice.

She eventually fell asleep before dawn and woke to the bright sun streaming through the windows. She felt warm and nauseous, but that wasn't right. It had only been a few days.

But their father was a God. Did that mean her pregnancy would be different?

Sunnëva made herself get up to put something in her stomach. Her feet tripped around the sheets as she went to the table to swallow down a stale piece of bread and pour herself more water. She took small sips as she blinked her achy, swollen eyes at the balcony windows dripping with rain. It took her a moment to realize it wasn't raining at all.

It was melting ice.

A sharp breath caught in her throat. Sunnëva walked toward the balcony with slow, hesitant steps, and shakily pushed on the glass doors. Warm sunlight fell over her skin as she stared at the kingdom outside.

The snow was melting.

Patches of grass appeared in spots where it had receded. The land was green with life. Tears sprung to her eyes. Freya's dream was, at last, coming to pass.

But ... the only way it would ever happen was if the God of Death was no more.

He left.

The realization struck her in the gut. She told him to leave, and he did. Pain lanced through her heart. A shrill wail slipped out of her mouth, leaving her body spasming. Sunnëva stumbled against the banister with a broken sob.

He left her.

The world closed in, and her lungs constricted. She couldn't take in any air. Her vision warped, and she gasped, forcing herself to suck in a painful breath.

She had to breathe.

Did he succeed in capturing Rune? What about the demons? What would happen now? Was the kingdom in danger? Sunnëva ran out of the room to find Aero.

The castle was unusually quiet. There were hardly any guards around, and the throne room was empty, as was the dining hall.

Did everyone leave? She stifled a sob, covering her mouth.

"My Queen?"

Sunnëva spun around with a gasp.

Tally and Gyda stood by the entryway of the kitchens, looking at her worriedly. "What's wrong?"

Sunnëva stumbled to the women and threw her arms around them. "They left. Everyone's gone."

"No, my lady," Tally said. "They're in the war room."

She immediately stopped crying and pulled back to stare at her.

They...

Then she was running. Sunnëva didn't think past getting to the war room. She had to see him. When she reached the third floor, voices drifted down the hallway. Arguing tones and worries.

"With the snow gone, so is our advantage," Garr said. "This changes everything."

"We have what we need to fight his army," Aero replied. "Our soldiers will be fitted with Nightstone and Moonstone."

"How about sunlight?" another asked. "Were you able to repurpose the Bloodstone?"

"No."

They cursed.

"However, I am working on an alternative with my associates from the Sun Guild."

"And meanwhile?" Garr said. "Rumiel will take this as a show of weakness. No magic is protecting this land now. His army will be at our gates soon, and we will be swarmed with demons."

"It's because you share power with *her*, sire," someone hissed. She froze at the door, her breath halting at the title. "The solution is obvious. Get rid of her and take it back—"

There was a cry that turned into a sharp, frightened keen. It was cut off with a crunch of bone. A chair screeched before she heard a body thud onto the floor.

Brief silence followed.

"We knew a great battle was coming, and the time is nigh." Her heart leaped at the sound of that cool voice. "Call on the clans to assemble the armies, Aero. The moment the Gate opened, we were at war."

"Right away, sire."

Sunnëva pressed on the door and it creaked open under her palm. The war room had crude brick walls displaying the Ice Phoenix banner. Sunlight spilled in from the large window on the eastern wall, glinting over the narrow table of dark marble in the center. Creatures and fae of every kind filled the seats.

Everyone's stares landed on her, but she was focused on the ice-blue eyes at the head of the table. Jökull lounged in his chair, indifferent and impassive, as if there was no danger to worry about. His expression didn't change at her arrival.

Seeing his face, her heart shook, and the first words out of her mouth were, "I can't." Sunnëva sobbed, snot and tears streaming down her cheeks. She was an emotional mess and didn't care if the court was witnessing it. "I can't," she said again. "I cannot exist without you."

Jökull rose from his chair, and his reply filled the room, low and harsh. *"Get out."*

Sunnëva withered on the spot.

He didn't want her anymore, not after what she said to him.

She took a step back, but chairs loudly scraped against the floor as everyone stood and started to leave the room. Garr and Quill gathered the body of some creature off the floor and carried it out, closing the door behind them.

He ... he had not meant her?

Jökull appeared in front of her. Pulling her to him, his forehead rested on hers, and he exhaled a low breath. "Sunnëva."

She clung to him, shaking. "I'm sorry for what I said. When I saw the land, I thought you left. I felt as if my world was gone, and I couldn't breathe."

He sighed and made her look at him. There was a softness on his face that he never showed anyone that wasn't her. "I am not going anywhere." His lips stole away the tears on her lashes. "My sweet apricity, it was decided a long time ago I wanted forever with you. Even if you cast me away, that will never change."

That merely reminded her why her heart chose him. He didn't heal her pain, or act as the hero that vanquished all of her troubles. He didn't try to fix what was broken or condemn the darkness she carried inside. Even when she hurt him and tried to push him away, he stayed.

She didn't know what this would mean for the world now, but she wasn't letting him go anymore.

Jökull brushed his lips along her throat. "And there was no damn way I would ever leave my mate, especially when she is carrying my heir."

She let out a shocked laugh. "You knew?"

"Of course I did." He cupped her cheek. "Gods can choose when their seed is planted, winter rose. This will not be an ordinary pregnancy by any means. And before you begin to worry, I promise you will be perfectly fine."

She smiled. "When did you know for certain?"

"I could smell it on you the morning after." Jökull dug his nose into her neck and inhaled her again. "Your scent changed. It's more heightened and sweet, mingled with mine. Your body changed, too. I feel it here." He fondled her breast, filling his hands with her. "And here." His hand slid up her dress to cup her where she was tender. She moaned as he stroked her between her thighs. He drew out his fingers and licked away her lust with a groan. "And I can taste the change in your body. We created a life together."

"More than one," she murmured.

He stared at her with a dumbfounded smile.

"Three." She touched her flat stomach. "Three pulses of life. Don't ask me how I know. I feel it."

His mouth crashed into her, devouring kisses that made her sigh. Grabbing her waist, He picked her up and placed her on the table.

"You smell so delicious." He was feral, inhaling her, touching her, licking her pulse. "I want to see."

Sunnëva laughed. "There is nothing to see yet. You won't see them for several months."

"No, love, I want to see *you*." Jökull lifted her dress and tore her undergarments apart in his claws. Her legs immediately fell open for him and he hissed at the sight of her, already wet with need. Kneeling, he pulled her to him and buried his nose in her core, moaning a curse. She squealed at the touch of his cool breath.

"I must have you." His large hands gripped her thighs and spread her wider. "Put your legs on my shoulders, love."

What? She stilled, both scandalized and pleased.

"Wrap your sweet thighs around my head as I have my way with you until you are pouring down my throat."

Heat flooded her core at his filthy words, her chest rising and falling with eager anticipation. "Here? What if someone walks in?"

Magic rippled around Jökull as his glamor fell away, and his true form appeared. All seven feet of ferocious beast made of pure muscle and menace.

"No one would dare if they value their lives," Jökull growled and from the savage possessiveness in his voice, she sensed he wouldn't hesitate to end whoever walked through that door. He laid his hand on her stomach. "You're mine, Sunnëva. And you're carrying my blood. I will tear apart anyone who comes near you. Now lay back and let me please you."

She did as he bade and put her legs up on his broad shoulders coated in feathers. They tickled against her sensitive flesh, shooting tingles into her stomach. He lowered and his shoulders pushed between her thighs, forcing her legs to spread wider to accommodate his frame. His breath sharpened at the sight of her, and he licked his lips.

The anticipation was maddening.

"I have to taste you again." The hungry desire on Jökull's face only made more heat flood her entrance. His eyes darkened and his grip shook where he held her. "Yes. That's it. I want you dripping all over this table."

His head lowered, and his icy tongue swiped her entrance. A cry ruptured out of her, and she arched her spine. A deep, content moan rolled through his chest. He swirled his tongue around her clit, and her hips bucked against him. He clamped her hips down, feasting on her as if he couldn't get enough.

She gripped his head, pulling his hair, pressing him harder against her. He growled and licked her hungrily in a rapid rhythm that had her panting. Sunnëva matched each stroke with the rock of her hips shamelessly, desperately. Racing toward that rapidly building orgasm.

Jökull speared her with his tongue, his fangs lightly pricking her folds. Sunnëva cried out, pulling at his feathers, squishing his head with her thighs. He growled as he gave it to her and shoved harder. Her cries went shrill, and her legs shook. His cold wings brushed against her skin with every thrust. Her core clenched, and he twirled his tongue in a way that seemed to touch the very end of her being. It slipped out of her and she whimpered in protest.

"Come for me, Sunnëva." He flicked her clit, taking it in his lips. "I want your sweet honey coating my tongue."

He thrust his tongue inside of her again, having his way with her there on the table like a rabid beast. An orgasm quickly crashed through her, leaving her body violently shaking as she let out a pleasure-filled scream. He swallowed every drop of her release.

"More. I need more," Jökull demanded. Before she even came down from that explosive orgasm, he devoured her sensitive flesh. Within seconds, she was crying and convulsing again.

As she shuddered on the table, Jökull stood. His mouth was covered in the glistening evidence of her arousal. He ran his thumb over his bottom lip, collecting what was left of her before sucking it clean. He looked so beautiful to her. Like the embodiment of the universe, made of night, stars, and ice. His white eyes were bright and full of only her.

Taking her neck, Jökull yanked her up to him. He kissed her so deeply she could taste herself on him. The grate of his rough voice sprouted goosebumps on her skin, making her shiver. "Turn around and hold on to the table."

She did, and he threw up her dress, exposing her sleek entrance to the air. He slipped into her in one thrust and they both cried out in a moan. He grabbed her hips and rode her with a madness, her pleasured cries filling the room.

As a Goddess, he no longer needed to be so careful with her and she loved it. The strength of his body, the vice grip of his clawed hands, and every hard plunge that would have snapped a human in half, proved how much he had restrained himself before. That fact, and his sheer virility, drove her to the edge. Sunnëva clenched around him, so close to coming.

He hauled her up and kissed her passionately, intimately, erotically as he thrust into her wildly, carrying her through the divine moment until they both ascended together.

41

One month. That was the duration of her pregnancy before she was at nearly full term. Sunnëva lay in the bath, frothing bubbles circling her belly protruding from the warm water. It faintly glowed with the divine power that constantly stirred in her womb like a soft current. This had to be all magic for her body to withstand such rapid growth with ease.

Despite the progression, Sunnëva hardly had any discomfort. No pain. No nausea. It was a perfect pregnancy, if such a thing could be said.

None of this was normal, even if she wasn't human anymore. Her mate assured her she would be fine, but Sunnëva still waited for something to go wrong. With either the health of her babies or a risk to their safety.

Primarily from Rune.

The fact that they were expecting also turned Jökull into a territorial, overprotective brute.

He ordered the lockdown of the castle, and the torches were lit day and night. The battlements were on constant watch. He left the preparation of their army to Aero and Garr while he worked nearly every day to cover the castle in warding spells with Tanzanite.

Sunnëva kept herself confined in their chambers to stay out of sight and to put her mate at ease. She sighed happily as his expert hands poured water over her scalp, running her hair through his fingers. He enjoyed washing her.

Her morning was interrupted by a loud rumble, and she groaned. The one thing she felt was constant hunger. She didn't seem to ever get full.

"Jökull," Sunnëva let out a whiny sigh when her stomach grumbled louder. She dropped her head on his wet shoulder as he finished washing her. "They are hungry again."

"I know." He chuckled and helped her out of the bath. Once her robe was on, Sunnëva waddled to the table where Tally had already come in to set their meal. Jökull dried her hair as she devoured a plate of food.

A knock came at the door and her snarly mate bared his teeth at it.

"Pardon me, sire," Aero called. "I'm here for her examination."

"Come in, Aero," Sunnëva said.

The mage entered and bowed. "My Queen, may I check on your progress?"

He came every three days and always politely asked. From a distance. It was probably due to Jökull menacingly standing guard over her like a feral creature.

Sunnëva nodded and patted his arm. "Sit, you menacing beast. You know he would never hurt me, and you also know he can't."

After he gutted two goblins for simply passing her in the hall, everyone quickly learned to stay away. Only a very small group of their closest companions were allowed in her vicinity, but even they couldn't approach her without permission.

Frowning, Jökull went to the bed, and she followed. He sat down with his back against the pillows, and she settled between his legs, her head resting on his chest. It seemed to calm him if she was in his arms. It also forced him not to attack anyone if she was in the way.

He drew the blanket up to her waist. Sunnëva let the robe fall open to expose her bulging belly, making sure to cover her chest.

Aero took slow, deliberate steps. He held out his hands for Jökull to see he was *not* a threat as he drew close. She stroked her tense mate, assuring him it was all right. It was his instinct to protect that was driving him now.

Aero carefully placed his hands on her stomach. A low, warning growl rumbled from Jökull.

"*Healer*," Aero reminded him absentmindedly as he pressed and felt the babies. His magic coursed into her gently. "You've grown another few inches. Their heartbeats are strong and healthy. You also look well. Any pain or discomfort?"

She shook her head. "None."

"She's immortal and a divine being. This won't harm her," Jökull said gruffly.

"Then I don't believe further examinations are necessary." Aero stepped back, clearing his throat. "If I continue to touch you, I risk losing a limb—or my head."

She smiled. "You're probably right. And how is Fen? Any progress?"

"Well, as you mentioned before, silver is indeed one of his weaknesses, and he continues to need confinement during the full moon. I have more theories to test, but I am convinced now it's very possible to give him human form again."

Sunnëva sighed happily in relief.

She hadn't seen Fenrin since her attack. He was mostly gone on raids with the soldiers to fight the demons that had been migrating north and attacking the clans. She sensed Fen gave them space so he wouldn't aggravate Jökull. She understood why, but she still missed her brother and sister terribly.

Sunnëva swallowed back the lump growing in her throat. "Thank you, Aero."

"Of course, my Queen."

"And what about your other project?" she asked hopefully.

"I am pleased to share that we have been successful. When you're able, come to the workroom so I may show you." The mage bowed and promptly excused himself.

It was good news, but Sunnëva didn't feel happy about it. Even after all he had done, she didn't want to hurt Rune. And she sensed her mate didn't want to either.

"I think your healer quit," Sunnëva said to change the subject. She glowered up at him playfully. "Fatal working conditions."

Jökull wrapped his arms around her and nuzzled her cheek. "You and these little ones are the most valuable thing in the universe to me. I can't help but want to keep everything else at bay."

She smiled. "Hmm, well, that makes it difficult for our friends to see me."

He grunted a dismissive sound.

"You know what else is harder to do while pregnant?"

"Feeling any sympathy for your enemies as you watch them slowly lose their life bleeding out on the battlefield?" he said nonchalantly.

She laughed. "No. I was going to say rolling over."

But his comment only reminded her of the reality outside the castle.

Sunnëva cupped her belly. It didn't seem real that this was happening to her. A few months ago, she was hunting in the woods, scavenging for food and hating everything that made her struggle. Now here she was, in the arms of a God, carrying life inside of her. It was so bizarre, sometimes she feared it was a dream.

Sunnëva gasped.

"What is it?" Jökull said, looking around the room wildly.

"They kicked." Another flutter brushed against her palm, and it was suddenly very real. She burst into sobs.

"Sunnëva?" Jökull looked down at her worriedly.

"I'm going to be a mother," she sniveled, not able to stop the rush of heightened emotions that seemed to hit her at random.

"Yes," Jökull said softly, laying a hand over hers. "You are."

Of course, she knew that already. It finally settled with that little kick. It filled her with such intense love and protectiveness, she now completely understood how Jökull felt. She curled around her belly as he held them close.

They would keep them safe.

Another knock came at the door. "Pardon me, my lady." Tally popped her head in. "A guest has arrived to see you."

"Me?" Sunnëva frowned. They weren't expecting anyone else.

"Come in," Jökull said, not at all perturbed.

Her guest came through the door, and more tears immediately started pouring in an endless stream.

"Ansa," she blubbered. "What are you doing here?"

Her sister gave her a watery smile. "I came to see you, silly. The King sent for me. He said his wife needed the comfort of her family."

Sunnëva started bawling again, and they chuckled at her reaction. "Thank you."

"I will be nearby if you need me." Jökull kissed her temple before he slid out from beneath her. He strode into the hall where Kerro lurked, leaving her with Tally and Ansa.

It had to have taken a great deal of his will to give her this moment. She adored him all the more for it.

Her labor came the following week. It was quick, and the pain was manageable. Jökull held her through it, praising her, as her sister encouraged her to push. They were all in awe as their children came into the world one by one. The first was a boy, which Gyda wrapped and passed to her. Then quickly came the second one in time for Tally to catch.

"A girl," she said, placing the baby in Sunnëva's arms.

The last was another boy. All of them had Jökull's white hair, but their eyes were tightly closed. They didn't make a sound.

"Why aren't they crying?" Sunnëva asked.

Jökull made quick work of cutting the umbilical cords, and he allowed Aero to take the babies to examine. Sunnëva finished the rest of her labor, left spent and panting in the bloodied sheets.

But the room had gone quiet. Aero, Tally, and Gyda hovered around the table, where they had set down their children.

"Are they all right?" Sunnëva asked, her voice breaking. "What's wrong?"

"They're perfectly fine," Gyda said.

They returned them to her, now clean. They were awake and alert, and gazing at her with glowing blue eyes. It wasn't until she heard that first gurgle that her heart burst open and she started sobbing from happiness and relief.

Once Aero confirmed all of them were perfectly healthy, they excused themselves to leave them alone with their new family.

She stayed in bed, watching Jökull. He stood by the open balcony beneath the moonlight, gently rocking all three sleeping babies. A tiny hand clutched his finger and his eyes welled. To everyone else, he was a beast, but in the privacy of their chambers, he was rendered completely helpless against the newborns in his arms.

"My little loves," he murmured to them. "My something great."

His voice was tender, his face full of such wonder. And she knew there was nothing he wouldn't do for them because they were already so very *loved*. Her children would have the father she never had.

And that thought made her silently weep.

42

Time passed them swiftly by as their children rapidly grew. Jökull had told her they would be different from humans, and it was true. Within three months, they already appeared to be six years old. They were bundles of mischief and magic, bringing life to the castle and earning the adoration of anyone who saw them.

But Sunnëva was troubled because she was happy—and afraid to be.

She sat on the stone bench outside in the courtyard, watching them play. They scampered through the castle gardens, laughing as Tally and Fenrin playfully gave chase. It was harder to catch them now that they learned how to spell themselves to run and leap faster.

But how long would they survive in a world of darkness? The dark, poisonous clouds above the Waste Lands were spreading. Without Jökull's magic, demons were constantly attempting to cross into the north. They reviewed more reports of clans seeking aid. They sent auxiliary forces, but she sensed this was only the beginning.

Rune was preparing.

And they were on constant alert.

The Castle Guards stood all around the courtyard, guarding the heirs as closely as she did. Jökull had called on friends and alliances.

The castle was full. They were ready to fight. But as Sunnëva looked at her children, she prayed for more time.

They were already so big, and they would keep growing.

How many more days would they have like this? How many more years? She was immortal now. Did that mean she would see them live and die within a blink of an eye?

Jökull came up beside her. He caressed her cheek, sensing her emotions.

She held it to her and closed her eyes. *Tell me they will have long lives. Tell me they won't leave me behind.*

"They will have very long lives," Jökull assured her. "They are demigods. Mortal, but with my gifts and extended lifespans. They will have many centuries of life."

"How do you know?"

"Because I am a demigod," Daiyu said as she joined them in the courtyard. The Princess chose to extend her stay with them for the season at Sunnëva's request. They needed all the help they could get to keep the castle guarded. Daiyu's three dragons circled the vast evening sky above them. "There are many of us out there, in fact."

Sunnëva gaped at her and at Jökull. "You didn't think this was something I should know?"

He shrugged. "I left that to her to disclose, if she wished."

"How much time passed before you became an adult?" she asked the princess.

"I grew to full maturity in one year," Daiyu said. "I am three hundred years old and expect to live several more centuries like my other cousins."

Cousins. That made her wonder how many demigods were wandering the world.

"But what about the Empress and Emperor? Are they not your parents?" Sunnëva asked.

She smiled fondly. "They are descendants of my mother. Each of them has cared for me like I am one of their own."

"My brothers had their indiscretions before they found their brides," Jökull explained. "But only humans can carry our blood."

"That's how you knew I would be fine." She narrowed her eyes at him. "Do you have any indiscretions I should know about?"

He smirked and tipped her chin. "Only you."

"Hmm." She then said to Daiyu, "Which one is...? If you don't mind saying."

"Zohar." The Dragon Princess crossed her arms and frowned. "The Spatial God. Not that he was much of a father. He likes to make an appearance every other decade."

"To visit you?"

"To convince me to become a Goddess and live with him in his Realm."

Sunnëva's heart leaped at the thought. "Have others done that?"

"Some. Not all of us are prone to the idea of living in a void, weaving the universe, while the rest of the world goes on. I would lose my home, my dragons, and everything I know." Daiyu shook her head. "No, I prefer to live, even if my mortal time eventually ends. That is life."

Seeing how happy her children were here, they probably wouldn't want to leave either.

"Hiram has three daughters who chose to be Goddesses," Jökull told her. "They became the Fates."

It was funny the workings of fate. As she gazed at her family, she was in disbelief at how much her life had changed so quickly. But she wouldn't change any of it.

When the sun started to descend, Sunnëva called out to her children, saying it was time to come inside. And was promptly ignored.

Tally laughed tiredly as she handed Sunnëva her wiggling daughter. "They are a sequence of chaos, my lady. Only Fenrin can keep up with them."

Her sons were climbing all over her poor brother, screeching like monkeys, pulling his ears and fur. "Oh, dear."

"No quarter!" Jorik bellowed where he straddled Fenrin's neck, waving his wooden sword. First out of the womb, he was an exact image of his father, with a temper to match. His white tresses fell to his shoulders, and he had a single braid coming down his left ear with one of her beads.

"No mercy!" Jalen dangled from Fen's tail, swinging himself like a pendulum. His short hair was a wild mop. He was her sweet one, always kind and curious, despite his rallying cry.

"Come, you little gremlins. Off to bed with you."

"No, I don't want to," her daughter whined, pouting. She squirmed out of Sunnëva's arms.

"Yes, Sana." Jökull picked her up and cradled her to his chest. "Now, boys."

Groaning, they obeyed their father's commanding voice. They slid down Fenrin's back, and her brother slumped, expelling a low relieved breath.

Groaning, they obeyed their father's commanding voice. They slid down Fenrin's back, and her brother slumped, expelling a low, relieved breath.

Jökull opened a portal into their children's bedroom. Spelled ore adorned the walls, toys were scattered on the floor, and it held one large bed for all three. Fenrin came in with them and flopped tiredly by the fireplace. He was always on guard duty.

It took more wrestling, but they eventually got their children washed and ready for bed.

"Can we blow out the candles?" Jorik grumbled as they tucked him in. "It bothers me when I sleep."

"No, darling," Sunnëva said, exchanging looks with her mate. "You know why."

They had already told them about their evil Shadow God uncle, who liked dark places.

"Mama, tell us a story," Sana said sleepily. Her little body was nearly swallowed up in the sea of pillows between her brothers.

Sunnëva sat on the edge of the bed as Jökull came to stand beside her. "Once upon a time, there was a cruel beast who lived in a castle of ice and roses. His magic coated the land in an endless winter."

"Until his bride came to burn it all down," Jökull said, and they shared a smile. "She was a fierce beauty, determined to vanquish him."

"Did she, Papa?" Jorik asked with a suspicious glower. He gripped his wooden sword to his chest.

"She did."

"Why didn't the beast bite her head off?"

"Aren't you listening?" Sana elbowed her brother. "She was too pretty."

Their father chuckled. "It wasn't because of that, though it might have been part of it."

"How?" Jalen asked, his pale eyes drifting close. "How did she defeat him?"

Jökull cupped her cheek, his thumb stroking her lips.

"She gave him her heart," Sunnëva answered faintly.

They chuckled when Jorik made a sound of disgust and rolled over. The room soon filled with the soft sounds of their deep breaths as they fell asleep.

She watched over her greatest accomplishment for a little while longer before she carefully slipped off the bed. Jökull quietly motioned at her to follow him to the balcony that connected their bedrooms.

Linking hands, Jökull led her to the balustrade. He held her to him, his arms wrapped around her waist as they looked up at the sky. It was bright with glittering stars.

Somewhere music started playing. It was the song they had danced to the night of the ball.

"Is that your magic, or do you have musicians playing for us somewhere?"

"Does it matter?" Jökull spun her around and dipped her.

No, it didn't. He pulled her back up and they danced.

This was nice. They hadn't been able to have a real moment alone since the birth. It was hard work raising three children while preparing for war. They had stolen kisses when they could, and escaped when someone could guard their children so they could have a passionate five minutes of release. But they were aware of the wary tension hovering over them, waiting for what came next.

And there was that other thing they both tried to ignore.

He looked past her shoulder at something in the distance. The Gate was glamored so no one but him could see it, but she felt its power calling to him.

She sighed. "Jökull."

He pulled her closer. "Don't think about our troubles tonight. Simply be here with me."

A portal opened beside them, and he guided her into the courtyard. The night was filled with the scent of roses as they danced under the moonlight, simply enjoying the peaceful stillness of this moment together. They had many things to worry about, but right now she wouldn't let any of them weigh down this rare snippet of time where she had him all to herself.

"That day in the village, when you proposed, did you think we would end up here?" Sunnëva asked.

"No. But I hoped for it. Even if your father had not offered your hand in marriage, I already decided I was taking you with me the moment you tried to kill me."

She laughed. "Demented beast. Is that why you agreed to his demands and mine? It seemed so extravagant of an ask, but you agreed without hesitation."

And she realized how significant that was with so little food to be found in the Everfrost.

Jökull caressed her cheek. "Sunnëva, you could have asked me for the moon itself and I would have given it to you. It didn't matter what it was. No cost was too great. If you had asked me to get on my knees, I would have done it in an instant."

You had me on my knees a long time ago.

"But wait, how did you get the extra grain?" she asked.

"It came from the castle reserves, but that wouldn't be enough to cover the rest. I had to form a trade agreement with Dagden. He will supplement the extra grain to Morkhàn and an additional half to the other clans for the next ten years until we can cultivate the land ourselves."

Her eyes widened. Snow and darkness didn't affect the Moor Lands, so they could grow food.

"In exchange for what?" she asked faintly.

"I released him from his fealty to the crown. He is now a king by right and the Moor Lands have become an independent kingdom from the Everfrost."

She gasped. "But at what cost?"

Because this would affect their government and army.

Jökull shook his head. "It was worth it, love. The thought had not occurred to me until I gave up the mountain. I could give up any land if it meant making you happy. All I knew was that here was this fierce woman I was waiting for and I would have her." Jökull tucked a loose strand of her hair behind her ear, the stroke of his finger tracing her jaw to lift her chin to him.

Sunnëva smiled as he inched closer to her lips. "What other secret plans have you made for the future?"

"Oh, I have plenty." He kissed her deeply, and it ignited an indulgent heat low in her stomach.

It couldn't be a more perfect night.

Until Rune's voice surfaced around them. "I wondered why the months of silence after your Gate opened." He laughed. "Then I realized you have been *busy*."

An awful chill sank through her body, stealing away all elation and warmth from her veins. They exchanged a frightened look. Jökull waved his hand, and a portal flared open beside them.

"You have given yourself three more reasons to no longer leave," Rune said as they leaped across it into the dark bedroom. "Well, now it is you who no longer has the choice."

The candlelight and the fire had gone out. She stood there, shaking, not able to move.

No...

Jökull rushed to the bed, calling their names.

"Funny thing, the minds of children. So curious and naughty. You did your best to protect them from me, *but I know every secret spoken in the dark.*"

The clouds parted, and the moonlight fell over the empty sheets. Sunnëva's chest heaved with rapid, sharp breaths as horror ripped through her heart. Her brother was gone, too.

"If you want them back, you will march through that Gate, Jökull. My dear little niece and nephews will keep me company until you do."

She whipped around, but Rune wasn't there. It was his shadows projecting his voice from the darkness, and they faded away with him.

"He took them." The words shuddered on her trembling lips and the room iced over with Sunnëva's gasping breaths. *"He took them!"*

Her scream ripped through the room. Ice shot out of her, shattering everything, and she collapsed.

43

Before all of this, Sunnëva had truly cared for Rune. She could have forgiven him for nearly everything, but not for this. Now, the only thing she felt for him was hate. They wasted no time gathering their generals and advisors. The war room was a hum of voices as they argued about what to do next.

"There is a great battle to come," Sunnëva said, and everyone fell silent. "Not merely for the future of the Everfrost, but for the world. If the war is lost, so are we all."

Jökull stood next to her. "You heard your Queen. Send word to the clans. We ride in force against the God of Shadows at dawn."

The rest of the night was spent rallying their armies and calling on sworn allegiances.

Sunnëva debated on whether to bring the princess into this, but when Daiyu entered the throne room she blurted out, "We need you."

She was trying to be strong, but her heart of a mother was unraveling her sanity. She needed all the help she could get to save her children.

At her declaration, the Dragon Princess bowed her head. "I stand with you, Sunnëva. Where do you need me?"

"I need you in the skies. Raining down fire on the Shadow Keep."

She nodded. "You have my dragons."

"My sword is yours in victory and defeat," the Earl of the Tanner clan declared next. They were the first to arrive. "Until death."

"Until death," the other Earls in the throne room echoed.

Six clans had come, except for Morkhàn, Adhar, and Rulem. They held allegiances to her father. He didn't answer her summons, and she didn't expect him to.

Dagden chose to remain neutral in this fight. As king, he reserved the right to refuse them. His territory was untouched by ice or darkness, so he was indifferent to the rest of the world's dilemma.

Those losses removed a significant number from Jökull's army, but there was one more they could call on.

They teleported into the Skelling Territory next. Sunnëva held her breath as her mate requested aid. They didn't have hope Kyrr would agree, but they couldn't afford pride with what was at stake.

Kyrr raised a clawed hand before they could finish their story. He stood to his full height and his people quieted. "We are with you, Jökull. I failed you once. I will not do so again."

The Skellings hooted their cry of agreement, the branches full of fluttering wings as they armed themselves. So many expressions crossed her mate's face, the strongest of them relief.

At dawn, they were ready.

Ansa and Tally helped Sunnëva into gold plated armor with a silver rose emblem embossed on the breastplate. Another gift from her husband. Sunnëva strapped on two swords at her waist. One of Nightstone and the other made for Rune.

She stared at her face in the mirror, painted with runes, hair braided away from her temples. That woman looked anxious because she was. The outcome of this day would change everything.

When Ansa and Tally finished, they stepped back. Sunnëva sensed their fear for their loved ones, but neither said a word.

Once again, lives were at stake except her own.

"They will come back to you," Sunnëva said, and her word as a Goddess rippled through the air. Even if she had to hold on to their souls herself.

They bowed to her deeply. Their faces were hidden beneath their hair, but she heard their faint weeping.

With a wave of her hand, Sunnëva opened a portal outside to the front of the castle. The sky was clear blue. She inhaled a deep breath, letting the crisp air fill her lungs. Their army was assembled in rows. Riders on crystal horses, fae still loyal to them, beasts, and the clans. A little over ten thousand soldiers, each armed with Nightstone.

The rays of the rising sun glinted off Jökull's new armor that matched hers, helmet in hand. He smiled as she strode to him. "You look like a Goddess of War."

She sighed and rested her forehead against his. "You are my strength."

"And you are mine," he murmured.

They stayed that way for a moment, simply breathing each other in. Then he conjured two crystal horses, and they mounted the saddles.

Promise me, we will send him back today, Sunnëva said through their bond.

Jökull nodded and put on his helmet. *There's no halfway with this. Today, we finish what we started.*

They moved to the front and held hands. A spark of blue light swirled in front of them and it expanded as they fed it more power. The portal grew and grew. It took a great deal of their magic to open one large enough to transfer their army as close as they could to the Waste Lands. Rune's wards kept them from teleporting into his territory, so they had to ride part of the way.

That didn't matter. They only needed to get close.

They led their army across the barren Waste Lands. It held nothing but desiccated trees, and the hot air reeked of sulfur and ash. Thunder boomed beyond the dark clouds overhead, leaving them under a constant night. The rumbling volcano of the Zafiro Mountains in the far distance constantly spilled molten lava, serving as the only source of light.

Moonstone wouldn't work here.

Torches were lit and spread amongst their men. Sunnëva was on high alert for any surprise attacks, but nothing else jumped out of the dark. A black tower appeared in the distance like a sharp talon, spearing the clouds.

The Shadow Keep.

And its Lord was waiting.

The God of Shadows was seated on his black steed, looking down at them from a crag. Shadows whisked around him, curling over his face and silhouette. The wind whipped his cloak as lightning flashed overhead, giving them a glimpse of his army below. Giants, demons, trolls, and fae. Drakon circled the sky above them. All carnivorous creatures double their number.

Rune told her he had been preparing for a long time and here was his proof. Sunnëva's heart pitched at the sight of the snarling wargs. She prayed Fenrin was still alive somewhere in one of those towers.

"He has a considerable force," Aero said behind them.

Jökull smirked. "Well, I have always enjoyed a challenge."

Garr grunted out a wry chuckle. "Aye. Not all of us will see daybreak tomorrow, sire, but what warrior ever dies a peaceful death? I go to mine with an axe in each hand!" he bellowed out.

Only half of their riders responded in agreement. Most of them looked afraid and Sunnëva was too, even if she was immortal.

They had so much to lose.

"This day will decide the future of the kingdom," Jökull said, his voice washing over their army. "For a land free of shadow and ice. Fae, human, or beast, that is what you're fighting for today. Your blades will cut back the darkness. Your shields will defend the lives we are fighting to protect. Death rides with you today. And if it's your time to march through the Gates, I will be right there to receive you."

Cheers went out among their riders, and it swarmed among the clans. Their banners rippled with their wary cry as they beat swords against their shields.

It moved her, but a seed of trepidation stirred in Sunnëva's chest when she looked at her mate. *You better not die on me.*

Jökull's mouth curved with a hint of a sly smile. *I don't plan to, love.*

They rode a ahead together, watching the God of Shadows. Rune vanished in a plume of smoke and appeared in front of them. They came to a stop between their armies. Sunnëva had to restrain herself from launching at him.

"Where are they?" she hissed.

He winked at her. "They are safely tucked away for you, sweetling. Don't worry."

She clenched the reins tightly, and ice coated her fists.

Rune canted his head as he took her in. Understanding crossed his face, and he smirked. Sunnëva stiffened when she realized her mistake. He knew what she was now and what that meant for her mate.

"So it has come to this," Jökull said.

"It certainly has." Rune's red eyes danced with flame. "What do you hope to gain today, brother? I have an army of thirty thousand, and you have perhaps a third of that. Your light tricks won't work here. You should have left when you had the chance."

Sunnëva schooled her expression, though inside her pulse was drumming. The sky rumbled with distant thunder.

"This does not have to end in bloodshed," her mate said evenly. He was cool and collected, nothing like she was. "Return them to us and we can end this peacefully. They are but children. No fault do they have in our conflict."

"If you want them back, get on your knees and *beg* for them."

Sunnëva hissed, baring her fangs. This was only a game to him. She knew Rune wouldn't keep his word, but Jökull didn't hesitate. He dismounted and lowered himself between their horses on the barren ground.

The kingdom kneels to you, Jökull once said. But he would bow for their children. He would bow in every effort to spare the lives of the people behind them.

Rune scoffed. "I begged you once, but it was not like this. I was crawling on my knees, clinging to your legs, weeping so pathetically onto your boots as I pleaded for your mercy."

Jökull sighed. "There was nothing I could do."

"Yet did you not do the impossible to save Sunnëva?" Rune snarled. "Was my bride's soul not worth holding onto?"

She was surprised he knew about that, but of course, he did.

"I am done gratifying your games, Rumiel." Jökull rose to his feet. The temperature dropped, and flurries formed in the air as his eyes glowed white. She'd been wrong. Her mate wasn't calm at all. He was only better at hiding it. "Return them to me unharmed," Jökull growled. "And we can end this without war."

"It ends when I take everything from you." Rune sent him a vicious smile and the malicious glint in his red eyes had them immediately stiffening. He tossed something at their feet.

It was a little white braid with a blue bead on the end.

Jorik's braid.

Sunnëva's lungs spasmed with shaky breaths. Fury surged out of her and ice tore through the air with her scream. Rune vanished into smoke, then reappeared at the front lines.

Drums began to beat, thrumming against her heart. It was all to provoke her, but she didn't care. She came with a purpose and wouldn't leave until it was accomplished.

Sunnëva drew her sword and kicked her heels. Her horse galloped head-on for the wall of demons. They snarled, their eyes reflecting in the darkness. Jökull raced beside her, scythe in hand. The ground rumbled as both armies charged.

They crashed into each other with a force of blades. Demons tore through the clans, and screams broke out all around. Sunnëva slashed through a warg coming down on Aero. He threw out his hand, releasing a purple wave of lightning through the enemy's ranks. She ducked under the jaws of a warg and turned it to dust with a swipe of her blade.

Blood and mud coated her face and armor. All she could taste was ash and despair as their numbers started to dwindle. It wouldn't stop.

Not until they stopped Rune. She had lost sight of him in the mayhem but the tower was ahead. That was her target. The battle continued as Sunnëva fought her way through.

"Hold the lines!" Garr bellowed. "Onward!"

Their riders fought on only to get crushed by giants and trolls. Their cries rang in her ears. Markus was on the ground, scrambling away from a Drakon. Sunnëva leaped and slashed her sword through its neck, severing the head. It dropped to her feet, blood gushing out. She helped the Earl up.

"Thank you, my Queen."

"I need to get to the Shadow Keep," she told him. "Gather your men—"

An arrow shot through his head and he went down.

"Archers!" Garr shouted in warning.

Sunnëva whipped around, noticing too late the demons on the tower battlements. Arrows rained through the dark, invisible until they were upon them. Aero conjured a translucent golden shield, and so did some of the fae, but many were hit.

The clans were falling. Demons tore through them endlessly, filling the field with more bodies every second. There was so much blood in the air she could taste it.

This wasn't a battle.

It was a slaughter.

Jökull was ahead, clearing a path for Rune. His scythe tore through the swarm of demons coming for him, their bodies vanishing in a scatter of ash. His fist speared into a troll's back and ripped out its spine. He rose on a pillar of ice above the masses and reaped a multitude of glowing souls. Bodies dropped all around him. Her mate convulsed as his tattoos flashed with the endless consumption of death.

And she felt how much strength it stole from him. He stumbled a step, panting heavily.

Wargs scaled up the pillar after him.

"Jökull!" Sunnëva shot out ice spears and killed them. She cut and slashed her way to him, Aero alongside her. "It's time," she told the mage.

Aero nodded. Purple electricity crackled around him as he looked up at the dark clouds. Lightning flashed behind them and thunder rumbled.

Jökull leaped off the pillar and landed by her when she reached him. He clasped her arm in assurance and they faced Rune together. He casually leaned against a crag, bodies piled all around him.

Sunnëva readied her sword. "I will make you bleed before this day is over."

He idly rose to his feet, playing with his shadows. "More than half of your army is gone, sweetling. You may as well surrender now before there are no humans left in the Everfrost."

"Every single one of them will fight to the death to see you defeated," Jökull said. "There will be no surrender. Not until one of us is no more."

Rune sneered. "I hoped you would say that."

He conjured a blade made of smoke and embers. Jökull's scythe became a sword spiraling with cerulean light. The Gods ran at each other and their weapons rang out in a clash of steel and magic. They moved so quickly that they were nearly a blur among the torch fires, marked only by the vivid red and blue streams in their wake.

Their movements were nearly perfectly matched until Jökull sliced him across the torso. The blow threw Rune back, and he caught himself in the air on a black cloud. He instantly healed and threw out spears of shadow. Jökull dodged, but one slashed past his shoulder, and he hissed. Sunnëva felt his pain echo through the bond.

Rune grinned at the blood dripping down his arm. "You will not win this fight."

At the flick of his hand, black mist lifted from the ground all across the battlefield. It spread and separated into many large, horned forms with glowing red eyes.

Demons of shadow.

"I've brought friends," he said.

Jökull smirked. "So did we."

A stream of fire blazed through the darkness and tore through Rune's army.

A roar bellowed overhead. Daiyu circled the sky on her silver dragon with two more in her wake. They filled the battlefield with flame. Aero parted a fissure in the toxic clouds and massive hawks poured through. The Skellings screeched out calls and fell upon the Drakon.

Rune snarled, furious.

Things were in their favor now.

"You're right, Jökull." Rune's face changed as he looked at him. Scales sprouted across his cheekbones and neck. His pupils turned into thin slits, his eyes becoming molten red. "It ends with us."

"Go!" Jökull shouted at her. His ice grew under Sunnëva's feet and moved her out of the way.

Rune shifted. His body grew and warped into his beast form.

An enormous black dragon.

His roar shook the earth, and the wind whipped with the might of his powerful wings. Jökull shifted into the Ice Phoenix. He slashed at the dragon's face with his talons and soared into the sky. Rune went after him. She was struck by how much larger he was than her mate. They crashed into each other in a beating of wings.

"My Queen." Garr and Aero came to her. "The battle is turning."

"Good. Break down the Keep's doors and get them out," Sunnëva said, briefly looking away from the aerial battle. "I'm counting on you."

They quickly put together a unit of men and ran off to rescue her children. But she lost sight of Rune and Jökull in the clouds. She needed to get up there. The waiting weapon at her hip vibrated as if it knew its purpose.

Daiyu flew down on her silver dragon and the ground shook as she landed. Ash blew around her, sticking to her face and armor. Her dragon riders flew down next. The princess gave an order in their language and one dismounted from the green dragon.

Daiyu motioned to Sunnëva. "Come."

"Thank you." She rushed forward and climbed onto the saddle. "Can you cover me?"

The princess nodded. "We will clear the air. Go. You know the commands."

"*Fei*," Sunnëva called. With a flap of its wings, the green dragon roared and soared into the sky.

Daiyu and the Skellings took down anything that tried to stop her. Sunnëva held her breath as she squinted through the toxic clouds, and worry strangled her when she felt Jökull's pain. She tugged on the link that connected them, and the bond led her north until she spotted them battling in the air ahead.

The black dragon dodged the Ice Phoenix's next attack and caught its throat in his jaws. Fright and anger wrenched through her chest.

Sunnëva flew to them and shouted, "*Huo!*"

Her dragon spat a stream of flame at Rune. He bellowed out a roar and released her mate. The Ice Phoenix flew back and it screeched at her.

Now, Sunnëva!

She leaped up onto her feet and threw herself off the saddle. She sailed through the air on her wings of ice and landed on the black dragon. Her second sword hummed as she drew it free. The blade glittered a vivid orange, the color of flames. It teemed with searing power.

"Let me introduce you to Sunstone," Sunnëva hissed, and she drove it into his back.

Rays of sunlight blazed out of the dragon's eyes and jaws. His scream of pain tore through the sky, and they plummeted through the air.

Sunnëva leaped off and the Ice Phoenix caught her. They watched the black dragon fall through the clouds and it crashed into the ground on the edge of the Waste Lands. Dust and smoke wafted into the air. When the debris settled, they flew down and landed.

The dragon shifted and Rune returned to his god form. He spat out blood, and gasped painfully as he sat up on his knees. The sword protruded from his stomach. Any attempt to pull it out burned his hands.

Rune sneered at her, but she saw the hurt behind it. "You stabbed me in the back, Su."

"You stabbed me in the heart first when you betrayed me, then you ripped it out when you took my children from me," Sunnëva said with a heavy sigh. She despised him for what he did, but this victory brought her no gratification. Her throat tightened as she fought the sting in her eyes. "You came at a time in my life when I really needed you, Rune. Our friendship was the one thing that helped me keep going. Thank you. And damn you for making me do this."

Guilt crossed his face and all the anger seemed to deflate out of him. He hunched over, more blood leaking from his mouth.

"It's over," Jökull said.

The Sunstone wouldn't kill him. Only a God could create their own undoing, but it had greatly weakened Rune and broken his wards. She sensed it the moment she stabbed him, and he finally noticed when the dark clouds began to dissipate.

Panic flashed across his face. "Don't."

Jökull opened a portal, revealing the arches of his Gate. The center glowed brightly with swirling blue light.

"Don't. Jökull, please," Rune pleaded, trying to move away. "I can't go back without her. I can't!"

Her? Sunnëva's eyes widened. Did he mean...?

Jökull's expression saddened. "I promised my wife I would send you back. All a man has is his word, brother. I'm sorry."

"You're not sorry," Rune snarled, his wet eyes flaming. "But you will be."

The force of his words struck her chest like a curse. She cast the feeling aside and shook her head with a sigh. It was a false threat because they both knew he had no power now.

"Greet father for me." Jökull grabbed Rune and tossed him through the portal.

His shout of rage cut off when he plunged into the light. He vanished, and so did the Gate.

The dark clouds above completely withdrew, and beams of golden sunlight fell over the smoking battlefield. The wargs disintegrated where they stood, the shadow demons sank into the receding darkness, and Rune's remaining army fled.

There was a stillness.

A quiet awe as their people looked at each other, realizing they were alive. The battle was won and the God of Shadows was vanquished. A wild cheer broke out. They beat on their shields, their voices rising in a roar.

"*Reigani*," they chanted, every single one lowering to their knees. "*Reigani!*"

The land was at last free.

Sunnëva closed her eyes against the warm sunlight basking over them. Finally, she kept her promise to Freya. And to herself.

A cool hand stroked her cheek.

She tearfully smiled at Jökull. His white hair blew with the wind as he smiled back. Blood and ash stained their faces, but they were still here together.

"Let's go get them," she said.

He shifted into the Ice Phoenix and she climbed onto his back again. He soared into the clear sky and they flew over their rejoicing army toward the black tower in the distance. When they reached the Shadow Keep, they rushed up the steps inside and found Garr and Aero in the tallest tower, discussing something.

"What's wrong?" Sunnëva asked them.

Aero's silver brows furrowed, and he exchanged an apprehensive look with the orc. "We can't get them out, my lady."

"We tried everything," Garr added.

"What do you mean?" She pushed past them.

A glowing red dome sealed off half of the chamber. Jorik, Jalen, and Sana were huddled inside, clutching onto Fenrin. They cried at the sight of her and Jökull.

"It's impenetrable." Aero hit the dome with a purple volt of electricity, but it merely crackled. "Whatever magic he used, none of my spells can break through."

Her mate strode up to the dome next and slashed it with his scythe. A burst of red power violently struck him, throwing him hard into the wall.

"Jökull!" Sunnëva rushed to him.

"I'm all right," he winced.

She helped him up, and he squeezed her trembling hand. They tried not to let their worry show, but they were thinking the same thing.

Their children were trapped in there without food or water. With their warg uncle, who would turn into a mindless beast when the full moon came.

Was this what Rune meant?

No, it couldn't be. He may have been wicked, but she didn't believe him evil enough to leave her children to die like this.

They are safely tucked away for you, sweetling. Don't worry.

She approached the crackling dome, feeling its dark energy prickle her skin.

"Sunnëva," Jökull called in warning.

She reached out and ... her hand went clean through. Power rippled against her skin like hot static, but it didn't stop her. She fully stepped in and the dome popped like a soap bubble.

It had deflected everyone except her. Why? Whatever Rune's reason, she was relieved to have gotten one thing right about him.

Her children ran to her. She gathered them in her arms, crying from relief.

Jorik wailed into her chest. "I am sorry for blowing out the candles, Mama. I'm sorry."

"Don't worry about that. I am only glad you're safe."

"Are you hurt?" Jökull asked them. "Did he harm you?"

They shook their heads.

"Only uncle, Fenrin," Sana said.

Her brother keened tiredly. He must have fought Rune to defend them. His fur was matted with dried blood from wounds long healed, but he was fine. She hugged him, too.

"Sire," Quill's deep voice called from the doorway. "You should see this."

The wariness in his tone had them both alert again.

Once they left their children in Aero's care, they were led into a crypt deep below the Shadow Keep. At the end of the steps, there was a single heavy door with faint light streaming from the small crack beneath. Sunnëva drew her sword and Jökull readied his scythe. He motioned for her to stand back, then he carefully opened the door. A pale red light fell on his face as he stared inside.

His shock swarmed through her.

"What is it?" She opened the door further.

The chamber walls were exquisitely carved, with a range of mountains and runes. In the center was a four-poster bed and on it lay a beautiful young woman with golden brown hair. She looked asleep, perfectly preserved by another enchanted red dome.

Sunnëva knew instantly who it was.

This was a tomb for Rune's bride.

After all this time, he still hadn't been able to let go. Sunnëva blinked away her misted vision. Regardless of what he had done, her heart broke for him, because if it had been the other way around...

She squeezed Jökull's hand, so grateful her family was together.

He closed the door and sealed it shut with magic. They stood there a moment, looking at the spelled door together. It went unsaid, but she felt his remorse. All Jökull could do for his brother now was to make sure no one disturbed her resting place.

Sighing, he said, "Let's go home."

44

Jökull opened a portal to the front gates of their castle. Their nearly
decimated army followed them through. Tally, Ansa, and Gyda
wept with relief at the sight of them. Tally threw herself at Aero
and kissed his face, covered in soot. Ansa traded between embracing
Kerro, Fenrin, and her nephews. Reunions happened all around.

Sunnëva stayed on their front steps as she fed on their joy. She
was too happy to do anything but watch her family together again.

Princess Daiyu and the Skellings had stayed behind in the Waste
Lands to hunt down any remaining demons, and to bring back their
dead. They should be put to rest with their families.

The kingdom was no longer shackled to an endless winter or the
threat of darkness. And the cost had been great. But now the air was
different. It was missing that faint pull of power from the east where
the Gate had been.

Jökull hugged her from behind, swaying to an unheard song.
"Once I sent him through, I rejected the call, and the Gate closed. I
plan to stay right here by your side for eternity."

Sunnëva sighed happily. "Do go on and tell me more sweet nothings," she said, repeating what she told him the day he gave her the Nightstone sword.

It was the day a lot of secrets came to light and the first seed of her love for him was planted. That seemed like so long ago.

"I only have eyes for you," Jökull murmured, and they shared a kiss. She smiled against his lips. "What now?"

"I can think of a few things—" His chuckle cut off with a sharp gasp. His body jerked, and white-hot pain shook the bond.

Sunnëva whipped around. Jökull blinked at her in confusion. Then they looked down at the black blade protruding from his chest.

A Skelling talon.

Her heart stopped. Her mind. Her world. Bright blood spilled from his lips.

"For the Everfrost," Thorstein said behind him, and he ripped it out.

Jökull keeled. Sunnëva screamed and lurched forward to catch him. Under his weight, she stumbled, and they fell on the steps.

"What have you done?" she cried. "Aero, Gyda, help me!"

Everyone rushed forward, their friends, their riders. Sunnëva pressed on the hole in Jökull's chest, feeding him her power, but it did nothing to repair his heart. His glamor faded away, revealing his true form. His weak heart pumped against her palm as blood seeped through her fingers. The glittering stars on his blue skin dimmed and his wings wilted.

He gasped for air, shaking in her arms. "Sunnëva..."

"Hold on, Jökull," she wept.

Aero held his hands above Jökull's chest and a mist of his purple Essence fell over him, but the wound refused to heal. He cast more spells, and each one failed. Gyda looked at her sadly, shaking her head.

"No, there has to be something you can do!"

"I told you this day would come, daughter," her father said indifferently.

The talon glistened in his fist with Jökull's blood. How did he have one? The talons were all disposed of. But that day in the throne room, she had only seen one and assumed the other was in the bag, too.

Rune—he must have kept it.

Thorstein stepped away at Fenrin's snarl as he stalked to her side. Aero and their soldiers were poised to attack, but her father wasn't daunted. Bjorn stood with him, in his armor and sword at his waist. He looked away from her teary face, lowering his head.

Electricity sparked around Aero, his eyes flaring vivid purple. "This is treason."

"*This* is prophecy," Thorstein said. "The age of the Ice Phoenix is over. The time has come for a new reign. Nothing you do will stop it."

Another army rode over the hill. They flew the gray banners for Morkhàn, the purple banners for Adhar, and the red banners of Rulem. About six thousand armed clansmen.

Their riders and the remaining loyal clans lined up at Garr's command. Kerro kept Ansa, Tally, and her children protected behind him. But they were outnumbered, wounded, and on their last leg.

Thorstein smirked. "Your army is spent, and your king is dying. We both know you cannot win this fight. Lay down your arms and yield peacefully."

Sunnëva stifled her sobs and sent more magic into Jökull, but it did nothing. Her power couldn't heal him. She looked around frantically, searching for something, anything, anyone who could help them.

"What do I do? Tell me what to do! How do I save you?"

"You can't..." More blood spilled from Jökull's quivering lips, and his pulse grew fainter under her fingers.

"No," she sobbed. "You have to stay with me. Please."

"Not all stories have good endings, but you were mine..." He smiled at her faintly and raised his trembling hand to her cheek. At the graze of his glowing fingertips, the last of his divine power sank into her like frost in her bones.

Then his hand fell.

He expelled his last breath.

And he went still in her arms.

There was a tearing in her chest with the destruction of her soul. The bond severed in half with a brutal snap, and all that remained was painful emptiness.

Sunnëva shook her head in disbelief, staring into those white eyes that could no longer see. "Jökull?" She touched his cold cheek with a trembling hand. "Jökull? Please wake up." She shook him, her voice rising in a cry. "No. No. *No! Jökull!*"

The golden light of his soul lifted off his body. Sunnëva tried to catch it from the air. She tried to hold on to it and put it back as he had done for her. But his soul slipped away and shot into the sky like a comet for the heavens, vanishing behind the clouds.

This wasn't real. It couldn't be.

It was only a nightmare she had to wake up from.

It was only a nightmare she had to wake up from.

The castle let out a horrid groan.

Crows cawed loudly and scattered into the sky. The surface cracked and bricks began to fall away. Aero told them to run. Ansa and Tally gathered her children, and her people fled as the windows shattered one by one. Every gargoyle statue on the roof fractured and broke apart, their fragments crashing to the ground. With the loss of Jökull's magic, the enchanted roses on the walls shriveled up and withered away.

Like her heart.

Every light in her went out, and that was when she accepted it.

Jökull was dead.

Then the source of all her strength crumbled. And Sunnëva couldn't do anything but hold on to him as her anguished wails echoed across the kingdom. They tore through the sky, each cry ripping through her heart and the pieces of her broken soul. The bond that had held it together was gone, leaving her internal scars to split open.

"His curse is cleansed from the land," Thorstein said. He looked at her crying children and gripped the talon. "And so will be all of his abominable creations."

Bjorn grabbed his arm. "What are you doing?" he asked in shock. "That is enough. Stop this."

Thorstein snarled and punched Bjorn, tossing him down. "No trace of that beast can be left after today."

He would slay them, too. His own grandchildren.

Shuddering, Sunnëva looked up at the man she once called father. Her breath came out frosty, her skin crackling as ice coated the stone steps beneath her and spread across the ground. She shook with the dark surge building inside of her. The air turned frigidly cold, storm clouds rolling overhead. Thorstein's eyes widened, and he slowly backed away.

All her life, he took from her. He took and took until there was nothing left but one thing.

Everything inside of her went still.

And she became *rage*.

From her throat ripped out a guttural, harrowing scream. It was the definition of grief and despair.

A cry of anguish.

A cry of heartbreak.

A cry of loss.

Of fury.

The wind whipped with the raging snowstorm she conjured, rising like the roar of a beast.

Ice shot out of her and ripped through Thorstein.

He burst into mist.

A rain of red on the snow.

Unmade.

Sunnëva stood, her chest heaving, and her clawed hands curling as she faced the opposing army. They pulsed with threads of life while her mate was cold and empty.

They had taken everything from her. Now they would know her pain.

A ravaging power rushed through her veins, and a scythe of ice appeared in her hand, crackling with frost. She ran and leaped on them. Her scythe cleaved through the ranks of the clans, throwing their dismembered limbs in her wake. They fell to her power as she shredded them apart. With a sweep of her hands, souls tore out of bodies by the hundreds.

She screamed and screamed as she killed them all.

Bjorn tried to flee on his horse, but her magic snatched him from the saddle. She lifted him in the air with her talons and began to peel the soul from his body.

"Stop! Sunnëva, stop this madness!"

She whipped around with a rageful snarl, but it wavered when she recognized Gyda.

The old woman shook her head. "Goddess of Death. Look at what you have done."

The land was riddled with bodies. With fresh bones.

At the quiet weeping, she saw her children cowering behind Ansa and Tally. Fenrin and Aero also backed away. They were afraid.

Of her.

Sunnëva's monstrous reflection looked back at her from the pool of blood at her feet. Her crown had reshaped itself into horns of ice, her eyes were completely white, and her face was gaunt like a skull.

She released Bjorn, and he collapsed, gasping for air. The remaining survivors fled on their horses without looking back.

"You came here to bring life, not take it," Gyda said.

"I found it, and they took him from me." Saying the words wrenched a sob from Sunnëva's throat, and she collapsed in the bloodied snow. Her dark power fell away, leaving the snowstorm to fade. Tears rolled down her cheeks as she looked up at the beautiful clear sky that no longer belonged in her world. "I want to destroy everything, so they know the destruction in my heart. I can't bear it, Gyda. I can't."

"Then I will bear it with you." The old woman held Sunnëva as sobs wracked her body.

It felt like the comfort of a mother. Of a friend.

45

There would be no funeral. Sunnëva refused to have one. Aero came to ask her about it, then Tally, Daiyu, and Ansa. She refused them all. *No fire* she screamed with such rage when they suggested a clan funeral. Sunnëva holed up in her bedroom for the next three days with Jökull's body, standing guard over the coffin of ice she encased him in. She couldn't bring herself to let him rot away.

"We can bury him at least," came Ansa's small voice beside her.

"No. Leave me alone with him," Sunnëva said, placing her palm on the coffin above his face. Tiny spikes of frost formed around her fingers, and her mouth trembled. "Please, please don't take him from me."

"Sunnëva." Ansa brushed the matted white hair from her face. "He can't stay with you."

"Leave me!" she screamed. Ice crystallized around her, and Ansa stumbled back, fear on her face. "I'm sorry," Sunnëva wept, each tear freezing on her cheeks. "I can't let him go. I love him."

Sunnëva sobbed harder when she realized she had never told him. Even when he said it, when her heart cried it out, why did it never occur to her to say it, too?

"I know," Ansa said, her voice breaking. "But your children need you. They lost their father. They can't lose their mother, too. Let us put him to rest for their sake."

Oh Gods, her children. They must be suffering, too. But Sunnëva hadn't seen them since ... she had turned into a monster. She was too ashamed. And too broken.

Grief was destroying her. The dark power she now held stirred inside, poisoned by her heart. It would become her darkness, and she would become a curse upon the world. That wasn't what her children deserved.

She had to let go.

Sunnëva covered her mouth and nodded, at last conceding. Aero came in with Tally.

"We will hold the funeral when the moon is at its highest point in the sky, my Queen," he said gently. "Burial or pyre?"

She wouldn't leave him in the cold ground. "Pyre..."

He bowed his head.

Sunnëva sank to the floor. Ansa held her and rocked her as Aero's purple Essence levitated the coffin out of the room. When the sight of Jökull fell away, she fell apart, feeling like she was losing him all over again.

Ansa got her into bed and held her until she cried herself to sleep. When she woke, it was hours later in the night. The room was so cold and empty. With it came the reminder she was alone. Grief strangled her and she couldn't breathe.

It was like death.

And she wanted it to take her away.

Sunnëva curled into herself and inhaled a deep breath. Air struggled to enter her aching lungs. She stifled her whimpers into the pillow, not wanting anyone to hear her break apart again.

Tomorrow ... she would pick up her pieces tomorrow.

The wispy clouds parted, and silvery moonlight streamed in through the tall balcony windows. It traveled across the floor and landed over the crystal dome set on the table. The single blue rose Jökull had given her softly glowed inside. Somehow, it was the only thing that had survived when his magic disappeared from the world, but even that was waning.

The rose had wilted, and one petal fluttered down.

In her sorrow, she lay there in the darkness, staring at it for hours. Another petal fell, and her heart quaked. Sunnëva prayed to the Gods for mercy. *Please don't take this from me, too.*

She closed her eyes, but all she saw was Jökull, impaled on the castle steps. A sob heaved in her throat.

Why?

Why did it come to this?

They were happy. They had a family. They won and saved the kingdom. Then it was all gone. Her heart and her world were gone.

What was the point of immortality if she was fated to mourn him until the world was reduced to dust?

The horrid moment of his death continued to repeat in her mind. She could not forget the image of the black talon tearing from his chest, and his blood spraying out.

No, you're not sorry ... but you will be.

Rune had been waiting for the opportune moment to get those talons, and because of her—he did. If only she had told Jökull about them from the beginning, they never would have left the north. She brought them here.

It was her fault.

Was that when everything went wrong? She thought of the riddle again, the words forever burned in her mind.

What is not a God but gives life?

What bleeds but doesn't die?

And is as unpredictable as the rising tide?

Memories of Jökull came to her in flashes as his voice answered each question.

Somehow, you gave him life.

You bleed, yet it is not fatal enough to die.
You're the tide that I am helpless against.

Tears rolled down Sunnëva's temples, and she dug her nails into her chest as heart-wrenching pain wracked through her body.

"Me..." The word came out like a strangled gasp before it turned into manic laughter. Air refused to enter her lungs and she couldn't breathe. There was no need to search for a way to kill him. She had prayed to be Jökull's downfall.

And her request was granted.

A horrid, dry sob broke out of her. "I killed the God of Death."

"Yes, you certainly did."

Her heart jumped at the sight of Ren standing in the moonlight, but it wasn't him.

The Druid sauntered into the room with a sly smile. "For love blinds even the clearest eye."

"You knew I would cause his death. Why didn't you tell me?" she shouted, shuddering with agony and anger. "Why give me your stupid riddle?"

"Well, I must admit, I do enjoy witnessing those who seek prophecy spiral in a pointless run, only to weave the threads of fate themselves."

He sat in a chair at the table and crossed one leg over the other. His green hair was tied at his nape, and he no longer wore a tattered black robe. An elegant bronze coat embroidered with oak trees adored his frame. He kicked up his feet on the table and his shiny black boots gleamed in the moonlight.

"Nevertheless, I am not permitted to tell you everything about the future." He frowned down at the gold rings on his fingers. "The God of Time denied us this. I suppose, to prevent Seers from taking advantage of their gifts for their own benefit. To disobey this rule is to lose our power, so one must be *very* careful."

His lashes rose, and his gold eyes stirred like liquid gold. Sunnëva had a feeling the Druid was searching for ways around this rule, and a chill shuddered down her spine at the thought.

415

"Why are you here?" she snapped. "Did you come merely to mock me in my grief?"

"Have you forgotten?" He nodded at the crystal dome. "I came for the rose you owe me."

Sunnëva jerked up in bed. "What?"

"A rose that was given. That was the payment for your riddle."

"No," she said through her clenched teeth.

His smile sharpened. "I am afraid you have no choice. A deal is a deal."

Sunnëva leaped out of bed with every intention of filling his body with spears of ice, but her finger burned like she wore a band of flame. She yanked off her ring to see the geas glowing like molten lava on her skin. It knocked her to the ground and her entire body burned like she was laying on a mound of lit coals. She bit back a scream, left helpless and convulsing on the ground.

The Druid lifted the dome in his arms. "Thank you. Our agreement is complete." He tutted at her wet glare. "I gave you what you asked for. Take it as a bargain well struck."

He had warned her that the cost would be painful, and it was. How cruel of him to take the rose now when it was her only solace.

"I will give you anything else for it," she said. "Our coffers are full of gold and jewels. Take it."

He laughed. "This rose was made by a god. It holds the power to mold *creation*. It is worth more than any amount of wealth in the world."

As he strode for the glass doors, the geas faded from her skin.

"Is this the purpose fate has given me?" she asked him. "Am I cursed to cause the death of everyone I love?"

The Druid paused on the balcony beneath the moonlight as he looked at her. "Only fools try to understand fate."

Sunnëva's heart withered further. "Please. I will give you anything else. That rose is all I have left of him."

"Is it? Did he not give you three progenies? They carry his blood. His life. As do you. He gave you his power, Goddess of Death. Yet you don't know what to do with it."

416

She stilled, sensing something hidden behind his words. He never said anything without intent.

"What does that mean?" she demanded. "I already tried putting his soul back into his body. It didn't work. It's too late. He's gone."

The Druid tsked as he walked away. "It seems you have not figured out my riddle after all."

Her eyes widened. Was there more?

"Wait!" Sunnëva hurried after him. "Come back!"

Her feet slid on the frosted floors as she dashed out onto the empty balcony. She ran into the banister and glimpsed the back of his head before he slipped into the trees of the desiccated garden below. Conjuring her wings, Sunnëva flew down and chased after his departing shadow. She halted before the dark forest when she lost sight of him.

The Druid vanished, leaving behind the puzzle of his words.

"No, please..." Sunnëva looked up at the Heavens, wanting to plead with the Gods again, but they would no longer hear her.

This couldn't be it. There had to be more.

Moonlight shone through the branches, and they fell over blue leaves on the canopy above her head, making them glimmer like flaming sapphires.

The Azure Tree towered before her. She could almost imagine Jökull beside her as he was the day they both stood right here together. Tears rolled as her eyes closed and she fell into the memory.

"You have an Azure Tree," she said into the darkness.

Jökull's faraway voice came to her again. *I do.*

"Did you make them, too?"

They are Elyön's creations. He seems to have a fondness for trees. These, in particular, appear at random in places of strong magic or intended fate. Azure Trees hold an unpredictable power and not even I know their true intention.

Sunnëva's eyes opened wide. An unpredictable power...

Her mind spun again, voices and memories bombarding her all at once.

Put me to fire, and you truly would have risen me from the ash.

417

Death claimed you a long time ago.

Impossible is a word used by those who don't believe.

You created something, Sunnëva...

Their paths had crossed because Jökull was her destiny. She came to him again because she was his fate. And this had all started with a magical rose.

She knew what to do.

Gasping for breath, Sunnëva snatched a branch from the Azure Tree and sprinted to the castle. A portal opened at her command and she crashed into Aero's dark workroom. Lighting a candle, she searched every box, and bottle, then his desk until she found what she needed.

Two enchanted blue petals lay nestled within a purple dome of magic.

Sunnëva lifted the dome with utter relief. Closing her eyes, she called on the magic living in her veins and gave the dying petals renewed life. Each one grew into a glowing blue rose.

What is not a God but gives life?

She laughed wetly. Not a God, but a Goddess. That dastardly Druid and his tricksy words.

Sunnëva returned one rose beneath the dome and cradled the other in her palms.

A flicker of light drew her eyes to the windows. The entire court, the clans, and the Skellings had gathered outside. They stood around Jökull's coffin, placed upon a pyre. And Aero held a torch.

"No, wait!" Sunnëva opened a portal and appeared outside in the cold night. "Stop!"

They all stared at her.

Aero shook his head. "My Queen—"

"You will wait," Sunnëva commanded. "Do not burn him yet."

She walked to her children where they stood silently crying while holding Tally and Ansa's hands. Crouching down before them, she smiled sadly. "My darlings, I need your help." She held out the rose to them. "Can I have a drop of your blood? Only a tiny bit."

Sana and Jalen shrunk away, but Jorik put on a brave face and held out his small hand. She removed her crown and used the sharp points of ice to prick his finger. A shimmering red droplet landed on the petals.

"For being first, I give to you your father's gift." Sunnëva touched his cheek and her fingertips glowed blue as she passed on their magic to him. "You hold the power over winter and death. You're the Ice Phoenix now."

She took a drop from Sana and Jalen next. Their cuts immediately healed.

What bleeds but doesn't die?

Standing, Sunnëva clutched the branch of the Azure Tree of unknown power with the rose.

And is as unpredictable as the rising tide?

At her nod, Aero lit the pyre. The flames caught the oiled firewood beneath and blazed brightly. The coffin of ice began to melt.

Sunnëva smiled at Fenrin faintly, patting his shoulder. Then she handed the crown to her sister and kissed her cheek. "I need to do something, Ansa. Trust that it will be all right. I only ask that you cover their eyes. They shouldn't see this part."

"What do you mean?" her sister asked, alarmed. "Sunnëva? What do you mean?"

She walked away to the pyre, and her children started calling after her.

Everything has a balance ... for only death pays for life.

Sunnëva stripped away her immortality like a glowing veil, letting it fall to the earth. And before the eyes of the court, she climbed onto Jökull's pyre.

Ansa screamed.

Aero shouted.

Tally and Fenrin wrestled her children back.

Lying beside her husband, Sunnëva placed the rose and branch on his chest, over his heart. Then she closed her eyes as the flames consumed them whole.

46

Sunnëva's soul floated through the cosmos. She was no more than a speck of light, drifting among space and time through a sea of the endless universe. The black sky was filled with millions of glinting stars and galaxies. It was all so incredibly breathtaking. If Sunnëva could cry, she would be.

Beyond appeared the Seven Gates. They surrounded her in an even circle. Each was carved and made of different pickets. The Netherworld Gate was made of bone and smoke. The Death Gate was made of smooth stone and ice. The Time Gate was made of white marble veined in black. The Mortal Gate was made of wood and flowers. The Spatial Gate was made of night and stars. Life's Gate was made of colorful misting clouds. And last was Heaven's Gate, made of gold and shining light.

But Sunnëva's soul was being guided toward a glowing nebula in the center of them. Her descent picked up speed, and she fell into it. Then she found herself in a plane of light.

Sunnëva blinked at her hands. Her body was back, yet it glowed and felt strange. Light as a feather, with no pain or feeling other than awe and some confusion.

Whatever brought her here left her on a white platform stirring with clouds, and Sunnëva looked up to find she wasn't alone. Before her was a dais, and on it were seven thrones of gold, but only three of them were filled.

She knew the Gods by sight alone, her spirit recognizing them.

Hiram, the God of Time. A striking male with dark skin, his eyes bright like liquid gold with a crown shaped like a sun on his dark hair. Behind him stood a woman with deep brown skin and her eyes were also gold, but warmer, with her black hair beautifully woven in a series of braids.

His human bride made a Goddess.

Beside him was the God of Mortals, the maker of earth and nature. Eitan had a delicate beauty with pale skin, soft lips, and vibrant green eyes. The purple flowers in his blond hair were the same color as the iridescent wings at his back, like that of the fae. A woven diadem of silver and gold adorned his forehead, matching the armored plate on his chest. Behind Eitan stood his bride. A man who was also as impressive, with dark red hair, and a crown of silver branches and blooms, butterflies fluttering around them both.

Then she met Zohar's glare, the God of Space and Dimension. He had features like the people of Xián Jīng. Dark eyes, midnight blue hair, and a crown of starlight. His bride on his left had similar features, her long black hair piled up in an elaborate knot adorned with gilded combs and jade. Her black gown held thousands of glittering stars, like the depths of the universe.

"It's *her*," said the Goddess of Time.

"Clearly." The Goddess of Space pursed her small red lips, eyeing her coolly.

An elaborate gown that shone like threaded silver had replaced Sunnëva's black mourning robes, and frosted wings fluttered behind her. Snow-white hair tumbled down her shoulders in silk strands, a crown of ice and pearls on her head.

"I am Sunnëva," she called up to the divine. "Jökull's bride. I have come for him."

"Why should we allow you to see him when you're the one responsible for his demise?" Hiram said, his voice booming around her.

She flinched, but her chest hitched with a sharp breath at the hope sprouting in her. *Allow her to see him?* That meant he was here. "I didn't want him to die."

"Oh, but you did," replied the Mortal God evenly. "We all heard your fervent prayers calling for his death."

"That was before they fell in love," his mate said with a kind smile. "I remember the day when I wanted to kill you, too, Eitan." He placed a hand on his shoulder and Eitan covered it with his. "If I am not mistaken, that is the sign of a God's bride." He shared a look with the others. "We all try to make them bleed."

The Goddesses shared a small smirk, remembering it fondly.

"You broke the rules," Hiram continued coolly. "You used the Death Gate to send Rumiel here. That is not his door."

"There was no other option," Sunnëva said. "As his bride is no more. Without her, his Gate cannot be opened."

The Gods exchanged a look.

"It was necessary," she insisted, clenching her fists. "He was disrupting the balance of the world."

"And now he threatens the balance of the Realms," Zohar replied tersely. "Our father and mother have enough to contend with, including keeping the Seven Gates in balance, without an impertinent son seeking to stir chaos within the Heavens."

"Please." Sunnëva dropped to her knees and bowed her head, shutting her eyes. "Please let Jökull come back. We need him. *I* need him. He is my world and without him, I am nothing."

There was a heavy pause, then a familiar cold power hovered above her head. She fell still, her breath halting.

"I told you not to do that."

Her heart leaped at the sound of his voice, and Sunnëva's entire being shook. She looked up at the most beautiful beast with eyes like snow. He glowed in this Realm. Light hovered off his midnight skin that glimmered with starlight. Long white tresses flowed around his face and a jagged crown of ice rested on his head.

"You bow to no one, Sunnëva." Jökull held out a clawed hand. Her trembling fingers landed in his palm, and she wept at how solid it was. He helped her stand, and they faced the Gods. "I am going home."

Not a question. Not a command. A simple statement that left no room for arguing.

"You know this cannot be forever," Hiram said. "We must all return to where we belong."

"And we will one day." Jökull brushed away the tear rolling down her cheek. "But right now, we belong with our family."

"She destroyed your godly flesh," Eitan reminded him. "You stripped yourself of your power for her, and she cast it away to come here. If you return, you will be remade with the little left she found of yours, but given mortal bodies without power or divine strength. Your immortality and dominion over life and death are now scattered in the ashes of your remains. You will have none of it again. The burden of guiding souls through the Gates will be passed on to your heirs until you leave the Mortal Realm to retake your place."

"I know," her mate said again, smiling at her. He sensed her concern for their children to endure such a thing and gently squeezed her hand. "We will be right there to guide them with that."

"You will age," Zohar added, in a last attempt to dissuade him. "You will be a helpless, pitiful human, Jökull. What will you do when Rumiel returns? We can't hold him here for long."

Sunnëva took a disheartened breath.

"And yet I do not care." Jökull looked up at them. "I have already spoken with Father about this and about the matter of Rumiel. We have come to an agreement. Nothing else you say will change my mind. You can rest on your grand thrones, comfortable in the lavishness of endless eternity. But I will go home and *live*."

She closed her eyes in utter joy, and Jökull kissed away the tears from her lashes. Hand in hand, they turned toward his Gate. It glowed brightly as it opened and swirled with blue light.

They took a step off the platform, and when she blinked again, Sunnëva awoke on a pile of ashes.

Movement shifted beside her, and Jökull hummed sleepily as he woke. Both of them were nude and coated in soot. She sat up, taking in her husband. He looked different: rounded ears, no claws, light blond hair fell around his shoulders, and he gazed at her with pale blue eyes that no longer glowed. His God's Mark was gone, along with all his tattoos.

Yet he was still hers.

There was a gasp, and she looked around to find their court had stood there all night, watching the pyre burn. Ansa broke in a sob and buried her face in Kerro's chest. Their children cried out and ran to them. Jorik reached them first. He threw his little body at them, then came Jalen and Sana.

Jökull caught them in his arms, laughing as he held them close. He pulled her to him and brushed his nose against hers. "You brought me back."

"I did." Sunnëva laughed wetly. "I love you. With every breath I breathe, to the depths of my soul. I love you."

His lips curved against hers. "You never had to say it."

The last golden embers hovering around them faded away with the dawn. They had risen from the ashes by some divine power, but a familiar energy lingered beneath them with the bones of their remains.

Among the ashes, Sunnëva spotted two seeds.

One pitch-black and the other pearly white. She scooped them up in her palm and felt the everlasting force humming inside.

They held the power of unendings and renewed beginnings.

There was a feast to celebrate the return of the King. The revelries continued long into the night and showed no sign of stopping when

they carried Jorik, Sana, and Jalen to bed. They cuddled together with their children for hours as they slept, simply holding them close.

When the gray of dawn arrived, Sunnëva and Jökull slipped away to their chambers next door. She lit a candle and sat at the table. Taking out a scroll and a well of ink, she began to write.

"What are you doing?" Jökull asked curiously. He brushed her hair aside and nipped her ear.

She smiled at the rush of heat sinking down her neck. "Give me a moment. I want to write down exactly what I did to resurrect you. It may be useful information one day."

"Hmm, how so?"

"What if I need to revive you again?"

Jökull chuckled as his lips skimmed the side of her throat. "If you kill me again, vicious little thorn, it will be permanent this time."

"How did you convince the God of Urn to send you back?"

"I didn't need to argue much. He allowed me to return for the same reason we were left behind in the first place. Man is not meant to be alone, and the same is true for Gods. I was incomplete without my bride, therefore I could not remain in the Heavens." Jökull gently took a fistful of her hair and tugged her head back to plant a deep kiss on her lips. "You are the other half of me, love."

"You're distracting me from very important work," she said between kisses. "These will be part of our legacy and added to the Sacred Scrolls."

His fingers were making quick work of undoing her bodice. "Sacred Scrolls?"

"That's what I have decided to call them. The parchments of sacred knowledge passed down by the Gods."

It was unlikely anyone would find their story for a long time. The details would probably change and other versions would be told. Most would likely assume it to be a fairy tale. Yet this wasn't a fairy tale.

It was a fable with a touch of destiny.

"We have all the time in the world to write our story," Jökull rumbled as he tugged down her sleeves to kiss her shoulders. "But right now, I want you. I want to be buried inside of you so deep I feel like a God again."

Sunnëva laughed. Well, she wouldn't argue against that.

Jökull picked her up and carried her to their bed. She watched unabashedly as he stripped away his clothes. Even human, he still held an otherworldly beauty. Still moved with the prowl of a predator, and she found his virility was the same.

Slipping between her open thighs, Jökull was everywhere all at once. His fingers tangled in her hair, his mouth crushing into hers in a claiming kiss. At her soft moan, his tongue slipped inside. His touch felt so incredible, she couldn't get enough. Sunnëva wrapped her legs around his waist and yanked him flush against her body. He growled in approval, and she whimpered at the gentle nip of his teeth on her neck.

"I would have broken down all Seven Gates to hear that sound again," he rumbled. "Merely to have your scent dripping all over me."

Jökull gently bit and kissed his way down to her chest, his teeth nipping her sensitive skin. When he got to the front of her gown, she gasped when he tore off her bodice. He made quick work of prying open the front of her dress, leaving her breasts free for his mouth to ravish.

"Perfection," he rumbled, his tongue circling one nipple while he fondled the other. Her core throbbed, begging for his attention.

The rest of her dress was shimmied off her body and tossed aside. His lips traveled down the valley of her breasts to her ribs. His hand hooked under her thigh and spread her open.

He kissed down her stomach slowly, her panting breaths growing sharper. She spasmed when he ran one of his fingers through her sleek folds.

"Already so wet for me, Sunnëva?" he asks teasingly.

"Yes." Her needy gaze met his. "Please."

He chuckled darkly. "You beg so prettily. How can I deny you when you look at me like that?" Jökull bent her knees upward, aligning his face with her sensitive flesh. "This is my favorite place to be."

He dragged his tongue along her folds. Sunnëva's moan was loud enough to fill the room. The sight of Jökull between her thighs nearly tipped her over the edge.

He growled in satisfaction. "Still as sweet."

His tongue flicked against her clit. Her back arched off the bed with a cry. Over and over again, he stroked her. She was trembling and writhing. Without warning, he plunged his tongue deep inside of her. Jökull wrapped her legs around his head and feasted on her until she was screaming and didn't stop until another orgasm swept through her with white-hot release.

Jökull licked every drop feverishly. His mouth moved its way up her trembling body before returning to her mouth. His gentle kisses left her floating. His blue eyes no longer glowed with power, but they were full of reverence for her.

"My winter rose," he said, the soft words falling like a gentle coating of frost on her skin.

His arm clamped around her back, and he hauled her up against his chest. He seated her on his cock in one firm thrust. She cried out, her head falling back. He nipped her shoulder and licked away the sting. "Mine."

There was no part of her that didn't belong to him. Her body was his to fill. Her every cry of pleasure was only his to hear. Everything from the weavings of her soul, the makings of her heart, and the depths of her mind were all his.

"You are mine," Jökull said again, sliding himself out. She bit her lip, moaning and writhing beneath him. He cradled her head before he slammed into her. Her walls clenched around him, not wanting to let go. "And so is this."

Jökull pumped into her, alternating between fast and slow, hitting the spot inside of her that had her entire body convulsing. Her cries echoed off the wall. The sensation was too much and her eyes squeezed close. Sweat dripped down her chest as her lungs seized. Her legs wrapped around his back and began to shake.

Her incoherent pleas came out as gasping whimpers. His hips pumped into her over and over again, so deep she could hardly breathe.

"Open your eyes, Sunnëva," he growled. "Look at me as I make you come."

She did at his deep thrust, and she arched with a scream. Bliss barreled into her body, and warmth spread from her stomach down to her toes. She was floating, trembling with aftershocks. Her vision slowly cleared, and she saw Jökull grinning down at her. While his fangs were gone, the canines still looked sharp.

"I think we scandalized the entire castle." He laughed. "They certainly heard that."

Sunnëva blushed. Gods, she hoped not.

He kissed her deeply, each press of his mouth searing into her soul. Claiming her. Adoring her. And she was looking forward to every kiss to come.

"How do you think our story will be told hundreds of years from now?" she asked, smiling up at him.

Jökull lifted himself over her, his lips skimming hers. "I don't know. I suppose our story will begin as all stories do." He planted a soft kiss on her neck. "With once..." She closed her eyes as he kissed both of her lashes. "Upon...." Then he brought his mouth to hers. "A time."

EPILOGUE

Deep in the castle gardens, everyone waited for Sunnëva. With Jökull's hand in hers, they joined their closest friends and family. Fenrin stood in the center. They were quiet as Gyda kneeled in the grass and ground the last enchanted rose in a mortar.

Sunnëva had finally figured out the missing ingredient. The night they first gave Fen the rose, the petals had been stained with drops of her blood. It's what had truly sired him to her.

This time, they needed something new to sire him. His own gene and something more. Sunnëva added drops of wolf blood to the bowl and the lock of Fenrin's hair from her bracelet. They mixed it with the rose oil until the solution shimmered brightly with magic.

Then the potion was ready.

Fenrin lapped it up, and they waited.

Nothing happened at first, but then he suddenly whined sharply. His body began to bend and warp. The two-legged warg dropped on four legs as his bones snapped and he keened, falling to the ground. Sunnëva squeezed Jökull's hand tightly.

Fenrin's body reformed itself into a large gray wolf with vivid blue eyes. He shifted again, and her brother appeared. Nude and matted, but completely whole.

Jökull tossed him a cloak, and Ansa and Sunnëva rushed forward to hug him tight. He was thick with muscle and much taller than she remembered, nearly as tall as her mate.

Fenrin laughed wetly, tears streaming down a face that she hadn't seen in nearly a year. "You did it," he said, his voice rough and garbled from lack of use. "You broke my curse."

"Look at you." Sunnëva clasped his broad shoulders. "You're a man now."

"You have remade him again," Gyda mused. She stood and rested against her staff. "He is a new species that is part warg, part wolf, and part of who he used to be. What is he to be called? A wargwolf?"

"Werewolf," she decided, brushing down her brother's messy hair. "The wargs vanished when the God of Shadows did, so now there is mostly wolf in him."

"Like Kyrr, you're the sire of your kind," Jökull told Fenrin. "Your bite can create more like you and they can birth others. Careful not to fill the world with too many werewolves that it should throw off the balance of life. And be careful not to breed pups outside of your kind. We do not know how this new curse would remake itself then. Nor do we know the extent of your abilities and your weaknesses. I suppose only time will tell."

Her brother looked perturbed by this new responsibility, but curious to discover more about himself.

"I was right." Daiyu gave Fen a flirty smile. "You are handsome."

He returned a roguish grin.

When it was time for the Dragon Princess to return home, Sunnëva and Jökull handed her a sealed vase containing their ashes. Daiyu placed it within a chest strapped to her dragon.

"Please take the ashes far away to a place where no one can find them. We must keep them separate from each other," Sunnëva said, touching her necklace with a locket containing the cursed seeds. "This type of power cannot fall into the wrong hands."

Rune would make his return one day. He'd be unstoppable if he somehow gained Jökull's power over life and death. And there was the pesky Druid who secretly schemed.

The Dragon Princess bowed her head. "I swear upon the Seven and the Seven Gates of old, I will do all to keep the ashes safe."

"Thank you." Sunnëva embraced her. "I am sad to see you go, but you're always welcome here."

Once they said their goodbyes, Daiyu crossed the landing to where Fenrin waited by the silver dragon. Her brother had decided he wanted to go explore the world, and perhaps find his place in it.

Sunnëva and Jökull waved to them as the dragons flew away to the vast west. They trusted Daiyu would find a place for their power somewhere among the many undiscovered lands or islands.

Safe from greedy hands.

Her vision welled with tears as the last glimpse of her brother vanished behind the clouds.

After that, Fenrin's visits became more sparing as time went on over the long years until he no longer returned. Last Sunnëva heard of him, he had formed Packs of werewolves all across Urn.

Ansa had five children with Kerro, half-human Skellings. Once Tally and Aero were wed, they started their family as well.

Bjorn, she never saw again. Their relationship couldn't recover after what she had nearly done to him, regardless of how many times she attempted to make amends. But Sunnëva knew he had become the Earl of the Morkhàn clan. Perhaps because he was no longer under their father's thumb, or because he gained wisdom, her brother led their people well.

The land thawed, and the clans thrived.

With the Ice Phoenix no longer ruling them, they adopted a new banner with a sigil of an interwoven, seven-pointed star. And their kingdom was no longer called the Everfrost, but instead named after a sacred blue tree.

They had fifty years of peace as the King and Queen of Azure.

There had been some battles and raids, but nothing they couldn't defeat together. A city eventually gathered in what became Old Tanzanite Keep. The castle was always cold, and the snow clung to the ground a deal longer in the winter. Their home may no longer have been made of ice, but it was always covered with climbing red roses.

Sunnëva watched her demigod children grow into amazing people, fall in love, and have families of their own. They led full lives filled with laughter and joy.

But with life came death, and Sunnëva sensed the end was near.

When it was time to go, both she and Jökull felt the power of the Death Gate opening. Magic pulsed in the air, thrumming against her heart like a soft call.

Sunnëva sat up in bed in the early dawn and looked at her husband. Jökull remained handsome in his old age with laugh lines around his mouth.

"It's time, isn't it?" she asked him tiredly, taking his soft hand.

He pressed a kiss to her wrinkly fingers. "It is."

"Does this mean Rune has returned?"

Jökull sighed. "Yes. We may hear news of demons being sighted soon, but I trust Elyōn has a plan. We have prepared the people for this day."

It was the agreement they made.

Elyon granted them exactly fifty years to be with their family. No more, no less. Jökull was to retake his place in the Heaven's at the same time Rune would break out of his confinement.

It must all have a purpose, so she had to put her faith in that.

That evening, they took a carriage ride to the Gate with their adult children, Ansa, and the rest of their friends, who they considered family.

Sunnëva sat between Jalen and Sana, both of them holding her hands. Jorik and Jökull sat across from her. Both wearing twin stoic frowns, quiet in their solemn sorrow. Goodbyes were hard, but they had spent every day being grateful for the time they had together with them, for her sons and daughter had decided they would live their lives in the Mortal Realm. They couldn't leave their families and everything they knew behind.

It was all right. Because she would always be around to watch over them.

The carriage rattled as it climbed a steep hill, and the magic crackling in the air marked their arrival. They stepped out of the carriage together. Aero, Tally, and their sixteen-year-old granddaughter climbed down from the driver's seat.

As mortals, they couldn't see past the warding magic, but at the wave of Aero's hand, the glamor cleared. It looked the same as Sunnëva remembered. A stone archway on a set of steps. It had a domed roof with elegantly carved pillars leading down a short passageway. The center glowered and swirled with light.

She and Jökull both took a deep breath as a rush of power washed over them. It rippled over her, sinking deep into her bones. The wrinkles faded from her skin as it became smooth again. Jökull's youthful beauty returned, along with his pointed ears and glowing eyes.

Their human lives had ended.

They were made Gods once more.

Choking on a sob, Sunnëva whipped around and held her children. She embraced Ansa, Tally, and Aero next.

"Thank you for everything," Ansa told her. "I love you."

Sunnëva sniffed. "I love you too. Both of you." She squeezed Tally's hand.

"Watch over my family, Aero," Jökull said.

The old mage bowed his head. "Of course, sire."

A rumble came from the distance.

In the far south, they glimpsed the edge of dark clouds forming where the Shadow Keep had once been. Rune was indeed back, and soon his darkness would spread across the world with no one powerful enough to stop him. The dark clouds spread, and her dread grew.

Whatever was coming, only the Gods knew. Sunnëva wished she could be here to help them fight, but that was not her fate.

"After we cross, I will once again be the God of Death, and you will no longer carry the burden of souls," Jökull told their sons and daughter. "But the power of the divine will remain strong in all of you. Everyone will always underestimate you. Some will dare to challenge you. Make them pay for it."

"We will, Father," Sana said. She had grown into a beautiful woman, fierce in her armor, and quick with a sword. Sunnëva saw herself in her.

"To our warrior, Jorik. The might of the Ice Phoenix is yours," Jökull said to him next. "You will carry my power over the frost, and it will pass on among your descendants. To be inherited by those with my blood and the blood of the Morkhàn line."

Jorik bowed his head.

"Sana, with intellect as sharp as a blade, to you we leave this." Sunnëva handed her a brass key. "You're the protector of its door and the secrets it contains."

The door led to many untold things they had gathered over the years that needed to be safeguarded, including certain Sacred Scrolls.

Her daughter accepted the key with a bow of her head.

"To Jalen, with a stout heart of kindness and wisdom, we leave the seeds," Jökull said next. Sunnëva removed her locket and placed it around his neck. "They must never be planted. For they would bear fruit not meant for this Realm."

Jalen bowed his head, too.

Sunnëva hugged and kissed them all again. She held Jalen the longest because he was the softest of them and she worried what the world would do to him once they were gone.

"My handsome boy, it's very clear," she said, cupping his cheeks.

"What is?"

"You were made with lots of love."

"Ugh, Mother!"

Laughing, they gazed at their family a little longer. The Gate was behind them, but neither of them could bring themselves to take the first step toward it. Even if she went, a piece of her heart would remain here.

That was fate's price.

Regardless, she still felt guilty, leaving them to face what she couldn't.

"Go," Jorik said, as brave as always. He was tall and handsome in his armor, so much like his father. "You taught us everything we know and prepared us for the war to come. Together, we will be enough to fight him. Don't worry."

His pale eyes glowed blue, and she saw the hint of ice wings on his back. Jalen and Sana nodded firmly, the air stirring with a crackle of their magic. Their little loves were no longer little. They were strong and powerful, everything they raised them to be.

"And you will have aid," Jökull said, looking up at the Heavens. White lights began to drop from the sky like falling stars. One of them was blue, the brightest of them all.

Sunnëva faintly gasped. "What are they?"

He smiled at her. "Seraphs. Watchers of the Heavens."

Tally held on to her granddaughter's arm as they observed the celestial beings with wonder. "Look, Sheli," she said. "The God of Urn sent help."

Sunnëva smiled then, finally feeling at ease.

With one last goodbye, she took Jökull's hand, and they walked into the Gate, ready for the next part of their forever.

THE END

ACKNOWLEDGMENTS

When the story of Jökull and Sunnëva first came to me, I had no idea what it would become. I only knew that it had to be told. I've always wanted to write a Beauty and the Beast fairy tale, and for it to mean something to every reader.

King's Bride is a love story about healing the scars in your heart, and about grieving over what you lost and never had, about growing and forgiving yourself. It's a dark tale based on impossibilities and how far you could go if you believe.

I embed a piece of heart and some of my tears in all of my books because I grow with these characters and I heal with them, too.

This book was no different.

I will always give thanks to my husband, Michael. My soulmate, my "Just George" (IYKYK), for always encouraging me and showing me what unconditional love is. Sometimes, his flirty lines make it onto my pages.

Thank you to my magical, super-patient wizard of an editor, Hina Babar. I don't know why you put up with my shenanigans, but I am grateful and I love you!

I am so thankful to my amazing beta readers Katie Ryan, Cher Martindill, Mimi Corpus, and Devyani Saini for reading through my messy drafts and helping me make it a hundred times better.

And I adore my smutty sweet potatoes, Veronica Frank, Madeeha Idrees, Lily Phan, Mimi Corpus, and Nicole Bonomini. Thank you for giving me the courage to put this book out there.

Always a massive thank you to my incredible street team. I cannot thank you enough for continuing to shout about my books to the world and for cheering me on when I needed it. Thank you to all the bloggers, Instagramers, Booktokers, and ARC readers who read *King's Bride* and gushed with me over how much they loved Jökull and Sunnëva.

I thank all of you from the bottom of my heart for joining me on this journey of discovery and wonder.

Here is to happily ever after,

Xoxo

Beck Michaels

WORLD GUIDE

LAND OF URN MAIN KINGDOMS:

The Everfrost: Located in Urn's chip, it is the eastern land connected to the rest of Urn by an isthmus. It later becomes the Kingdom of Azure.

Magos Empire: Kingdom of the mages, which is separated into three guilds; Sun, Lunar and Earth. The magic of the guilds is limited to their element.

Xián Jīng Dynasty: Set on the west coast of Urn. They are a prominent power in this era and the center of trade.

Vale of the Elves: Set in the midwest before the kingdom was split into Red Highland and Greenwood.

ENCHANTED ORE:

Nightstone: Black crystal used to slay demons.

Moonstone: White crystal used to reflect moonlight to deter or slay demons. Can be spelled for other uses.

Bloodstone: Red ore created with blood magic to contain the wearer within a perimeter. Over the years, its use was taken over by slave keepers to contain their captives.

Tanztone: Also known as Tanzanite. It is a versatile crystal used to hold spells. However, the crystal can only be spelled once.

Sunstone: Orange crystal used to reflect sunlight to deter or slay demons. Can be spelled for other uses.

TERRITORIES IN URN'S CHIP BEFORE THE RISE OF THE AZURE KINGDOM:

The Everfrost: territory of the God of Death and the clans.

The Frost Lands: territory of the Skellings.

The Moor Lands: territory of the Wild Fae.

The Waste Lands: territory of the God of Shadows.

THE GODS:

Elyōn: the God of Life and maker of the Gods and the Gates.

Gavriel: Goddess of the Heavens oversees the gathering of souls

Hiram: The God of Time who oversees the past, present, and future.

Zohar: The God of Space and Dimension, who oversees the bridges between the Realms.

Eitan: The God of Mortals who oversees the natural laws of life.

Rumiel: The God of Shadows who oversees the Netherworld.

Jökull: The God of Death who guides souls through the Seven Gates at their beginning and at their end.

.

℘RONUNCIATIONS

NAMES:

Jökull: Joh-cull *(His name is an Icelandic word that means glacier. The true pronunciation is much different.)*

Sunnëva: Sue-neh-vah

Elyōn: Ehl-yon

Thorstein: Thors-tain

Bjorn: B-yorn

Aero: Eh-row

Tally: Tah-lee

Daiyu: Dah-yu

Gyda: Gee-duh

PLACES:

Magos: Mah-goes

Xián Jīng : She-an-ging

Saxe Sea: Sah-x

Argyle: Ar-guy-el

Azure: Ah-z-her

Arthall: Ar-thall (separate continent from Urn)

FOR MORE INFO ON THIS VAST WORLD VISIT:
WWW.BECKMICHAELS.COM/THE-LAND-OF-URN

ALSO BY BECK MICHAELS

The Guardians of the Maiden series:
Divine Blood
Bonded Fate
Shattered Souls
Rising Dawn

ABOUT THE AUTHOR

BECK MICHAELS is the bestselling author of the enchanting epic fantasy series *The Guardians of the Maiden,* and *The Chronicles of Urn.* Beck lives in Indiana with her husband and two children, where she spends her time reading and daydreaming of stories in faraway lands.

WWW.BECKMICHAELS.COM

PLUMA
PRESS

Made in the USA
Las Vegas, NV
13 October 2023

79042305R00266